The Reluctant Widow

Author of over fifty books, Georgette Heyer is one of the best-known and best-loved of all historical novelists, making the Regency period her own. Her first novel, *The Black Moth*, published in 1921, was written at the age of fifteen to amuse her convalescent brother; her last was *My Lord John*. Although most famous for her historical novels, she also wrote twelve detective stories. Georgette Heyer died in 1974 at the age of seventy-one.

The Black Moth

Powder and Patch

Simon the Coldheart

These Old Shades

The Masqueraders

Beauvallet

The Conqueror

Devil's Cub

The Convenient Marriage

Regency Buck

The Talisman Ring

An Infamous Army

Royal Escape

The Spanish Bride

The Corinthian

Faro's Daughter

Friday's Child

The Reluctant Widow

The Foundling

Arabella

The Grand Sophy

The Quiet Gentleman

Cotillion

The Toll-Gate

Bath Tangle

Sprig Muslin

April Lady

Sylvester

Venetia

The Unknown Ajax

Pistols for Two

A Civil Contract

The Nonesuch

False Colours

Frederica

Black Sheep

Cousin Kate

Charity Girl

Lady of Quality

My Lord John

Mysteries

Footsteps in the Dark

Why Shoot a Butler?

The Unfinished Clue

Death in the Stocks

Behold, Here's Poison

They Found Him Dead

A Blunt Instrument

No Wind of Blame

Envious Casca

Penhallow

Duplicate Death

Detection Unlimited

The Reluctant Widow

Georgette Heyer

arrow books

22

Arrow Books
20 Vauxhall Bridge Road
London SW1V 2SA

Arrow Books is part of the Penguin Random House group of companies
whose addresses can be found at global.penguinrandomhouse.com

First published in the United Kingdom in 1939 by William Heinemann

Published by Arrow Books in 2004

www.penguin.co.uk

A CIP catalogue record for this book is available from the British Library

ISBN 978 0 09 946807 3

Typeset by SX Composing DTP, Rayleigh, Essex

Penguin Random House is committed to a sustainable
future for our business, our readers and our planet. This
book is made from Forest Stewardship Council® certified
paper.

Printed and bound in Great Britain by Clays Ltd, Elcograf S.p.A.

The authorised representative in the EEA is Penguin Random House Ireland,
Morrison Chambers, 32 Nassau Street, Dublin D02 YH68.

One

It was dusk when the London to Little Hampton
stagecoach lurched into the village of Billingshurst,
and a cold mist was beginning to creep knee-high over
the dimly seen countryside. The coach drew up at an inn, and
the steps were let down to enable a passenger to alight. A lady,
soberly dressed in a drab-coloured pelisse and a round bonnet
without a feather, descended on to the road. While she waited for
a corded trunk and a valise to be extricated from the boot, the
coachman, finding himself to be some minutes ahead of his time-
sheet, hitched up his reins, clambered down from the box, and in
defiance of the regulations governing the conduct of stage-
coachmen, rolled into the tap-room in search of such stimulant
as would enable him to accomplish the remainder of the journey
without endangering an apparently enfeebled constitution.

The passenger, meanwhile, stood in the roadway with her
trunk at her feet, and looked about her in a little uncertainty. She
was expecting to be met, but as her experience had taught her
that the gig was more commonly employed for the purpose of
picking up the new governess than the carriage used by her
employers, she hesitated to approach the only conveyance she
could perceive, which was a light travelling coach, drawn up on
the opposite side of the road. While she stood looking about her,
however, a servant jumped down from the box, and came up to
her, touching his hat, and enquiring whether she would be the
young lady who had come down from London in answer to
the advertisement. Upon her assenting, he made her a little bow,

picked up the valise, and led the way across the road to the travelling coach. She stepped up into it, her spirits insensibly rising at this unlooked-for-attention to her comfort; and was further gratified by the servant's spreading a rug over her knees and expressing the hope that she would not feel chilled by the evening air. The steps were put up, the door shut, the trunk bestowed on the roof, and in a very few moments the coach moved forward, bowling along in a well-sprung manner that formed a pleasing contrast to the jolting the stage-coach passenger had been enduring for several hours.

She leaned back against the squabs with a sigh of relief. The stage had been crowded, and her journey an uncomfortable one. She wondered whether she would ever become accustomed to the disagreeable economies of poverty. Since she had had ever opportunity of inuring herself to these over a period of six years, it seemed unlikely. Dispirited, but determined not to give way to melancholy reflections, she turned her thoughts away from the evils of her situation, and tried instead to speculate upon the probable character of her new post.

It had been with no high hopes that she had set out from London earlier in the day. Her employer, seen once only in a quelling interview at Fenton's Hotel, had disclosed no hint of the kindly impulse that must have caused her to send her own carriage to meet the governess. Miss Elinor Rochdale had been misled into thinking her massive bosom as hard as her rather prominent eyes, and, had any other choice offered, would have had no hesitation in declining a post in her household. But no other choice had offered. There were too often young gentlemen at a susceptible age in families requiring a governess, and Miss Rochdale was too young and too well-favoured to be eligible, in the eyes of most provident Mamas, for the position. Happily, however – for Miss Rochdale's savings were negligible, and her pride still too great to allow of her remaining longer as the guest of her own old governess – Mrs Macclesfield's only male offspring was a sturdy lad of seven. He was, by his mother's account, high-spirited, and of so sensitive a temperament that the exercise of the greatest tact and persuasion was necessary to control his activities. Six years earlier, Miss Rochdale would have shrunk from the horrors so clearly in store for her, but those years had taught her that the ideal situation was rarely to be found, and that where there was no spoiled child to make the governess's life a burden, she would in all likelihood be expected to save her employer's purse by performing the menial tasks generally allotted to the second housemaid.

Miss Rochdale tucked the rug more closely round her legs. A thick sheepskin mat upon the floor of the coach protected her feet from the draught, and she snuggled them into it gratefully, almost able to fancy herself once more Miss Rochdale of Feldenhall, travelling in her father's carriage to an evening party. The style of servant who had been sent to fetch her, and the elegance of the equipage, had a little surprised her: she had not supposed Mrs. Macclesfield to have been in such comfortable circumstances. Upon first perceiving the coach, she had thought she had seen a crest upon the door-panel, but in the failing light it was easy to be mistaken. She fell to pondering the probable degree of gentility of the establishment ahead of her, and the various characters of its inmates, and since she was of a humorous turn of mind, soon lost herself in the weaving of several very improbable histories.

She was recalled to her surroundings by a perceptible slackening in the pace of the horses, and, looking out of the window, saw that the darkness had by this time closed in. The moon not having yet risen it was impossible to discern anything of the country through which she was being driven, but she gained the impression of a narrow and certainly tortuous lane. She did not know for how long she had been in the coach, but it seemed to be a considerable time. She recollected that Mrs. Macclesfield had described her home at Five Mile Ash as being within a short distance of Billingshurst, and could only suppose that the way to it must be more than ordinarily circuitous. But as time went on it became apparent that either Mrs. Macclesfield's notions of distance were country ones, or she had been deliberately mendacious.

The journey began to seem unending, but just as Miss Rochdale was entertaining a suspicion that the coachman had lost his way in the darkness the horses slowed from a jog-trot to a walk, and the vehicle swung round at a sharp angle, its wheels encountering an uneven gravel surface, as of a carriage-drive ill-kept. The pace was picked up again, and maintained for a few hundred yards. The coach then drew to a standstill, and the groom once more jumped down from the box.

A faint silver light had begun to illumine the scene, and as she stepped out of the coach Miss Rochdale was just able to see that the house she was about to enter was of a respectable size, although built in a rambling and rather low-pitched style. Two sharp gables, and some very tall chimney-stacks were silhouetted against the night-sky; and a lamp burning in one of the rooms showed that the windows were latticed.

The groom had tugged at the big iron bell some moments before, and the echoes of its distant clanging still sounded when the door was opened. An elderly man in shabby livery held it for Miss Rochdale to enter the house, favouring her, as she passed him, with an intent, and rather anxious scrutiny. She scarcely heeded this, for her attention was claimed by her surroundings, which were surprising enough to cause her to check on the threshold, looking about her in a good deal of bewilderment. What, her startled brain demanded, had the woman she had seen at Fenton's Hotel to do with all this decayed grandeur?

The hall in which she found herself was a large, irregularly shaped room, with a superb oaken stairway at one end of it, and at the other a huge stone fireplace, big enough for the roasting of an ox, thought Miss Rochdale, and with a chimney which might be depended on to gush forth smoke any time some unwise person kindled a fire on the flags beneath it. The plaster ceiling, blackened between the oak beams, showed how correct was Miss Rochdale's prosaic reflection. The stairs and the floor of the hall were alike uncarpeted, and lacked polish; long brocade curtains which had once been handsome but were now faded and in places worn threadbare, were drawn across the windows; a

4

heavy gateleg table in the centre of the room bore, besides a film of dust, a riding-whip, a glove, a crumpled newspaper, a tarnished brass bowl possibly intended to hold flowers, but just now full of odds and ends, two pewter mugs, and a snuff-jar; a rusted suit of armour stood near the bottom of the staircase; there was a carved chest against one wall, with a welter of coats cast on the top of it; several chairs, one with a broken cane seat, and the others upholstered in rubbed leather, were scattered about; and on the walls were a number of pictures in heavy gilded frames, three moth-eaten foxes' masks, two pairs of antlers, and a number of ancient horse-pistols and fowling-pieces.

Miss Rochdale's astonished gaze alighted presently on the servant who had admitted her, and she found that he was regarding her with a kind of melancholy curiosity. Something in his demeanour, coupled as it was with the depressing dilapidation all around her, put her forcibly in mind of the more lurid romances to be obtained from a circulating-library. She could almost fancy herself to have been kidnapped, and was forced to summon up all her common sense to dispel the ridiculous notion.

She said, in her pleasant, musical voice: 'I had not thought it had been so far from the coach-stop. I have arrived later than I expected.'

'It's all of twelve miles, miss,' responded the retainer. 'You're to come this way, if you please.'

She followed him across the uneven floor to one of the doors that gave on to the hall. He opened it, but his notion of announcing her seemed to consist merely of a jerk of the head, signifying that she was to enter. After a moment's hesitation, she did so, still more bewildered, and conscious by this time of a little feeling of trepidation.

She found herself in a library. It was quite as untidy as the hall, but a quantity of candles in tarnished wall-brackets threw a warm light over it, and a log fire burned in the grate at the far end of it. Before this fire, one hand resting on the mantelpiece, one booted foot on the fender, stood a gentleman in buckskin breeches and a mulberry coat, staring down at the leaping flames. As the door closed behind Miss Rochdale, he looked up, and across at her, in a measuring way that might have disconcerted one less accustomed to being weighed up like so much merchandize offered for sale.

He might have been any age between thirty and forty. Miss Rochdale realized that he must be her employer's husband, and was a good deal cheered to discover that besides being a very gentlemanlike-looking man, with a well-favoured countenance and a distinct air of breeding, he was dressed with a neatness and a propriety at welcome variance with his surroundings. He had, in fact, all the appearance of a man of fashion.

He did not move to meet her, so Miss Rochdale advanced into the room, saying: 'Good evening. The servant desired me to enter this room, but perhaps –?'

It seemed to her that there was a faint look of surprise in his face, but he replied in a cool voice: 'Yes, that was by my orders. Pray be seated! I trust you were not kept waiting at the coach-stop?'

'No, indeed!' she said, taking a chair by the table, and folding her hands over her reticule in her lap. 'The carriage was waiting for me. I must thank you for having sent it.'

'I should certainly doubt of there being a suitable conveyance in these stables,' he said.

This remark, uttered as it was in an indifferent tone, seemed extremely odd to Miss Rochdale. She must have shown that she was taken aback, for he added stiffly: 'I believe that the exact nature of the position offered to you was explained in London?'

'I believe so,' she returned.

'I chose that you should be brought here directly,' he said.

She looked startled. 'I thought – I was under the impression – that this was my destination!'

'It is,' he said, rather grimly. 'However, I do not desire that you should be under any misapprehension. I am giving you the opportunity to see with your own eyes what may not have been adequately described to you, before we come to any definite bargain.' His level gray eyes swept the disordered room as he spoke, and then returned to their scrutiny of her countenance.

She hoped that she succeeded in preserving it. She said: 'I do not understand you, sir. For my part, I considered myself definitely engaged when I set out from London to come here.'

He bowed slightly. 'Oh, yes! If you still wish it!'

She could not be sure that she did, but the alternative prospect of returning to town to seek another post caused her to say cheerfully: 'I shall do my best, sir, to fill the position satisfactory.' She detected irony in his steady gaze, and was disconcerted by it. She added, with a slightly heightened colour: 'I was not aware, however, that it was you who had engaged me. I thought –'

'It was unnecessary that you should know it,' he said. 'Once you have made up your mind to the bargain, I have nothing more to say in the matter.'

From what she had seen of his wife she could readily believe this; the only surprise she felt was at his having had any say at all in the matter. Yet his manner was very much that of a man accustomed to command. Feeling herself to be at a loss, she said, after a short pause: 'Perhaps it would be as well if I were to lose no time in making the acquaintance of my charge.'

His lip curled. 'An apt term!' he remarked dryly. 'By all means, but your charge is not at the moment on the premises. You shall see him presently. If what you must already have observed has not daunted you, you encourage me to hope that your resolution will not fail when you are brought face to face with him.'

'I trust not, indeed,' she said, with a smile. 'I was given to understand, I own, that I might find him a trifle – a trifle high-spirited, perhaps.'

'You have either a genius for understatement, ma'am, or the truth was not told you, if that is what you understand.'

She laughed. 'Well, you are very frank, sir! I should not expect to be told quite all the truth, but I might collect it, reading between the lines, I fancy.'

'You are a brave woman!' he said.

Her amusement grew. 'I am sure I am no such thing! I can but contrive as best I may. I dare say he has been a little spoilt?'

'I doubt of there being anything to spoil,' he replied.

The coldly dispassionate tone in which he uttered this remark made her reply in equally chilly accents: 'You do not desire me, I am persuaded, to refine too much upon your words, sir. I am very hopeful of teaching him to mind me in time.'

'Teaching him to mind you?' he repeated, with a strong inflexion of astonishment in his voice. 'You will have performed something indeed if you succeed in doing so! You will have, moreover, the distinction of being the only person to whom he has attended in all his life!'

'Surely, sir, you –?' she faltered.

'Good God, no!' he said impatiently.

'Well – well, I must put forth my best efforts,' she said.

'If you mean to remain here, you would be better advised to turn your attention to the evils you can more easily remedy,' he said, with another glance of dislike around the room.

She was nettled, and allowed herself to reply with a touch of asperity; 'I was not informed, sir, that it was to fill the position of housekeeper that I was engaged. I am accustomed to keep my own apartment neat and clean, but I can assure you I shall not meddle in the general management of the house.'

He shrugged, and turned away from her to stir the now smouldering log with his foot. 'You will do as seems best to you,' he said. 'It is no concern of mine. But rid your mind of whatever romantic notions it may cherish! Your charge, as you choose to call him, may be induced to accept you, but that is because I can force him to do so, and for not other reason. Do not flatter yourself that he will regard you with complaisance! I do not expect you to remain above a week: you need not remain as long, unless you choose to do so.'

'Not remain above a week!' she exclaimed. 'He cannot be as bad as you would have me think, sir! It is absurd to speak in such a way! Pardon me, but you should not talk so!'

'I wish you to know the truth, to have the opportunity to

reconsider your decision.'

A good deal dismayed, she could only say: 'I must do what I can. I own, I had not supposed – but I am not in a position – in a position lightly to decline –'

'No, so, indeed, I apprehended,' he said. 'It could not have been otherwise.'

She stared at him. 'Well! This is frank indeed! I am sure I am at a loss to guess why, having engaged me, you should now be so set on turning me away, sir!'

At that he smiled, which made his somewhat forbidding countenance appear very much more pleasing. 'It is certainly absurd,' he agreed. 'You are not what I had expected, ma'am. I must tell you that I think you too young.'

Her spirits sank. 'I made no secret of my age, sir. I am perhaps older than you imagine. I am six-and-twenty.'

'You look younger,' he commented.

'I hope it need not signify, sir. I assure you, I am not without experience.'

'You can hardly have had experience of what now lies before you,' he retorted.

A dreadful suspicion crossed Miss Rochdale's mind. 'Good heavens, he is not – he surely cannot be – *deranged*, sir?' she exclaimed.

'No, he is quite sane,' he answered. 'It is brandy, not madness, to which the greater part of his propensity for evil is attributable.'

'*Brandy?*' she gasped.

He raised his brows. 'Yes, I thought you had not been told the whole,' he said. 'I am sorry. I intended – and indeed ordered – otherwise.'

Miss Rochdale now realized that not her charge but her employer was mentally deranged. She rose to her feet, saying with a firmness which she hoped concealed her inward alarm: 'I thank you sir, it would be best that I should present myself without further loss of time to Mrs. Macclesfield.'

'To whom?' he asked, rather blankly.

'Your wife!' she said, retreating strategically towards the door.

He said with unruffled calm: 'I am not married.'

'Not married?' she cried. 'Then – Have I been under a misapprehension? Are you not Mr. Macclesfield?'

'Certainly not,' he replied. 'I am Carlyon.'

He appeared to think that this statement was sufficient to apprise her of all she could possibly wish to know about him. She was wholly bewildered, and could only stammer: 'I beg your pardon! I thought – But where, then, is Mrs. Macclesfield?'

'I do not think I know the lady.'

'You do not know her! Is this not her house, sir?'

'No,' he said.

'Oh, there has been some dreadful mistake!' she cried distressfully. 'I do not know how it can have come about! Indeed, I am very sorry, Mr. Carlyon, but I think I am come to the wrong house!'

'So it would appear, ma'am.'

'It is the most mortifying circumstance! I do beg your pardon! But when the servant asked me if I was come in answer to the advertisement I thought – But I should have enquired more particularly!'

'Did you come in answer to the advertisement?' he interrupted, his brow creasing. 'Not mine, I fancy!'

'Oh, no! I was hired by Mrs. Macclesfield to be governess to her children – more particularly, her little boy.' In spite of herself, she began to laugh. 'Oh, dear, could anything be more nonsensical? You may conceive what an effect your words had upon me!'

'I imagine you must have supposed me to be mad.'

'I did. But it is no laughing matter after all! Pray, where am I, sir?'

'You are at Highnoons, ma'am. Where do you wish to be?'

'Mrs. Macclesfield's residence is at Five Mile Ash,' she answered. 'I hope it may not be far removed from here?'

'I am afraid it is quite sixteen or more miles to the east of this place,' he responded. 'You will hardly reach it to-night.'

'Good God, sir, what in the world am I to do? I fear she will be much offended, and I am sure I do not know how to explain my folly to her!'

He did not seem to be attending very closely. He asked abruptly: 'Was there no other female got down from the stage at Billingshurst?'

'No, there was no one got down but myself,' she assured him.

'I suppose her courage deserted her,' he remarked. 'It is not surprising.'

'I collect that you too were expecting someone. It is indeed a chapter of accidents. I wish I knew how to contrive to be well out of such a fix!'

He favoured her with another of his measuring glances. 'Well, we may yet turn it to good account. Before you decide to present yourself at Five Mile Ash you might do worse than consider the post I have to offer.'

'You do not require a governess, sir!'

'No. I require a female – preferably a respectable female – who would be willing, upon terms, to marry a young relative of mine,' he replied.

She was for several moments deprived of all power of speech. Finding her tongue at last, she demanded: 'Are you in earnest?'

'Certainly.'

'I think you must indeed be mad!'

'I am not, but I dare say it may appear so.'

'To marry a young relative of yours!' she said scornfully. 'No doubt the gentleman whose evil propensities are attributable to brandy!'

'Precisely.'

'Mr. Carlyon,' said Miss Rochdale roundly, 'I am in no mood for such trifling as this! Be as good as to –'

'I am not trifling with you, and I am not Mr. Carlyon.'

'I beg your pardon! It is what you told me!'

'You have my name correctly, but it will be more proper for you to address me as Lord Carlyon.'

'Oh!' said Miss Rochdale. 'Well, that makes it no better, sir!'

'Makes what no better?'

'This – this preposterous and ill-timed jest of yours!'

'My proposal may be preposterous, but it is not a jest. There are reasons why I am anxious to see my cousin married as soon as possible.'

'I do not pretend to understand you, my lord, but if that is so your cousin would be better advised to offer for some lady of his acquaintance.'

'Undoubtedly. But his character is too well known to make him acceptable to any female of his acquaintance. Nor has he any longer the recommendation of a respectable fortune.'

'Upon my word!' exclaimed Miss Rochdale, hardly knowing whether to laugh or to be indignant. 'And why, pray, should you suppose that this monster might be acceptable to me?'

'I don't suppose it,' he replied calmly. 'You may leave him at the church door, if you choose. In fact, I think you should do so.'

'Either I am dreaming,' said Miss Rochdale, maintaining her composure with a strong effort, 'or you are indeed mad!'

Two

He looked a little amused at this, but only replied with a shake of his head. Quite provoked by such conduct, Miss Rochdale said sharply: 'It does not signify talking! Be so good as to tell me how I may reach Five Miles Ash before it is too late to set out!'

He glanced at the bracket-clock on the mantelpiece, but as this had stopped, drew out his watch. 'It is already too late,' he said. 'It wants only ten minutes to nine.'

'Good God!' she exclaimed, turning quite pale. 'What am I to do?'

'Since I appear to have been in some sort responsible for your predicament you will do best to trust me to provide for you.'

'You are very obliging, my lord,' she retorted, 'but I prefer not to place my trust in one whose senses are clearly disordered!'

'Don't be foolish!' he replied, in much the same tone as she might herself have used in addressing a troublesome child. 'You know very well that my senses are not in the least disordered. You will do well to sit down again while I procure you some refreshment.'

His manner had the effect of soothing her exasperated nerves, and she could not but acknowledge that his offer of refreshment was welcome. She had not eaten since the morning. She went back to her chair, but said suspiciously: 'I do not know how you may mean to provide for me, for I am certainly not going to marry your cousin!'

'That is as you wish,' he returned, tugging at the bell-pull.

'From what I have seen of your establishment,' remarked Miss Rochdale waspishly, 'that bell is very likely broken.'

'More than probable,' he agreed, walking towards the door. 'But this is not my establishment.'

Miss Rochdale put a hand to her brow. 'I begin to think my own senses are becoming disordered!' she complained. 'If this is neither your house nor Mrs. Macclesfield's, whose, pray, is it?'

'My cousin's.'

'Your cousin's! But I cannot remain here!' she cried. 'You cannot mean to keep me here, sir!'

'Certainly not. It would be quite ineligible,' he said, and left the room.

Wild ideas of precipitate flight crossed Miss Rochdale's mind, but since she did not want for common sense, she rejected them. To be wandering about an unknown countryside all night would scarcely ameliorate her difficulties, and although her host's behaviour might be extraordinary he did not appear to entertain any notion of constraining her against her will. She sat still therefore, and waited for him to reappear.

This he presently did, saying as he entered the room: 'There seems to be nothing but cold meat in the house, but I have ordered them to do what they can.'

'Some tea and bread-and-butter is all I require,' she assured him.

'It will be here directly.'

'Thank you.' She drew off her gloves, and folded them. 'I have been wondering what to do for the best. Is there any carriage, or post-chaise, perhaps, which I might hire to convey me to Five Mile Ash, sir?'

'As to that, I would convey you in my own carriage, but you will hardly endear yourself to your future employer by arriving at midnight.'

The truth of this observation most forcibly struck her. The image of the redoubtable Mrs. Macclesfield rose before her mind's eye, and almost caused her to shudder.

'There is a decent inn at Wisborough Green where you may

put up for the night,' he said. 'In the morning, if you are determined to stick to your purpose, I will have you driven to Five Mile Ash.'

'I am very much obliged to you,' she faltered. 'But what shall I say to Mrs. Macclesfield? The truth will not serve: she would think it fantastic!'

'It will certainly be awkward. You had better tell her that you mistook the day, and have but this instant arrived in Sussex.'

'I am much afraid that she will be justly angry, and perhaps turn me away.'

'In that case, you may return to me.'

'Yes! To be married to your odious cousin!' she said. 'I thank you, I am not yet reduced to such straits!'

'You are the best judge of that,' he replied imperturbably. 'I am naturally not very conversant with the duties a governess is expected to perform, but from all I have heard I should have supposed that almost anything would be preferable.'

There was so much truth in what he said that she was obliged to suppress a sigh. She said in a milder tone: 'Yes, but not marriage to a drunkard, I assure you.'

'He is not likely to live long,' he offered.

She began to feel a good deal of curiosity now that her alarm had been allayed, and looked an enquiry.

'His constitution has always been sickly,' he explained. 'If he does not meet his death through violence, which is by no means improbable, the brandy will soon finish him.'

'Oh!' said Miss Rochdale weakly. 'But why do you wish to see him married?'

'If he dies unmarried I must inherit his estate,' he answered.

She could only stare at him. Happily, since she was for the moment unable to find words to express her bewilderment, the servant came into the room just then, with a tray of tea, bread-and-butter, and cold meat, which he set down on the table beside her. He looked towards Carlyon, and said in a worried voice: 'Mr. Eustace is not come in yet, my lord.'

'It is of no moment.'

'If he is not in some scrape!' the man murmured. 'He went off in one of his quirks, my lord.'

Carlyon shrugged his disinterest. The servant sighed, and withdrew. Miss Rochdale, having drawn up her chair to the table, and poured out a cup of tea, addressed herself gratefully to the cold mutton, and began to feel more able to grapple with her circumstances. 'I should not wish to appear vulgarly inquisitive, my lord,' she said, 'but did you say that you would inherit the estate if your cousin were to die unwed?'

'I did.'

'But don't you wish to inherit it?' she demanded.

'Not at all.'

She recruited herself with a sip of tea. 'It seems very odd!' was all she could think of to say.

He came up to the table, and took a chair opposite her. 'I dare say it may, but it is the truth. I should explain to you that I was for five unenviable years my cousin's guardian.' He paused, and she saw his lips tighten. After a moment, he continued in the same level voice: 'His career at Eton came to an abrupt end, for which most of his paternal relatives held me to blame.'

'Why, how could that be?' she asked, surprised.

'I have no idea. It was commonly said that if his father had not died during his infancy, or if my aunt had appointed one of her brothers-in-law to be his guardian in preference to myself, his disposition would have been wholly different.'

'Well, to be sure, that seems very hard! But – pardon me! – was it not strange that you should have been chosen to be his guardian? You must have been very young!'

'Your own age. I was six-and-twenty. It was natural enough. My aunt was my mother's elder sister; she inherited this estate from grandfather. My own estates lie within seven miles of it, and the intercourse between our two families had been constant. I had myself been fatherless for many years, a circumstance that perhaps made me older than my years. I found myself, at the age of eighteen, the head of a family whose youngest members were still in the nursery.'

'Good heavens, do not tell me you were called upon to take charge of a family at that age!' Miss Rochdale exclaimed.

He smiled. 'No, not quite that. My mother was then living, but she did not enjoy good heath, and it was natural that they should look to me.'

She regarded him wonderingly. 'They?'

'I have three brothers, and three sisters, ma'am.'

'All in your charge!'

'Oh no! My sisters are now married; one of my brothers is on Sir Rowland Hill's staff, in the Peninsula; another is secretary to Lord Sidmouth at the Home Office, and in general resides in London. You may say that I have only the youngest on my hands. He is in his first year at Oxford. But at the time of which I speak they were all at home.' The smile again lit his eyes. 'Your own experience must tell you, ma'am, that a family of six, ranging in age from infancy to sixteen years, is no light burden to cast upon a delicate female.'

'No, indeed!' she said feelingly. 'But you had tutors – governesses?'

'Yes, I lost count of them,' he agreed. 'Two of my brothers had the most ingenious ways of getting rid of their preceptors. But I do not know why I am boring on about my affairs, after all! I meant merely to explain how it was that my aunt came to leave her son to my care. I must confess that I most signally failed either to curb his inclination for all the more disastrous forms of dissipation, or to influence him in any way for the better. I only succeeded in giving him a profound dislike of me. I cannot blame him: his dislike of me can be nothing compared with the sentiments I have always cherished in regard to him.' He looked across the table at her, and added with deliberation: 'It is not an easy task to deal fairly with a youth for whom you can feel nothing but contempt and dislike, ma'am. One of my cousin's uncles would tell you that I was always hard on him. It may have been so: I did not mean to be. When I was obliged to remove him from Eton, I put him in charge of an excellent tutor. It did not answer. A great noise was made over my refusal to entertain the notion of letting him go to

Oxford. There was, in fact, little likelihood of his proving himself eligible, but on every count I should have opposed it. I was held, however, to have acted from spite.'

'I wonder you should have listened to such ill-natured nonsense!' Miss Rochdale observed, quite hotly.

'I did not. After various vicissitudes, the boy took up a fancy to enter the Army. I thought if he could be removed from the society that was ruining him there might be some hope of his achieving respectability, so I bought him a pair of colours. I was instantly held to nourish designs on his inheritance, and to have chosen this way of putting a period to his existence. Happily for my reputation, he was asked to send in his papers before he had seen any active service. By that time he was of age, and my responsibility had come to an end.'

'I am astonished you should not have washed your hands of him!'

'To a great extent I did, but as his interpretation of our relationship included a belief that he was at liberty not only to pledge my credit, but to attach my signature to various bills, it was a trifle difficult to ignore him.'

She was very much shocked. 'And his paternal relatives blame you! Upon my word, it is too bad!'

'Yes, it becomes a little wearisome,' he acknowledged. 'I blame myself for having lent a certain amount of colour to their suspicions by once taking up a mortgage on part of the unencumbered land. I really meant it for the best, but I should have known better than to have done it. Were he to die now, and his property to come into hands, it would be freely said in certain quarters that I had not only encouraged him to commit all the excesses that led to his end, but had, by some unspecified means, prevented him from marrying.'

'I own it is very disagreeable for you,' she said, 'but I am persuaded your own family, your friends, would not believe such slander!'

'By no means.'

'You should not allow yourself to regard it.'

'No, perhaps I should not, if I had only myself to consider. But such whisperings can be extremely mischievous. My brother John, for instance, might find them embarrassing, and I have no desire to throw any rub, however unwitting, in his way. And Nicky – no, Nicky would never bear to hear me slandered!' He broke off, as though recollecting that he was addressing a stranger, and said abruptly: 'The simplest way to put a stop to all this nonsense is to provide my cousin with a wife, and that is what I am determined to do.'

'But I do not properly understand, sir! If, as you say, your cousin dislikes you, why would he not himself look about him for a wife? He cannot wish you to inherit his possessions!'

'Not at all. But not all the representations of his doctor have been enough to convince him that his life is not worth the purchase of a guinea. He considers that there is time and to spare before he need burden himself with a wife.'

'If this is so, how have you been able to persuade him to be married to some unknown female whom, I collect, you have found for him through advertisement? It must be preposterous!'

'I have said that I will meet his present debts if he does so.'

She regarded him with some shrewdness. 'But he would be left with the burden of a wife on his hands. Or have you also undertaken to provide for this unfortunate female, sir?'

'Of course,' he said matter-of-factly. 'There has been no suggestion on my part that the marriage should be more than a form. Indeed, I would ask no woman to live with my cousin.'

She wrinkled her brow, and said with a faint flush: 'Can your purpose be achieved so? Forgive me, I think you cannot have considered, sir! To exclude you from the succession must there not be an heir?'

'No, it is immaterial. The property is most foolishly left. My cousin inherited it from his and my grandfather, through his mother, but her marriage to Lionel Cheviot had so much displeased my grandfather that he was at pains to prevent its falling into his hands, or on to those of his family. With this aim, he settled it upon his grandson, with the proviso that if Eustace died unmarried it must revert to his younger daughter, or her eldest son: myself, in fact.'

'It is entailed, I collect?'

'No, it is not an entail precisely. On the day Eustace marries he may dispose of the property as he wishes. It is an awkward arrangement, and I have often wondered what maggot can have entered my grandfather's head. He had some odd fancies, one of them being a strong persuasion that early marriages are beneficial to young men. That may have been in his mind when he made these provisions. I cannot tell.' He paused, and added calmly: 'You must acknowledge, ma'am, that my present scheme is not as fantastic as it may at first appear.'

She could not help smiling at this, but merely said: 'Will you find any female ready to lend herself to such a marriage? I must hold that to be in grave doubt.'

'On the contrary, I hope I may have done so,' he retorted.

She resolutely shook her head. 'No, my lord, you have not, if you have me in your mind. I could not entertain such a notion.'

'Why could you not?' he asked.

She blinked at him. '*Why* could I not?' she repeated.

'Yes, tell me!'

She found herself quite unable to comply with this request, although she was sure that she knew her own reasons. After struggling to put these into words, she sought refuge in evasion, and replied crossly: 'It must be perfectly plain why I could not!'

'Not to me.'

Apparently he was not to be so put off. Eyeing him with some resentment, Miss Rochdale said: You do not appear to me to want for sense!'

'No, nor am I so set up in my conceit that I cannot be convinced. I am waiting for you to do so.'

This very reasonable speech caused Miss Rochdale to feel a quite justifiable annoyance. She said coldly: 'I cannot undertake to do so. You may say, if you please, that I still have enough pride to recoil from such a contract.'

'What I please to say cannot possibly signify,' he replied patiently. 'Is this all your reason?'

'Yes – no! You must know that it is impossible to put into words what I feel! Every feeling must be offended!'

'Are you betrothed?' he asked.

'No, I am not!'

'You are perhaps in the expectation of becoming so?'

'I have told you that I am six-and-twenty,' snapped Miss Rochdale. 'It is in the highest degree unlikely that I shall ever be betrothed!'

'In that case,' he returned prosaically, 'you might do very much worse for yourself than to strike this bargain with me.' He saw how her colour rose, and smiled with a good deal of understanding at her. 'No, do not fly out upon me! Consider for a moment! You appear to be committed to a life of drudgery. I do not even know your name, but it is apparent to me – was apparent from the outset – that you were not born to the position you now occupy. If you are without the expectation of contracting an eligible alliance, what does the future hold for you? You must be too well aware of the evils of your situation to make it necessary for me to point these out to you. Marry my cousin: you must own that the advantages of such an alliance would outweigh the drawbacks which, I assure you, I perceive as clearly as you do yourself. His character is disgraceful, but he comes of a good family: as Mrs. Cheviot, with an easy competence to call your own, you must command respect. You need do no more than take my cousin's hand in church: I will engage for it that he shall not afterwards molest you. You may pass the rest of your life in comfort; you may even marry a second time, for I am in earnest when I say that my cousin cannot hope to continue long in his present way of life. Think soberly before you make me an answer!'

She heard him out in silence, meeting his steady regard at first, but presently lowering her eyes to the contemplation of her own hands, tightly clasped in her lap. It was impossible for her to listen to him unmoved. It was rarely that she had encountered a fellow-creature who understood any part of the ills of her

21

situation. Such casual acquaintances as she possessed seemed to think that the genteel nature of her chosen occupation must make it acceptable to her. But this strange, curt man, with his rather hard eyes and his almost blighting matter-of-factness, had called her life a drudgery. He had said it without a trace of sympathy in either face or voice, but he had said it, and only those who had endured such a life could know how true it was.

She hoped that she had too much delicacy of principle to allow the temptation she felt to overcome her scruples. That it was a temptation it would be useless to deny. Her future was indeed uncertain, and she was being offered, merely for giving her hand in nominal marriage, security, perhaps even the means of commanding again some of the elegancies of life. To remain steady in refusing must be a struggle; it was a minute or two before she could trust herself to look up. She tried to smile; it was a woeful attempt. She shook her head. 'I cannot. Do not press me further, I beg of you! My mind is made up.'

He bowed slightly. 'As you wish.'

'I think you must perceive that I could not do it, sir.'

'You have asked me not to press you further, and I shall not do so. You shall be conveyed to Five Mile Ash at whatever hour of the day you choose to-morrow.'

'You are very good,' she said gratefully. 'I wish Mrs. Macclesfield may not turn me from her door! I am persuaded she would do so if she knew the truth!'

'You will have time to think of some acceptable explanation. Drink your tea! When you have done so, I will conduct you to the inn I spoke of, and arrange for your accommodation there.'

She thanked him meekly, and picked up her cup. She was relieved to find that he did not appear to be vexed, or even disappointed at her refusal to fall in with his schemes. She felt herself impelled to say: 'I am sorry to disoblige you, my lord.'

'I know of no reason why you should be expected to oblige me,' he answered. He took his snuff-box from his pocket, and opened it. 'You still have the advantage of me,' he remarked easily. 'May I know your name?'

'My name is Rochdale,' she replied, after a second's hesitation. 'Elinor Rochdale.'

His hand remained poised above his open box; he looked up quickly, and repeated in an expressionless tone: 'Rochdale.'

She was conscious of a heightening of the colour in cheeks; she said defiantly; 'Of Feldenhall!'

He inclined his head in a gesture betokening nothing more than an indifferent civility, but she was very sure that he knew her history. She watched him inhale his snuff, and suddenly said: 'You are correct in what you are thinking, sir: I am the daughter of a man who, between unlucky speculation and the gaming-table, came to ruin, and shot himself.'

If she had expected to embarrass him, she was doomed to disappointment. He restored his snuff-box to his pocket, remarking merely: 'I should not have supposed it to have been necessary for Miss Rochdale of Feldenhall to pursue the calling of a governess, whatever her father's misfortunes may have been.'

'My dear sir, I have not a penny in the world but what I have earned!' she said tartly.

'I can readily believe it, but you are not, I fancy, without relatives.'

'Again you are correct! But I am the oddest creature! If I must be a drudge, as you have described me, I prefer to receive a wage for my labours!'

'You are certainly unlucky in your relatives.' He commented.

'Well,' she said candidly, 'I cannot quite blame them, after all. It is no light matter to have a penniless girl foisted on to one, I am sure. And one, moreover, to whose name a disagreeable stigma is attached. You yourself know something of what it means to be whispered about: you should be able to understand my resolve not to cause either my relatives or my friends embarrassment. You will say that I might have called myself by some other name! I might perhaps have done so had I had less pride.'

'I should not say any such thing,' he answered calmly. 'I will agree, however, that you have a great deal of pride – and some of it false.'

'False!' she exclaimed, quite taken aback.

'Certainly. It has led you to exaggerate the consequences of your father's death.'

'You cannot know the circumstances that led to it,' she said, in a low voice.

'On the contrary. But I have yet to learn that you were in any way concerned in them.'

'Perhaps you are right, and I have allowed myself to be too much mortified. My first experience of how the world must look upon our affairs was an unhappy one. You must know that I was betrothed to a certain gentleman at the time of my father's death who – who was excessively relieved to be released from his obligations.' She lifted her chin, adding: 'Not that I cared a button for that, I assure you!'

He remained entirely unmoved. 'How should you, indeed?'

She would have spurned any expression of pity, but she felt irrationally annoyed by this unfeeling response, and said rather sharply: 'Well, it is no very pleasant thing to be jilted, after all!'

'Very true, but the knowledge that you were well rid of a bad bargain must soon have allayed your chagrin, I image.'

A reluctant twinkle came into her eye. 'I have not the most distant guess, my lord, why the extreme good sense of your remarks should put me out of charity with you, but so it is!' she said. 'You will do well to conduct me to your decent inn before I am provoked into answering you in a style quite unsuited to our different degrees!'

He smiled. 'Why, I am sorry if I have vexed you, Miss Rochdale. But I cannot conceive that expressions of sympathy on my part could in any way benefit you, or, in fact, be acceptable to you.'

She began to drawn on her gloves. 'How odious it is in you always to be so precisely right! Do your friends in general feel themselves to be remarkably foolish when they are with you?'

'As I am fortunate in having a good many friends, I believe no,' he replied gravely.

She laughed, and rose to her feet. As she did so, a bell pealed vigorously, as though pulled by a very urgent hand. It startled her, and she turned her eyes towards Carlyon in a look of dismayed enquiry. He had risen when she did, and he moved towards the door, saying: 'That is doubtless my cousin. You will not wish to meet him. Do not be alarmed! I will not let him come into this room.'

'It is his own house after all!' she said, amused. 'I suppose he will not eat me!'

'Unlikely, I think. But he will probably be drunk, and I should be loth to subject you to any more annoyance than you have already suffered.'

The servant must have been nearer at hand than either of them knew, for before Carlyon could reach the door voices were heard in the hall, a hasty footstep sounded, and a tall, slender young gentleman fairly burst into the room, exclaiming in accents of heartfelt relief: 'Oh, Ned, thank God you are here! I had nearly rid home, only that Hitchen told me in the very nick of time that you had driven over here! I am in the devil of a pucker! In fact, I don't know what's to be done, and I thought I had best come to you at once, even if you are not quite pleased with me!'

One glance at this fair-headed, fresh-faced youth, with his open blue eyes, and tanned cheeks, had been enough to convince Miss Rochdale that whoever else he might be he was not Carlyon's dissolute cousin. A second glance was needed to enable her to discern an indefinable likeness in him to Carlyon, for it was not marked. He was plainly in considerable agitation, and he looked more than a little scared. Her experience of Carlyon, brief as it was, prevented her from feeling any surprise at his damping response to the young man's impetuous speech.

'Yes, certainly it was the best thing to do,' he said. 'But I cannot believe there is any occasion for all this commotion, Nicky. What have you been doing?'

His young brother heaved a large sigh, and smiled blindingly at him. 'Oh, Ned, you always make a fellow feel there is nothing so desperately bad after all! But indeed there is! I'm excessively sorry, but I have killed Eustace Cheviot!'

Three

A shocked silence fell upon the room. Carlyon stood perfectly still, staring at his brother under suddenly frowning brows. Nicky returned his gaze, deprecatingly, but not unhopefully. He put Miss Rochdale strongly in mind of a puppy, who, having chewed up his master's shoes, was doubtful of winning approval.

It was Carlyon who broke the silence. 'The devil you have!' he said slowly.

'Yes,' Nicky said. 'And I know you won't like it, Ned, but indeed I never meant to do it! You see, it was – Well, you now how he –'

'Just a moment, Nicky! Let me have this from the start! What are you doing in Sussex?'

'Oh, I've been rusticated!' Nicky explained. 'I was on my way home when –'

'Why?' interrupted Carlyon.

'Well, it is nothing very bad, Ned. You see, there was a performing bear.'

'Oh!' said Carlyon. 'I see.'

Nicky grinned at him. 'I knew you would! Keighley was with me – just kicking up a lark, you know! And, of course, when I saw that bear – well, I *had* to borrow it, Ned!'

'Of course,' Carlyon agreed dryly.

'The Bag-wig said I stole it, but that's fudge! As though I would do such a thing! That made me as mad as fire, I can tell you! Well, I don't mind his abusing me like a pick-pocket for setting the brute on to tree two of the Nobs – it did, Ned! It was the most famous thing you ever saw in your life!'

'I dare say, but I didn't see it.'

'No, and I wish you might have done so, for I do think you must have enjoyed it. Well, there it was, and of course I expected I should have to fork out my knocking-in money, or some such thing, and I didn't care a fig for that. But then, as I say, the Dean would have it I had stolen the bear, in spite of my telling him that I had only borrowed it, and I fired up at last, and said I'd no need to steal bears because if you knew I wanted one you would very likely give me one –'

'It is the last thing in the world I would give you.'

'Well, I don't want one; I should not know what to do with it. But I dare say my saying that put him in a worse pet, for the long and the short of it is that I am rusticated for the rest of the term. But I don't think the Bag-wig was so very angry, you know, because for one thing he don't like one of the Nobs the bear chased, and for another, I'll go bail he had a twinkle in his eye, for I saw it. He's a great gun!'

'Very well, and what happened next?'

'Oh, then, of course, I had to come down! Keighley drove me to London in his new phaeton. He has the prettiest pair of bays, Ned! Regular sixteen-mile-an-hour tits, and –'

'Never mind that! I want to hear the rest of this story.'

'Oh, yes! Well, from London I had to come the rest of the way on the stage-coach to Wisborough Green –'

'Why, in heaven's name?'

'Oh, pockets to let! To tell you the truth, when I'd paid my fare I'd only a couple of benders left.'

'That I can well believe, but could you not have gone to Mount Street?'

'Yes, but I thought very likely John would be there, and you know what he is, Ned! He would have been prosing on and on, and I don't mind if you take me to task, but I won't have John preaching sermons to me, because he's not my guardian, after all, and it only makes me mad!'

'You are quite out of luck: John is at home.'

'Yes, I know he is: Hitchen told me so. I wish he were not, for he is bound to pull a long face over what has happened, and say I had no business to have done it, just as though he would not have done it himself, which I know he must have, for with all his prosy ways he's right one, isn't he, Ned?'

'Yes; and what is it that he must have done?'

'I was coming to that. I thought, when I reached Wisborough Green, that I would go into the Bull, and borrow old Hitchin's gig to take me up to the Hall. And Jem said he was in the coffee-room, and I went in, and he was, and that damned fellow, Eustace, was there too. Everything would have been all right and tight had it not been for that, Ned!'

'Was anyone else in the coffee-room?'

'No, only Hitchen and me. Well, I was quite civil to Eustace, and he was too – to me, I mean. And Hitchin said I might borrow the gig, and while the nag was being harnessed would I have some supper? I was devilish hungry, I can tell you, and Hitchin had a rare ham there, so I said I would. And that's when it all began. Because while I was eating the ham there Eustace sat, grumbling himself into a fit of the sullens. You know how he does! I wasn't paying much heed to him, and I would not have, only that he started on you, Ned.' He broke off, and his boyish countenance hardened. Miss Rochdale, curiously watching him, thought that he ground his teeth. 'He said such things there was no bearing it!'

'No, I see. Was he foxed, Nicky?'

Nicky gave this his consideration. 'Well, he wasn't as drunk as a wheelbarrow,' he explained. 'Just a trifle bosky, you know. He always is. I warned him I'd not sit by while he abused you, but it was all to no purpose. He said – Well, that's no matter! I knocked him down – and so would John have done!'

'Yes, never mind that! Go on!'

'He never could bear to have his cork drawn, and I did – landed him a regular facer! He was ready to murder me! Picked himself up, and came at me, and before you could turn round we

28

were at it, milling away! I floored him again, and the table went over in the flurry, and all the plates and things were on the ground, and the big knife Hitchen used to carve the ham. By God, Ned, Eustace is a shocking loose-screw! Do you know, he snatched up that knife, and tried to stab me with it? We had the devil of a struggle, and there was Hitchin, trying to help me wrench the knife out of his hold, and only getting in the way, and – O God, Ned, I don't know how it happened, and I swear I never meant to do it! I had hold of the knife, and suddenly he let go, and whether he tripped, or it was Hitchin trying to grasp him – though I don't mean to say it was anyone's fault but mine! – but however it was he fell forward, and before I knew – before I had time to move –!' He broke off, covering his face with his hands.

'In fact, it was an accident?'

'Yes, it was an accident. Of course it was an accident! Why, is it likely I would –'

'No, certainly not. But there is no need to be so agitated, if that is what happened. The case is not desperate.'

'Oh, Ned, do you think so indeed? Shall I have to stand my trial? Will they say I murdered Eustace? For I suppose that is what I have done, though I did not mean to.'

'Nothing of the sort! Don't be silly, Nicky! As for standing your trial, it won't come to that. You will have to face a Coroner's inquest, but Hitchin's evidence must clear you of blame.'

'Oh, yes!' Nicky said naïvely. 'Hitchin told me not to put myself in a pucker, because if it had been ten times as bad as he would swear the devil out of hell for one of us!'

'I dare say he may have said so, but you will do better not to repeat it.'

'No, of course not. Besides, he has only to tell the truth, for it happened exactly as I have told you. And it is not that I am sorry he's dead, because I'm not, but I never thought it would have been so horrid! When I think of the way that knife slid into Eustace I feel quite sick!'

'No useful purpose is served by your thinking of it any more.'

'No. Well, I will not, but I can tell you, Ned, it almost makes me wish I had not been rusticated at all!'

At this point, Miss Rochdale, who had all the time been standing by the table, listening with gradually increasing appreciation to young Mr. Carlyon's artless recital, was betrayed into uttering a sound between a choke and a gasp. It brought Carlyon's head round quickly; he said: 'We are both of us forgetful of our manners. You will allow me to introduce my brother Nicholas to you, Miss Rochdale. Nicky, you do not know Miss Rochdale, I think.'

'Oh, no! I beg pardon! I did not immediately perceive – How do you do?' Nicky stammered, making his bow.

She gave her hand. 'Pray do not regard it! It was very natural you should not. I should have left you with your brother but that I do not know my way about this house, and had no very clear notion where I should go. Perhaps, my lord, I might await you in –'

'No, I beg you will be seated, Miss Rochdale. I shall not detain you for many more minutes, I trust.'

'Ned, you do not say so, but I know very well you cannot like this!' Nicky burst out. 'And indeed I would rather by far that you should curse me for putting you in such a fix, for of course I see that is just what I have done, though I never meant to, and Bedlington, and the rest of them, will set it about that you wanted me to pick a quarrel with Eustace, and I can't see how it will all end!'

'No, I don't like it at all,' Carlyon replied, 'but there would be very little sense in my cursing you for what you could not help. It has been an unlucky mischance, but we must trust to come about. I dare say we shall do so. Did the knife enter some vital organ? Was he killed instantly?'

'Oh, no! In fact, I did not at first think – it seemed so unlikely that I could possibly have – But when Greenlaw saw him –'

'Greenlaw is there?' Carlyon interrupted.

'Yes – oh, yes! Well, of course, as soon as I knew what had occurred I ran instantly to fetch him. I thought you would say I should do so, though I never supposed it was anything but what might be easily mended. But Greenlaw says he will not last the night, and –'

'Are you telling me that Eustace is still alive?' Carlyon asked sharply.

'I don't know, but I fancy so. Greenlaw said it could not be many hours, but –'

'Good God, Nicky, why did you not tell me this before? It puts quite a different complexion on the matter!'

'Does it make it better?' Nicky asked hopefully.

'Most certainly it does! One evil consequence may at least be averted. How came you here? In Hitchin's gig?'

'Yes – and now I come to think of it I have left it standing outside, so I had best –'

'Matthew may drive it back to Wisborough Green. Tell him so! You will find my travelling carriage in the stable yard: desire Steyning to convey you to the Hall, and say I shall not need him again to-night. Now go, Nicky! And mind you do not talk of this to any save John!'

'Yes, but, Ned, I had as lief –'

'No, do as I bid you!'

'Yes, but where do you go, Ned?'

'I am going to Eustace, of course, to try what I can do to untangle this coil.'

'Well, I think I should come with you. For, after all –'

'You would be very much in the way. Make your bow to Miss Rochdale, and be off!'

He was obeyed, but reluctantly. As the door closed behind him, Carlyon turned to Elinor, and said without preamble: 'It is a fortunate circumstance that you were here. I fancy I have no need to explain to you that the man now lying at Wisborough Green is my cousin?'

'Indeed, no! I had collected that he must be the man I was supposed to be going to marry.'

'He is the man you *are* going to marry,' he replied, with decision.

She stared at him. 'What can you possible mean?'

'You heard my brother: Cheviot is not yet dead. If we can reach Wisborough Green while he still breathes, and is in possession of his senses, you may be married to him, and he may leave his estate away from me. Come, I have not time to lose!'

'No!' she cried. 'No, I will not do it!'

'You must do it: the matter is now become of too much moment to allow of my permitting you to talk yourself out of arguments. While there was no immediate prospect of Eustace's death I might respect the scruples which led you to refuse to marry him, but all that is changed. In doing what I tell you now you will run no risk of discovering disagreeable consequences in the future. You will be a widow before the morning.'

'There is one consequence that remains unchanged!' she retorted. 'You are asking me to sell myself, to marry a dying man for the advantages it may bring me, and every feeling must be offered by such –'

'I am doing no such thing. I offer you nothing.'

'You said – you gave me to understand I was to become, in plain words, your pensioner!'

'What I said an hour ago is no longer to the purpose. I am asking you to help me.'

'Oh, it is wrong! I knew it is wrong, and crazy beside!' she exclaimed, wringing her hands. 'How can you think to put me in such a position? Can you not perceive –'

'Yes, I can perceive, but I am not thinking very much of you at this present. I will engage to shield you to the best of my power from scandalous whisperings, and I believe I know how that may be achieved, but all that is for the future.'

'Oh, you are abominable!' she said indignantly.

'I am anything you please, Miss Rochdale, but there will be time enough to tell me so later. I am going now to fetch my curricle up to the house. I shall not be many minutes.'

'Lord Carlyon, I will not go with you!'

He paused, with his hand on the door, and looked back at her. 'Miss Rochdale, you have been very frank with me, and I with you. We know each other's circumstances. I tell you now that in doing as I bid you have nothing to lose. Have no fear that the world will look on you askance! Curiosity and conjecture there may be, but who will dare to cast a slur on you while you are acknowledged by Carlyon? Behave like the sensible woman I believe you to be, and do not make a piece of work about nothing! Now, I have stayed talking too long already, and must go for my curricle.'

She was left without a word to say. The conviction that the affair was not as simple, almost as commonplace, as it seemed when he described it, could not be banished, but, whether from being a good deal tired by the events of the day, or from her acknowledged dread of having to present herself at Five Mile Ash on the morrow with a lame excuse trembling on her lips, she felt herself to be quite unequal either to continue arguing, or to defy one who seemed to be too much in the habit of ordering the lives of others to broke any opposition to his will. Accordingly, when the old servant came into the room a few minutes later to tell her that his lordship was waiting for her at the door, she rose up meekly out of her chair, and accompanied him out to the curricle. She was able to see, in the now bright moonlight, that her trunk and her valise were already corded on to the boot, and, absurdly enough, that seemed to settle the matter, she took Carlyon's hand, which he had stretched down to her, and mounted into the carriage beside him. His horses were fidgeting, but he kept them standing. 'You will be cold, I am afraid,' he said, critically surveying her pelisse. 'Barrow, fetch out a greatcoat to me directly, if you please! One of Mr. Cheviot's: it does not signify which. Tuck the rug well round you, Miss Rochdale: fortunately we have only some six miles to travel, and the night is fine.'

She did as he recommended, torn between amusement and vexation. His manner showed neither relief nor triumph at her capitulation. She suspected that it had not occurred to him that she might not do as he desired, and began to be strongly of the opinion that he stood in urgent need of a sharp set-down.

The servant came out of the house again with a heavy

driving-coat, which he handed up to Carlyon. Miss Rochdale was huddled into it; the horses sprang into their collars, and the curricle rolled forward at a smart pace. Once beyond the gates, the pace quickened rather alarmingly. Carlyon said: 'You will not object to driving rather fast, I hope. It is quite safe: I am only too familiar with this road.'

'Yes that is very pretty talking,' said Elinor, 'when you know very well you have no intention of slackening this shocking pace, whatever I may say!'

She thought he sounded as though he were amused. 'True. You have really no need to be anxious, however, I shall not overturn you.'

'I am not anxious,' she said coldly. 'You appear to me to be a competent whip.'

'You should certainly be a judge, for your father was one.'

She was taken off her guard, and replied wistfully: 'He was, was he not? I remember –' She checked herself, feeling unable to continue.

He did not seem to notice her hesitation. 'Yes, what we call a nonpareil – quite a nonesuch! As I recall, he was used to drive a pair of grays in a perch-phaeton he had. I have often coveted them.'

'All the driving-men did so. I believe Sir Henry Peyton bought them when – You are a member of the F.H.C. yourself, I dare say?'

'Yes, though I am not frequently in London. To own the truth, to be continually driving a barouche to Salt Hill and back becomes a trifle flat.'

'Yes, indeed, and always at a strict trot!'

'You drive yourself, Miss Rochdale?'

'I was used to. My father had a phaeton built for me.' Again she turned the subject. 'You are a hunting-man also, sir?'

'Yes, but I rarely hunt in Sussex. It is indifferent country. I have a little place in Leicestershire.'

She relapsed into silence, which was unbroken until she suddenly said: 'Oh, this is absurd! I must surely wake up soon, and find that I have been dreaming!'

34

'I am afraid you must be tired indeed,' was all he replied.

She was so much provoked that she sat for some time cudgelling her brain to think of some remark that might disconcert him. She found it. 'I am sure I do not know why you have forced me into this carriage, or why you are in such haste to bring me to your cousin, my lord,' she said, 'for without a licence, I cannot possibly be married.'

'No, you are very right,' he replied. 'I have it in my pocket.'

In a shaking voice she uttered: 'I might have known you would have!'

'I dare say you may not have thought of it before.'

No adequate words with which to answer him presented themselves to her. She could only say: 'I suppose you have even provided for the necessary clergyman to perform the ceremony?'

'We are going to halt at the parsonage on our way,' he said.

'Then I hope very much that the parson may refuse to go with us!' she cried.

'He will certainly crowd us,' he agreed, 'but it will not be for very many minutes, after all.'

Her bosom swelled. 'I have a very good mind to tell him that I am being constrained against my will, and have no desire to marry your cousin!'

'You have not the least need to tell him so; you have only to tell me,' he responded calmly.

There was another pause. 'I suppose you think me excessively silly!' Elinor said resentfully.

'No, I am well aware of the awkwardness of your situation. You may be pardoned for feeling some irritation of the nerves. But if you could not bring yourself to trust me you would do very well. Do not be for ever teasing yourself with thoughts of what is to happen next! I will take care of that.'

She was mollified, and although she would not for any consideration have acknowledged it, the prospect of being able to cast her burdens on his shoulders could not but attract her. She said no more, but ceased to sit bolt upright beside him, and leaned back instead, as though by this relaxation of her body her mind relaxed also. She still cherished a hazy notion that she must regret this adventure, but the night air was making her sleepy; it was pleasant to be bowling along with a light breeze fanning her cheek; the disagreeable necessity of confronting an irate employer no longer loomed before her; and it was fatally easy to allow herself to be carried into a fantastic dream wherein she was only expected to do as she was bid.

When he pulled up his horses before the parsonage gate, Carlyon handed the reins over to her, saying: 'If I am gone above ten minutes, will you walk them, Miss Rochdale?'

'Yes,' she said, in a docile voice.

She was obliged to do so, but she had not taken more than one turn when he rejoined her, this time with a stout little man at his heels. She wondered what arguments had been used to persuade the cleric into performing what must surely be an unorthodox ceremony, but she was not really surprised that they had succeeded. She made room for Mr. Presteign to sit beside her, and gave the reins back to Carlyon. He thanked her, and said: 'This is Miss Rochdale, Presteign.'

Mr. Presteign said how-do-you-do in a flustered voice. He added: 'Of course, if you have the licence there is no objection on that score. But, you know, my lord, if either party should be unwilling, I could not, even to oblige your lordship – not that I mean to suggest that you would – for hope I have too great a respect for your lordship's benevolence to suppose –'

'My dear sir, you know the circumstances! Unusual they may be, but irregular I have taken care they shall not be. My cousin you will find – if we find him at all – very willing to do what he believes must spite me; the lady may draw back from the contract at any moment she chooses so to do.'

The parson seemed satisfied; Miss Rochdale could only reflect on the perversity of her own disposition, which made it impossible for her to draw back the instant she was offered the opportunity of doing so.

It was not far from the parsonage to the inn at Wisborough

Green. Miss Rochdale was soon being ushered into a pleasant a parlour, where a small fire burned, at which she was glad enough to warm her chilled fingers. Mr. Presteign joined her, and she saw, in the full candlelight, that he was a jolly-looking cleric, with rosy cheeks, and a pair of rather innocent blue eyes, just now opened wider than their wont in an expression of mingled nervousness and curiosity.

A servant whom Carlyon addressed as Jem had received them. Elinor heard him say, with a strong Sussex accent, that the doctor was with Mr. Eustace in the best bedroom, and that I was a hem set-out, surelye, but in no ways master Nick's fault, as everyone, whether present or not, would testify to the Crowner.

'Nonsense! Where is Hitchin?' Carlyon asked, stripping off his driving-gloves.

'I'll fetch him to your lordship,' replied the tapster, waiting to help Carlyon to take off his long, many-caped coat. 'He should ought to be in the coffee-room. Lamentable put-about, he is. Well, surely, I disremember when we had such a set-out at the Bull, and your lordship knows I've been with Mr. Hitchin a dunnamany years.'

The landlord, a respectable, middle-aged man, whose ordinarily cheerful countenance was just now overlaid with gloom, came in at that moment. His brow lightened at sight of Carlyon, and he said: 'I don't know when I've been more glad to see your lordship. I've been thinking to myself it was a lucky chance I happened to see your lordship on the road to Highnoons, so it was, for poor master Nick was in a rare taking, and small blame to him! But what I say, and will swear to anywhen, my lord, is that he never had no thought to go sticking my knife into Mr. Eustace! And as for the start of it all, I'll tell the Crowner to his head Master Nick was speaking comely as you please to Mr. Eustace, until Mr. Eustace went beyond what flesh and blood could stand, let alone a high-couraged young gentleman, which we all know Master Nick is!'

'Is Mr. Eustace alive?' demanded Carlyon.

'Oh, ay, me lord! He's alive, but none so valiant, by what I hear from the doctor. Don't you be afeared for Master Nick, my lord! I saw the whole, and there's no Crowner going to shake me.'

'The whole village will just about say as how it were Mr. Eustace as done the thing!' said the helpful Jem eagerly.

'I'll go up to Mr. Eustace. Do you keep this fool, Jem, from ruining all, Hitchin! And bring coffee for the lady, and for Mr. Presteign!'

He left the room, the landlord at his heels, and strode up the short corridor to the staircase. Hitchin said: 'I see your lordship's brought Parson along, but asking your pardon, it ain't a parson Mr. Eustace is in the mood to see, nor ever was. I misdoubt me Parson won't like it, for he's got no know, though a pleasant enough gentleman, and preaches a comfortable sermon, I'm sure. Howsoever, it's as well to have everything shipshape and above-board, I dare say.'

'Exactly so!' Carlyon said.

Four

The room which Carlyon softly entered at the head of the staircase was a wainscoted apartment, hung with dimity curtains, and containing a four-poster bed, which stood out into the room. Under the patchwork quilt, and propped up by pillows, lay a young man, his head a little fallen to one side. One lock of his lank, dark hair was tumbled across his brow; his lips, which were almost bloodless, were slightly parted; and he was breathing short and fast. The light cast by a branch of candles on a nearby table showed that his countenance had assumed a ghastly pallor; he seemed to be sleeping.

A grizzled man, wearing the conventional frock-coat, but not the wig, of a doctor of medicine, was seated by the bedside, but he looked up when he heard the door open, and at once rose, and went to meet Carlyon. 'I thought you would come, my lord,' he said, in a lowered tone. 'Upon my soul, this is a bad business – a very bad business!'

'As you say. How is he?'

'I can do nothing for him. The knife entered the stomach. He is sinking, and I do not expect him to outlive the night.'

'Is he in possession of his faculties?'

The doctor smiled grimly. 'Quite enough so to be casting about in his mind for some means of doing you an injury, my lord.'

Carlyon glanced towards the bed. 'I hope he may not have hit upon the only way in which he can accomplish it.'

'He has done so, but you need feel no alarm on that score.'

'He has done so?'

'Oh, yes! But no one but Hitchen and myself has heard what he has to say. When I found what he would be at I took care to send the nurse about her business. If this had to happen it is as well it has happened where he is too well known to have the power of working mischief.'

'What are you talking of?'

The doctor looked at him under his brows. 'No, it would not occur to you, I suppose, my lord. Mr. Cheviot, however, knows well that he can best hurt you through your brothers. He has told me that Mr. Nicholas set out to murder him, and at your instigation. He would like to think that he could bring Mr. Nick to the scaffold.'

For a moment Carlyon did not speak; the light, flickering in a little draught, cast his features into relief against the wall; the doctor watched a muscle twitch beside his strong mouth. Then he said: 'Let him think of it. I can trust Hitchin. I shall hope to give his thoughts another direction. Can he go through a ceremony of marriage?'

The doctor's brows rose quickly. 'So you are at that, are you?' he muttered. 'Yes, but whom will you find, my lord? It has been in my mind, but I see no way of accomplishing it. There is too little time left.'

'I have brought a lady with me who is willing to marry him. She is below-stairs, with Presteign.'

The doctor stared at him, a look of appreciative amusement creeping into his eyes. 'You have, eh? My lord, after all the years I have known you, ay, and after the scrapes I've seen you in, and the bones I've set for you, I wonder that you should still have the power to surprise me! But will he consent?'

'Yes, for you could never bring him to believe that I do not covet his estate. He has suspected me ever since I first broached the matter to him of nourishing some evil design for which his marriage was to serve as a mask.'

He stopped, for Eustace Cheviot had stirred, and opened his eyes. The doctor stepped up to the bed, and felt his pulse.

'Damn you, take you hands off me!' Eustace whispered. 'I know I am done for!'

Carlyon walked forward to the other side of the bed, and stood there, looking down at him. The clouded eyes regarded him stupidly for a moment, and seemed gradually to regain intelligence. An expression of malevolence crossed the sharp features; Eustace uttered in a faint voice: 'I wish I had married to spite you, by God, I do! You thought you could gammon me, but I wasn't as green as you thought, Carlyon!'

'Were you not?' Carlyon said evenly.

'You had some precious scheme to throw dust in the eyes of the world. I don't know the whole, but I fancy I was to be married so that it might appear that you had no designs upon Highnoons. And then you would have disposed of me, would you not? Ah, but I am more up to smoke than you thought for, my dear cousin, and I would have willed Highnoons away from you within an hour of leaving the church. You thought I had not sense enough to make my will speedily, but I had!'

'You do yourself harm by talking so much, Mr. Cheviot,' interposed the doctor.

A spasm of pain twisted Cheviot's face; his eyes closed for an instant, but opened again, and fixed themselves once more on Carlyon's face. 'Your precious Nick was too quick for you!' he sneered.

'Too quick for you as well, Eustace.'

Eustace moved his head restlessly on the pillow. 'Yes, by God!' he muttered. 'You'll have it all! Damn you, damn you!'

'Yes, I shall have it all.'

'Ay, but I'll turn it to dust and ashes for you! You will have to see Nick stand his trial! He murdered me, do you hear? He meant to murder me!'

'I may have to see him stand his trial, but his credit is better than yours, cousin, and the only witness to your quarrel is devoted to my interest. I shall see Nick acquitted.'

The calm certainty with which he spoke had its effect. The dying man gave a groan, and made a convulsive attempt to drag himself up on his elbow.

'For God's sake, my lord, take care what you are about!' the doctor muttered, restraining him.

'But he will have to stand his trial!' Eustace gasped. 'Your pride won't stomach that, whatever the event!'

'No,' Carlyon agreed. 'Both my schemes and yours have miscarried. You would see your estate safe from my machinations; I would save Nicky from yours, if I could. Well, I do not value Highnoons above Nicky: I will let it go.'

Cheviot glared at him, his befogged brain only half comprehending what was said to him, clinging obstinately to its one idea. 'How? How?' he panted.

'You may be married, here and now, and bequeath Highnoons to your wife.'

Cheviot frowned, as though trying to concentrate his wits. 'How will that serve you?' he asked suspiciously.

'It will serve me.'

'And you will not step into my shoes?'

'I shall not step into your shoes.'

'I'll do it!' Cheviot said, plucking at the sheet. 'Yes, I'll do it! I don't care about Nick. I'll die happy to think I've foiled you!'

Carlyon nodded, and walked to the door. The doctor followed him out on to the landing. 'You will not do it, my lord!'

'I shall do it. It is what he wishes.'

'He does not understand above half of what you would be at! In all the years of my practice I never met a creature so wholly devoid of good! Well I know what patience you have used towards him, what forbearance! It seems to make him hate you the more. He is a vile fellow! But this –! No, it will not do, my lord!'

'It will do very well. He does not know why I do it, but it is what he wants, and since I have no purpose in my head but to escape an inheritance I do not desire, I shall not sleep the less sound for having in some sort deceived him.'

'Ay, but will it answer, my lord?' the doctor urged. 'To marry him out of hand now might not prove of service to Mr. Nicholas. It must seem –'

'Oh, I am not thinking of Nicky!' Carlyon said. 'He stands in no danger. But it will be better for the lady if it is not generally known that she sees Cheviot for the first time this evening. I think that may be contrived.'

'Good God!' said the doctor weakly. 'Is it so indeed? You go quite beyond me, my lord! How will you contrive it?'

'Oh, a long-standing betrothal, perhaps – kept secret.'

'Kept secret!' exploded Greenlaw. 'And why?'

Carlyon was half-way down the first flight of stairs, but he paused, and looked up, his rather rare smile softening his face. 'My dear sir! For fear of my devilish stratagems, of course!'

'Mr. Edward!' pronounced Greenlaw awfully. 'That is, my Lord Carlyon!'

'Yes?'

The doctor stared down at him with a fulminating eye. 'Nothing!' he said, and went back to his patient.

Carlyon was met at the foot of the stairs by the landlord, who came out of the coffee-room to intercept him. 'My lord, the lady would not partake of any refreshment,' he said. 'And Parson took a fancy to a drop of Hollands, as is his custom.'

'Very well. Have you a pen, ink, and some paper?'

The landlord admitted, with a puzzled frown, that he had these commodities. His brow cleared suddenly. 'To be sure! Mr. Eustace will be wishful to make his Will!' he discovered. 'But it queers me a trifle to know – well, my lord – the lady!'

'The lady is betrothed to Mr. Eustace.'

Hitchin's eyes started at him. 'Betrothed to Mr. Eustace!' he gasped. 'And her so pleasant-spoken and genteel!'

'And Mr. Eustace,' pursued Carlyon, ignoring this involuntary outburst, 'is desirous of marrying her, so that she may be provided for after his death.'

The landlord appeared to have difficulty in controlling his voice. He succeeded in enunciating: 'Yes, my lord!' and tottered away to find the pen and paper. He found, after some search, a serviceable quill. He regarded it severely, and made it the recipient of a pithy confidence. 'Mr. Eustace, is it?' he said scathingly. 'Adone-do! Mr. Eustace never took no such notion into his wicked head, and well you know it! Mr. Eustace to be worriting himself over such things! Ay, just about, he would! Out of your head that came, my lord, don't tell me!'

The quill, very naturally, returned no answer. Hitchin sniffed, and picked up the ink-pot. 'And a hem good thing for you it will be to be shut of Mr. Eustace!' he said.

Carlyon, meanwhile, had entered the parlour. He found Miss Rochdale and the parson seated on either side of the fireplace. Miss Rochdale looked tired, and a little pale, and there was a rather scared look in the eyes which she raised to his. He smiled reassuringly at her, and said: 'Now, if you will come upstairs with me, Miss Rochdale, if you please!'

She said nothing; Mr. Presteign got up from his chair, and asked nervously: 'My lord, am I to infer that Mr. Cheviot is willing to have this ceremony performed?'

'Very willing.'

'Lord Carlyon!' said Miss Rochdale faintly.

'Yes, Miss Rochdale, in a little while. There is nothing to alarm you. Come!'

She rose, and laid her hand on his proffered arm. He patted it briefly, and led her to the door. She whispered: 'Oh, pray do not – I am sure –'

'No, just trust me!' he said.

She could think of no reason why she should, but it did not seem possible to say so; she went with him up the stairs, and into the sick-room.

Eustace Cheviot's eyes were open, his head turned towards the door. Miss Rochdale gazed at him almost fearfully, but he was not looking at her. His eyes remained riveted to his cousin's face, searching it in suspicion and a kind of avid eagerness which gave him something of the look of a bird of prey. Miss Rochdale's clutch tightened on Carlyon's arm instinctively.

He did not seem to notice it, but led her forward. 'Are you of the same mind as ever, Eustace?' he asked, in his cool way.

'Yes, I tell you!'

The doctor was looking curiously at Miss Rochdale. She felt the colour mount to her cheeks, and was glad to stand at the bed-head, out of the direct light of the candles. It did not occur to her until some time afterwards that neither then, nor at any time during the unreal ceremony did her bridegroom look at her. She felt stupid, as though she had been drugged, or hypnotized into acting without her own volition. She watched the doctor, the parson, Carlyon, seeing how they conferred together, but without comprehending what they said; observing their movements, but so divorced from them that she could never afterwards remember quite what had happened in that grim room hung with dimity curtains. All that imprinted itself on her memory was the pattern of the wallpaper, the gay lozenges of colour which made up the patchwork quilt covering the bed, and the way one lock of Cheviot's hair clung dankly to his brow. When her hand was put into his, she started, and looked round wildly. The labouring voice from amongst the tumbled pillows was whispering after the parson words which he had to bend his head to catch.

'Repeat after me . . .'

'I, Elinor Mary . . .' she said obediently.

There was a pause; the parson was looking flustered, raising anguished brows at Carlyon, standing on the other side of the bed. Carlyon moved, dragging the signet ring from his finger, and putting it into his cousin's hand. But it was he who pushed the ring over Elinor's knuckle, guiding Cheviot's weak hand. She remained entirely passive, not moving until presently her arm was taken in a firm hold, and she was led to the table which stood against the wall, and required to sign her name. She did so, and was rather surprised to find that her hand did not shake. The paper was taken from her, and to the bed; she watched the doctor support Cheviot while he slowly traced his signature. Then Carlyon came back to her, and again took her arm, and led her to the door.

'There, that is all,' he said. 'Go down to the parlour: I shall not be very long in coming to you.'

He shut the door upon her, casting a frowning glance towards the bed. The doctor had measured out a cordial, and was holding it to Cheviot's parted lips. He met Carlyon's glance with a significant look. Mr. Presteign said: 'Indeed, I trust I have done right! I do trust I have! I am sure I have never –'

Cheviot's eyes opened. 'Right? Ay! The best day's work of your life, parson!' he uttered. 'But I won't die till I've made my Will! Paper – ink, you damned sawbones! Where's my cousin? He'd cheat me if he could, but I'll live long enough to spite him, see if I don't!'

'Mr. Cheviot, Mr. Cheviot, will you not make your peace with your maker?' implored Presteign.

Cheviot had fallen against his pillows, exhausted by his fit of passion, his eyelids dropping. The doctor stayed by him, his fingers counting the feeble pulse, his eyes watchful on the livid face. At the table Carlyon was writing steadily. Once he paused, and looked thoughtfully at Cheviot, as if considering. Then his quill resumed its searching.

Cheviot roused again from his stupor. 'My Will! Lights! I can't see plain in this infernal darkness!'

'Gently! You shall sign your Will in good time,' Carlyon said, not raising his head.

Cheviot peered across the room at him. 'You're there, are you?'

'Yes, I am here.'

'I always hated you,' Cheviot remarked conversationally.

'Mr. Cheviot, I most earnestly conjure you to put these thoughts out of your mind, and before it too late to –'

'Leave him, man, for God's sake!' Greenlaw said, under his breath.

'Yes, I always hated you,' repeated Cheviot. 'I don't know why.'

Carlyon shook the sand from his paper, and rose with it in his hand, and came to bed. 'Are you able to sign your Will, cousin?' he asked.

'Yes, yes!' Cheviot whispered eagerly, trying to grasp the quill that was placed between his fingers.

'You bequeath all the property of which you die possessed to your wife, Elinor Mary Cheviot: is that your wish?'

A little laugh shook Cheviot. He caught his breath on a stab of pain, and gasped: 'Yes, yes, I don't care! If only I could see more plain!'

'Hold the candle nearer!'

Mr. Presteign picked up the branch in a shaking hand.

'It's not that, my lord,' the doctor muttered.

'I know. Come, Eustace, here is the pen, and there is enough light now. Write down your name!'

The dying man seemed to make a great effort. For a moment, held up in Carlyon's arms, he peered stupidly at the paper under his hand; then his eyes cleared a little, and his aimless clutch on the quill tightened. Slowly he traced his signature at the foot of the paper. The pen slipped from his fingers, the ink on it staining the quilt. 'Oh, I know what I should do!' he said, as though someone had challenged this. 'Put my – put my hand on it, and say – and say – give this as my last will and testament. That's it. By God, I beat you at the post, Carlyon!'

Carlyon lowered him on to the pillows, and removed the paper from under his hand. 'You two are witnesses,' he told the other men. 'Sign it, if you please!'

'If he is of sound mind –' Presteign said doubtfully.

The doctor smiled sourly. 'Don't tease yourself on that score! His mind is as sound as ever it was.'

'Oh, if *you* are assured of that –!' Presteign said, and wrote his name quickly on the paper.

Someone scratched on the door; Carlyon went to it, and opened it, to find Hitchin there, with the intelligence that Mr. Carlyon was below-stairs.

'Mr. Carlyon?'

'Mr. John, my lord. I've shown him into the parlour. Mr. Carlyon is very wishful to see your lordship.'

'Very well, I will come directly.'

The doctor rose from the table, and gave Cheviot's Will back to Carlyon. 'There, it's done, and I hope you may not regret this night's work, my lord,' he said.

'Thank you; I do not expect to regret it.'

'To be throwing a good estate to the four winds for a scruple!' the doctor grumbled.

Carlyon shook his head, and went out of the room. Downstairs, he found Elinor seated by the fire in the parlour, and his brother, John Carlyon, standing in the middle of the room, and staring at her in perplexity. He turned as he heard the door open, and said quickly: 'Ned! For God's sake, what is this farrago of nonsense? I am met by that fool Hitchen, who tells me I shall find Cheviot's betrothed in the parlour, and now this lady informs me that she is married to him!'

'Yes, that is quite true,' Carlyon replied. 'My brother John, Mrs. Cheviot. I am glad you are here, John: you are the very man I need.'

'Ned!' said Mr. Carlyon explosively. 'What the devil have you been about?'

'Just what you knew I meant to be about. Did Nicky tell you what had chanced?'

'Yes, Nicky did tell me!' John said grimly. 'Very pretty tidings, upon my word! But he did not tell me the whole!'

'No, for he did not know it. I have been fortunate in finding a lady willing to marry Eustace, and I stand very much in her debt.' He smiled slightly at Elinor as he spoke, and added: 'Miss Rochdale – or, rather, Mrs. Cheviot – you are very tired, and must be anxious to retire. It has been a fatiguing day for you.'

'Yes,' agreed Elinor, regarding him with a fascinated eye. 'It – it has been just a little fatiguing!'

'Well, I am going to put you in my brother's charge. He will take care of you, and drive you to my home. John, how came you here?'

'I rode.'

'Very well. Leave your horse for me, and take Mrs. Cheviot in my curricle. Tell Mrs. Rugby to see her comfortable bestowed, and be sure that she has some refreshment before she retires.'

'Well – yes, certainly! Of course! But you, Ned?'

'I must stay. I shall come later.'

'Is Eustace alive?'

'Yes, he's alive. I'll tell you the whole presently. Do you take Mrs. Cheviot home now, there's a good fellow!'

'I thought,' said Elinor feebly, 'that I was to put up here for the night.'

'Circumstances have changed, however, and I think you will be more comfortable at the Hall. You will be quite safe in my brother's hands, and you will find my housekeeper very ready to attend to all your wants. John, Mrs Cheviot's baggage is already bestowed in the curricle, so you have nothing to wait for.'

'But what am I going to do?' Elinor asked helplessly.

'We will discuss that to-morrow,' replied Carlyon.

He left the room, just nodding to his brother as he passed him, and Mrs. Cheviot and Mr. Carlyon were left to eye one another doubtfully. 'I will go and bring the curricle round to the door,' said John heavily.

'I don't think I should go.'

'Oh, yes, indeed I think you should! You will not wish to stay here with that creature dying above-stairs.' He checked himself, and coloured. 'I beg pardon! I was forgetting –'

'You need not beg my pardon. I never saw your cousin until an hour ago,' she said.

'You – Mrs. Cheviot, you do not tell me that *you* responded to the advertisement which my brother caused to be –'

'Oh, no! It was all a mistake. I am a governess: I came to take up a position in quite another household, and, in error, stepped into your brother's carriage, which was waiting at the coach-stop. But why I have allowed myself to be thrust into marrying your dreadful cousin I cannot tell! I think I must be as mad as your brother!'

'Well, it is all very odd,' said John, 'but if Carlyon thought you should marry Cheviot you may depend upon it you have done the right thing. You must not be thinking that he is mad: indeed, I can't think how you should do so, for I never knew anyone with a better understanding. I will go and fetch the curricle.'

Elinor had perforce to acquiesce, and in a very few minutes was stepping up once more into this vehicle. John was careful to wrap the rug securely about her, and drove off, holding the horses to a steady trot.

'You know, if you should not object, I should be very glad to know how all this business came about,' he suggested.

She told him her share in the evening's events. He listened in a good deal of surprise, and his comments were those of a sensible man. He had a deliberate way of speaking, and she thought that he resembled Carlyon more nearly than did his youngest brother. In appearance, he was very like him, although half ahead shorter. Both air and address were good, and his manners were conciliating. Elinor found it easy to confide in him, for although he appeared to be quite uncritical to Carlyon's actions, he appreciated the delicacy of her position, and fully entered into her feelings upon the event.

'It is an awkward business indeed!' he said. 'It is too bad of Nicky! As though my brother had not had enough to bear without this catastrophe!'

She ventured to suggest that Nicky seemed not to have been able to avoid the encounter.

'No, but it is all of a piece! Setting bears on to the dons! I might have guessed how it would be! And I dare say Ned never so much as told him he should not have done so!'

'No,' she reflected. 'I believe he did not.'

'No!' he ejaculated. 'But so it is always!' He drove on in fuming silence for a little while.

She said diffidently: 'I think your brother Nicholas was very much shocked by what had happened.'

'I should hope he might be indeed! To be putting Ned to all this trouble! It beats everything! I was never more angry with him in life!'

She was silent. After a moment he said in a severe tone: 'I do not mean to say that there is any harm in Nicky, but he is a great deal too thoughtless, and now we see where it has led him.

50

However, I suppose Carlyon will settle it all, and we must hope that it will be a lesson to Nick.'

'Yes,' she said, smiling a little. 'Mr. Nicholas seemed to think also that his brother would settle it all.'

'Ay, he and Harry were always the same!' John exclaimed. 'For ever getting into scrapes, and running to Ned to pull them out again! While as for my sister Georgiana – But I should not be talking in this way! You know, Miss – Mrs. Cheviot – Ned is the best of good fellows, and it vexes me beyond bearing when I see him so imposed on! Take that creature, Eustace Cheviot! I dare say no one knows the half of what Ned had done for him, or the forbearance he has shown, but does he get one word of gratitude for it? No! I believe Cheviot veritably hated him!'

She shivered. 'You are very right. When I saw him, there was such an expression of enmity in his eyes, when they rested on your brother, that I was almost afraid. Why should it be? It is very terrible!'

He agreed to it, adding: 'There are some men, ma'am, who have such twisted natures that they cannot see virtue in another without hating it. My cousin was such an one. He resented my brother's authority; when Carlyon has rescued him again and again from the consequences of his own conduct it has but increased his jealous hatred of him. It is a good thing for us that he is dead. But I wish he had not met his end at Nick's hands.'

He relapsed into brooding silence, which remained unbroken until the curricle turned in through a pair of great wrought-iron gates, when he roused himself from his abstraction to say: 'We have only a little way to go now. You will be glad to warm yourself at a good fire, I dare say. It has grown chilly.'

The curricle soon drew up before a large, stone-built mansion; and in a very short space of time Elinor was being led across a lofty hall to a pleasant saloon, furnished in the first style of elegance, and lit by a great many candles. Nicholas Carlyon jumped up from a wing-chair by the fire, and demanded eagerly: 'Did you see Ned? How has it gone? Is Eustace dead? Where is Ned?'

'Ned will be here presently. Do, for God's sake, mind your manners, Nick! Set a chair for Mrs. Cheviot this instant! If you will be seated, ma'am, I will desire the housekeeper to prepare a room for you.'

He left the room immediately, and Nicky, blushing at his rebuke, made haste to conduct Elinor to a seat by the fire. 'I beg pardon!' he stammered. 'But what is this? John said – but you are not Mrs. Cheviot!'

'You may well wonder at it,' she said. 'Your brother constrained me to marry your cousin, so I suppose I must be Mrs. Cheviot.'

'He did?' Nicky cried. 'Oh, that's famous! I was afraid I had ruined all! I might have guessed Ned would never allow himself to be out-jockeyed!'

'It may seem famous to you,' retorted Elinor, with some tartness, 'but I can assure you it does not to me! I have not the smallest desire to be married to your odious cousin!'

'No, but I dare say he may be dead by now,' said Nicky encouraging. 'There's no harm done!'

'Yes, there is! There is a great deal of harm, for I was to have gone to Five Miles Ash as governess to Mrs. Macclesfield's family, and now I do not know what is to become of me!'

'Oh, my brother will arrange everything!' Nicky assured her. 'You have no need to be in a fret, ma'am. Ned always knows what one should do. Besides, you would not like to go as a governess, would you? You are not at all like any that my sisters had! I believe you are bamming me!'

She did not feel equal to arguing the matter with him. She untied the strings of her bonnet, and removed it, with a sigh of relief. Her soft brown ringlets were sadly crushed; she tried to tidy them, but was really too weary to care much for her appearance, and soon relapsed into immobility, her cheek propped on one hand, her eyes drowsily watching the flames in the hearth. She was roused presently by the entrance of Mr. Carlyon, who came in with a tray in his hands, which he set down on the table at her elbow.

'I think you should take a glass of wine, ma'am,' he said, pouring one out for her. 'The housekeeper will have your bedchamber ready directly. Will you take a biscuit?'

She accepted it, and sat sipping her wine, and listening to a brief exchange of conversation between the two brothers, until the housekeeper came in to fetch her to bed. She went very willingly, only wondering what John Carlyon could have told the housekeeper to make that comfortable woman accept her with such seeming placidity. She was conducted up a broad, shallow stairway to such a bedchamber as she had not occupied since her father's death. A servant was passing a warming-pan between the sheets of the bed; a fire had been kindled in the hearth; and her brushes and combs laid out upon the dressing-table. The housekeeper assured herself that all was in order, desired Mrs. Cheviot to ring the bell if she should require anything, bade her a respectful good night, and withdrew.

Mrs. Cheviot, leaving the future to take care of itself, prepared to give herself up to the present luxury of a warm bed, and within half an hour was deeply and dreamlessly asleep.

Five

*D*ownstairs, in the saloon, Mr. John Carlyon told his young brother severely that the best thing he could now do would be to go to bed. This suggestion having been indignantly spurned, he said; 'There is nothing more for you to do, and Ned may not reach home until morning. He will not leave while Eustace is still alive, I dare say.'

'Well, I shall sit up till he comes,' Nicky said. 'Good God, I could not sleep a wink! How can you think of it? But, John, how came that lady to be with Ned at Highnoons? I have been puzzling my head over it. It seems very strange!'

'You had best ask Ned,' John replied uncommunicatively.

'Well, and so I shall, and, what is more, he will tell me!' said Nicky, rather nettled.

'Very likely.'

'At all events,' said Nicky, 'the affair is not as bad as it might have been, is it? For if Eustace married that lady –'

'Not as bad as it might have been!' John exclaimed. 'I do not know how it could well be worse! And all come about through a prank I wonder you should not be ashamed to think of perpetrating at your age!'

Nick retired to the chair by the fire, and cast himself into it, saying: 'Oh, fudge! There was nothing in that, I am sure! Why, when Harry was up, you know very well he –'

'Yes, I am aware that there was never anything to choose between you and Harry, more's the pity! But at least Harry was never such a young fool that he would allow himself to be dragged into a quarrel with Eustace Cheviot!'

'John!' said Nicky despairingly, 'I keep on telling you I stood it for as long as I might, but there was no bearing it! If he had abused me I would not have cared, but to hear him say such things of Ned was more than flesh and blood could stand! Besides, I never meant to do more than mill him down, after all!'

John grunted, but upon his young brother's attempting to justify himself still further, interrupted to read him so stern a lecture on the subject of his volatility, thoughtlessness, and general instability of character that Nicky was silenced, and had to sit enduring in dumb resentment this comprehensive homily. When it came to an end, he hunched an offended shoulder, and pretended to bury himself in the *Morning Post*, which lay providentially to hand. John went over to the desk, and busied himself with some papers of his which were lying there.

It was rather more than an hour later, and the brothers had not exchanged any further conversation, when a firm tread was heard to cross the hall, and Carlyon entered the room.

Nicky sprang up. 'Ned, what has been the end of it?' he asked anxiously. 'I thought you would never come! Is Eustace dead?'

'Yes, he is now. You should be in bed, Nicky. Did you see Miss Rochdale safely bestowed, John?'

'Is that her name? Yes, she went up to bed over an hour ago. You have been a thought high-handed in that quarter, have you not?'

'I am afraid so indeed. There was really nothing else to be done, matters having been pushed to a crisis.'

'Ned, you know I am as sorry as I could be!' Nicky said, 'I wouldn't have put you in a fix for the world!'

'Yes, that is what you always say,' interposed John. 'But you go from one scrape to another! Now it has come to this, that you may think yourself fortunate if you do not have to stand your trial for manslaughter!'

'I know,' Nicky said. 'Of course I know that! And perhaps they won't believe it was an accident.'

'My dear Nicky, none of this is likely to go beyond the Coroner's inquest,' Carlyon said. 'You go up to bed, and don't tease yourself any more to-night!'

Nicky sighed, and John, perceiving that he was looking pale and very tired, said roughly: 'Don't worry! We shall not let them hale you off to prison, Nick!'

Nicky smiled sleepily but gratefully at him, and took himself off.

'Incorrigible!' John said. 'Did he tell you why he has been sent down?'

'Yes, there was a performing bear,' Carlyon answered absently.

'I suppose that is sufficient to explain all!'

'Well, it was sufficient to explain it all to me,' Carlyon admitted. 'Once a performing bear had entered Nicky's orbit the rest was inevitable. Have you been waiting up for me? You should not have done so.'

'You look fagged to death!' John said, in his brusque way. 'Sit down, while I pour you a glass of wine!'

Carlyon took a chair by the fire, and stretched his booted legs out before him. 'I am tired,' he owned. 'I hope I may not be called upon to attend any more such death-beds. But we shall brush through this very well if Hitchin does not let his loyalty run away with him.'

John handed him a glass of wine. 'Oh, I don't doubt we shall come about, but we should never have been put into such a situation! It is what I have been saying to you for ever, Ned: you are by far too easy with Nick! There's not an ounce of harm in the boy, but he is a great deal too wild. It is as I said a while back: he plunges into scrapes, and then runs to you to extricate him.'

'Well, thank God he does run to me!' said Carlyon.

'Yes, that is all very well, but why you must needs encourage him to steal bears, and to –'

'My dear John, in what possible way can I be held to have encouraged Nick to do any such thing?' protested Carlyon.

'No, well, I did not mean that precisely, but I know as well as if I had been present that you have not told him how wrong he has been!'

'He knows that without my telling him.'

'He needs to be hauled well over the coals!'

'I expect you have done so already.'

'He does not attend to me as he does to you.'

'He might do so, however, if you would be more sparing of your homilies.'

John shrugged, and said no more for a few moments. When he spoke again it was on another subject. 'Who is this female to whom you married Cheviot?' he asked.

'She is a daughter of Tom Rochdale of Feldenhall.'

'That man! Good God! Then that is how she comes to be a governess! Poor thing! But what is now to become of her?'

'Well, I do not as yet know how Cheviot's affairs may stand, but I dare say something may be saved from the wreck. He made his will in her favour.'

'Made his will in her favour?' John repeated incredulously. 'Ned, was that his doing, or yours?'

'Mine, of course.'

'Well,' John said dubiously, 'I suppose some compensation had to be made her, and, to be sure, I was never in favour of its coming out of your pocket. But ought not the estate to have gone to the next of kin?'

'Old Bedlington, for instance,' said Carlyon.

'Yes, I suppose so, for, after all, he is his uncle.'

'But I don't want old Bedlington to be living within a stone's throw of me,' said Carlyon.

'No, my God!' John agreed, struck by this eminently reasonable point of view. 'I dare say he will kick up the devil of a dust, though.'

'I don't think it. He had never any expectation of inheriting the estate.'

'You will have him down upon you as soon as he hears of this,' John said gloomily. 'Depend upon it, he will blame you for the whole. I suppose he must be the only person alive who had a kindness for Eustace – and if he had known what we knew even he might not have caressed and encouraged him so much!'

'I suppose his own son cannot be a source of much satisfaction to him,' Carlyon said, yawning.

'A source of expense, more like, but I never heard that Francis Cheviot was a commoner like his cousin! Not but what he is like to ruin Bedlington, if he goes on his present pace. I heard that he dropped five thousand at Almack's last week, and I dare say that's not the half of it. I should be sorry for Bedlington, if he were not such an old fool.' He gave a short laugh. 'He is in a great way over the trouble they are in at the Horse Guards.' Carlyon raised his brows in lazy enquiry. 'Oh, information leaking out! Not my department, thank God! It's for ever happening. Bonaparte's agents know their business very well.'

'I thought you were looking a little grave. Is it serious?'

'Serious enough, but they're all as close as oysters over it. Of course, things do leak out – well, if you have old fools like Bedlington dabbling their fingers in state affairs what can you expect? There are plenty of people like him who can't keep their tongues still. Oh, they don't mean to give secrets away, but they're damned indiscreet! That's why Wellington has been keeping his plans so dark this time. But from what Bathurst told the Doctor there's something more than indiscretion in this business. You won't repeat this, Ned, but there's an important memorandum gone astray, and they're all in an uproar over it. By what I can make out, it's to do with his lordship's campaign for this spring, and there are only two copies in existence. You may guess what Bonaparte would give to have an inkling of what Wellington means to do, whether he will march on Madrid a second time, or strike in some new direction!'

'I can indeed! Do you say this memorandum has been stolen?'

'No, I don't say that, but I do know it is missing. However, from all I have ever seen of the way they go on at the Horse Guards it will very likely turn up in the wrong file, or some such thing.'

'You are severe!' Carlyon said, looking amused.

'Why, I dare say Torrens would say the same, for you must know that there are too many of Prinny's creatures foisted on them at the Horse Guards, and a shabbier set of fellows you'd be hard put to it to find than most of 'em! Such jobbery!'

'Oh, now you are back at Bedlington!'

'Him, and some others. Lord Bedlington!' John enunciated scornfully. 'And why, pray?'

'Distinguished military career,' murmured Carlyon.

'Distinguished military fiddlesticks!' snorted John. 'A.D.C. to the Regent! Pander to the Regent, more like! But, there! I do not know why I am boring on in this way. Will you be able to bring Nick off safe, do you think?'

'Yes. Though Eustace would have been glad to have injured him if he could have done it.'

'What a damned fellow he was!' John said warmly. 'I should like to know what harm Nicky ever did him!'

'Well, he seems to have treated him very roughly tonight,' Carlyon pointed out. 'But it was not Nicky he meant to hurt so much as me, through Nicky. Fortunately Greenlaw sent the nurse away as soon as Eustace began to talk, so there's no harm done.'

'Oh, you had Greenlaw there, had you? Well, he's a disrespectful old dog, but safe enough! I'd give something to know what he must have thought of your freaks this night!'

Carlyon smiled. 'Oh, I tried his civility too high, and he got to remembering helping me down from the church steeple, and digging the shot out of your leg, John, that time we stole one of my father's fowling-pieces, and I peppered you so finely – do you remember? He was within an ace of giving me as stern a homily as you have probably given Nick.'

'Impudent old rascal!' John said, grinning. 'I wish he had done so! But, Ned! This Will! Is it in order? Might it not be contested?'

'I believe it is legal enough. I shall certainly not contest it.'

'Not you, no! But Bedlington must be next of kin to Eustace, and it occurs to me that he might try to set the Will aside on that score. For once Eustace was married –'

'No, you are forgetting. By the terms of the original settlement, in default of appointment by Eustace, the estate must have devolved upon me. To invalidate the Will would not benefit Bedlington.'

'True, so it was! Did you think to name an executor?'

'Yes, myself and Finsbury.'

'That was a good thought, to bring a lawyer into it,' John approved. 'But, I must say, I wish you were well out of the business!'

'Why, so I soon shall be, I trust,' Carlyon said, setting down his empty glass, and rising to his feet.

'It seems to me you are left with this widow on your hands!'

'Nonsense! Once probate has been granted I dare say she will sell the estate, and I hope she may be able to live very comfortably upon the proceeds.'

'It has been so mismanaged since Eustace came of age that she may find it hard to find a purchaser,' John said pessimistically. 'Ten to one, too, there will be so many charges on it that the poor girl will find herself in a worse case than ever. Was he in the moneylenders' hands, do you know?'

'I don't, but I should think very likely. His debts will have to be paid, of course.'

'Not by you!' John said sharply.

'Well, we shall see how it goes. How long are you staying with us, John?'

'I must be in London to-morrow, but I shall come back, of course, now that thing have turned out in this way.'

'You need not.'

'Oh, I don't doubt you will manage it very well without me!' John said, smiling at him. 'But that young rascal will have to give his evidence at the inquest, and naturally I shall not stay away at such a time.'

Carlyon nodded. 'As you please. Snuff the candles, if you are coming to bed: I told the servants they need not sit up longer.'

'I have a letter I must finish first. Good night, old fellow!'

'Good night,' Carlyon picked up the branch of candles that stood on one of the tables, and went to the door.

John had seated himself at the desk again, but he looked round. 'I don't know why I should be surprised at Nicky's wild ways, after all!' he remarked. 'I still have the scars of those shots in my leg!'

Carlyon laughed, and went out, closing the door behind him. John stayed looking after him for a moment, a half-smile on his lips, then he sighed, shook his head, and turned back to his correspondence.

Mrs. Cheviot slept late into the morning, being awakened at last by a maidservant, who brought her a cup of chocolate, and the information that breakfast would be served in the parlour at the foot of the stairs. She placed a brass can of hot water on the washstand, and after ascertaining that Madam required no assistance at her toilet, withdrew again.

Elinor sat up in bed, luxuriously sipping her chocolate, and wondering how many of the fantastic events of the precious day had had existence only in her imagination. Her presence in this well-ordered household seemed to indicate that some at least of them had been real. She was unable to refrain from contrasting her present situation with what would have in all probability been her lot in Mrs. Macclefield's house, and she would have been more than human had she not enjoyed the very striking difference. She got up presently, and looked out of the window. It commanded a view of some formal gardens, just now showing only some snowdrops in flower, and beyond these the outskirts of a park. Lord Carlyon was evidently a man of consequence and fortune, and nothing, she reflected, could be more unlike the squalor of his cousin's house than the quiet elegance of his own establishment.

She dressed herself in one of her sober-hued round gowns, and putting a Paisley shawl over his shoulders, betook herself downstairs. While she hesitated in the hall, not quite knowing where she should go, the butler came through a door at the back of the house, and bowed civilly to her, and ushered her into a snug-parlour, where her host and his two brothers were awaiting her before a bright fire.

Carlyon came forward at once, to take her hand. 'Good morning. I trust you are rested, ma'am?'

'Yes, indeed, thank you. I do not think I can have stirred the whole night through.' She smiled, and bowed to the other two men. 'I fear I have kept you waiting.'

'No, no such thing. Will you not be seated? The coffee will be brought in directly.'

She took her place at the table, feeling shy, and glad of the butler's presence in the room, which made it impossible for the conversation to go beyond the commonplace. While Carlyon exchanged views with John on the probable nature of the weather, she took covert stock of him. He proved, when seen in the light of the day, to be quite as personable a man as she had fancied him to be. Without being precisely handsome, his features were good, his carriage easy, and his shoulders, under a well-cut of superfine cloth, very broad. He was dressed with neatness and propriety, and although he wore breeches and top-boots in preference to the pantaloons and Hessians favoured by town-dwellers, there was no suggestion in his appearance to the slovenly country squire. His brother John was similarly neat; but the high shirt collar affected by Nicky, and his complicated cravat, indicated to Elinor's experienced eye an incipient dandyism. That Nicky's attire had been the subject of argument soon became apparent, for at the first opportunity he said in a contumacious tone: 'I do not see how I should well wear mourning for Eustace. I mean, when you consider –'

'I did not say you should wear mourning,' interrupted John. 'But that waistcoat you have on is the outside of enough!'

'Let me tell you,' said Nicky indignantly, 'that this fashion in waistcoats is all the crack up at Oxford!'

'I dare say it may be, but you are not, more shame to you, up at Oxford at this present, and it would be grossly improper for you to be going about the countryside, with our cousin but just dead, in a cherry-striped waistcoat.'

'Ned, do you think so?' Nicky said, turning in appeal to Carlyon.

'Yes, or at any other time,' responded his mentor unfeelingly.

Nicky subsided, with a sotto voce animadversion on old-fashioned prejudice, and applied himself to a formidable plateful of cold roast sirloin. Carlyon signed to the butler to leave the room, and when he had done so, smiled faintly at Elinor, and said: 'Well, now, Mrs. Cheviot, we have to consider what is next to be done.'

'I do wish you will not call me by that name!' she said.

'I am afraid you will have to accustom yourself to being called by it,' he replied.

She put down the slice of bread and butter she had been in the act of raising to her lips. 'My lord, did you *indeed* marry me to that man?' she demanded.

'Certainly not: I am not in orders. You were married by the vicar of the parish.'

'That is nothing to the purpose! You know very well it was all your doing! But I hoped I might have dreamed it! Oh, dear, what a coil it is! How came I to do such a thing?'

'You did it to oblige me,' he said soothingly.

'I did not. Oblige you indeed! When you as good as kidnapped me!'

'Kidnapped you?' exclaimed John. 'No, no, I am sure he would not do such a thing, ma'am! Ned, you were not so mad?'

'Of course I was not. Accident brought you to Highnoons, Mrs. Cheviot, and if, when you were there, I over-persuaded you a trifle –'

'Well, that is what you say, but from what I have been privileged to see of you, my lord, I should not be surprised to find it had all been a plot to entrap me! I was asked by the servant if I had come in answer to the *advertisement*. Did you indeed advertise for a wife for your cousin!'

'Yes, I did,' he replied. 'In the columns of *The Times*. You may often see such advertisements.'

She regarded him speechlessly. John said: 'It is very true. But

I own I do not consider it a respectable thing to do. I was always against it. Heaven knows what kind of a female might have arrived at Highnoons! But as it chances it has all turned out for the best.'

She turned her eyes towards him. They were remarkably fine eyes, particularly so when sparkling with indignation. 'It may have turned out for the best as far as you are concerned, sir,' she said, 'but what about the abominable situation in which *I* now find myself? I do not know how I am any longer to possess any degree of credit with the world!'

'Have no fears on that score!' Carlyon said. 'I have already set it about that your betrothal to my cousin was of a long-standing, though secret, nature.'

'Oh, this passes all bounds!' she cried. 'I do not scruple to tell you, my lord, that nothing would have induced me to have entered into an engagement to marry such an odious person as your cousin!'

'A very pardonable sentiment,' he agreed.

She choked over her coffee.

'Mrs. Cheviot's feelings are perfectly understandable,' John said reprovingly. 'I am sure no one can wonder at them.'

'Yes, but Eustace is dead!' objected Nicky. 'I cannot see why she should feel it so particularly! Why, by Jupiter, ma'am, now I come to think of it, you are a widow!'

'But I do not want to be a widow!' declared Elinor.

'I am afraid it is now too late in the day to alter that,' said Carlyon.

'Besides, if you had known my cousin better you *would* have wanted to be a widow,' Nicky assured her.

'Be quiet, Nicky!' Carlyon said.

Elinor bit her lip resolutely.

'That is much better,' Carlyon encouraged her. 'I do indeed appreciate your feelings upon this event, but it is quite useless to be crying over split milk. Moreover, I do not think you will find that the consequences of your marriage will be as disagreeable as you suppose.'

'No, depend upon it we shall see to it that they shall not be,' said John. 'There may be a little awkwardness in some quarters, but my brother's protection must guard you from ill-natured gossip. If *we* are seen to accept you with complaisance there can be no food for scandal, you know.'

She sighed. 'I see, of course, that there can be no undoing it now. I have come by my deserts, for I knew all along that I was acting wrongly. But I do not mean to tease you to no purpose! I suppose I can be a governess as well widowed as single.'

'Undoubtedly, but I trust there will be no need for you to continue in what I am persuaded must be a distasteful calling,' said Carlyon.

She looked quickly round at him. 'No, no, I told you I would not be your pensioner, my lord, and to that at least I shall hold fast!'

'No such thing. My cousin signed a Will leaving the whole of his property to you.'

'What?' she cried, turning quite pale. 'Oh, good God, you are not in earnest?'

'Certainly I am in earnest.'

'But I could not – It would be quite shocking in me –!' she stammered.

'Are you imagining that you have become a rich woman overnight?' Carlyon enquired. 'I wish it may be found so, but I fear it will be no such thing. You are more likely to discover that you are liable for God knows how many debts.'

The widow sought in vain for words in which to express her feelings.

'Lord, yes!' said Nicky cheerfully. 'Eustace had never a feather to fly with, and it's my belief the gull-gropers had their talons fast in him!'

'And I,' said Elinor, controlling her voice with a strong effort, 'am in the happy position of inheriting these debts?'

'No, no!' said John. 'They must be paid out of the estate, of course! Fortunately, he could not mortgage the land – not that you will get much for it, if you should decide to sell it, for since my brother ceased to administer it everything has been allowed to go to ruin.'

'But what a charming prospect for me!' Elinor said, with awful irony. 'Saddled with a ruined estate, crushed by debt, widowed before ever I was a wife – it is the most abominable thing I ever heard of!'

'Oh, it will scarcely prove to be as bad as that!' Carlyon said. 'When all is done, I hope you will find yourself with a respectable competence.'

'Indeed, I hope so too, my lord, for I begin to think I shall have earned it!' she retorted.

'Now you are talking like a sensible woman,' he said. 'Are you willing to be guided by me in how you should go on?'

She looked at him in some indecision. 'Is there no way in which I can escape this inheritance?'

'None at all.'

'But if I were to disappear, which I should like very much to do –'

'I am persuaded you will not be so poor-spirited as to draw back at this juncture.'

She swallowed this, and after a moment said in a resigned voice: 'What ought I to do, then?'

'I have already considered that, and I believe it will be most natural for you to take up your residence at Highnoons,' he said.

'At Highnoons! Oh, no, indeed, I had rather not!' she said, looking very much alarmed.

'Why had you rather not?' he asked.

'It would look so presumptuous in me to be residing there!'

'Presumptuous to be residing in your husband's house?'

'How can you talk so? The circumstances –'

'The circumstances are precisely what we all of us wish to conceal. It would be ineligible for you to remain under my roof, for mine is a bachelor-household.'

'I have no desire to remain under your roof!'

'Then we need not waste time upon that point. You might, with perfect propriety, seek refuge with some relative of your own, but you will be obliged to attend to a good deal of business, and since I shall be joined with you in that it will be more convenient if you are within reach of this place.'

'I would not go to my relatives in such a predicament as this for any consideration in the world!' Elinor declared, with a shudder.

'In that case, you have really no choice in the matter.'

'But show shall I go on in such a place?' she demanded. 'I am sure it is quote covered in dust and cobwebs, and very likely overrun with rats and black-beetles, for I saw quite enough of it yesterday to convince me that it has been shockingly neglected!'

'Exactly so, and that is one reason why I should be glad to see you there.'

The widow's bosom swelled. 'Is it indeed, my lord? I might have guessed you would say something odious!'

'I am not saying anything odious. If we are to dispose of Highnoons advantageously, it must be put into some kind of order. I will engage to do what I can with the land, but I cannot undertake to set the house to rights. By doing that you will at once oblige me, and give yourself an occupation that will divert your mind from all these troubles which you imagine to be gathering about your head.'

'To oblige you must of course be an object with me,' said Elinor, in a trembling tone.

'Thank you: you are very good!' he responded, with unimpaired calm.

A chuckle escaped Nicky. He grinned across the table at Elinor. 'Oh, I beg pardon, but you know it is never the least use disputing with Ned, for he has always the best of it! He is the most complete hand! And I'll tell you what! If you should find that there are rats at Highnoons I'll come over with my dog, and we will have some famous sport!'

'Now, Nicky, do hold your tongue!' begged John. 'But you know, ma'am, there is a great deal of sense in what Carlyon says. The place cannot be left without anyone to manage things, and I am sure I do not know who else is to go there.'

'But the servants!' she protested. 'What must they think if I am suddenly foisted upon them?'

'So far as I am aware, only Barrow and his wife were lately employed by Eustace,' said Carlyon. 'Which reminds me that you will do well to hire a couple of girls to work in the house. But you need entertain no qualms: Barrow has been at Highnoons for many years, and is necessarily conversant with all the circumstances that led up to the ceremony you took part in yesterday. He was greatly attached to my aunt, for which reason he has remained with my cousin. Neither he nor his wife is likely to cause you the smallest embarrassment. But I fear you will not find him an efficient butler: he was used to be a groom, and only came into the house when no other servant would remain there.'

'You know, Ned, I think Mrs. Cheviot should have some respectable female to bear her company there,' John interposed.

'Certainly she should, and I will discover one for her.'

'If I wanted a respectable female to live with me in that horrid house, I should beg my own old governess to come to me!' said Elinor.

'An excellent suggestion. If you will give me her direction, I will have a letter conveyed to her immediately,' said Carlyon.

Elinor, feeling herself quite overborne, meekly said that she would write to Miss Beccles.

'And you must not think that you will be lonely,' Nicky assured her. 'For we shall come over to visit you, you know.'

She thanked him, but turned once more to Carlyon. 'And what is to be done about Mrs. Macclesfield?' she asked.

'It is very uncivil of us, no doubt, but I am inclined to think that we shall do best to let Mrs. Macclesfield pass out of our lives without embarking on explanations which cannot be other than awkward,' he replied.

Upon reflection she was obliged to agree with him.

Six

Shortly after noon, resigned but by no means reconciled, Mrs. Cheviot was driven to Highnoons by her host. They went in his lordship's carriage, very sedately, and his lordship beguiled the tedium by pointing out to the lady various landmarks, happy falls of country, or glimpses of woodland, which, he told her, would later on be carpeted with bluebells. Mrs. Cheviot responded with cold civility, and inaugurated no topic of conversation.

'This country is not in the grand style,' said Carlyon, 'but there are some very pretty rides near Highnoons, which I will show you one day.'

'Indeed?' she said.

'Certainly – when you have recovered from your sulks.'

'I am not in the sulks,' she said tartly. 'Anyone with the least sensibility would feel for me in this pass you have brought me to! How can you expect me to be in spirits? You have no sensibility at all, my lord!'

'No, I am afraid that is so,' he replied seriously. 'It is an accusation which has often been cast at me, and I believe it to be true.'

She turned her head to look at him in some little curiosity. 'Pray, who has accused you of it, sir?' she asked suspiciously.

'My sisters, when I have been unable to enter into their feelings upon certain events.'

'I am surprised. I had collected that your brothers and sisters were all devoted to you.'

He smiled. 'You would wish me to understand, I dare say, that the strong degree of attachment which exists between us has aggravated a naturally overbearing disposition.'

She was obliged to laugh. 'I must tell you, my lord, that I find this habit you have got into to reducing to the most uncompromising terms what has been expressed with the utmost delicacy, quite odious! What is more, I am much disposed to think that if I had the toothache, and told you I was dying of the pain, you would be at pains to announce to me that one does not die of the toothache!'

'Undoubtedly I should,' he agreed, 'if I thought you entertained any fears on that score.'

'Odious!' she said.

They had by this time reached Highnoons, and were driving up the neglected carriage-way, between dense thickets of overgrown shrubs, and trees whose branches almost met over their heads.

'How forcibly it puts one in mind of all one's favourite romances!' remarked Mrs. Cheviot affably.

'The greater part of those bushes should be cleared away, and the rest pruned,' he responded. 'Some of these branches need lopping, and I have seen at least three trees which are dead, and must be cut down.'

'Cut down? My dear sir, you will destroy the whole character of the place! I hope there may be a blasted oak. I do not ask if a spectre walks the passages with its head under its arm: that would be a great piece of folly!'

'It would,' he agreed, smiling.

'Naturally! The house is clearly haunted. I have not the least doubt that that is why only two sinister retainers can be brought to remain in it. I dare say I shall be found, after a night spent within these walls, a witless wreck whom you will be obliged to convey to Bedlam without more ado.'

'I have a greater dependence on the fortitude of your mind, ma'am.'

The carriage had drawn to a standstill before the house by this

70

time. Elinor allowed herself to be handed out of it, and stood for a moment critically surveying her surroundings.

As much of the pleasure gardens as she could see were overgrown with weeds, and she gave them scant attention. The house itself, now that she saw it in the daylight, she found to be a beautiful building, two hundred years old, with chamfered windows, and tall chimneys. It was perhaps built in too long and rambling a style for modern taste, and much of its mellow brickwork was masked by thick tangles of creepers; but Elinor was obliged to own to herself that she was pleasantly surprised by it.

'All that ivy shall be stripped away,' said Carlyon, also surveying the frontage.

'No such thing!' said Elinor. 'Only see how it overhangs some of the windows! I dare say one can scarcely see to set a stitch in those rooms on the brightest day! Then, too, consider how the least wind must set the tendrils tapping at the window-panes like ghostly fingers! How can you talk of stripping it away? You are not at all romantic!'

'No, not at all. Come, you will take cold if you stand any longer in this east wind! Let us go in.'

The door had already been opened by old Barrow. It was apparent to Elinor that this was not Carlyon's first visit to Highnoons since he had left it in her company on the previous evening. Barrow looked at her certainly with curiosity, but there was no surprise in his face; and a glance round the hall showed Elinor that an attempt had been made to render it habitable.

'Barrow, here is your mistress,' Carlyon said, laying his hat down on the table. 'Mrs. Cheviot, you will find Barrow very attentive to your comfort. You will wish to see Mrs. Barrow presently, I dare say, and to give her your orders. Meanwhile, I will conduct you over the house, if you are not too tired by the drive.'

'Not at all,' said Elinor feebly.

'Mrs Barrow and the young wench your lordship fetched over from the Hall have redded up the Yellow Room for the Mistress,' disclosed the retainer. 'Them not thinking Mistress would care to

71

sleep in poor Mr. Eustace's room, not but what he didn't take and die there, when all's said. Howsever –'

'Yes, that will do!' interrupted Carlyon. 'Mrs. Cheviot, the book-room you have seen already. The dining-parlour is here.' He opened the door into a room on the left of the entrance-lobby. 'It is not handsome – none of the rooms here are large, and the pitch is everywhere low – but I have known it when it has looked very pretty.'

'Ay, that you have, my lord,' agreed Barrow, with a reminiscent sigh.

'Barrow, be so good as to go and desire Mrs. Barrow to send some coffee to the book-room for Mrs. Cheviot!'

The retainer having been thus shaken off, Carlyon led Elinor over the rest of the house. She found it rather bewildering, for it was made up of what seemed to be a multitude of small rooms, and very long passages. Many of the rooms were wainscoted to the ceiling, and the furniture was all old-fashioned, and more often than not coated with dust.

'Most of these apartments have not been in use since my aunt died,' Carlyon explained.

'Why in the name of heaven did no one put the chairs under holland covers?' exclaimed Elinor, her housewifely instincts quite revolted. 'Good God, what a task you have set me, my lord!'

'I know very little about these matters, but I imagine you will have your hands full.' He added: 'That may keep you from indulging your fancy with thoughts of headless spectres.'

She cast him a very speaking look, and preceded him into the apartment which had been prepared for her use. This at least showed signs of having been scrubbed and polished, and, since it faced south, the pale spring sunlight came in through the leaded window-panes, and gave it a cheerful aspect. Elinor took off her bonnet and her pelisse, and laid them down on the bed. 'Well, at all events, Mrs. Barrow showed her good sense in her choice of bedchamber for me,' she observed. 'And who, by the by, is the young wench you brought over from the Hall, my lord?'

'I do not know her name, but Mrs. Rugby thought that she would prove a suitable and an obliging maid for you. You will of course engage what servants you deem necessary, but in the meantime this girl is here to wait on you.'

She was touched by this thought for her comfort, but merely said: 'You are very good, my lord. But, regarding the servants you have recommended me to engage, pray, how are their wages to be paid?'

'They will be paid out of the estate,' he returned indifferently.

'But, as I collect, sir, that the estate is already grossly encumbered –'

'It need not concern you; there will be funds enough to cover such necessary expense.'

'Oh!' she said, a little doubtfully.

They were interrupted. 'There had ought to be the hatchment up over the door,' said Barrow severely.

Carlyon turned quickly. The retainer was standing on the threshold, gloomily surveying them. 'Hatchment,' he repeated.

'Nonsense!' Carlyon said impatiently. 'Situated as this place is in the country I see not the least need for such a display.'

'When Mistress took and died,' said Barrow obstinately, 'we had the hatchment set up in proper style.'

'Then pray set it up over the door again!' said Elinor.

Barrow regarded her with approval. 'And the knocker tied up with crape, missus?' he asked.

'By all means!'

'That'll be primer-looking, that will,' nodded Barrow, and went off to attend to these matters.

'You are a woman of decision,' remarked Carlyon.

'I trust I have my wits about me, my lord. No good purpose could be served by offending the notions of these people.'

'My cousin had so cut himself off from county society that I doubt of your being troubled by visitors.'

'Indeed, I hope you may be right, sir!' was all that she replied.

They went downstairs again, and to the book-room, where a fire burned, and the coffee-cups had already been laid out.

Carlyon declined partaking of this refreshment, but Elinor sat down by the table, and poured out a cup for herself. It overflowed with papers, and after a cursory glance he shut it again, saying: 'I must come here in a day or two, with the lawyer, and go through all these papers. It will be best, Mrs. Cheviot, if you leave any that you find for me to deal with.'

'Certainly,' she responded calmly. 'If you are an executor of that infamous Will, as I have little doubt you must be, you should lock up the desk, I believe.'

'I expect I should,' he agreed. 'But as there does not appear to be a key to the desk, and I am persuaded I can trust you to keep all intact, I must dispense with that formality. I imagine there can be little here worthy of the trouble.' He left the desk, and came to her, holding out his hand. 'I shall leave you now, ma'am. Rest assured that your letter shall be conveyed to Miss Beccles without loss of time. I shall hope to see her safely installed here within a very few days.'

She took his hand, but said with a little loss of composure: 'Thank you. But you will not leave me alone here for long?'

'No, indeed. If you should desire my attendance, send over to the Hall, and I will come. This affair has cast a good deal of business upon me, and I may be away from home for a day or two, but a message will soon bring me. I will send Nicky over in the morning to see how you go on. Goodbye! Believe me, though I have little sensibility I am fully conscious of the debt I owe you.'

He was gone, and she was left in some lowness of spirits, wondering how she should contrive, and what would be the end of this strange adventure. A period of quiet reflection helped to calm the natural agitation of her mind; since she had consented to take up her residence in this mouldering house she must do as best she might. To this end she presently rang the bell, forgetting that the wire was broken. After an interval, she was obliged to go in search of the servants, and so found her way for the first time to the kitchens.

These were old-fashioned, but she was glad to perceive that the floor and the table were both well-scrubbed. Both the

Barrows were there, with a respectable-looking abigail, and a groom, who lost no time in effacing himself. Mrs. Barrow was a woman of clean aspect, and comfortable proportions. She at once rose to her feet, and dropped a curtsy.

Elinor thought it wisest to adopt an open manner with the Barrows, and she soon discovered that they were under no awkward misapprehensions as to the nature of her marriage. Mrs. Barrow, having presented the abigail to her, sent the girl off upon an errand, and waited with her hands folded over her apron to hear what her new mistress had to say.

Elinor said, with a little difficulty, that she must think it strange to have an unknown mistress set over her, in such circumstances, but Mrs. Barrow at once replied: 'Oh, no, ma'am! Not if my lord thought it right!'

Such a dependence on Carlyon's judgement in servants who were not his own seemed strange, but Mrs Barrow's acceptance of his infallibility was presently explained by her informing Elinor that she had been a housemaid up at the Hall until her marriage to Barrow. She was more genteel than her husband, whom she plainly kept in order, and seldom allowed her speech to lapse into the broad Sussex dialect which came most readily to Barrow's tongue. She at once volunteered to conduct Elinor once more round the house, and to show her in more detail than had Carlyon what could be cleaned or renovated, and what must be thrown away. 'For, questionless, ma'am, things are come to a bad pass, and such as must make my poor mistress turn in her grave, but what can one woman do, when all's said, and me with no help in the kitchen, and not bred to kitchen work? But it was for my mistress's sake me and Barrow has stayed with Mr. Eustace. Ah, there was a sainted lady, to be sure, and so nice in her ways – well, there, it does no good to talk, but what we have always said, and shall say, is that Cheviot blood was never no good, and never will be, and Mr. Eustace was all Cheviot! A Wincanton, my late mistress was, and her late ladyship too, for they were sisters, and that attached you never saw the like! Her ladyship was younger than my mistress by two years, and old Mr.

Wincanton he left Highnoons to my mistress, and tied up, so they say, in his lordship.'

'Ay, old master he never reckoned nowt to the Cheviots,' interpolated Barrow. 'A foreigner, Mr. Cheviot was. Come out of Kent, so I believe.'

'Hush!' said his wife reprovingly. 'Not but what it's true enough, ma'am. No one hereabouts reckoned much to Mr. Cheviot, and it was for mistress's sake we stayed here when she died.'

'Besides the pension,' Barrow assured Elinor.

Elinor allowed Mrs. Barrow to run on in this fashion while she went over the house with her, inspecting closets and linen-cupboards, for she had no wish to alienate the good woman by snubbing her, and was, moreover, sufficiently curious not to object to listening to some gossip. She gathered that her late husband's career had been one of ruinous dissipation, and that when he had visited his home, which was not often, it was usually in the company of a set of men – and sometimes not men only, said Mrs. Barrow repressively – association with whom could scarcely have been expected to have improved the tone of his mind.

'And to think he should not have been in the house above a day when he should have met his end like he did!' Mrs. Barrow said. 'And at Master Nicky's hands, too, which does beat all, I will say! I was never more upset in my days, ma'am, me having known Master Nicky from the cradle. But his lordship will settle it!'

Elinor soon found that Carlyon was the great man of the neighbourhood, a good landlord, as his father had been before him, and, in Mrs. Barrow's estimation, a personage whose will was law, and whose actions were above criticism. She had to suppress a smile as she listened, but while making every allowance for the loyalty of a woman born on his estate, and attached to his family by every interest, she gained the impression of an estimable character who had the trick of endearing himself to his dependents.

The afternoon was soon gone, but not without certain plans having been made between the two women, and decisions arrived at. By the time Elinor sat down to an early dinner, it had been agreed that a niece of Mrs. Barrow's should be engaged on the morrow, and the old coachman's wife summoned up from the lodge to scrub and to scour; and Elinor had found time to walk round the neglected gardens. There was a shrubbery, which must once have made a pleasant winter walk, but which was so overgrown that in some places it was almost impassable. Elinor made up her mind to set the groom to clear it, a resolve which was highly applauded by Barrow, who had had some qualms lest she should have settled on himself as being the properest person for the task.

She went back to the book-room after dinner, and sent Barrow for some working-candles. The linen-chest had yielded tasks enough for the most zealous needlewoman, and a formidable pile of sheets, towels, and tablecloths had been brought downstairs to be mended. Until Barrow presently brought in the tea-tray, Elinor remained occupied with this work, her brain busy at once with schemes for the immediate future, and with reflection upon all that had passed since she had come into Sussex. With the coming of the tea-tray, she laid aside her work, and began to look along the dusty bookshelves in search of something to divert her mind for an hour. None of the books were of very recent date, and quite a large amount of space seemed to be devoted to collections of sermons, very dry histories, and the ancient classical authors, bound in crumbling calf; but after wandering round the shelves for some time in growing disappointment, she came upon some books clearly acquired by the late Mrs. Cheviot. Here, jumbled amongst some bound copies of the *Lady's Magazine*, were all Elinor's favourite poets, and a number of novels in marbled boards. Most of these were already known to her, but just as she was hesitating between Mrs. Edgeworth's *Tales of Fashionable Life*, and a battered copy of *Thaddeus of Warsaw*, her eye was caught by a title which seemed so apposite to her situation that she could not help but be diverted. She drew *The School for Widows* out, and stood for some moments turning over the pages. Unfortunately, too many were found to be missing to make the perusal of this work eligible. She restored it to its place, and took out instead a promising, but not so well-worn, novel by the same author, entitled *The Old English Baron*. With this in her hand she retired again to her chair, put another log on the fire, and settled down to be cosy for an hour before retiring to bed.

For one who had had little leisure of late years to indulge a taste for light reading this was luxury indeed, and not even the desponding tone of Miss Clara Reeve's story, or the lachrymose behaviour of her heroine had the power to disgust Elinor. She read on, heedless of the time, alternately amused and interested by the exploits of the perfect Orlando, and very wisely skimming over his Monimia's all too frequent fainting-fits. The guttering of one of the candles at last recalled her to a sense of the time; she glanced instinctively up at the bracket-clock on the mantelpiece, but its hands till pointed mendaciously to a quarter to five. The candles, however, had burned so low in their sockets that it was evident the hour was far advanced. Elinor got up, feeling a little guilty, as though an irate employer might later demand of her why she had so grossly wasted the candles; and restored her novel to its place on the shelf. A slight sound, as of a creaking stair, made her start. She realized that all had been silent in the house for a long time, and had certainly supposed that the servants must long since have gone up to bed. For a moment she was frightened; then she recollected how old stairs would creak long after they had been trodden on, picked up the bedroom candlestick which Barrow had brought in to her, and kindled the wick at one of those still burning in the room. A glance at the grate, to assure herself that there was no danger of the smouldering remnant of the log's falling out to set the house on fire, and she snuffed the candles in the chandelier, and walked over to the door. She opened it, and stepped out into the hall, only to be brought up short by the unnerving sight of a complete stranger, in the act of crossing it in the direction of the book-room.

78

She gave a gasp of shock, and for an instant felt her heart stand still. But, unlike Miss Smith's Monimia, she did not suffer from an excess of sensibility, but was, on the contrary, a very level-headed young woman, and it did not take her more than a moment to perceive that the stranger was looking quite as aghast as she herself felt.

The oil-lamp left burning on the hall table showed him to be a gentlemanly-looking young man, dressed in riding-breeches and a blue coat, and with a drab Benjamin over all. He had his hat on his head, but after the first few seconds' astonished immobility he pulled this off, and bowed, stammering: 'I beg a thousand pardons! I did not know! I had no notion – Forgive, I beg!'

He spoke with the faintest trace of a foreign accent. The removal of his hat showed him to be dark-eyed, and dark-haired. He looked, at the moment, to be extremely discomfited, but his air and manner were both good, and the cast of his countenance spoke a reassuring degree of refinement. Elinor, feeling all the awkwardness of her own situation, blushed, and replied: 'I fear you must have come, sir, to see one who is no longer here. I do not know how it is that the servant should leave you standing in the hall. Indeed, I did not hear the door-bell ring, and had supposed Barrow to have gone to bed.' As she spoke, her eyes alighted on the tall-case clock, and she perceived with a start that the time wanted but ten minutes to midnight. She turned her amazed gaze upon the unknown visitor.

He appeared to be fully conscious of the need for an explanation, but in doubt as to how best to make it. After some hesitation he said: I did not ring, madame. It is so late! Mr. Cheviot and I are friends of such long standing that I have been in the habit of walking into the house without announcement. In effect, knowing that the good Barrow must be in bed, I came in by a side-door. But I did not know – I had not the least notion –'

'Came in by a side-door!' she repeated in a blank tone.

His embarrassment increased. 'I have been upon such terms with Mr. Cheviot, madame – and seeing a light burning in one of the parlours I made so bold – But had I known – You must understand that I am staying with friends in the neighbourhood, and I had hoped – indeed, I had expected to have had the pleasure of meeting Mr. Cheviot at – at a little soirée this evening. He did not come, and so, fearing he might be perhaps indisposed, and not desiring to leave the neighbourhood without seeing him – in short, madame, I rode over. But you said, I think, that he is not here?'

'Mr. Cheviot met with – with a fatal accident last night, sir, and I regret to be obliged to inform you that he is dead,' said Elinor.

He looked thunderstruck, and almost incredulous. 'Dead!' he ejaculated.

She bowed her head. There was silence for a moment. He broke it, saying in a voice which he strove to render calm: 'If you please, how is this? I am very much shocked. I can scarcely believe it can be possible!'

'It is very true, however. Mr. Cheviot fell into a dispute at an inn last night, and was accidentally killed.'

A flash of anger kindled his dark eyes. He exclaimed: 'Oh, *sapristi!* He was drunk, in effect! The fool!'

She returned no answer. After another pause, during which he stayed frowning, and jerking at the lash of his riding-whip, he said: 'This occurred last night, you say? It was in London, no doubt?'

'No, sir, it was here, at Wisborough Green.'

'Then he came here yesterday!'

'So I believe,' she concurred.

His eyes wandered round the hall, as though in search of inspiration. He brought them back to her face, and said with a forced smile: 'Pardon! I am so much shocked! But you, madame? I do not perfectly understand –?'

She had foreseen this question, and now answered it as coolly as she might. 'I am Mrs. Cheviot, sir.'

A look of the blankest amazement came into his face. He stood staring at her, and could only repeat: 'Mrs. Cheviot!'

'Yes,' said Elinor stonily.

'But – You would say my friend's wife?'

'His widow, sir.'

'Good God!'

'I dare say this news comes as a surprise to you, sir,' she said, 'but it is true. My – my husband's friends are of course welcome to his house, but you will readily understand, I am persuaded, that at this late hour, and under such circumstances, I am unable to extend to you that hospitality which – which –'

He pulled himself together, saying quickly: 'Perfectly! I will instantly leave you, madame, and with the most profound apologies! But, forgive me! You are young, and alone, is it not? And this terrible tragedy has come upon you with a suddenness one does not care to think of! As a close friend of this poor Cheviot I should wish to be of all possible service! Alas, I fear all will be found to be in great disorder, for well I know that he had not the habit of – in short, madam, if I could be of assistance to you I should count myself honoured!'

'You are extremely obliging, sir, but Mr. Cheviot's affairs are in the hands of his cousin, Lord Carlyon, and I hope not to want for assistance.'

'Ah, in that case – ! That changes the affair, for Lord Carlyon, one is assured, will do all that one could wish. My poor friend's papers, for instance, in such turmoil as they were – for you must know that I have been much in his confidence! – but Lord Carlyon will have taken all into his hands, I am assured.'

'He will certainly do so, sir,' she agreed. 'If you are concerned in any of Mr. Cheviot's affairs you should consult his lordship. I am sure you will find him very ready to oblige you. I believe he is at this present a good deal occupied with the – with the sad consequences of his cousin's death, but I expect to see him here within the next day or so, with Mr. Cheviot's lawyer, to go through whatever papers Mr. Cheviot may have had.'

'Oh, no, no!' he said. 'I am not concerned in that way, madame! It was merely that I wished, if I might, to be of assistance. But I perceive that you are left in good hands, and I will leave you immediately, with renewed apologies for my intrusion upon you at such a time!'

She acknowledged his bow with an inclination of her head, and went past him to the front door, to open it. The bolts were in place, and the chain up, and the young man at once hurried to Elinor's side to relieve her of the necessity of drawing the bolts back. He soon had the door open, and was bowing gracefully over her hand, begging her not to stand in the cold night air. She was glad enough to shut the door upon him, and to put the chain up again, for although his manner was unexceptionable she could not like to be alone with a complete stranger at this hour of night.

She was about to mount the stairs to her bedchamber when she recollected that the visitor had entered by a side-door. She could not go to bed with any degree of comfort while a door stood unlocked into the house, so she turned back, and went to see which door it might be.

But the most zealous search failed to discover any door that was unbolted, a circumstance that puzzled her sadly. It began to seem as though the gentleman had prevaricated a little, and had in fact made his entrance by way of a window. But Elinor, going with her candle from room to room, could find none that was not secure, and her surprise gave place to a feeling of great uneasiness. Some natural explanation of the visitor's presence there must be, she told herself, but she could not think of one, and at last went up to bed with a heart that beat rather fast. Had the young man been less amiable and apologetic she would have been much inclined to have roused the household, but she could not believe that his motive in entering so mysteriously had been sinister, and as he must by now have ridden away there could be little object in waking Barrow to go after him. But however amiable he might be it was no very pleasant thought that strangers could apparently enter the house at will, and in despite of bolted doors and windows. Elinor was glad to see a key in the lock of her own bedroom door, and had no hesitation in turning it.

She lay awake for some time in the firelight, listening intently, but no sound disturbed the silence of the house, and she fell asleep at last, and slept soundly until morning.

Seven

*E*linor lost no time on the following morning in acquainting both the Barrows with what had occurred during the night. Barrow instantly professed himself ready to swear through an inch-board that he had secured every door and window against intruders, but Mrs. Barrow said in a very wifely spirit that he took no care for anything, and if her eye was not upon every task none was performed.

'But it is true that when I went to find and lock the door I could not discover any that was unbolted,' Elinor said. 'Indeed, I have been puzzling my head over it, for I cannot imagine how anyone can have entered the house. Is there some door I do not know of? And yet –'

'Never trouble your head, ma'am!' Mrs. Barrow told her robustly. 'Depend upon it, the man climbed in through one of the windows! But I am put about that such a thing should have happened, and I wish you had roused me, for I would have sent my fine gentleman about his business very speedily.'

'There was not the least need for me to rouse you. I do not mean to say that the gentleman caused me annoyance, for he was very civil, and quite as taken-aback as I was myself.'

'Well, it queers me who it may have been, ma'am,' Mrs. Barrow declared. 'Not but what – I wonder, was it the Honourable Francis Cheviot, perhaps? Him as is son to Lord Bedlington, which is uncle to poor Mr. Eustace.'

'I do not know. It was stupidly done of me, but I forgot to ask him what his name was.'

'A dentical fine gentleman?' said Barrow. 'Nursed in cotton, as they say?'

'N-no. At least, I do not know. He had an air of fashion, but he did not look to be a dandy precisely. He was dark, and quite young. Oh, he spoke with a slight foreign accent!'

'Oh, *him!*' said Barrow disparagingly. 'That'll be the Frenchy, that will. I've seen him before, but I disremember that he ever came climbing in at the window.'

'A Frenchman! Why, yes, he uttered a French oath, now you put me in mind of it! Pray, who is he?'

'He came with Mr. Francis one time,' mused Barrow. 'He had some outlandish name, but I don't know what it was. Came to England in a basket of cabbage, he did.'

'Came to England in a basket of cabbages!'

'Adone-do, Barrow!' said his wife indignantly. 'It was no such thing, ma'am!'

'It was what Mr. Eustace told me,' argued Barrow. 'The Frenchy being naught but a baby, and went into the basket as snug as a mouse in a cheese, I dare say.'

'It was a cart full of cabbages, and to be sure he did not come all the way to England in it! It was at the start of that nasty Revolution they had, ma'am, and they do say there was no way for decent folks, and the Quality, and such, to get away but by smuggling themselves out of the town in all manner of disguises, and such shifts.'

'Ay, no end to the outlandish tricks them Frenchies get up to,' nodded Barrow. 'Not but what I don't believe all I hear, and I always reckoned that was a loud one.'

'An émigré family! I see!' Elinor said. 'I should have guessed it, indeed.'

'I don't know what kind of a family it might be,' said Barrow cautiously, 'but what should take him to come visiting Mr. Eustace at that hour of night? I never saw him above a couple of times in my life, and for all he's a Frenchy he came in at the front door like a Christian.'

'I think he said that he was visiting friends in the neighbourhood.'

Barrow seemed inclined to cavil at this. He scratched his chin. 'Well, he's not visiting his lordship, that's sure. Nor he's not at the Priory, for old Sir Matthew he's tedious set against all Frenchies. And he won't be at Elm House, for a decenter couple of ladies than Miss Lynton and Miss Elizabeth you won't find, and to be having gentlemen to stay is what they wouldn't do. And if it's the Hurst he meant, Mr. Frinton and his lady has gone up to London, and won't be back this se'nnight.'

'Likely he came from the Hill,' suggested Mrs. Barrow comfortably. 'I'm sure it's no matter.'

'Ay, likely he did,' agreed Barrow. 'There's no saying what they'll do, them as live on the Hill.'

Having expressed himself suitably as a Weald man, he seemed to think the problem settled, and went off to make an inventory of all the silver in the house.

Elinor let the subject drop, and was soon immersed in household details with Mrs. Barrow. But when that lady had sailed off kitchenwards her thoughts reverted to the episode, and while she set about the several tasks that lay nearest to her hand she found herself still puzzling over it.

At eleven o'clock the sound of hoof-beats on the carriage-drive made her look out of the window. She saw the Hon. Nicholas Carlyon trotting up to the house on a stylish bay, a cross-bred dog, half lurcher, half mastiff, bounding a long beside his horse. He caught sight of her, and waved his whip, calling out: 'How d'ye do? Ned told me I should come over to see if you were tolerably comfortable.'

'I am much obliged to you both!' she returned. 'Do but take your horse to the stables, and I will come down and let you in!'

By the time he had done this she was already standing in the porch. He came striding along, and at once pulled off his hat, and said: 'Good morning, ma'am! Shall you object to Bouncer? I will leave him outside if you wish, only if I do I dare say he will be off hunting, and the thing is that Sir Matthew Kendal's preserves abut on to this land, and he don't above half like to have Bouncer on them.'

'No, indeed, that would never do,' she said. 'I have not the least objection to him, for you must know I have been used to dogs all my life. Pray bring him in with you!'

He looked gratified, and called the dog to heel. Barrow, who happened to be crossing the hall at that moment, looked with a good deal of reproach at his mistress, and gave it as his considered opinion that if Master Nicky was to bring his dogs in, spannelling the floors, there could be no sense in summoning the gardener's wife up to scrub them. The intelligent hound, however, lifted a lip at him, and he made off, muttering.

'My brother has gone off somewhere in his chaise, Mrs. Cheviot,' announced Nicky, following his hostess into the book-room. 'Oh! You do not like it when one calls you by that name! Well, you know, I have been thinking, and if you should not dislike it excessively I believe I should call you Cousin Elinor. For you are our cousin, are you not?'

'By marriage, I suppose I must be,' acknowledged Elinor. 'I do not dislike you to call me so, at all events – Cousin Nicholas.'

'Oh, no! I wish you will not call me Nicholas!' he protested. 'No one ever does, except John sometimes, when he reads me one of his lectures! Ned never does so. Why, how you have changed everything here already! I declare, this is first-rate!'

She invited him to sit down by the fire; he declined partaking of any refreshment, but was anxious to know if there was any way in which he could be of use to her. 'For you must know that I am quite at leisure,' he told her. 'And Ned said I could make myself useful.'

She did not feel that his assistance in sorting linen would be of much practical help, but it occurred to her that he might be able to throw light on the identity at least of her midnight visitor. She described the encounter to him, therefore. He listened with much interest, and at the end said that his cousin Eustace had been a very loose screw, and that any friends of his were likely to prove ugly customers. But he was less concerned with the Frenchman's name than with the manner of his entry.

'Too smoky by half, cousin!' he said. 'A fellow don't go

creeping into a man's house at midnight if he's up to any good. Depend upon it, Eustace was concerned in some devilry or other!'

'I hope you may be wrong!' she said. 'For if you are not I dare not think of the odd persons who may seek to gain admittance here in the expectation of finding him!'

'Very true. Are you quite sure there was no door left open?'

'I could not find one. It is the strangest thing! I own I cannot be at my ease over it.'

'I'll tell you what it is, Cousin Elinor!' said Nicky, his eyes sparkling. 'I should not be at all surprised if there were a secret way into the house we do not know of!'

She regarded him in considerable dismay. 'No, pray do not put such uncomfortable notions into my head!' she begged.

'Yes, but I dare say there is,' he insisted. 'You know, it was used to be said that Charles II hid in this house after Worcester. Ned says that's all fudge, and he was never within ten miles of Highnoons, but only fancy if it were so!'

'Only fancy!' echoed Elinor in a hollow tone.

Nicky jumped to his feet, and began to walk round the room, inspecting the walls. 'I dare say there may be a sliding panel somewhere, just as I saw in some old house or another, with a passage into the garden.'

'It is not in this room,' said Elinor firmly. 'He did not enter here – and I wish you will not talk in such a way! I shall not sleep a wink all night!'

'No, indeed! I should think you would not!' Nicky agreed. 'We must find it, of course! By Jove, this is capital sport!'

Nothing would do for him but to be allowed to search the house. Elinor went with him, torn between amusement at his enthusiasm, and a horrid fear that he might indeed discover a hidden door. The dog Bouncer accompanied them, hopeful of rats, but presently grew disgusted with the lack of sport, and lay down, yawning cavernously. Nicky tapped all the pannelling in the ground-floor rooms without producing the hollow note he so ardently desired to hear, and Elinor was just beginning to breathe again, when he insisted on going upstairs. She felt that it was unlikely that a secret way into the house should be found in any of the bedrooms, but Nicky said he had seen one that started from a cheese-room at the very top of a house.

'Good God, there is a large loft here which was very likely used as a cheese-room in former times!' Elinor cried, quite aghast.

'Is there, by Jupiter?' Nicky exclaimed. 'I'll go up there this instant!'

She did not accompany him, and he presently reappeared, slightly cast down at having been unable to discover even as much as a priest's hole in the cheese-room. He put Elinor so forcibly in mind of the schoolboy brothers of several of her late pupils that she very soon abandoned all formality with him, an arrangement which seemed to suit him very well. His conviction that the large cupboard built into the wall of her bedchamber was just the place where one might reasonably expect to find a hidden trap-door provoked her into apostrophizing him as an odious boy, a form of address to which he seemed to be accustomed, for he grinned, and said: 'I know, but what sport if it were so, Cousin Elinor! Only consider!'

'I am considering it,' she said. 'and let me tell you, Nicky, that if you are trying to make my flesh creep you are wasting your time. Recollect that I have been a governess, and governesses, you know, have no romantic notions, and seldom indulge themselves with swooning, or the vapours!'

'Oh, don't they just!' he retorted. 'My sisters once had one who was for ever swooning! We told her the Hall was haunted, and Gussie – my sister, Augusta, you know – dressed up in a sheet, and Harry and I clanked chains, and made the most famous groaning noises! She did not stay with us above a month.'

'I am astonished she stayed with you as long,' said Elinor. 'I had thought my lot a hard one, but I perceive I have considerable cause to be thankful that at least I was never hired to instruct your sisters.'

He laughed. 'Oh, we should not have served you so, for you are not at all like a governess. May I go in this room?'

'Do, by all means!' she said cordially. 'If you should find any skeletons behind the wainscoting, do not hesitate to call me! I shall be in the still-room, at the end of the corridor.'

She parted from him, and went off to check the stores. She was engaged in arranging a row of preserve-jars on a shelf when she heard Nicky shout to her in a voice of great excitement. She stepped out on to the corridor, saying calmly: 'You have discovered a skull. How delightful it is, to be sure!'

'No, no, I have not, but only come and see, Cousin Elinor! I'm not gammoning you! Only come!'

'Very well, but I do not scruple to tell you that my expectations are high, and nothing less than a skull will do for me.'

He led her into a small, square apartment, wainscoted to the ceiling, and containing little besides a bed, a carved chest, and two chairs. 'You're quizzing me, but you will not do so when you have seen what I have discovered! Now, look about you, cousin! You would not suppose that there was anything out of the ordinary here, would you?'

'I should not,' she agreed. 'But having closely inspected this house I am aware that there is a concealed cupboard on the right of the fireplace. In fact, it is by no means perfectly concealed, and has been used, I fancy, as a wardrobe.'

'Yes,' he interrupted, in no way damped. 'But do you know what is in that cupboard?'

She looked at him suspiciously. 'Nicky, if you have placed something horrid there, just to see me go into strong convulsions —'

'I tell you I'm not bamming, ma'am! Why, is it likely I would do such an unhandsome thing?'

'Yes,' said Elinor frankly. 'Extremely likely!'

'Well, I would not. Watch!'

He stepped up to the panel which formed the door of the cupboard, and slid it back. Elinor looked warily inside, but the cupboard was empty. She glanced enquiringly at Nicky, and found that his innocent blue eyes were fairly blazing with excitement.

'For heaven's sake, tell me instantly what it is!' she begged.

'Watch!' he said again, and stepped into the shallow

cupboard, and dropped on to his knees, and with some difficulty prised up a triangular section of the oaken boards that formed the floor. These were so cunningly joined together that when the trap-door they formed was in place only a close inspection revealed the fact that the floor was not solid. With starting eyes Elinor watched the section come up, and a dark, narrow cavity appear at her feet.

'It is easier lifted from below,' Nicky explained, propping the triangular section up against the wall.

'Easier lifted from below!' echoed Elinor, in a failing voice.

'Yes, for I have tested it. I dare say, in the old days, they may have had some contrivance for opening it on this side, for you can see how the boards have shrunk, so that I can get my nails under them, and that cannot have been so when the place was used in earnest. Look, Cousin Elinor, do you see? It is a secret stair, going down the big chimney-stack!'

'Good God!' she said faintly.

'I knew you would be surprised!' he nodded. 'I wonder if Ned knows of this?'

She regarded him with a fulminating eye. 'If I find that your – your *odious* brother knew of such a thing, and left me here at the mercy of any marauder who has a fancy to steal into the house at dead of night – oh, it is too abominable of him! Where does that horrid little stair lead?'

'I don't know yet. I would not explore it until you had seen it, for it is your house, after all, and it would be rather too bad if I were to keep all the fun to myself.'

'That was thoughtful of you. I am so much obliged to you!' Elinor said feelingly. 'I wonder if there is any hartshorn in the house?'

'Oh, now you are quizzing me again! But do not let us be wasting time! Shall I go first?'

'Down that dreadful stair?' gasped Elinor. 'Do you imagine, you horrid creature, that I am going to set foot on it?'

He looked at her in a little surprise. 'Will you not indeed? Oh, you are thinking that it is bound to be dusty! Well, I dare say it may be, but I shan't regard that. Do you stay here, and I will soon find where it leads!'

She started forward, and clutched his sleeve. 'Nicky, for heaven's sake do not venture down there without even a candle! You do not know what you may discover!'

'Fudge! I am sure there is enough light for me! It must lead into the garden, of course, but how is it we have not seen the door? There is nothing to be afraid of, Cousin Elinor!'

'You cannot know that! You may fall, and break your leg, or find something there – oh, I wish you will not go!'

He grinned at her. 'Don't I hope I may find something, that's all! If there is a skull, I will fetch it up to you!'

'Do not dare do anything of the sort!' she said, shuddering. 'If you are set on going down, only let me call Barrow to go with you!'

'Barrow! No, I thank you! I don't mean to tell him of this!' said Nicky, disappearing through the gap.

Elinor waited at the top, quite sick with apprehension, and calling from time to time to know if he were still safe. He assured her that he was, and that there was light enough penetrating through the opening for him to see his way. She retired to a chair, and sank into it to await events. It seemed an age before he reappeared, but he did so at last, and stepped into the room, brushing the dust from his clothes. 'It is the most famous thing!' he informed her. 'It is just as I supposed! The stair goes down the chimney-stack – it is the bakehouse chimney, you know! And there is a door at the bottom, only it is so covered over with creepers you would never see it unless you searched particularly for it! I wonder how they hid it in the old days?'

'I wonder?' said Elinor, gazing at him in a fascinated way. 'I suppose there is no difficulty in opening the door from outside?'

'On, not the least in the world! There is a latch: you have only to part the creepers, and you may see it as plain as anything! Cousin Elinor, I was never more pleased with anything in my life! It is first-rate! Why, we have nothing like this up at the Hall!'

'How wretched for you!' said Elinor.

'Well, I do think it is unfair that a paltry fellow like Eustace should have such a bang-up thing, when I dare say he never made the least use of it! Only think what Harry and I could have done if we had had such a passage up at the Hall!'

'I prefer not to think of it,' said Elinor. 'But I wish with all my heart you had got it up at the Hall!'

'Yes,' he said wistfully. 'But it is of no use to be thinking of that. Only it does seem rather too bad that I never knew of it till now. By Jupiter, I wish Harry were here! If he had but seen this when we were boys he would have thought of something famous to do with it, for he was always the most complete hand, you know! Why, we might have given Eustace the fright of his life! Harry is one of my brothers, you understand. He is in the Peninsula, and I do wish he were not! You would like him excessively!'

'I am sure I should,' said Elinor sympathetically. 'He sounds to be a delightful creature! But meanwhile I shall be obliged to you if you will instantly find a hammer and some strong nails, and secure the hidden door!'

'Nail it up! But, Cousin Elinor, do you not realize that the man you found in the house last night must have entered by this way?' he exclaimed.

Elinor closed her eyes for a pregnant moment. 'Yes, Nicky, I do realize that,' she said. 'And since I have not the least desire that he should repeat his visit I wish you will secure that door!'

'Well, I am by no means certain that that is what we should do,' he said, frowning. 'The more I think of it the more I'm persuaded there is something dashed smoky about the business. Only consider, cousin! A man who must needs come creeping into a house by a secret stair can be up to no good!'

'Very true. There is a want of openness about such behaviour that strikes one forcibly, and makes me at least disinclined to pursue the acquaintance.'

His brows were still knit. 'Why should he have done so, if he did not know that Eustace was dead, and you here in his place? Or do you suppose that he was not a friend of Eustace's at all, and wished to get into the house without his knowing of it?'

She thought it over. 'No,' she said at last. 'He must have perceived the light shining under the door into the book-room, and thought that you cousin was there. I have no doubt that he was coming towards that room when I stepped out of it. Indeed, he must have heard me walking about in the room! Had he not wished to be seen he must have hidden himself, for he certainly had time enough to have done so. I am persuaded he expected to see your cousin.'

Nicky's eyes had begun to spark again. 'Jupiter, only fancy if we should have stumbled on some plot he and Eustace were hatching between them! I wonder what it can have been? Depend upon it, he came by the secret way so that the servants should not know of his visit! Tell me again just what he said to you!'

She complied with this request to the best of her ability. He listened attentively, questioning her closely upon the various heads of her narrative. He shook his head over it. 'It's deuced odd!' he said. 'Mind you, though I own I don't see what he would be at, I don't believe he was so innocent as you think! Well, if he were he would not have been on such terms with my cousin as he described! Said he had been intimate with him, did he not?'

'Yes, decidedly. In fact, he spoke of being aware of the confusion your cousin's affairs must be in, and he offered to assist me in getting his papers into order.'

Nicky looked fixedly at her. 'He did, did he? Now, why should you need the help of some stranger when it is perfectly well known that my cousin had any number of relatives whom you would apply to if you needed help? By Jove, you have hit upon it, ma'am! Your precious visitor came here to get something from Eustace, and his wanting to go through his papers proves it! Oh, this is famous! Let us go downstairs at once, and hunt for what it may be!'

'No, that you shall not!' declared Elinor roundly. 'Your brother left all those papers in my charge, and no one must look at them but himself and the lawyer who is joined with him as an executor to your cousin's Will! Besides, it is nonsense! What could there be that anyone should want?'

'I don't know, but I'll swear there is something! Of course, it may not be a paper: I wonder if Eustace had stolen something of value? He was always under the hatches, and –'

'I will not allow it to be possible!' said Elinor. 'Do you wish me to believe that your cousin was a common thief? Such a notion must be absurd!'

'Well, he stole Harry's best fishing-rod once,' argued Nicky. 'Harry drew his cork for it, what's more, and he ran to my aunt saying how brutally he had been used. He was the most cow-hearted fellow imaginable!'

'I dare say, but there is a difference between a boy's borrowing what does not belong to him, and –'

'He didn't borrow it! He stole it, and swore he had no notion where it was! Only Harry had a pretty strong guess where he had hidden it, and he found it. If you don't believe me, you may ask Ned! And though it is not a thing we speak of in a general way it was for stealing that he was expelled from Eton. At least, he would have been, only that Ned prevailed on them to let him remove him, with nothing said as to the cause.'

'Good God!' said Elinor bitterly. 'A pretty husband I was married to, to be sure!'

'Oh, he was a shocking fellow!' said Nicky cheerfully. 'So you see –'

'I do not care how shocking he may have been, I will not permit you to tamper with his papers!' said Elinor, with resolution. 'It would be most improper in me. Besides, I do not set the least store by all this nonsense! You have refined too much upon what must have some quite simple explanation.'

'I'll lay you odds you are wrong!' offered Nicky. 'Of course, if you think I should not look at Eustace's papers I will not do so. I think I should go back to the Hall, and tell Ned what we have discovered. I dare say he may have returned by this time.'

'Yes, I think you should,' said Elinor thankfully. 'But I wish you will secure that door before you go!'

'No, no, we must on no account do so!' he replied. 'I am in great hopes that that fellow will come back again. Indeed, I would wager a pony he will, and we don't wish to scare him off!' he smiled engagingly at his fascinated hostess. 'Now, *do* we, Cousin Elinor?'

'Certainly not!' she said, rising nobly to this occasion. 'If he should come again, I will offer him refreshment. If only I had thought of it earlier! I do trust my inhospitality may not have given him a distaste of this house!'

'I knew you were a right one!' Nicky said. 'But do be serious, ma'am! You see, if I am in the right of it, and I do think I may be, he will come to get whatever it is he wants, and we must lie in wait for him, and catch him red-handed. I know Ned would way so!'

'I can readily believe he would,' said Elinor sardonically.

Nicky replaced the trap-door, and shut the cupboard. 'I do not see that there is anything more we can do here at this present,' he said. 'Let us go downstairs again, cousin. And you must not say a word of this to the Barrows, you know, for besides that we do not wish anyone to know what we have discovered, ten to one they would take fright, and run away, leaving you alone here, and that would not do at all.'

'At last you have uttered a sentiment with which I find myself in profound agreement!' said Elinor. 'But do not delude yourself into fancying that I mean to spend another night in this house with that dreadful door unsecured, for nothing would induce me to do so! Though, to be sure, I have not the least expectation of receiving another such visit from that man!'

He followed her down the stairs. 'Well, if you have not, you cannot have the least objection to my leaving that door open,' he said reasonably.

She entered the book-room, and sat down by the fire. 'I should not, I know,' she confessed. 'But females have such unaccountable fancies! You will think me as paltry a creature as your cousin, I dare say, but I must own that there is something very disagreeable to me in the thought that there is a way into this house which issued by one whom you have assured me must be an ugly customer. In fact, even now, in broad daylight, I find

I cannot be easy in my mind, and quite dread being obliged to go upstairs.'

'Oh, you need be under no apprehension, ma'am!' he assured her. 'There can be no fear of anyone's entering that door during the daylight! But I'll tell you what? While I ride back to the Hall to tell Ned about this, I'll leave Bouncer to guard you. You will be quite at your ease then, for he is pretty fierce, I can tell you! He took a bite out of the blacksmith's leg only the other day. He is a splendid dog, and only quite young yet!'

She looked dubiously at the dog, who was stretched out before the fire, fast asleep. 'Well, if you think. . . . But perhaps he will not stay, if you go.'

'Yes, he will. I have been training him to do all manner of tricks! Here, Bouncer! Here, boy!'

The hound awoke, and sat up, dipping his ears, and panting fondly at his master. Nicky patted him invigoratingly. 'Good dog, Bouncer!' he said. 'Now, you stay here, and guard her! Do you understand, sir? Sit! That's it! On guard, Bouncer, mind!' He straightened himself, regarding his pet proudly. 'You can see how he understands me, can you not?' he said. 'I'll be off at once. Don't put yourself to the trouble of coming to the door with me! And don't be in the fidgets, will you, cousin? I shall be back almost directly, and I will bring Ned to you, *Sit*, Bouncer! On guard!'

He left the room as he spoke, taking the precaution of shutting the door behind him. The faithful Bouncer bounded over to it, sniffed long and loud at the crack, uttered a whine, and scratched at the panel. Finding it immovable, he returned to the fire, and lay down with his head on his paws, and his eyes fixed on Elinor.

She leaned back in her chair, really a good deal upset by the discovery of the secret stairway, and feeling the need of a period of quiet during which she might compose her mind. Common sense assured her that Nicky's theories could be nothing more than the products of an ardent imagination, but try as she would she could not hit upon a more reasonable explanation of the Frenchman's presence in the house on the previous night. He had not seemed to her at all the sort of young man to have made use of the secret door from a high-spirited desire to give his host a fright; nor could she believe him to have been a common housebreaker. Some motive he must have had, but what this was she was much inclined to think no one but himself would ever know. That he would return in the same manner seemed other to go beyond the bounds of probability, yet however irrational it might be she could not think of that secret stair without feeling her pulse beat fast with trepidation.

She did her best to shake off such foolish fears, and told herself she would be better employed in sorting the linen than in sitting thinking herself into nervous spasms. She got up out of her chair, and would have walked over to the door had it not been unmistakably brought home to her that the intelligent hound at her feet was labouring under some confusion of ideas. He too rose, and with bristles lifting all along his back, and his lips curling away from a set of admirable teeth, placed himself before her, growling.

Elinor stood still, looking down at him doubtfully. 'Good dog!' she said, in what she hoped was a reassuring voice. 'Lie down, sir!'

Bouncer barked at her.

'You stupid creature, he did not mean you to keep me chained to my chair!' scolded Elinor. 'Lie down this instant!'

Bouncer stood his ground, and went on growling, in a sort of crescendo which could not be regarded as other than menacing. Elinor sat down again. Pleased with his success, Bouncer followed suit, and lolled his tongue out, and panted gently.

Eight

Since the clock in the book-room did not go, Elinor had no means of ascertaining for how long she was left confronting Nicky's zealous pet. It seemed a very long time. While she remained still, Bouncer lay peaceably enough, with his head on his paws, and his eyes half-closed; but the smallest movement brought his head and his bristles up, while an attempt to win him over by blandishments he took in such bad part that Elinor thought it prudent to desist. Her workbox, and the pile of linen to be mended were alike out of her reach, but she found that by stretching out her arm she could reach the what-not that stood near her chair. There was a small book upon one of its shelves, and she managed to secure this without incurring censure from her guardian. It proved to be a copy of the *Turf Remembrancer*, and for the next hour and more it was Elinor's only solace. She culled from it much valuable information, such as had not before come in her way, and followed with bewildered interest the careers of several animals who rejoiced in names which ranged from the comparatively commonplace to the wildly fanciful. She could conjure up little enthusiasm for Lightning or Thunderbolt, but read with satisfaction an account of parentage and prowess of Watch-them-and-catch-them, and of Fear-not-Victorious, and would have been almost ready to have answered a catechism on their form, and the weights they would be likely to carry in any forthcoming race.

But however entrancing the names of race-horses might be the *Turf Remembrancer* could not but pall upon her. By the time Barrow came into the room, midway through the afternoon, she was heartily sick of it, and would have been hard put to it not to have thrown it at Nicky's head had it been he, and not Barrow, who entered.

'You never ate the luncheon Mrs. Barrow sent up to the dining-parlour, ma'am,' observed Barrow reproachfully. 'She made sure you'd be glad of a bite, too.'

'Yes, and so I should,' said Elinor crossly, 'but this stupid dog of Mr. Nicholas's will not let me move from my chair! Do, pray, call him off!'

'Whatever did Master Nicky take and leave that nasty brute here for?' demanded Barrow, eyeing Bouncer with dislike.

'He – well, he thought I should have him to guard me!' explained Elinor rather lamely.

'Have him to guard you?' said Barrow incredulously. 'It's midsummer moon with Master Nick, surelye! What would you be wanting with a guard, ma'am?'

'I don't want one at all, and I wish you will call him away!'

Barrow looked with considerable misgiving at the dog, Bouncer returned the stare enigmatically. 'The thing is,' said Barrow, 'that there dog is a tedious fierce brute, ma'am, and I'd as lief let Master Nick call him off.'

'But Master nick is not here!'

Barrow looked nonplussed. As his mistress clearly expected him to do something, he patted his leg in a tentative way, and invited Bouncer to come to him. Bouncer growled at him. This caused the servitor to retreat strategically into the doorway, seeing which Bouncer rose to his feet and barked with all the zest of a dog who finds his threats succeed beyond his expectations.

'Try to tempt him away with some meat!' commanded the exasperated prisoner.

'Ay, that's what I'll do!' agreed Barrow, and went off to procure some of the mutton laid out for Elinor's refreshment.

He returned with this, and with Mrs. Barrow too, who stalked in armed with a long-handled broom, declaring her intention of soon ridding Mistress of the plaguey creature. Bouncer, not unnaturally, took instant exception to the broom, and such a pandemonium of barking, scolding, and growling ensured that Elinor could only beg her would-be rescuer to go away. Barrow then held down the plate of meat, and chirped at Bouncer, who made one of his short rushes at him, and so caused him to drop the plate, and leap back to the door. Bouncer hastily consumed the offering, licked his lips, and waited expectantly for more.

'There's only one thing to be done, ma'am,' said Barrow. 'I'll have to shoot him, that's what I'll have to do.'

'Good God, no!' cried Elinor. 'I would not have you do such a thing for the world! Why, whatever would Master Nicky say?'

'Master Nicky indeed!' exclaimed Mrs. Barrow indignantly. 'I'll Master Nicky him when I see him! The idea of his playing off his tricks on you, ma'am! I've a very good mind to tell his lordship what a naughty boy he is!'

'Indeed, I – I think he meant it for the best!' said Elinor. 'And he said he would come back presently. Do you think you could contrive to bring a tray to me, with some bread-and-butter and coffee? And perhaps you might also push that table to where I may reach it, so that I may at least occupy myself with darning those tablecloths!'

Bouncer seemed disinclined at first to permit this disarrangement of the room, but Mrs. Barrow had the happy notion of bribing him with a large marrow-bone. He accepted this, and lay down with it between his paws, gnawing it, and beyond growling in a minatory fashion made no further objection to the table's being pushed towards Elinor. He seemed so intent on his bone that she tried the experiment of rising from her chair. This was going too far, however, and she was obliged to sit down again in a hurry. Bouncer then returned to his bone. His teeth appeared to be in excellent condition. When Mrs. Barrow cautiously came back into the room with a tray, he cocked a watchful eye at her, and paused in his work of demolition to consider the possibilities of the tray. He evidently thought it worth while to investigate it, for he rose, and approached the table. Mrs. Barrow told him to be off, so he chased her from the room, and returned to try what blackmail could achieve in the way of sustenance. Elinor gave him a crust, which he rejected scornfully. He went back to his bone, and remained happily occupied with it for some time, and finally buried what remained of it under one of the sofa cushions.

'You are an odious animal!' Elinor said severely. 'I hope your master beats you!'

He yawned at her contemptuously, cast himself down before the fire again, and resumed his vigil.

Not until nearly five o'clock did Nicky return to Highnoons, and by that time Elinor was in such a temper that she could happily have boxed his ears. He was admitted by Barrow, who had evidently told him how his plan had miscarried, for he came at once to the book-room, laughing delightedly, and saying: 'Oh, Cousin Elinor, indeed I beg your pardon! Have you been there all day? I don't mean to laugh, but it is the drollest thing!' He bent over Bouncer, who was frisking round him joyfully. 'You rascal, what have you been about? Yes, good dog, down! down!'

'He is not a good dog! He is an excessively bad dog!' said Elinor, quite exasperated. 'It is all very well for you to stand there laughing, and encouraging that horrid creature, but I am quite out of patience with you!'

'Well, I am really excessively sorry,' Nicky said penitently, 'but it was not Bouncer's fault! He did not perfectly understand me! But only fancy his guarding you like that all this while! I cannot help being pleased with him, for, you know, I was not above half sure that he would guard anything! You must own that he is a clever fellow!'

'I own nothing of the sort,' said Elinor, getting up, and shaking out her skirts. 'He appears to me to have a very disordered intellect. And pray what have you been about all this time? And where is your brother?'

'Oh, he is not here!' Nicky said blithely. 'When I reached home again our butler told me that he was gone up to London.

He will not be back until to-morrow, I dare say. But do not be in a pucker, ma'am! I mean to stay with you, and only fancy if we caught that stranger without Ned's knowing anything about it! That would be something, wouldn't it?'

'Nicky, I am in no humour for this nonsense, and so I warn you!' said Elinor. 'If Lord Carlyon is away from home, I insist on your securing that door!'

'Oh, no, I have a much better notion than that!' Nicky said blithely. 'If you should not dislike it, I mean to spend the night in that room above-stairs, and then, if anyone comes up the secret stair, I shall catch him.'

The outraged widow gave him to understand in the plainest terms that nothing could exceed her dislike of this project. He remained entirely unconvinced, merely setting himself to coax and cajole her into relenting. After twenty minutes of his persuasive eloquence she began to weaken, partly because she was a kind-hearted woman, and perceived that a refusal to let him amuse himself in this way would bitterly disappoint him; and partly because from having had a good deal to do with young gentlemen of tender years she was well aware that however weary of the argument she might be he would be ready to continue it with unabated vigour until a late hour of the night. She gave way at last, and with an acid reference to the well-known effect of the dropping of water upon stones, said that he might do as he pleased.

Passing over this rider with all the air of one too well-accustomed to listen to such odious comparisons to pay any heed to them, Nicky favoured her with one of his blinding smiles, and said that he had known all along that she was pluck to the backbone. She thanked him for this tribute, and enquired how he meant to account for his presence in the house to the Barrows.

'Oh, there can be no difficulty!' he answered. 'I shall say you are in the fidgets because of what happened last night, and I am come so that you may be comfortable.'

'Well, if you are set on keeping watch over that stair, I think you should tell Barrow the whole, and let him bear you company,' she said.

This, however, he would by no means agree to, indignantly demanding whether she thought him to be incapable of dealing unassisted with any midnight marauder. She mendaciously assured him that she had every confidence in his ability to capture, single-handed, any number of desperate persons, and he relented enough to show her a serviceable pistol which he had had the forethought to bring with him.

She eyed this weapon with misgiving. 'Is it loaded?' she asked.

'Loaded! Ay, of course it is loaded!' he said impatiently. 'What would be the use of it if it were not, pray? It is not cocked, however, so if you are thinking that it may go off you may be quite easy on that score.'

'Oh!' she said. 'Is it your own pistol?'

'Well, no,' he admitted airily. 'As it happens, it is one of Ned's. But he will not object to my having borrowed it.'

'Oh!' said Elinor again. She added carelessly: 'I dare say you are quite in the habit of using firearms?'

'Good God, yes!' he replied. 'Why, what a flat you must be thinking me! Ned taught me to handle a gun when I was scarcely breeched!'

'Did he indeed?' said Elinor politely. 'What a prodigy you must have been! I had no notion of it! You must forgive me!'

He grinned. 'Well, I am sure I was no more than twelve, at all events. And naturally I have shot at Manton's times out of mind. I don't mean to say that I am a crack shot, like Ned and Harry, but I have more than once culped a wafer.'

'You put me quite at my ease. And yet I cannot help thinking that perhaps it might be as well if you did not shoot at anyone unless you found yourself absolutely obliged to.'

'Indeed I shall not! Particularly now that his inquest is hanging over us all. I don't wish to be putting Ned to more trouble, you know.'

'No,' she agreed. 'I do feel that to expect him to bring you off safe from two such enquiries might tax even his ingenuity a little far.'

'Oh, he would contrive it, never fear!' he said cheerfully. 'But don't put yourself in a pucker! I don't mean to do more than hold the fellow up, and discover what mischief he is up to. And I'll tell you what, Cousin Elinor! If he does come again, I shall not show myself immediately. I shall follow him, to see where he goes, and what he finds. I think that is what I should do, don't you?'

She agreed to it, tactfully concealing from him her comfortable conviction that no midnight visitor was at all likely to reward his vigil. Had she had any real fear that the Frenchman would return she must, she believed, have alienated her youthful guest for ever by divulging the whole to Barrow. She was happy in not feeling herself obliged to spoil sport in this dreary fashion, and volunteered instead to acquaint the Barrows with his intention of spending the night at Highnoons.

The information was greeted in the kitchen with scant favour. Mrs. Barrow opined darkly that she knew Master Nick well enough to being no doubt that he was up to some mischief; while Barrow said that in his opinion to have Master Nick capering about like a fly in a tar-box could afford no comfort whatsoever to anyone suffering from nervous qualms. 'I tell you to your head, ma'am, that Master Nick, not to wrap it up in clean linen, is tedious loose in the hilts!' he said severely.

Mrs. Barrow, with a passing admonition to him to hold his tongue, informed her mistress that this bodeful pronouncement meant merely that Master Nick, being but a lad, was scarcely to be relied on. 'But it's no matter!' she said. 'He'll be company for you, I dare say, ma'am. But mind you make him tie that nasty dog of his up!'

This, in the event, proved to be unnecessary. Nicky had already decided that Bouncer must be shut up in one of the loose-boxes, for fear of his giving tongue at the approach of a stranger. The faithful hound, therefore, after being regaled with a large plateful of meat and broken biscuits, was led off stablewards, bearing in his jaws the remnants of the bone with which his hostess had thoughtfully presented him. His attitude to her now was that of one who in the execution of his duty yet bore no malice towards his victim. She could not acquit him of grinning at her, and told him that he was a vile creature, a tribute which he accepted with a flattening of his ears, and a perfunctory wag of the tail.

Mrs. Cheviot and the Hon. Nicholas Carlyon dined very cosily together off a neck of veal, stewed with rice, onions, and peppercorns, followed by pippin-tarts, and some ramekins which moved Nicky to send a message to the kitchen assuring Mrs. Barrow of favourable treatment if ever she should desire a post as cook up at the Hall. Barrow then set a decanter of port on the table, and Elinor very correctly withdrew to the book-room, whither her guest soon followed her, with a suggestion that they should while away the evening with a rubber or two of piquet. As the pockets of both gamesters were, in Nicky's phrase, wholly to let, they played for fabulous but imaginary stakes, with the result that when the tea-tray was brought in, Elinor found herself several thousand pounds to the good. Nicky very handsomely said that he only wished he could pay her the half of such a sum, and they sat down to drink their tea in perfect amity.

Nicholas favoured his hostess with some reminiscences of his past career, which made her laugh heartily; in her turn she entranced him with an account of her father's exploits in every realm of sport, and in this way an hour or two was very pleasantly beguiled. In fact, on such easy terms with Nicky did Elinor feel herself to be by the time they went up to bed that she seriously jeopardized the honourable position she held in his esteem by suggesting that he should allow her to have the bed made up in the room he meant to occupy, so that he might pass the night in comfort. His shocked face recalled her to her senses, however, and she made haste to beg pardon, assuring him that she had spoken without thinking. He explained to her with the utmost patience that the sight of a gentleman sleeping in that room would effectually scare any intruder into a precipitate retreat; she confessed that she had been shatter-brained from a child; and they parted on the best of terms, she to lie awake for some time smiling over the simple enthusiasm of an engaging boy, he to stretch himself out on the unmade bed in the little square room, determined on no account to fall asleep.

This, after the first hour, proved to be more difficult than he had bargained for, and he more than once thought wistfully of the bed made up for him in the best spare bedchamber. He had removed his riding-boots, and hidden them behind a chair, and his feet grew steadily colder as the night advanced. He was obliged at last to cast one of his pillows over them, which alleviated his discomfort so much that he presently began to drop asleep. Had Elinor but known it, he only half believed in his own arguments, and had no very real conviction that an adventure did in very truth await him. He was at that stage in his development when, without having giving up all hope that the wonderful would happen, only a part of his eager brain expected it. For this reason, it was with a feeling of delighted incredulity that he was aroused, when just slipping over the border between waking and sleeping, by a sound coming from the direction of the concealed cupboard. It jerked him fully awake, and he raised himself on his elbow, hardly believing his own ears. But there could be no doubt about it: someone was lifting the trap-door in the cupboard.

With a gasp of excitement, Nicky snatched up the pillow covering his feet, restored it to its place at the head of the four-poster, and slid from the bed to the floor on the father side of it, his pistol firmly held in one hand. The moon was not shining in at the unshuttered window, but there was a faint grey light in the room, enabling him to discern the outlines of the few pieces of furniture.

He heard the scroop of the panel sliding back, and caught the reflection of a beam of yellow light cast on the wall. Whoever had entered by the secret stair had brought a lantern with him. Nicky's heart beat fast, but although his mouth certainly felt a little dry suddenly he was honestly delighted. He took care to remain crouched down behind the bedstead, and breathlessly awaited events. The beam of light shifted; he heard shod feet softly crossing the room in the direction of the doorway, and could scarcely refrain from raising his head to peep. The door-handle turned with a tiny scraping sound, and a creeping draught informed Nicky that the door stood open. He tried to peer under the bed, and was rewarded by a glimpse of an oblong of that yellow light, lying on the threshold of the room. Another instant, and it disappeared: the unknown visitor had stepped out on to the corridor. Nicky resolutely counted up to twenty before he allowed himself to rise from the floor. He was alone in the dim room, and the door, as he had guessed, stood open. He stole to it, taking care to cock his pistol, and saw the yellow light at the head of the uncarpeted stair. Again it halted; the unknown stood still, probably listening for any sound of stirring in the house, Nicky thought. As his eyes grew accustomed to the darkness, he could vaguely perceive the outline of a figure. He flattened himself against the wall, and waited. Apparently satisfied that the house slept, the figure moved again, going stealthily down the stairs. Nicky followed at a discreet interval, his stockinged feet making no sound on the wood-floor. He was so excited by this time that the heavy thudding of his heart made him feel almost sick. He stole down the stairs, sliding his hand along the baluster-rail, and letting it take most of his weight, to obviate any treacherous creaking of the stair-boards. The hall below was closely shuttered, and in dense darkness, save for the oblong of light cast by the intruder's lantern. Nicky reached the foot of the stairs in time to see the beam light up the door of the book-room. It stopped suddenly, and veered round, as though its holder had heard some sound, and was turning to discover the cause of it. Nicky instinctively stepped back, collided with the suit of rusted armour behind him, and brought it clattering to the ground, himself with it. With an exasperated oath he scrambled up, thankful that his finger had not been upon the trigger of his gun, and called out: 'Stand fast! I have you covered!'

The beam of light found him out; before he was fairly on his feet again there was a flash of whiter light, a loud report, and he was knocked over again, and knew, as he fell, that he had been hit. He managed to get up on to one elbow, and to fire in the direction of the lantern, but although his ball shattered the lantern it missed its holder, who became lost in the thick darkness. Nicky heard the shriek of bolts drawn back, and shouted frantically; 'Barrow! Barrow!' The next instant a shaft of moonlight, and a current of cold air streamed in through the open front-door, and he knew that his quarry had made good his escape.

Upstairs, in the Yellow bedchamber, Mrs. Cheviot had just dropped off to sleep. The first shot roused her, and even as she started up, scarcely crediting her ears, the second followed it, and brought her out of bed in a flash, groping for her slippers. She had kept an oil-lamp burning low beside her bed, and she turned it up with trembling fingers. Hastily struggling into her dressing-gown she ran out of the room, calling: 'Nicky, where are you? Oh, what in the world are you about?'

'I'm in the hall,' his voice answered her, a trifle faintly, but reassuringly cheerful. 'The devil's in it that I missed the fellow!'

She hurried down the stairs, holding the lamp up, and saw him rather unsteadily picking himself up. 'Nicky! Good God, do not tell me he did indeed come back?'

'Come back? Of course he did!' Nicky said, cautiously feeling his shoulder. 'What's more, I should have had him if you would not keep a damned suit of armour in the stupidest place anyone every thought of! Oh, I beg pardon! But indeed it is enough to try the patience of a saint!'

'Nicky, you are hurt!' she cried, quite horrified. 'Oh, if I had dreamt that anything was likely to happen I would never – My poor boy, lean on me! Did he fire at you? I heard two shots, and I was never more shocked in my life! Good God, you are bleeding! Let me help you into a chair this instant!'

'I think he winged me,' said Nicky, allowing himself to be assisted to a tattered leather chair, and sinking down into it. 'I never touched him, but I did shatter his lantern, and that would have been pretty fair shooting, I can tell you, if I had been aiming at it. But it is the most curst mischance, cousin! I have no notion who he was, or what he wanted, except that he was making for the book-room, which I guessed he would be in any event.'

'Oh, never mind that!' she said, setting the lamp down on the table, and running to shut the front door. 'As long as you are not

108

badly wounded! Oh, what in the world will Lord Carlyon say to this? I am culpably to blame!'

Nicky grinned feebly. 'He'll say it was just like me to make such a botch of it. Don't be in a taking! It's only a scratch!'

By this time Barrow had appeared on the scene, a tallow candle held waveringly in one hand, and on his face an expression compound of amazement and consternation. He was sketchily attired in breeches and his night-shirt, but he forgot this unconventional raiment when he saw Nicky clutching one hand to his left shoulder, and came hurrying down the stairs, clucking with dismay. He was almost immediately followed by his spouse, scolding and exclaiming at once. Between them, she and Elinor eased the coat from Nicky's shoulders, and laid bare a wound which, though it bled nastily, Mrs. Barrow announced to be not by any means desperate.

'I believe you are right!' Elinor said, with a sigh of relief. 'It is too high to have touched any fatal spot! But a doctor must be fetched instantly!'

'Oh, fudge! It's nothing!' Nicky said, trying to shake them off.

'Be still, Master Nicky, will you?' said Mrs. Barrow. 'Likely you have the ball lodged in you! But who fired at you? Sakes alive, what is the world a-coming to? Barrow, don't stand there gawping! Fetch some of Mr. Eustace's brandy to me straight, man! Oh dear, what a hem set out this is, to be sure!'

Elinor, meanwhile, had snatched Barrow's candle from him, and hurried into the book-room. She came back with one of the tablecloths she had been mending in her hand, and began to tear it into serviceable strips. Nicky was looking very faint, and had his eyes closed, but he revived when Barrow forced some brandy down his throat, choked, coughed, and again said that it was only a scratch. Elinor ordered Barrow to support him upstairs to the spare bedroom, and followed anxiously in their wake, carrying the torn cloth, and the brandy bottle. By the time Nicky had been laid upon the bed, Mrs. Barrow had fetched a bowl of water, and was ready to bathe his wound. She and Elinor staunched the bleeding, and bound the shoulder as tightly as they could. The patient smiled sweetly up at them, and murmured: 'What a rout you do make! I shall be as right as a trivet by morning.'

'Great boast, small roast!' grunted Barrow, covering him with the quilt. 'I'd best ride for the doctor, no question. But who shot you, Master Nicky? Don't tell me that plaguey Frenchy was in the house again, because I doubled-bolted every door, and so I'll swear to, sure as check!'

'I don't know if it was he or another,' Nicky replied, shifting uneasily on his pillows. 'I didn't meant to tell you, but he came in by a secret stair that goes down the bake-house chimney. I found it this morning.'

Mrs. Barrow gave a scream, and dropped the strip of linen she was rolling into a bandage.

'Do-adone, Martha!' said Barrow, happy to be able to take a lofty tone with her. 'Master Nicky's gammoning you. That old stair's been shut this many a year!'

'Well, it has not,' said Nicky, nettled to find that Barrow knew of his discovery. 'And I'm not gammoning you! I was in that room where the entrance to it is, and I saw this fellow come out of the cupboard.'

Mrs. Barrow sat down plump upon the nearest chair, and expressed her conviction that she was unlikely ever to recover from the shock her nerves had sustained.

'You shouldn't ought to have stayed there without me to see you didn't come to no harm, Master Nick!' said Barrow. 'That cat's in the cream-pot now, surelye, for what his lordship will have to say about this night's work I daren't, for my ears, think on! If it ain't like you, sir, to be flying at all game, and never no thought taken to what may come of it! Ah, well, I'll saddle one of the horses, and fetch Dr. Greenlaw to you straight!'

'But what in the name of heaven can anyone want in this house?' demanded Elinor.

'There's no saying what any Frenchy may want,' said Barrow austerely, 'but you can lay your life, ma'am, it ain't anything good.'

Nine

*I*t was fully an hour later when the welcome sound of voices in the hall informed Elinor that the doctor had arrived at Highnoons. She had found time to dress herself; Mrs. Barrow had roused the obliging wench from the Hall, and told her to make up the smouldering fire in the kitchen, and to set water on it to boil, while she herself, taking a high tone with Nicky, bullied and coaxed him into permitting her to undress him, and get him between sheets. He was so much discomfited by some of the more embarrassing reminiscences of his extreme youth which she saw fit to recall to his memory that his protests lacked conviction, and she had less trouble with him than might have been expected.

Dr. Greenlaw opened his eyes a little at sight of Elinor, but bowed to her very civilly before turning his attention to his patient.

Nicky smiled at him. 'You are never done with us, Greenlaw!' he remarked.

'Very true, Mr. Nick, but I am sorry to find you in this case,' replied the doctor, beginning to unwind the bandages. 'What scrape are you in now, pray?'

'The devil's in it that I don't precisely know,' confessed Nicky. 'But if only I had not missed the fellow I should not care!'

'Barrow has been babbling some nonsense about Frenchmen. Was it a housebreaker, sir?'

'Yes, of course,' Nicky said, with a warning glance cast in Elinor's direction. 'Well, what's the damage? It's only a scratch, isn't it?'

'Ay, you were born under a lucky star, sir, as I have told you before,' said Greenlaw, opening a case of horrid-looking instruments.

'Yes, when I fell off the stable-roof, and broke my leg,' said Nicky, eyeing his preparations with some misgiving. 'What are you meaning to do to me, you murderer?'

'I must extract the ball, Mr. Nicky, and I fear I shall hurt you a trifle. Some hot water, ma'am, if I might trouble you!'

'I have it here,' Elinor said, picking up the brass can from before the fire, and hoping that she did not look as queasy as she was beginning to feel.

But she and Nicky alike underwent the ordeal with great fortitude, Elinor by dint of turning her eyes away from the doctor's probing hands, and Nicky by gritting his teeth, and bracing every muscle. The doctor encouraged them both with a gentle flow of irrelevant conversation to which neither attended. Elinor was glad to discover that he was deft and quick. The ball was not deeply lodged, and was soon extracted, and the wound washed, and dressed with basilicum powder. Greenlaw bound it up comfortably, measured out a cordial, and obliged Nicky to swallow it. 'There, you will do very well, sir!' he said, drawing the bedclothes over his patient. 'I shan't bleed you.'

'No, that you won't!' retorted Nicky, faint but indomitable.

'Until to-morrow,' finished Greenlaw grimly.

He then beckoned Elinor out of the room, gave her a few instructions, told her that as Nicky would in all probability sleep soundly now for several hours she might as well go back to her bed, and, after promising to return later in the day, took himself off. Nicky did indeed seem sleepy, so as soon as she had taken the precaution of locking the door into the room that gave access to the secret stair, Elinor retired to her own room again, and once more went to bed.

It was long before she slept, however. Setting aside his desperate behaviour, the return of her mysterious visitor most seriously alarmed her. That he did indeed want something from Highnoons was now established, and since his conduct clearly indicated that he would stop at nothing to obtain it she was unable to view with the smallest equanimity a continued sojourn in the house. The scutter of a mouse across the floor made her jump nearly out of her skin, and she was kept awake for a long time by an uncontrollable anxiety to strain her ears on the chance of catching any alien noise in the house. Her dreams, when she did at last fall asleep, were troubled, and she arose in the morning feeling very little rested, and considerably incensed with Carlyon for having placed her at Highnoons.

Nicky, whom she found sitting up in bed and partaking of a substantial breakfast, seemed to be little the worse for his adventure. Mrs. Barrow had fashioned a sling for his left arm, and whenever he did not need the use of this arm he gratified her by slipping it into the sling. He too had been thinking over the night's adventure, and he greeted Elinor with the pleasing suggestion that his assailant had been a French spy.

'A spy!' she exclaimed. 'Oh, do not say so!'

'Well, one of Boney's agents,' he amended. 'John says he has any number of them, and we do not know them all by any means.'

'But what should a French agent want with your cousin?'

'I don't know, and, to tell you the truth, I should not have thought Eustace was the kind of fellow to be of the least use to anyone,' he replied. 'But depend upon it, that is what it is!' He inserted a generous portion of cold beef into his mouth, and added, somewhat thickly: 'I dare say we have not seen the last of that fellow, not by a very long way. Why, for anything we know we have stumbled upon a really bang-up adventure!'

It was plain that he viewed the prospect with enthusiasm. Elinor could not share it. She said, with a shiver: 'I wish you will not talk so! If it were true, only consider what might happen to us in this dreadful house!'

'Just what I was thinking,' nodded Nicky, spreading mustard over another portion of beef. 'There is no saying indeed! I shall stay here.'

'Well, I shall not!' declared Elinor tartly. 'I have no desire to lead a life of such adventure!'

'You would not like to catch one of Boney's agents?' said Nicky incredulously.

'Not at all. I should not know what to do with him if I did. Yes, I should, though! I should set your horrid dog to guard him!'

'Yes, and he would do so, wouldn't he?' grinned Nicky. 'Oh, Cousin Elinor, would you be so very obliging as to let the old fellow out of the stables? I told Barrow to do so, but he would not. He is a paltry creature!'

'Will he bite me if I do?' demanded Elinor.

'Oh, I should not think he would do so!' Nicky said encouragingly. 'But pray do not let him make off! I should not like Sir Matthew's curst keepers to shoot him.'

'I should!' retorted Elinor, going off to release the prisoner.

Bouncer, so far from offering to bite her, greeted her as a benefactress from whom he had been parted for years. He jumped up at her several times, barking on a high, ear-splitting note, dashed three times round the stable-yard at speed, and finally brought her an unwieldy branch of wood which he seemed to think she might like to throw for him. She declined to enter upon a sport of which, she guessed, he would not readily tire, and invited him to accompany her to the house. Picking up his branch, he trotted along beside her. He would have carried his toy into the hall had she not prevented him. Since he remained deaf to her adjurations to him to drop it, she laid hold of one end, and tried to pull it away from him. Pleased that she was ready to play a game he knew and liked, he threw himself whole-heartedly into a tug-of-war, growling in a blood-curdling way, and wagging his tail furiously. Fortunately, since Elinor was no match for him, the groom came round the corner of the house just then, and Bouncer, perceiving him, let go of the branch in order to chase him back to his proper quarters. Elinor hastily threw the branch into a thicket of brambles. Bouncer soon returned to her, prancing along in the manner of a dog who has acquitted himself well, and cocked his ears at her expectantly. He consented to accompany her into the house, but obviously thought poorly of her taste in choosing to be indoors on a fine morning. But when she took him upstairs to Nicky's room nothing could have exceeded his joy at being reunited with the master whom he had not seen for ten hours. He leaped up on to the bed, uttering screaming barks, and ecstatically licked Nicky's face. After that, being forcibly adjured thereto, he jumped down again, cast himself down by the fire, and lay panting.

'What he needs, of course, is a good run,' said Nicky, fondly regarding him.

'Oh, yes?' said Elinor politely.

'I was only thinking, cousin, that if you did happen to be going out for a walk you might like to take him with you,' he explained.

'I know that that is what you were thinking,' she returned. 'I am well able to imagine what that walk would be like, I thank you!'

'Oh, but he is quite well-behaved now!' Nicky assured her. 'I have very nearly trained him not to kill chickens, or chase sheep, and if only you do not meet any other dogs you will not have the least trouble with him.'

'He has already had a very nice run, chasing the groom,' said Elinor hard-heartedly. 'And I do not mean to go out walking to-day.'

'Oh, well, I dare say I shall be able to take him myself presently!' he said.

'You will not get up to-day!'

'Not get up? Good God, of course I shall! There is nothing amiss with me beyond this hole in my shoulder!'

She extracted a promise that at least he would not get up until Dr. Greenlaw had seen him, and went off to confer with Mrs. Barrow. By the time she had emerged from the kitchen the doctor's gig was at the door, and he was taking off his greatcoat in the hall. She was able to give him a comfortable account of his patient, but begged him, as she led him upstairs, not to permit of Nicky's leaving his bed that day. He said dryly that he doubted whether anyone could keep Nicky in bed if he had taken it into his head to get up.

'I wish his brother were here!' she said.

'Ay, Mr. Nicholas would mind him,' he agreed.

'I hold myself entirely to blame for what has happened!'

He looked surprised. 'I am sure I do not know why you should, ma'am.'

She recollected that Nicky had not taken him into his confidence, and said quickly. 'For permitting him to remain here last night, I mean!'

'Ah, well!' he said. 'If it not one thing with Mr. Nick, it must needs be another! He has taken no serious hurt, ma'am.'

When he saw Nicky, he found that the wound was healing quite as well as could be expected, and that the pulse, though a little fast, was by no means tumultuous. He condemned in round terms the breakfast which he learned, upon enquiry, that Nicky had consumed, and said that he would bleed him, to be on the safe side.

'Oh, no, you will not!' Nicky said, drawing the bedclothes up to his chin.

'Ay, but I will, Mr. Nick,' said Greenlaw, once more getting out his bag of instruments. 'We do not want to run the risk of any fever.'

'I have no fever, and I'll be damned if I'll let you cup me!'

'Now, sir, you know I have often done so, and you have been the better for it!'

Nicky would by no means allow it to have been so, and vociferated his protests so loudly that Bouncer sat up, bristling. He had not so far paid any heed to the doctor, with whom he was acquainted, but he now clearly perceived that his attitude was menacing, and with a growl of warning he bounded up on to the bed, and stood astride Nicky's legs, daring Greenlaw to touch him.

Nicky gave a shout of laughter, and grasped him by the scruff of his neck. 'Good dog, Bouncer! Sick him off, then!'

'Very well,' said Greenlaw, smiling reluctantly. 'But if you are in a high fever by nightfall, do not blame me, sir!'

After this episode, Elinor was not surprised, an hour later, to encounter Nicky somewhat shakily negotiating the stairs. He was wearing a dressing-gown of such startling design and varied colour that she blinked at him. He told her that he had bought it in Oxford, and that it was all the crack. 'Only fancy that old rascal's wanting to bleed me!' he said. 'Why, I must have lost pints already, for I'm as weak as a cat!'

'Of course you are, and you should be in bed!' she said. 'You must lie on the sofa in the book-room, and, mind! if you do not stay there quietly to bed you must and shall go!'

He made a face at her, but he was glad enough to stretch himself out on the sofa, and to allow her to rearrange his sling more comfortably. But he became very recalcitrant when Barrow brought in a bowl of gruel, and said that if there was any ale in the house he would like a tankard of it, with a sandwich to eat with it. These being firmly denied him, he agreed to compromise with a bowl of chicken-broth, and a glass of white wine whey. Having disposed of this light repast, he then settled down to discuss exhaustively with Elinor what ought next to be done to entrap the foe. He had not pursued the subject very far, however, when the front-door bell clanged in the distance, and Bouncer rose, growling.

Such was the irritation of nerves which Elinor laboured under that she could not repress a start, or banish from her mind the fear that whoever stood at the front door had come to the house with a fell purpose in view. Something of the same nature seemed to be in Nicky's brain too, for he sat with his head a little tilted, listening intently. Bouncer padded over to the door, and set his nose to the crack under it, tail and hackles well up. Barrow crossed the hall in his usual leisurely fashion, and a murmur of voices sounded. Bouncer's bristles sank, and he began to wag his trail, and to snuff loudly.

'It's Ned!' exclaimed Nicky, his face lightening.

'Oh, I do hope it is indeed!' cried Elinor, and ran to the door, and opened it.

She would not have believed, twenty-four hours earlier, that the sight of that tall figure, in the long, many-caped driving-coat, could be so welcome to her. 'Than God you are come, my lord!'

she uttered, in accents of heartfelt relief. Then her eyes alighted on a little, old lady standing beside Carlyon, in an old-fashioned bonnet, and a drab pelisse over a plain, round gown and a spencer, and she cried out: 'Becky!' and started forward, to clasp the little lady in a warm embrace.

'My love!' said Miss Beccles. 'My dear Mrs. Cheviot!'

'Oh, Becky, pray do not call me so!' Elinor begged. She turned to Carlyon, her cheeks in a glow. 'I had no notion you meant to bring her to me so speedily, sir! I am so very much obliged to you! Oh, dear, it makes me wish more than ever that I had not served you such a trick –! I do not know what you will say when you hear of it, but indeed I never dreamed, when I let him stay – But do pray come into the book-room!'

He had been allowing Bouncer to tug at his gloves, but he looked up at that, his brows lifting. 'My dear Mrs. Cheviot, how can you possibly have served me a trick? Is anything amiss?'

'Everything!' she declared.

He maintained his usual calm, merely looking a little surprised, and saying: 'That is certainly comprehensive. I see you have Nicky here. Yes, that will do, Bouncer! Be quiet!'

Nicky at this moment appeared in the doorway of the book-room, his left arm reposing interestingly in its sling. 'I say, Ned, I'm devilish glad to see you!' he remarked. 'We have had such a lark here!'

Carlyon regarded him without betraying either dismay or astonishment. 'Now what have you been about?' he asked, in a resigned tone.

'Well, I'll tell you, but take off your coat, and come in!'

'Very well, but make your bow to Miss Beccles. My youngest brother, ma'am.'

Miss Beccles dropped a curtsy, saying in her soft voice: 'I am very happy to make your acquaintance, sir, but should you be standing there in the draught, do you think? Forgive me, but you do not look to me to be quite well!'

'No, of course he should not be standing there!' said Elinor, recalled to a sense of her responsibility. 'He should be in bed! I wish you will go back to the sofa, Nicky! What a tiresome boy you are!'

Carlyon looked a little amused. 'Do as you are bid, Nicky! I think Miss Beccles would be glad of a bowl of soup, Mrs. Cheviot: it was cold during the drive.'

'Oh, no!' murmured the little lady, looking up at him gratefully. 'I was so well wrapped up! Such a luxurious chaise, and every kind attention to my comfort!'

'Indeed you must have some soup, and a glass of wine as well!' Elinor said, drawing her towards the book-room. 'Barrow, pray tell Mrs. Barrow! There is the chicken-broth that was made for Mr. Nick. Come in, Becky dear!'

'By Jove, yes, she may have *all* my chicken-broth, and that white wine whey too!' said Nicky generously.

Miss Beccles walked over to the sofa, and plumped up the cushions, smiling invitingly at him. He thanked her, and lay down again on it. 'I will make you a panada presently,' she said. 'You will like that, sir.'

'Shall I?' he asked doubtfully.

'Yes,' she said, with gentle certainty. She looked at Elinor, and said: 'My love, if you should desire to be private with his lordship I will go upstairs and set about unpacking my trunks.'

'No, no, Becky, do not go! I do not mean to remain another night in this dreadful house, but since you are come to it is only right that you should know what manner of things happen to one here!'

'You alarm, me, Mrs. Cheviot,' interposed Carlyon. 'Are you going to tell me that you have indeed encountered a headless spectre?'

'Yes,' she said bitterly. 'I might have known you would make light of it, sir!'

'I may do so, perhaps, but I will engage not to until I know what it is that has so much distressed you. How are you hurt, Nicky?'

'I was shot at!' replied Nicky impressively.

'You were shot at!'

'Yes, but the ball only lodged in my shoulder, and Greenlaw soon dug it out.'

'But who shot at you, and why?'

'That's just it, Ned! We haven't a notion who it was! It is the most famous affair, and only think! if I had not been sent down it would not have happened, and we might never have known anything about it!'

'I think,' said Carlyon, 'that you had better tell me this story from the start, if I am to understand it.'

'Well, the start of it was Cousin Elinor's part of the adventure. I was not here. Tell him how it all began, cousin!'

'Yes, pray do!' said Carlyon, walking over to the fire, and standing with his back to it. 'I am happy, at all events, to discover that you are so far reconciled to your lot, ma'am, as to accept the – er – relationship that exists between us.'

She was obliged to smile. 'Well, I had rather be called by almost any other name than Cheviot!' she said.

'I will bear it in mind. Now, what has been the matter here?'

Beginning to feel, quite irrationally, that she had been making a mountain out of a molehill, she described as briefly as she could her encounter with the young Frenchman. He heard her in attentive silence. Miss Beccles quietly removed her bonnet and pelisse, and sat down in a chair with her hands placidly folded in her lap.

'You say he was young, and dark, and spoke with only a slight accent, ma'am?'

She agreed to it, adding that the Frenchman was of medium height and slim build, and wore neat side-whiskers.

Carlyon opened his snuff-box, and took a meditative pinch. 'Then I fancy he must have been young De Castres,' he said.

Nicky sat up. 'What, Louis De Castres?' he exclaimed. 'But, Ned, he is quite the thing! Why, you may meet him everywhere!'

'Very true. Mrs. Cheviot seems even to have met him here.'

'No, dash it, Ned, he is not the kind of loose screw to be breaking into houses at dead of night! Because the story he told Cousin Elinor was a pack of lies! You do not know the whole yet!'

'Well, I may be mistaken,' Carlyon said. 'I merely suppose it may have been he from the fact of my having once or twice seen him in Cheviot's company.'

'Good God, I should not have thought he would have made a friend of a fellow like Eustace!' said Nicky, quite shocked. 'I believe him to be tolerably well-acquainted with Francis Cheviot, but there's nothing in that, after all! I don't care for Francis myself, but he is very good *ton* – all the crack, in fact!'

The door opened to admit Barrow, who came in with a tray which he set down on the table at Miss Beccles's elbow.

'Barrow,' said Carlyon, 'do you know the name of any Frenchman whom Mr. Cheviot may have been acquainted with?'

'I did hear what his name was, my lord,' admitted Barrow. 'But I didn't take no account of it, not holding with Frenchies.'

'Was it De Castres?'

'Ay, that'll be it,' nodded the henchman. 'I knew it was something outlandish, my lord.'

'Well, by Jupiter!' ejaculated Nicky. 'But – oh, wait till you hear the rest, Ned!'

Carlyon nodded dismissal to Barrow, who went away again. Miss Beccles, drawing up her chair to the table, said: 'Dear me, how commonplace it seems, to be sure, to be eating and drinking – such an excellent broth, too! – with so much excitement on hand!'

The placidity in her voice caused her late pupil to look at her reproachfully. 'I do not desire any more such excitement, Becky!'

'No, my love, but I expect his lordship will know what it to be done. I am sure you may be quite easy in your mind.'

Elinor perceived that her old governess had fallen all too easily under the calming spell his lordship seemed to hold over his admirers, and gave a defiant sniff.

'But, Ned, listen to what followed!' interrupted Nicky. 'When I rode over yesterday, as you bade me, Cousin Elinor told me the whole, and of course I remembered at once how it is said that Charles II hid in this house, and I thought very likely there might be a secret way into it –'

'Did you find it?'

The widow's colour rose. She fixed a pair of accusing eyes on Carlyon's face, and demanded: 'My lord, answer me this, if you please! Did you know of that secret stair when you brought me here?'

'Yes, certainly I knew of it, but I thought it had been closed these many years,' he replied.

'Oh, this is too much!' Elinor cried. 'And pray why did you not tell me of it?'

'I was afraid it might add to your distaste of the house,' he explained.

She struggled to maintain her composure. 'Oh, no, how came you to think such a thing?' she said sarcastically. 'I am sure it was the only thing needed to make me quite comfortable!'

He smiled. 'Indeed, you have cause to be vexed with me,' he acknowledged. 'I beg your pardon! I collect that the stair is not, as I had supposed, closed?'

'Closed! Nothing of the sort! All kinds of desperate person are at liberty to come up it any time they choose!'

'That is certainly quite undesirable,' he said imperturbably. 'If you have not already attended to the matter, I think steps should be taken to secure the entrance.'

'You amaze me, my lord! I had not looked for so much consideration! Let me tell you that had I not allowed my judgement to be overborne by your brother's pleading that door would have been sealed yesterday, and he would not now be lying there with his arm in a sling! Nicky, do pray, put it back! Dr. Greenlaw said you should keep it still, remember!'

'Oh, it's no matter, cousin! Ned, I am persuaded you would not have had me shut up the stair! The more I thought about the occurrence the more I became convinced that fellow – De Castres, I mean, if it really can have been he – had come for some secret purpose. I told Cousin Elinor we should seek to discover what that might be, and I said I would spend the night in that little spare bedchamber where the trap-door is, just on the chance of the fellow's coming back to have another touch at it.'

Carlyon nodded. 'To own the truth,' Nicky confessed, 'I did not above half expect that he would.'

'And I did not expect it at all!' interpolated Elinor. 'I do beg of you to believe, sir, that nothing would have induced me to have allowed Nicky to prevail upon me to let him stay in that room had I had the least notion of what was to happen! I am so distressed! If you are angry with me I cannot blame you!'

'My dear ma'am, how should I be angry with you?'

'Ned, I know it has all gone awry, but I did right to leave the stair open, didn't I?' Nicky demanded.

'Yes, quite right. I collect that your visitor did indeed return?'

'Yes, and I crept after him down the stairs. There was never anything like it! To think of such an adventure's happening, and all because I was rusticated! I never expected any very particular good to come from that, you know, but only fancy!'

'A very observable instance of the workings of providence,' agreed Carlyon. 'How came you to be shot?'

'Oh, that was the most curst mischance! The fellow was making for this room, and I had reached the foot of the stairs, when all at once he stopped, and looked about him. I stepped back quickly that he might not see me, and what must I do but fall over the stupid suit of armour Cousin Elinor must needs keep at the bottom of the stairs!'

'I do not keep it there!' said Elinor indignantly. 'I found it there!'

'Well, I do not know how that may be, but I should have thought you would have moved it to a better place. However, it's no matter, except that it ruined all. I had your pearl-mounted pistol in my hand, Ned, and I shouted out to the fellow to stand, for I had him covered, but he fired at me before I well knew what he would be about, and over I went again. I shot at once, and smashed the lantern he was carrying, but I don't think I can have hit him, for he escaped by the front door before anyone could come to my aid. And the devil of it is that I still don't know what it is that he wants, and I have a great fear that now he knows the game is up he will not come again. I have made wretched work of it!'

123

'Yes, it is a pity he should have discovered your presence,' agreed Carlyon. 'However, it is of no use to repine over what cannot be mended. This is certainly very interesting, Nicky.'

'Yes, indeed! What it not diverting?' struck in Elinor.

He looked at her thoughtfully, but said nothing.

'What are you thinking, Ned?' asked Nicky eagerly.

'I was wishing John had not gone back to London,' Carlyon replied unexpectedly. 'Never mind! He will be here again the day after to-morrow!'

'John!' exclaimed Nicky. 'Why, what use would he be, I should like to know?'

'He was telling me something which I cannot help feeling may have some bearing on this extraordinary event.'

Nicky's face was alight. 'Oh, Ned, do you think – Is it possible that – You know, I told Cousin Elinor this morning I thought very likely that fellow might be one of Boney's agents, only then you said it was De Castres, and I thought it had not been possible!'

'It is certainly unexpected. Yet I believe it would not be quite the first time a scion of one of these émigré families has thrown in his lot with Bonaparte.'

'How very shocking, to be sure!' said Miss Beccles, shaking her head. 'It makes one feel so very particularly for their poor parents. But young persons are often very thoughtless, I fear.'

'It cannot be so!' Elinor said. 'Why, I have in the past known several such families, and they would be disgusted by the very thought of such a thing!'

'No doubt the elder members of such families would be, ma'am, but there is no doubt that Bonaparte's career, and the régime he has set up, have kindled an enthusiasm for his cause in some of the younger men's breasts. It is no wonder, after all! They have little to hope for in England, and, one supposes, can find little to inspire them with hope in the Bourbon King, and the set of men he keeps about him. But these are only surmises! We are running ahead a great deal too fast.'

Nicky, who had been sitting with knit brows, said: 'It is very well, Ned, but how should Eustace have had anything to say to French spies? *I* never thought that he had even common sense!'

'A very unreliable agent, one would have said,' concurred Carlyon. He frowned down at the lid of his snuff-box. 'And yet,' he said, 'I will own that I have sometimes wondered where Eustace found the money to pay for some of his more-expensive pleasures. This might be the answer.'

'A Bonapartist agent!' said Elinor. 'Well, I thought I had known the worst of my bridegroom, but it seems I was at fault!'

'I should think,' said Carlyon, 'that he was, rather, a go-between.'

'I do not see that that would make him any better!'

'On the contrary, decidedly worse.'

'Oh, what an abominable man you are!' cried Elinor, quite out of patience.

'Hush, my love!' interposed Miss Beccles, in gentle reproof. 'A lady should never be uncivil, you know. His lordship must be quite shocked to hear you express yourself with such unbecoming violence.'

'I wish I might shock him!' said Elinor bitterly.

'Well, I do not see why you should wish so!' said Nicky, firing up. 'And Ned is not an abominable man!'

'A gentleman, Nicky,' said Carlyon, grave as a judge, 'should never contradict a lady.'

Miss Beccles nodded her innocent agreement with this dictum. The widow eyed his lordship smoulderingly, but maintained a prudent silence.

Carlyon, after casting her a somewhat quizzical look, seemed to become wrapped in his own meditations. Nicky, fidgeting restlessly for a little while, at last burst out with: 'Do you think we should shut up the secret way? I mean —'

'Oh, yes!' Carlyon replied absently. 'I do not think we can hope for him to come by that way a third time.'

'Well, but, Ned, what must we do, then? It would be too flat to leave it as it now stands!'

'Certainly not. But as the matter appears to be of considerable urgency I hardly think that we should be permitted to leave it. Some new form of approach must be expected. Time will show what this may be.'

'Not to me!' said Elinor, with resolution. 'I will not spend another night in this house, and so I tell you!'

'Oh, Cousin Elinor, you would not be so poor-spirited!' Nicky cried incredulously. 'Besides, what should you be afraid of when you will have me with you, and Miss Beccles, and Bouncer too?'

'How you can have the effrontery, Nicky, to offer me that horrid dog as consolation is something that gives me a very poor idea of your chivalry!' retorted Elinor. 'What is more, I am not so callous that I would ask my dear Becky to remain an hour in this place! It is not at all what she has been accustomed to, I assure you.'

'Very true, my love,' sighed Miss Beccles. 'When I was young I used to wish very much that I could meet with an adventure, but none ever came my way, and in the end I did not think of it any more. And now it has come to me, and all through my lord, who so kindly brought me to you!'

'Becky, all my dependence is on you!' almost wailed Elinor. 'You cannot wish to remain in this dreadful house!'

'But, my dear Mrs. Cheviot, it seems to me such a comfortable house! And now that my lord is to close up the secret door, which, I own, I should not quite like to have open, I cannot see the least cause for you to leave it. And I am sure that if the dear doggie is to stay with us we must be quite safe.'

The intelligent hound, who had sat up at the first mention of his name, flattened his ears, and lolled his tongue out gratefully.

'If you knew as much of the dear doggie as I do,' declared Elinor, 'you would scarcely stay in the same room with him!' She turned to Carlyon, and added: 'Upon being told to guard me, the creature kept me in my chair for the better part of a day!'

'Well, that was quite my fault!' argued Nicky. 'He did not perfectly understand what I said to him. And you must own he stayed at his post like a regular bulldog!'

'Yes! And consumed a plate of meat, and a large marrow-bone, which he buried behind the sofa cushions!'

'Poor old fellow!' said Miss Beccles, is caressing accents.

Bouncer, recognizing a well-wisher, got up, and thrust his cold, wet nose under her hand, assuming as he did so the soulful expression of a dog who takes but a benevolent interest in cats, livestock, and stray visitors. Miss Beccles stroked his head, and murmured dulcetly to him.

Elinor fixed her eyes upon Carlyon. 'My lord, do you expect me to remain here?' she asked straitly.

'Yes, Mrs. Cheviot, I do,' he replied.

'But I may be murdered in my bed!'

'Improbable, I think.'

She swallowed. 'But what would you have me do?'

He looked consideringly at her. 'I believe you would be well-advised to set about the procuring of mourning-clothes,' he said. 'I appreciate that your time, since I left you here, has been a little taken up by other matters, but this should have been thought of. I will send my carriage over to be at your orders, in case you should like to drive to Chichester. You will find a tolerable silk-warehouse there, and may choose something suitable to your condition.'

'But who is to receive any French agents who may call while I am gone?' she retorted.

'Oh, I will do that!' grinned Nicky.

'My dear Nicky, I am about to convey you home. I dare say Mrs. Cheviot has had a surfeit of your company by this time.'

'Oh, Ned, no!' Nicky cried, aghast. 'You could not ask me to leave Highnoons now! Why, anything might happen!'

'Nothing is likely to happen.'

'I do not know what makes you think so, my lord,' remarked Elinor. 'A man who will twice break into a house, and fire upon anyone who discovers him –'

'I am inclined to think that that was a mistake.'

'A mistake, was it!' said Nicky, ruefully feeling his shoulder.

'I dare say you startled him, my dear boy, and he fired before he had time to consider what he was about. He cannot have wished to make such a stir. In fact, his whole manner of conducting this affair appears to me to be the work of a novice. Depend upon it, someone must be behind De Castres, if De Castres it was.'

'Someone more cunning, I dare say?' said Elinor politely.

'Undoubtedly.'

'And who will perhaps descend upon me in his turn?'

He smiled. 'Perhaps,' he agreed.

'And all the advice you have to give me is that I should go to Chichester to choose mourning-clothes which I assure you I don't mean to wear!'

'I hope you will think better of that decision, ma'am. It is always a pity to put up the backs of people. I see that you have already made this room at least more habitable. But there must still be a great deal of work to be done in the house, which should keep you occupied for some little time. I believe you have no need to feel any undue alarm: violence cannot serve these people, and they are unlikely to attempt anything in the same nature again. What we have now to look for is something a trifle more subtle.'

'Well, then, Ned, don't you think I should remain here?' urged Nicky. 'Cousin Elinor will be more comfortable if I do, will you not, cousin?'

'Of course there can be no question of your leaving while you are still so weak!' she said. 'You will scarcely take him out in this cold when he ought to be in his bed, my lord! I assure you, Miss Beccles and I will take every care of him.'

'I have no doubt of that, and am very much obliged to you both. Have either you or he looked through the contents of that desk, on the chance of discovering any clue to your mystery?'

'No, but I would have done so!' said Nicky. 'Cousin Elinor would not permit it, however.'

'Extremely proper. I am expecting Finsbury in Sussex to-morrow, and shall bring him here. But in the event it will be wise to assure ourselves that no dangerous document lies in that desk.' He walked over to it as he spoke, and sat down before it, pulling open the top drawer. A welter of papers was disclosed, which

Carlyon sorted out, laying them in separate heaps. The other drawers were in much the same condition, and Nicky's eagerly expressed conviction that the desk possessed a secret hiding-place was found to be without foundation.

Carlyon restored the papers, saying calmly: 'There is very little here beyond bills and vowels.'

'Good God!' said Elinor. 'Then I suppose I may look next to be dunned! How sobering it is to reflect that had I never met you, my lord, I might even now be peacefully established in Mrs. Macclesfield's house!'

'Sobering indeed. If am persuaded you would have discovered her to be an overbearing female, and the children all grossly indulged.'

'Nonsense! I dare say a most agreeable household,' said Elinor firmly.

'Now, my love, you know you had no very pleasant notion of Mrs. Macclesfield's character!' Miss Beccles reminded her. 'I have been telling his lordship how bravely you have borne all your reverses, and how thankful I am you are now in such good hands.'

'Good hands?' gasped the affronted widow. 'Becky, are you in your senses? If you refer to Lord Carlyon, I really think you cannot be! I never did him the least injury, and only consider how he has served me! He forced me to marry a creature given over to every form of vice; he brought me to his house where everything is in dust and tatters, mice run across my bedchamber floor, and French agents walk in and out at will, shooting at anyone who dares to say them nay; he discloses to me with what I can only describe as the most callous unconcern imaginable that my late husband died apparently under a load of debt, which I shall no doubt be called upon to settle; and when I ask him what I am to do, all he can think of is to suggest that I should buy myself mourning-clothes!'

Miss Beccles smiled at his lordship. 'Dear Elinor was always such a lively girl!' she murmured. 'So spirited! I know your lordship will make allowances.'

'I should be happy to do so,' he returned. 'But I do not find her at all spirited. On the contrary, she appears to me to take an unnecessarily despondent view of her situation. There is really no need that I am aware of, Mrs. Cheviot, for you to put yourself in a fret.'

'Oh, she is not as chicken-hearted as you would suppose, Ned!' Nicky said blithely.

Mrs. Cheviot, speech failing her, rose, and took several agitated turns about the room. Carlyon went to her, and took her hand. 'Come!' he said reassuringly. 'I should not leave you here, you know, if I thought you stood in any danger. To run away must be nonsensical. By remaining, like a sensible woman, you may be very helpful. I am persuaded you must see, in the light of what has happened, that my placing you in charge here was a very lucky chance.'

Elinor gazed at him. 'A very lucky chance!' she echoed faintly. 'My lord, when I first encountered you the suspicion crossed my mind that your intellect was disordered. I am now certain that this is so!'

Ten

An exhaustive search of Eustace Cheviot's bedroom having brought to light nothing but some more crumpled bills, and several irrelevant papers tucked into the pockets of various coats, it became apparent that if Eustace had indeed had in his possession any document destined for French eyes he had hidden it away in some place where it was unlikely papers would be looked for. Even Nicky was a little daunted by the prospect of being obliged to search minutely a house crammed with chests, cupboards, commodes, drum-tables, and old coffers. 'And when we have ransacked every drawer in the place, ten to one it will be found poked up a chimney, or stuffed into the lining of a chair!' he said pessimistically. 'I do not know how we are to do!'

'I suppose,' said Elinor, who, in spite of herself, had begun to take an interest in these proceedings, 'that it was not upon his person?'

Carlyon shook his head. 'I have everything that was in his pockets,' he replied.

'I wonder,' said Miss Beccles diffidently, 'if he perhaps put it between the leaves of a book? I cannot help feeling that that would be a very good hiding-place, and I noticed that there were a great many books in that room below-stairs. If you should like it, my lord, dear Mrs. Cheviot and I can busy ourselves to-morrow with taking them all out, and dusting them at the same time.'

'A very excellent notion,' Carlyon said. 'I am much obliged to you, ma'am.'

'So am not I!' said Elinor. 'Why, I dare say there are more than a thousand books on the shelves!'

Nicky, who was beginning to feel tired, sat down on the edge of the bed, and said disgustedly; 'Oh, lord! There is no end to the places where we should search!'

'Do you not think, sir, that if a warming-pan was brought up, as I dare say it might be directly, and the fire kindled in your bedchamber, you would be more comfortable in your bed?' suggested Miss Beccles, in her gentle way.

Nicky naturally scouted this idea, declaring that he should not retire before dinner; but upon being assured that he should not be fobbed off with gruel, but should be supplied with a tray loaded with sustaining and palatable viands, he began to think more kindly of his bed, and finally consented in a magniloquent spirit to get between the sheets again. Carlyon went downstairs to give orders for the securing of the secret door; and Elinor took Miss Beccles off to install her in the bedchamber next to her own. Miss Beccles sighed her pleasure at sight of the fire already burning in the heart, and smiled mistily upon her hostess. 'It should not be, my love, but such a comfort to one! I do not know if I stand on my head or my heels! From the moment of his lordship's coming I have been cast into such a flutter! I declare I could not believe the evidence of my ears when Polly – you remember Polly, my love: a very obliging girl! – when Polly came to tell me my Lord Carlyon wished to see me! And me in my old olive-green merino, for you must know I was engaged in polishing the furniture, and not in the least expecting to receive a visitor, much less so noble a visitor! But I dare say he would not notice, for thank heaven I had my wits about me enough to strip off my apron, and thrust it under a cushion. But to see such a fine gentleman in my poor little room –! I declare I was so overcome I had scarcely strength enough to drop him a curtsey! But he is most truly the gentleman! I was rendered easy in a trice!'

'Lord Carlyon's manners are certainly well-bred, but –'

'Oh, my love, I perceived at a glance that he was used to move in the first circles! And the beeswax lying on the table, and an old rag, and my merino so crushed! I was almost over-powered! And what he could want with me I knew no more than Polly, but that was soon told. You may imagine my astonishment! I fear he must have supposed me to have less than common sense, for I was obliged to beg him to repeat the whole before I could credit it!'

'I do no wonder at it! You must have been excessively shocked to hear what a dreadful tangle I was got into!'

'I own, my first reflections upon the event were of so agitating a nature that I was obliged to sit down plump upon the nearest chair. But all was soon explained! And then to learn that I was to come into Sussex the very next day, to be with you! I was left with my head in such a whirl I scarcely knew what I was about, or how I should contrive!'

'Poor Becky, you have been shamefully used!' Elinor said warmly. 'I would not for the world have had you pack up in such uncomfortable haste! But I might have known how it would be! He is the most abominable creature, and thinks everyone's convenience must give way to his!'

'Oh, no, my love, indeed I do not know how you can talk in such a way! Only fancy his calling to take me up into his own chaise, a sitting beside me all the way, just as though I had been a person of the first consequence! Alas, dear Mrs. Cheviot, you must know as well as I how seldom it is that one meets with any extraordinary civility when one is only a governess!'

'Yes, indeed I do know, but –'

'Every observance was shown me! The most distinguishing notice! And such kind attentions! And I in so much agitation that every faculty was in danger of becoming suspended! I am sure he must think me the most antiquated fidget, for what must I do but forget my netting-box! I am quite ashamed to think that I should have exclaimed that I believed I had not brought it, for his lordship, without the least show of being vexed, instantly ordered the postilions to turn back! And a glass of ratafia and a macaroon on the road, though I assured him I was not accustomed to take anything in the middle of the day!'

'I will allow him to be thoughtful in such matters as that, but –'

'And such a well-informed mind, my love! I did not look for him to put himself to the trouble of talking to me, I'm sure, but he was all that was most amiable! You may judge of my relief to know that you were in the care of one whom I could so truly respect!'

'Becky, let me make it plain to you that I am *not* in Carlyon's care! How I came to let myself be thrust into this imbroglio I cannot imagine! And now to hear you, whom I have all my life believed to be a model of propriety, talking as though a piece of good fortune had come to me, puts me out of all patience! For it is quite shocking, Becky!'

'Indeed, my love, I do partake of your sentiments, but depend upon it you did right to trust his lordship to be the best judge of your actions.'

'Did right to let myself be married and widowed within a couple of hours? How can you say so?'

'To be sure, when you speak of it in such terms as that it does sound a trifle unusual,' Miss Beccles admitted. 'But I have never been able to support the thought of your being condemned to the life I have been obliged to lead. And you know, my dear Elinor – if I may still call you so, though I know I should not – from all his lordship was condescending enough to tell me it does seem as though it is a merciful dispensation of providence that the young man is dead. Not that one would wish to say anything unkind, but I cannot think that he was quite the thing, and I dare say must have made you a sad husband. How often has one been forced to observe that the most tragic events are for the best!'

It was plainly useless to expect the little governess to enter into her feelings on the matter, so Elinor left her to her unpacking, and went downstairs to discover what Carlyon meant to do next.

She found that he had put on his coat again, and was upon the point of departure. As she descended the stairs, he looked up, and said: 'The door is now fast, ma'am, and I do not anticipate that you need feel any further alarm. Remember, I beg, that all is as yet no more than conjecture! We should be ill-advised to refine too much upon what has happened, until we are given more positive proof that our suspicions are well-grounded. I shall be visiting you in the morning, with my cousin's lawyer. Meanwhile, I have procured a wedding-ring for you, which I trust may fit your finger more nearly than that signet of mine.'

He held it out to her, so that she was obliged to take it, and to give him back his own. He seemed to have judged the size of her finger with tolerable accuracy. She slipped the ring on, but demanded: 'My lord, how long do you mean to keep me in this house?'

'I fear I cannot answer you until I learn more precisely how matters stand.'

'I dare say you would not be in the least moved if you came to-morrow, and found us all lying dead in our beds!' she said bitterly.

'On the contrary, I should be a good deal surprised.'

She could not help laughing. 'Odious creature! Very well, I see you have a heart of stone, and I waste my time in useless entreaties! What would you have me do, sir?'

'My advice to you you found so unpalatable that I hesitate to repeat it, Mrs. Cheviot.'

'Oh, yes! you would have me decked out in black crape! I am not such a hypocrite!'

'I do not know what will be proper for you to wear, but I must point out to you that it is in the highest degree likely that my cousin's uncle, Lord Bedlington, will come into Sussex to attend the funeral, if not the inquest, and he will certainly wait on you. Your wearing colours will occasion some remark.'

'You have a reasonable answer for everything, my lord. It is what one particularly dislikes in you! Pray, what am I to say to Lord Bedlington?'

'I will engage to say all that is needful. It will be best for him to suppose that you had been for long betrothed to my cousin. As for last night's affair, Nicky assures me that he allowed Greenlaw to suppose that he had been shot by a common housebreaker. I have already desired the Barrows to tell the same tale. Our care must now be not to do or say anything that could betray our suspicions.'

'Very true! How shocking if we should frighten any spies away!'

'Yes, I think you must see that it would be shocking indeed,' he agreed, smiling, and putting out his hand. 'I shall leave you now. If you should be nervous, I recommend you to let Nicky's dog roam at will over the house during the night. He would certainly give tongue at the approach to any stranger.'

'How little one guesses what one may come to!' she remarked, turning her head to look at Bouncer, who was enjoying a satisfactory roll on the hearth-rug. 'Never did I think I should live to be grateful to that horrid animal!'

He laughed, shook hands, and went away. Bouncer stood up, shook himself, and wagged his tail expectantly.

'If it's your dinner you are thinking about,' said Elinor severely, 'You had best come and be civil to Mrs. Barrow.'

He pranced ahead of her down the long stone-paved corridor that led to the kitchens. Nothing could have exceeded his affability there, but only Elinor's persuasion induced Mrs. Barrow to bestow a plate of scraps on him. She said that he had already had the shoulder of mutton designed for Elinor's own dinner. But the sagacious hound listened to Elinor's reproaches with an expression compound of innocence and such gnawing hunger that she found it hard to believe such a thing of him, and insisted that he should be fed. There was nothing in the manner in which he disposed of his portion to lend the least colour to the allegation made against his character.

The evening passed tranquilly. Miss Beccles, who had lost no time in getting upon good terms with Mrs. Barrow, made a panada for the invalid, which he pronounced to be first rate; Elinor lost to him all the vast sums she had won at piquet on the previous night; and Bouncer suddenly achieved popularity with Mrs. Barrow by catching a large rat in the larder, whither he had repaired in search of something to maintain his strength during the night watches. Mrs. Barrow was moved to bestow on him a large ham-bone. He subsequently hid his under Elinor's bed, and his recollection of its whereabouts in the middle of the night, and insistent demands to be admitted into her room, were all that occurred to spoil her rest that night.

The morning found her spirits fast recovering their tone. Nicky seemed to be much amended; and the presence of Miss Beccles was at once so comfortable and so calming that she received the news that his lordship's carriage was at the door, ready to carry her to Chichester, with a docility surprising in one so high-spirited. The two ladies set off in this luxurious vehicle, and spent an agreeable few hours shopping, returning in the afternoon with so many band-boxes piled up on the seat before them that Nicky said he wondered they had not thought to hire a wagon, or even Pickford's van.

It would have been useless for Elinor to have attempted to pretend that her mind was too elevated an order to rejoice in the possession of new clothes, and she lost no time in running up to her room to try on the dove-gray muslin, with black ribbons, and the handsome black silk, trimmed with lace, and a treble flounce. She was just trying the effect of a very pretty lace cap, with lappets that tied under her chin with a black bow, when she heard Bouncer set up a great barking in the hall. The next moment Nicky was thumping on her door, and telling her to make haste and come downstairs, for a post-chaise had just driven up to the door.

'It's old Bedlington, cousin, for I craned out of my window, and had the plainest view of him! Lord, I wonder what he will say when he finds you here! I wish Ned were here still to enjoy the jest!'

She ran to the door, and opened it. 'Oh, Nicky, what shall I say to him? Where is your brother?'

'Oh, he is gone back to the Hall! He and Finsbury took all Eustace's papers away with them, and wasted I do not know how much time trying to discover what his keys might fit. I dare say the most of them belong to things in Cork Street – he had rooms there, you know. Oh, and Ned told me to say that he begged pardon, but had forgot to inform you that he took the liberty of paying off Eustace's valet, when he went to Cork Street yesterday, because you will scarcely need him, and he is a mean sort of a fellow, up to every trick. By Jove, Cousin Elinor, if that gown is not the most bang-up thing I ever saw! You look all the crack!'

'Nicky, pray come downstairs with me!' she begged. 'I am quite at a loss to know what I shall say to Lord Bedlington!'

'Well, I don't mind owning I would give a monkey only to see his face,' said Nicky frankly. 'But Ned said, if he should chance to arrive here I was not to show myself, on account of the awkwardness of its being my fault that Eustace is dead.'

'Good God, yes, indeed! I had quite forgotten that circumstance! My dependence must be all on Becky. Is my cap quite straight?'

He assured her that it was, and she went down the stairs, taking some comfort in the imposing rustle of her silk skirts, but pale enough from fright to pass for an inconsolable widow.

Barrow had ushered the visitor into the front parlour, where Miss Beccles was engaged in disposing the chairs more comfortably round the newly-kindled fire. Mrs. Cheviot, softly entering the room, was in time to hear her assuring his lordship, with unshaken placidity, that Mrs. Cheviot would be downstairs directly.

'Here she is, indeed!' she said, catching sight of Elinor. 'My dear Mrs. Cheviot, here is my Lord Bedlington come to pay you a visit of condolence!'

Elinor curtsied, wondering at her meek little chaperon's effrontery.

'Mrs. Cheviot!' ejaculated Bedlington. 'Upon my word, I do not know what to say! I am quite at a loss!'

He passed his handkerchief across his face as he spoke, and she was able to steal a look at him. He was a portly gentleman, of some fifty years, of medium stature, and a round face, in which small blue eyes were habitually open to their widest. He wore very tight Inexpressibles, and very high and rigidly starched shirt-points, which made it hard for him to turn his head; and when he bowed a slight creaking betrayed that a swelling paunch was confined by stays. The yellow lining to his coat, and the Prince's buttons, which embellished it, proclaimed his office.

'My dear ma'am – this shocking intelligence – my poor nephew! I was so much upset I was obliged to have half a pint of blood taken from me!' he uttered.

'Ah, a wise precaution, my lord!' nodded Miss Beccles. 'I have the greatest faith in the good effects of judicious cupping.'

He turned to her eagerly. 'There is nothing like it!' he assured her. 'My dear friend, his Royal Highness the Prince Regent, swears by it, you know! I do not know how many pints he has not had taken from him! But this is not to the point! My poor nephew! Ah, no one but myself had a value for the boy!'

Elinor thought it prudent to keep her gaze discreetly lowered.

His lordship applied his handkerchief to his eyes again. 'Carried off so young!' he sighed. 'I had always a kindness for him, for you must know he was so like my dear brother it could not but affect me profoundly! But I do not properly understand – in short, ma'am, had no notion he was married! Indeed, I doubted that it could be so, but I perceive – It is very strange!'

'My marriage to Mr. Cheviot, sir,' said Elinor, in a low tone, 'took place when he lay upon his death-bed. Our – our betrothal was a secret known only to – known only to my Lord Carlyon!'

He looked much struck. 'Known to Carlyon! You amaze me, ma'am! I had not supposed – He cannot have known of this marriage!'

She replied with more firmness: 'You are mistaken: I owe my marriage solely to Lord Carlyon's exertions to bring it about.'

'Impossible!' he exclaimed. 'Why, it cuts up all his hopes! That is, if the poor boy made his Will before he died, but I dare say he had no time.'

'On the contrary, my lord, Mr. Cheviot drew up his Will in my favour.'

'You do not mean it! This is most astonishing news! A strange man, Carlyon! There is no understanding him at all! Ah, my dear, had my poor sister-in-law left things otherwise, who shall say that I should be standing here to-day, upon this melancholy occasion!'

She was constrained to say: 'I believe my Lord Carlyon cannot be blamed for your – for my husband's untimely death, sir.'

'Ah, I dare say not, but I shall always say that he used the poor lad with unmerited harshness! But how did it come about? I saw Eustace in town not five days since, and he was in good health! But I collect he met with some accident?'

'Yes. That is – Pardon me, but it is painful to me to be obliged to discuss – I am sure my Lord Carlyon will inform you better than I can how it was!'

'Ah, no wonder!' he sighed, taking her hand, and squeezing it feelingly. 'This is painful for you indeed! A secret betrothal! It is easy to see why it must have so! Yet poor Eustace might have told me! I have always stood his friend. And you say Carlyon assisted at your marriage? Well! I am all admiration, do not pretend to understand how it can have been so! But, my dear, tell me! Who is there to support and advise you in all the business to be undertaken now? I speak to you without reserve: I fear poor Eustace's affairs will be found to be in a sad tangle. It is well that I was able to snatch a day to journey down to visit you! You will let me relive you of the burden – the sad duty – of settling the effects! It is proper that I should help you, ma'am, for you must know that I was greatly attached to Eustace. In spite of his youthful follies, be it understood! I do not deny that he was not always conducted himself as he should, but we shall not speak ill of the dead.'

'You are very good, sir,' she managed to say. 'But I believe – that is, I know – that my Lord Carlyon is an executor of the Will, and has taken all into his hands. I have nothing to do.'

He looked to be a good deal affronted by this, and reddened, exclaiming: 'Without a word to me! I hope I am not one to rate my claims too high, but as poor Eustace's nearest relative I might have expected to be consulted before Carlyon took it upon himself – But so it has been always! He is a man of so little sensibility that I dare say he may not even think that there are relics I must wish to posses! The Wincanton interest is all he cares for, but my poor brother was Eustace's father, little though any of the Wincantons or the Carlyons may have regarded him! I do not care to think of Carlyon's turning over papers that can be of no interest to anyone but my brother's own kin! My letters to him! – I believe all were preserved! I should wish them to be destroyed, or handed back to me.'

She could only suggest to him that he should approach Carlyon in the matter. His little red mouth pouted disconsolately; he said that he wondered he had not been sent for; and seemed to be labouring under such a sense of wounded dignity that she found herself apologizing to him for an oversight which was none of hers. Upon learning from her that Carlyon had removed all Eustace Cheviot's papers from Highnoons, he said something about encroaching ways which she judged it better to ignore. Miss Beccles suggested solicitously that he must need some refreshment after his drive; and while a tray of wine and cakes was sent for he was induced to sit down by the fire. He seemed to be very much put out by the discovery that his support and advice were not needed by the widow, and she soon perceived that he was a man with a very high notion of his own consequence. She said all that was conciliatory, and had the satisfaction of seeing him grow more mellow towards her. He offered to remain at Highnoons until after the funeral, and she was hard put to it to know how to decline without giving offence. He was evidently much affected by his nephew's death, and sat sighing gustily, and shaking his head over it until she began to wonder whether he would ever take himself off. But in the end he did so, saying he should drive to the Hall, and demand the whole truth from Carlyon. He told Elinor that although he was much occupied with state affairs he should certainly attend the funeral, and, once more taking her hand between both of his, said that he should claim the privilege of an uncle in desiring her to allow him to put up at Highnoons for a night.

Civility compelled her to assure him that he would be welcome; he thanked her; and at last climbed up again into his chaise, and was driven away.

'Prosy old fool!' said Nicky. 'Did you brush through it pretty well, cousin? What did he say? I thought he was staying here for ever, and wondered whether I could not set Bouncer on to drive him away! But then I thought very likely you would not like it if I did, so I kept the old fellow with me. But I dare say he would like to take a bite out of fat old Bedlington, wouldn't you, Bouncer?'

Bouncer jumped up at him ecstatically, apparently under the impression that this treat was indeed in store for him.

Eleven

There was nothing amongst Eustace Cheviot's papers to occupy the two executors' minds for long, and it was soon agreed between them that the first step towards winding up his estate must to be ascertain the exact number of his obligations. This task the lawyer took in hand, sighing, and pulling down the corners of his mouth, and saying that he feared the half of them were not yet known. He perused Cheviot's Will in a disapproving way, but although he audibly tut-tutted, and shook his head sadly, he allowed that it was sufficiently well drawn up to serve. 'But, my lord,' he added severely, 'I must not be understood to say that this document is drawn up in quite such terms as I should have used, had I been called upon to serve my late client in this matter. However, it appears to be valid, and I shall apply for probate directly.'

He then tied such papers as he proposed taking away with him with a piece of tape; excused himself from remaining at the Hall that night, as he was civilly invited to do, on the score of having already hired a room at the inn at Wisborough Green; assured Carlyon that he would not fail to be present at the inquest on the following morning; and bowed himself out.

He had hardly been gone ten minutes when the door into Carlyon's study was again opened, and his brother John walked into the room, rubbing his hands together, and exclaiming against the inclemency of the weather.

'My dear John!' Carlyon said. 'I did not expect to see you until to-morrow!'

'No, well, I thought I might arrive too late if I put off the journey, and so applied to Sidmouth for leave to absent myself immediately. I found him in a good humour, and so here I am,' John replied, walking over to the fire, and bending over it to warm his hands.

'I am extremely glad to see you. Did you come post?'

'No, I drove myself, and damned cold it was! How has all gone since I saw you? Where is Nicky?'

'Nicky is at Highnoons, with a hole in his shoulder,' replied Carlyon, going over to the table on which the butler had set out a decanter and some glasses. 'Sherry, John?'

'Nicky is *what*?' demanded John, straightening himself with a jerk.

'It's not serious,' Carlyon said, pouring sherry into two of the glasses.

'Good God, Ned, cannot Nicky keep out of trouble for as much as two days?'

'Apparently not, but he cannot be blamed for this adventure. Sit down, and I'll tell you the whole: I fancy it should interest you.'

John cast himself into a deep chair by the fire, saying caustically: 'You need not tell me *you* do not blame him! Well, what mischief is he in now?'

But when he had heard Carlyon's matter-of-fact account of the happenings at Highnoons he abandoned his sceptical attitude, and stared at his brother with his brows knit. 'Good God!' he said slowly. 'But –' He stopped, and appeared to sink into deep abstraction. 'Good God!' he said again, and rose, and went to pour himself out another glass of sherry. He stood holding this in his hand for a minute or two before returning to his chair by the fire. 'Eustace Cheviot?' he said, on a note of incredulity. 'Who would be fool enough to employ a drunken sot on such work? I cannot credit it!'

'No, it does seem unlikely,' Carlyon agreed, polishing his quizzing-glass, and holding it up to observe the result. 'But I must admit that he had always a marked propensity for intrigue. However, I dare say this suspicion had not crossed my mind but for what you were saying to me the other night, about leakages of information. I shall be happy to learn that my reflection upon this subject are far-fetched and nonsensical?' He looked enquiringly at John as he spoke, but found him still heavily frowning. 'What, if anything, do you know of Louis De Castres?'

'Nothing. He is not suspected, to the best of my knowledge. But it would be useless to deny that there have been instances where men as well-born as he – It must be investigated, Ned!'

Carlyon nodded. John began to poke the fire rather vindictively. 'The devil! I wish – But that's nothing to the purpose, of course! If there should be any truth in this, Ned, it will raise the deuce of a scandal. I own, I wish we were well out of it. You found nothing amongst Eustace's papers?'

'No, nothing.'

'Nicky did not know who it was who fired at him?'

'No. But the very fact of his entering the house by the secret stair would seem to preclude his having been any common thief. Moreover, the book-room would scarcely have attracted a common thief, and one must assume that the house was well-known to the man. He appears to have had no hesitation upon entering it, but made his way straight to the book-room.'

John grunted, and went on jabbing at the log in the hearth. 'What do you mean to do?'

'Wait upon events.'

John glanced up at him under his brows. 'You are thinking it may be that memorandum I spoke of, are you not?' he asked bluntly. 'If it were so indeed it must be found!'

'Certainly, but I think it quite as important to discover the man who sold it to De Castres.'

'By God, yes! But, Ned, I cannot quite agree with you in this! Boney's people would give much to have a copy of it, but to steal the thing itself advertises to us that Wellington's plans are known!'

'The season is already some way advanced. Would it be possible, in your judgment, for Wellington to alter his plans?'

John stared at him. 'How can I say? No, I must suppose. The

transports –' He broke off, recollecting himself. 'Hang it, Ned, I will not believe it can be so! Even if it is now too late to alter whatever dispositions his lordship has made, to inform him that these are known must be the work of an idiot! Boney's agents know their work a little too well for that!'

'So I should imagine, and have already told myself. Yet I fancy there might be several answers to that argument. If any suspicion of Eustace's intentions existed in the mind of De Castres, he might have demanded to see the memorandum itself. Consider for a moment what must be the disastrous result to the French if Eustace had given deliberately false information! To concentrate troops without incontrovertible proof that it is precisely in that direction a powerful enemy will strike would be to take a risk I cannot think any general would hazard.'

'You would think so indeed. You think De Castres had bargained for a sight of the memorandum, either to carry it off with him, or to make his own copy of it?'

'Something of that kind, perhaps. You yourself said it would very likely be discovered in a wrong file. It may have been intended to have restored it in just such a way.'

'I spoke in jest! It can never have been in a file, of course. I tell you the thing is most secret!'

'There might still be ways of restoring it.'

'Yes, I suppose there might – but not ways known to Eustace Cheviot, Ned! Now, for heaven's sake, my dear fellow, do but consider! You knew Eustace as well as anyone! This will not do!'

Carlyon got up to replenish his own glass. 'Very true, but I never imagined Eustace could be more than a go-between. If all these suspicions are correct, someone of far more importance than Eustace must stand behind him. Someone who is afraid to appear in the matter himself, and so employs a tool.'

'I will not allow it to be possible!' John said explosively. 'I never knew such a fellow as you are, Ned, for doing or saying the most outrageous things, and then making them seem the merest commonplace! It is a great deal too bad of you, and I know you rather too well to be drawn in!'

'Now, what have I ever done or said to deserve this from you?' asked Carlyon mildly.

'I could recite to you a score of things!' John retorted. 'But one will suffice! If it was not the most outrageous thing imaginable to force that unfortunate young female into marriage with Eustace, then I know nothing of the matter! And do not explain to me how it comes to be the most reasonable and ordinary thing to have done, because I shall end by believing you, and I know very well it was no such thing!'

Carlyon laughed. 'Very well, I will not, but I cannot believe your judgment to be so easily overpowered.'

'If Eustace was indeed selling information to the French,' said John, 'then I must set it all at Bedlington's door! I dare say Eustace has very often visited him at the Horse Guards, and I will take my oath he would know how to make the most of his opportunities! He was never a fool: indeed, he had the sort of cunning there is no keeping pace with. You should know that! I should not be at all surprised if Bedlington had dropped some hint, without in the least meaning to, but enough for Eustace! We cannot tell how it may have been, but to be trying to implicate someone of real consequence – Bathurst, no doubt! – is the outside of enough!'

'No, I was not thinking of Bathurst,' said Carlyon calmly.

'This is something indeed!' said John, with awful irony. 'Depend upon it, Ned, this is all a figment of the imagination, and whatever it was that De Castres wanted will be found to have nothing whatsoever to do with any state affair!'

'I hope you may be right. I am really not anxious to plunge the whole family into such a scandal as you have already foreseen.'

The butler came into the room, and bowed. 'I beg your lordship's pardon, but my Lord Bedlington has called, and would wish to have speech with your lordship immediately. I have ushered his lordship into the Crimson Saloon.'

John choked over his sherry, and was taken with a fit of coughing. After an infinitesimal pause, Carlyon said: 'Inform his lordship that I shall be with him directly, and carry sherry and

Madeira into the Crimson Saloon. You had better instruct Mrs. Rugby to prepare the Blue Suite, since no doubt his lordship will be spending the night here.'

The butler bowed again, and withdrew. Carlyon glanced down at his brother. 'Now what have you to say?' he enquired.

'Damme, Ned!' said John, still coughing. 'It was only his being announced so pat! You must have expected him to come here!'

'I did,' replied Carlyon. 'But not before he had received my letter, notifying him of Eustace's death.'

'What?' John exclaimed. 'You inserted a notice in the *Gazette*, of course! He has seen that!'

'He can hardly have done so, since it does not appear until to-morrow,' Carlyon retorted.

John heaved himself up out of his chair, staring. 'Ned! You mean you believe Bedlington – You think that De Castres told Bedlington – It's not possible!'

'No, that was not what was in my mind,' Carlyon replied. 'I was thinking of one whom I know to be a close friend of De Castres.'

'Francis Cheviot! That frippery dandy!'

'Well, the thought cannot but occur to one,' Carlyon said. 'He is Bedlington's son – and here we have Bedlington, twenty-four hours before he should be in Sussex.'

'Yes, I know, but – a fellow who cares for nothing but the set of his cravat, and the blend of his snuff!'

'Ah!' said Carlyon pensively. 'But I recall that upon at least three occasions in the past I have found Francis Cheviot by no means lacking in intelligence. In fact, my dear John, I would never underrate him as an opponent. I have known him to be – quite amazing ruthless when he has set out to attain his own ends.'

'I would not have credited it! Of course, you have been better acquainted with him than I ever was. I cannot stand the fellow!'

'Nor I,' said Carlyon. 'Were you not telling me that he had suffered severe losses over the gaming-table?'

'Yes, so I believe. He plays devilish high – but one must be just, even to Francis Cheviot, you know, and he did inherit his mother's fortune! Not but what I should doubt whether it can have been handsome enough to stand – But this is to no purpose, Ned!'

'Very true. Let us go and welcome our guest!'

They found the butler arranging decanters on a table in the Crimson Saloon, and Lord Bedlington fidgeting in front of the fire. He started forward as Carlyon came into the room, exclaiming: 'Carlyon, what is this terrible business? I came at once – though I could ill be spared! I was never more shocked in my life! And I must tell you that I wonder at your not having advised me immediately of the event! Oh, how d'ye do, John!'

'I called at your house in town, but was so unfortunate as to find you away from home,' said Carlyon, shaking hands. 'So I wrote you a letter, which I fancy will reach your house to-morrow. Tell me, from what source did you learn of Eustace's death?'

The round blue eyes stared at him. There was a perceptible pause before Bedlington replied testily: 'How can one tell how such news may get about?'

'I cannot, certainly. Where did you learn it, sir?'

'My poor nephew's valet told my man. It will be all over town by now! But how did it happen? What accident befell Eustace? Some talk of a brawl in an inn! I came to you to hear the truth!'

'You shall do so, but you may believe that the truth is as painful to me to relate as it will be to you to hear. Eustace met his death at my brother Nicky's hands.'

'Carlyon!' gasped Bedlington, falling back a pace, and grasping at a chair-back to steady himself. 'My God, has it come to this?'

'Has what come to this?' demanded John, bristling.

Thus challenged, his lordship sought refuge in his handkerchief, and uttered in broken accents that he would never have believed such a thing.

'Believed such a thing as what?' pursued John, remorselessly adhering to his sledge-hammer tactics.

'I do wish you would be quiet, John!' said Carlyon. 'Pray sit down, sir! I need hardly tell you that the whole affair was an accident. If Eustace had had his way it would have been Nicky who had been killed, and that, I am constrained to tell you, would have been a clear case of murder.'

'Ah, you were always unjust to the poor lad! I might depend upon you to shield your brother!'

'Certainly you might, but happily this affair does not rest upon my testimony. To be brief with you, Bedlington, Eustace was, as usual, in his cups, and in this condition was unwise enough to provoke Nicky into knocking him down. Upon which, he seized a carving-knife, and tried to murder Nicky. In the scuffle, during which Nicky contrived to wrest the knife from him, he seems to have tripped and fallen on the knife. He died some hours later. I regret the occurrence as much as anyone, but I cannot hold Nicky to blame.'

'No, nor anyone else!' John said roughly.

Bedlington, who appeared to be quite overcome, only moaned behind his handkerchief. Carlyon poured out a glass of wine, and took it to him. 'Come, sir! I appreciate your concern, but to be blunt with you I cannot altogether deplore a taking-off that I am much inclined to think may have come just in time to prevent Eustace from plunging all of us into a scandal we must be thankful to be spared.'

Bedlington emerged from his handkerchief to demand in trembling accents: 'What can you mean? A few irregularities – the extravagances of youth – ay, and of a youth brought up under the rule of one – but I say no more! You best know how much you are to blame for the poor lad's excesses!'

'By God, that's too much!' exploded John, his complexion darkening.

'Then do not add to it, John. Had you no suspicion, sir, that these irregularities might have gone beyond the bounds of what ever you could pardon?'

Bedlington flushed. 'This is base slander! You never liked Eustace! I shall not listen to you! I do not know what you would be at, but my brother's son –! No, no, I will not listen to you!'

Carlyon bowed slightly, and waited in silence while he gulped down the wine in his glass. This seemed a little to restore the balance of his lordship's mind. He allowed John to refill the glass, asking abruptly: 'How came he to marry that young woman I found installed at Highnoons? Yes, I have been there already, and I do not know when I have been more taken-aback! Who is she, and how can such a thing have come about? I do not understand why Eustace should have excluded me from his confidence!'

'She is the daughter of Rochdale of Feldenhall,' replied Carlyon.

The blue eyes started at him. 'What! He who shot himself, and left his widow and family destitute?'

Carlyon bowed.

'Well!' Bedlington said, puffing out his lips. 'If that is so, of course I perceive why he should not have cared to tell me! I do not like the match; I must have done my possible to have prevented it. This is marvellous indeed! And it was you who contrived the wedding? I do not know what to say! She told me all was left to her!'

Carlyon bowed again.

'Wonderful!' Bedlington said, shaking his head. 'You are a strange man, Carlyon! There is no getting to the bottom of you!'

'You flatter me, sir. If you could but bring yourself to believe that I have never wanted to inherit Highnoons you would not find me at all unfathomable.'

'Well, Carlyon, I must own that I have wronged you!' Bedlington said, sighing. 'But this tragedy has so overset me I do not know what I say!'

'It is very natural,' said Carlyon. 'I dare say you will wish to be alone. Let me take you up to the rooms I have had prepared for you! Dinner will be served in an hour.'

'You are very good. I own I shall be glad of a period of quiet reflection,' said Bedlington, rising with a groan, and tottering in his host's wake to the door.

John remained in the saloon, waiting in some impatience for

his brother's return. It was some time before Carlyon rejoined him, and when he did, it was to say: 'Really, John, you are as foolish as Nicky! Must you take up the cudgels in my defence quite so violently?'

'Never mind that!' said John. 'I can't stand those play-acting ways of his, and never could! What did you think of him?'

'Nothing very much.'

'Well, by God, I didn't believe what you were saying to me, but I'll swear the man's in the devil of a pucker! I wondered to hear you give him such a hint of what you suspect!'

'I wanted to see what the effect of it might be on him. I cannot be said to have got much good by it.'

'I think he was frightened.'

'Very well. That can do no harm. If he himself has no suspicion, I have told him nothing; if, as I think might well be, he has reason to think that Francis Cheviot might be up to some mischief I hope I may have pricked him into taking the matter into his own hands. I should be glad to see it out of mine!'

'Did you believe his story of having learnt of Eustace's death from his valet?'

Carlyon shrugged. 'It might be. No, I don't think I did.'

John looked dissatisfied. 'Well! And what had he to say to you above-stairs? You were long enough away!'

'He was boring me with recollection of Uncle Lionel. I may add that none of these tallied with my own, but let that pass. He would be glad to regain possession of the letters he wrote to him. But as I have found none I was unable to oblige him in the matter.'

'Ned, was he trying to discover whether you had come upon this damned memorandum amongst Eustace's papers?' John demanded.

'My dear John, Bedlington may be an old fool, but he has not worked in a Government department without learning not to commit himself! If I choose to give my suspicions rein, I may read into his enquiries just such an object; if, on the other hand, I keep an open mind, I need see nothing in them but the natural desire of a fond uncle to be informed as to the exact nature of his nephew's follies and obligations. I was quite frank with him.'

'Quite frank with him?' ejaculated John, rather dismayed.

'Yes, I gave him to understand that I had come upon little beyond bills, vowels, and some amatory correspondence which I propose to burn,' responded Carlyon tranquilly.

John burst out laughing. 'You are the most complete hand! You did not tell him of Nicky's last adventure?'

'On the contrary, I told him that Mrs. Cheviot had been sadly discomposed by a thief's breaking into the house.'

'What had he to say to that?'

'He said that he hoped no valuables had been stolen.'

'Well? Well? And then?'

'I said that, so far as we could ascertain, nothing had been stolen,' replied Carlyon.

'I wonder what he will do next!' John said.

'He informs me that he must return to London in the morning, but will be in Sussex again to attend the funeral. Upon which occasion,' Carlyon added, taking a pinch of snuff, 'he will put up for the night at Highnoons.'

'Good God, Ned, I begin to believe you may have been right!'

'Yes, I can see you do,' said Carlyon. 'But I begin to think I may have been wrong!'

Twelve

*W*hen he reappeared, in time for dinner, Lord
Bedlington seemed to have shaken off his petulance.
He sighed heavily from time to time, and twice was
obliged to wipe his eyes, but his hosts were gratified to observe
that his bereavement had not affected his appetite. He partook
lavishly of every dish, and was so much moved by the excellence
of the Davenport fowls, stuffed, parboiled, and stewed in butter,
that he sent a complimentary message to the cook, and
congratulated Carlyon on having acquired such a treasure. By
the time he had worked his way from the Hessian soup and
ragout which began the repast, through a baked carp, dressed in
the Portuguese way, some beef-steaks with oyster sauce, the fowls,
and a Floating Island, with a fruit-pie as a remove, he was so far
reconciled to his nephew's death as to be able to recount three of
the latest good stories circulating town, and to confide to Carlyon,
as he ecstatically savoured the bouquet of the port, that he really
could not agree with his old friend Brummell in deeming it a wine
only fit for the lower orders to drink. He certainly drank a great
many glasses of it, but whatever hopes John might have cherished
of his tongue's being loosened soon vanished. My Lord
Bedlington had not kept company with the Regent for years
without acquiring a hard head and the digestion of an ostrich.
Mellow he might become, and indiscreet stories he certainly told,
but not his worst enemy would have accused him of being foxed.

When he could at last be parted from the decanters, Carlyon
took him off to his library, firmly excluding John, by saying that

he knew he had letters he wished to write. John made a face at him, but bowed to this decree, and went off to kick his heels in one of the saloons.

After commenting on the comfort of a log fire, the luxury of the chair he was sitting in, and the superlative qualities of the brandy he was rolling round his palate, his lordship seemed to bethink him of his nephew again, and to recall the sad circumstance which had brought him into Sussex. He very handsomely owned that he believed Carlyon had acted always with the best of intentions, and even confessed that his own partiality for his dear brother's only son might have made him over-lenient towards faults in Eustace which he perceived as clearly as anyone could wish. He blamed the most of them on to the bad company which Eustace had kept, and, lowering his tone to a confidential note, asked Carlyon if he had any reason to fear that Eustace might have been in some worse scrape than any of them suspected.

'I have sometimes wondered whence he obtained the means to live as expensively as he did,' responded Carlyon, in his level voice.

'Yes!' Bedlington said eagerly. 'Yes, indeed, and I too have wondered! I do trust we may not find anything seriously amiss! I cannot flatter myself the poor boy took me as much into his confidence as I could have wished.'

'He certainly did not take me into it.'

'No, well! I do not desire to mar the harmony of this evening by reproaching you, and I shall accordingly say nothing of that. Yet I cannot but feel that had you treated him with more sympathy –'

'My dear sir, you, I am persuaded, treated him with a marked degree of sympathy, but it does not appear to have won you his confidence.'

'True. It is very true! Sometimes I have asked myself if I caressed him too much, allowed him too much licence. You know, he has been free to treat my house as his home ever since his poor father's death – that is to say, ever since he was of an age to be glad of a house in town where he might be sure of a welcome. Indeed, if have treated him like my own son, but I do not know that it answered. I hope I have not been the innocent means of leading him into temptation!'

Carlyon looked faintly surprised. 'How should you be, indeed?'

'Oh, as to that –! In an establishment such as mine, you understand: my position as A.D.C. to the Regent: I need not say more! I am sure I do not know the half of the people who come to the house, and how could I tell whom poor Eustace might be meeting there? Young men cannot always be trusted to keep the line, and, alas, there was a weakness in him – one must own it! – that might have led him to allow himself to be drawn into the wrong company.'

He went on in this strain for some time, but as his host remained politely unresponsive abandoned it at last, and relapsed into melancholy abstraction. He roused himself to enquire about the funeral arrangements, desiring Carlyon to postpone the date to enable him to attend the ceremony, and almost tearfully begging him not to neglect the least pompous detail of it. Upon hearing that the cortège would set out from the chapel where Eustace's body was at present lying, and not from Highnoons, he looked very much shocked, and could not think it right. He wished to know the style of the cards Carlyon had no doubt sent out, and the number of carriages he had ordered, not to mention the mutes, and the plumes, and was only silenced by Carlyon's saying that since Eustace, after making himself odious to the entire neighbourhood, had met his end in a drunken brawl that must still further lessen his credit with his acquaintances, the more private and unostentatious his obsequies were the better it would be for all concerned.

'I shall attend the funeral!' Bedlington declared. 'I mean to spend a night with the poor young creature at Highnoons. I dare say she will be glad of the counsel of an old man: I am sure I do not know what is to become of her, for it is not to be expected that Eustace has left her in affluence. That crazy old house, very nearly in ruins, from what I could see of it! It would cost a fortune to put it in order, and there she is, saddled with its upkeep, and none to support or guide her!'

'Mrs. Cheviot does not reside there alone: she has an elderly companion with her.'

'Yes, yes, a poor little dab of a woman! I don't know what your notions may be, Carlyon, but I should advise selling the place, if any could be found to buy such a ramshackle, old-fashioned house.'

'No doubt she will do so, but until we have probate it is too early to be making plans.'

'Of course: that is understood! But she cannot like to have such a place on her hands, and to be put to the expense of paying the wages of I dare say four or five servants. I feel I should do all I can for her – poor Eustace's bride, you know, and her circumstances so uncomfortable, for there is no blinking the fact that her father died under a cloud! I declare, I have a good mind to invite her to come up to London with me, and to stay in Brook Street until she knows how things may stand! Then the servants may be paid off, and the house closed. What do you say to that, eh?'

'I cannot advocate the leaving of the house untenanted, sir,' was all the answer he could win from Carlyon.

He very soon took himself off to bed, and Carlyon was able to join John, whom he found yawning over a dying fire.

'Hallo!' John said. 'Has he been boring on for ever? You should have let me bear you company!'

'No, you are too severe with him: he cannot talk at his ease in face of your grim scowls. I find it hard myself.'

'You!' John said, bursting out into a laugh. 'Well, had he anything to say that was to the point?'

'He is very uneasy, I fancy. There was some talk of his having unwittingly led Eustace into temptation, as though he had a suspicion some worse mischief than he knows of might have been on hand.'

'Led him into temptation! Pray, how?'

'Apparently he feels that his house is for ever full of evil company. He says he does not know the half of the people who frequent it, and ascribes this to his being the Regent's A.D.C.,' Carlyon said, with only a flicker of a smile.

'A delightful reflection upon Prinny! Refreshingly honest, I swear!'

'I am going to bed,' Carlyon said. 'An evening spent in Bedlington's company is the most fatiguing thing I know. I pity Mrs. Cheviot! He is a dead bore!'

'Oh, he still stands by his threat to inflict himself upon her, does he?'

'Yes, and to invite her to return to Brook Street with him, while Highnoons is shut up, and the servants dismissed.'

'Ha! So that me may search the place at his leisure!' said John, grinning. 'Much obliged to him!' He accompanied his brother out into the hall, and picked up his bedroom candle. 'When have you arranged the funeral? Should I attend?'

'As you wish. I must do so, at all events. It is postponed for two days, Bedlington having affairs that must keep him in town.'

'Deuce take the old fidget!' John growled. 'You will be glad to be done with this, Ned, and know Eustace safe underground!'

'I shall certainly be glad to be done with it, and wish I saw my way through it.'

John gripped his elbow, roughly squeezing it. 'Ay, it has been the devil of a business. As for seeing your way, I do not wonder you cannot! Here is this widow left on your hands, as I told you before! Well, it serves you right, old fellow!'

'Nonsense!' Carlyon said.

In the morning, Lord Bedlington made his appearance dressed for his journey. A somewhat malicious suggestion, put forward by John, that he must surely wish to attend the inquest, which was to be held in the coffee-room of the inn at Wisborough Green, he greeted with a strong shudder. His mind seemed to be divided between horror at an inquest's having to be held over any member of his family, and a shocked realization that he had come into Sussex quite improperly clad. His anxiety to put himself into mourning at once, coupled with a fear that

Schultz, his tailor, might not be able to supply his needs in due time, formed the subjects of his breakfast-table conversation, and certainly hastened his departure. By ten o'clock his chaise was bowling away down the avenue, and Carlyon was giving orders for his own carriage to be brought up to the house.

He and John drove to Highnoons, to take up Nicky, and discovered this young gentleman to be almost completely restored to health, his spirits only damped by the thought of what lay before him. He smiled gratefully at John, and said it was devilish good of him to have come down from London.

'Well, of course I have come!' John said severely. 'If that is a sling you have hanging round your neck, put your arm in it, and see you keep it there!'

'Oh, the wound scarcely troubles me at all! I don't need the sling, and only wear it to please Becky!' said Nicky, who had lost no time in getting upon terms with Miss Beccles.

'Very likely, but it will present a good appearance. I know these Sussex juries!'

'Yes, but I did not get hurt in that fight with Eustace!' objected Nicky.

'No need to say so unless you are asked, and then you will say you were wounded in repelling housebreakers,' said his cynical brother. 'Either way will serve as well.'

He turned to shake Elinor warmly by the hand, and to make his bow to Miss Beccles. Carlyon addressed some observation to Elinor; she replied to it; and then, waiting in vain for any comment on her gray gown, with its black ribbons and lace, rallied him with: 'Well! You perceive, I trust, that I am gone into half-mourning at least! I expect to be heartily commended!'

'You look charmingly, ma'am,' he replied.

She was put out of countenance. 'Oh, no, no, no! I was not asking to be complimented on my looks, but upon my docility!'

There was an amused expression in his eyes; he answered, however, with perfect gravity: 'You forget that I have three sisters. I trust I have learnt from them to avoid making such remarks as must be reckoned tactless in the extreme.'

She laughed out at that. 'Well! It is very hard if I am not to be praised for showing myself so biddable! I received my Lord Bedlington yesterday in the most sombre black imaginable. He has been with you, I think: has he told you of his intention to stay at Highnoons for the funeral?'

'Yes, and I am aware that you have cause for complaint. Believe me, I did not intend you to undergo such hardship when I begged you to take up your residence here.'

'No! It quite spoils the tranquillity of my sojourn here!' she countered. 'When all has been so agreeable until now!'

He smiled, but only said: 'I trust your rest was undisturbed last night?'

'No such thing! Your brother's odious dog scratched so vigorously at my door that I was obliged to get up out of my bed to let him in!'

'He must have taken a marked fancy to you, ma'am,' he said politely.

'He had a marked fancy for the ham-bone he had laid under my bed!' she retorted.

He laughed. 'Well, that is a great deal too bad, certainly, but never mind! I am relieving you of both him and my graceless brother.'

'Oh, no!' she exclaimed quickly. 'No, pray, do not, sir! He is an excellent watch-dog, and gives me the greatest feeling of security! Only fancy! He would not allow the baker to come within fifty yards of the house!'

'What's that?' Nicky demanded. 'You will not make me go back to the Hall yet, Ned! I am set on searching for that precious document, whatever it may be. Besides, Cousin Elinor will not like to be left without Bouncer, and you know he will never stay if I go.'

Both Elinor and Miss Beccles added their earnest entreaties to his, and it was finally agreed that Nicky should return to Highnoons after the inquest. He naïvely informed his brother that he had found an attic stuffed with old lumber, and meant to have a rare time poking about amongst the entrancing relics he had discovered there. 'You can have no notion, Ned! There is an old pistol, I dare say as old as Queen Anne, and a couple of rapiers all rusted over, and I do not know what more besides!'

'Famous!' said John sardonically. 'The very place where you would expect to find a state paper!'

'Well, as to that, there's no saying where it might be, after all,' argued Nicky. 'But only think, John! Do you remember that first-rate kite Eustace had, and would never let Harry fly? I found it there, under a heap of rubbish, and recognized it on the instant!'

'No!' John exclaimed, much struck. 'Why, it must be years old! I wonder you should remember it!'

'Oh, yes! It had red stripes! I could not forget!'

'Yes, that's true. And a long tail, which Harry snipped off when Eustace was so mean-spirited as to refuse to let him fly the thing! Well, upon my word!'

It began to seem as though rummaging amongst half-forgotten playthings, instead of attending an inquest, was to be the order of the day, but the two brothers were recalled to a sense of the occasion by Carlyon, and rather regretfully followed him out to the carriage. Miss Beccles softened the rebuke by suggesting that they should fly the kite later.

'By Jove, yes! Do let us, John!' Nicky exclaimed.

'Nonsense!' said John. 'Kites, indeed! I wonder if it is as good as ever?'

The carriage drove away with them, and the two ladies returned to their interrupted task of dragging all the books from their shelves in the library, clapping them together, dusting the covers, and restoring them to their places. It was exhausting work, and the clouds of dust that thickened the air, and made the ladies sneeze, seemed to indicate that Eustace Cheviot had not been of a bookish turn of mind. Such extraneous matter as floated to the floor when the books were clapped plainly had been placed between the leaves by feminine hands. Several dried flowers were discovered, an old laundry-list, and a recipe for making eel broth, which Miss Beccles thought would be a sustaining diet for an invalid. But of state secrets there was no trace, and although Miss Beccles derived great satisfaction from knowing that no dust, cobwebs, or spiders any longer lurked on the shelves, Elinor could not but feel that she had been wasting her time.

They were just sitting down to a nuncheon of cold meat, fruit, and tea, when the Carlyon carriage once more pulled up at the front door, and the three brothers alighted. Elinor ran out at once to enquire whether all were well, and was met by Nicky, who called cheerfully: 'They have not put me in irons, Cousin Elinor! The Crowner was a great gun! I had not thought it had all been so simple! To tell you the truth, I did not above half like the notion of having to give my evidence, but no one could have been more civil! I was soon feeling at home to a peg. And Hitchin spoke in bang-up style! It was brought in Accidental Death, and only fancy! half of the people who had crowded in to listen to the case set up a cheer! I can tell you I was glad to be able to jump up into the carriage, and get away!'

'Oh, I am so heartily thankful!' Elinor cried. 'It must have been so, of course, but one could not help being a little anxious.'

She put out her hand impulsively to Carlyon, as she spoke, and he shook it, saying: 'Thank you. It is happily over, and did indeed go without the least rub.' He added, a smile in his eyes: 'Judging from the demeanour of the spectators, it would have gone hard with the jury had they brought in another verdict! I was obliged to hustle Nicky away, for what must some of the villagers do but try to shake him by the hand, as though he had been a public benefactor!'

'Well, it was improper, but one cannot wonder at it,' said John. 'Cheviot left no stone unturned to render himself odious in these parts.'

She led them into the dining-parlour, and pressed them to partake of some cold meat. Nicky exclaimed: 'What, mawdling your insides with tea again! No, I thank you!'

'Yes, indeed, it is very wrong to be drinking tea at such an hour as this,' confessed Miss Beccles. 'But such an agreeable luxury!'

Happily for Nicky, Barrow had seen the carriage drive up to the house, and now brought a large jug of ale into the room, and three tankards. The gentlemen were thus able to enjoy a very tolerable nuncheon, during which they discussed the inquest with the ladies, informed them what arrangements had been made for the funeral, and announced their intention of spending the afternoon at Highnoons, to search for any secret document there might be there.

Carlyon's part in the search was methodical, and unhurried. For some time he was ably assisted by John, both brothers sitting in the book-room, Carlyon before an antique commode, whose drawers and cupboards were crammed with the accumulations of years; and John on the sofa, with a battered wooden box at his feet, which one of Eustace's keys had been found to fit. This was full of papers, old account-books, ledgers, and bundles of letters, and these were all in such disorder that he was very glad to accept Elinor's offer of assistance in sorting them out. But after half an hour's steady work an interruption occurred. Nicky looked into the room, saying: 'Look, is not this the very one, John?'

'Ay, that is it,' John replied, glancing up at the gaudy, if somewhat faded, kite he was being shown.

'Well, do you mean to come and try if it will fly?'

'Flying kites at my age! I should rather think not! Cannot you see that I am busy?'

'Oh, fusty work!' Nicky said, disappearing again.

John returned to his task, but happening to raise his head a few minutes later caught sight of Nicky in the garden. His attention remained riveted, and he presently ejaculated: 'One would fancy him a school-boy! Incurable folly!'

Neither Carlyon nor Elinor returned any answer, and after a slight pause, during which he continued to look out of the window, he said testily: 'That's no way to go about it! Why does he not take it into the meadow? There cannot be wind enough in this hollow!'

'Here is a book of household accounts twenty years old,' said Elinor. 'Shall I lay it aside to be burnt?'

'Yes, certainly,' he said absently. 'There! You have got it entangled in the hedge! Ned, that boy will be hurting his shoulder if he persists! I'll go out to him!'

He left the room abruptly as he spoke, and five minutes later Elinor had an excellent view of him upon the lawn, arguing with Nicky. Both brothers then departed in the direction of the meadow, Bouncer at their heels, and were no more seen until the light began to fail, and Carlyon had called for his carriage. They came in then, flushed and untidy, but full of satisfaction in having found the kite to be in famous shape, and very hot against their deceased cousin for the selfishness which had made him refuse to allow them to fly it years ago, when, as John rather unconvincingly said, they might really have enjoyed such a childish pastime. He looked a little conscious when he realized how late it was, and said that he begged pardon for having left his task. 'But I thought I had best make sure Nicky did himself no injury,' he explained. 'Besides, I don't believe there is anything in this rubbish-heap of a house but what had better have been burnt years ago!'

'I began to agree with you,' said Carlyon, ruefully regarding the huge pile of waste-paper on the floor. 'Nevertheless, the work had to be done, and whether I find anything of value or not I must continue until it is finished. Mrs. Cheviot, I beg you will not exhaust yourself in this search! I shall return to-morrow, and there is not the least need for you to be turning out any more drawers and cupboards to-day.'

Both he and John took their leave of her, John saying that although he must return to London on the morrow he should try to be in Sussex to attend the funeral. As they left the house, Bouncer entered it, very much out of breath, and generously plastered with mud. Miss Beccles uttered a shriek of dismay, and ran at once for a cloth, with which she proceeded to dry his legs and paws, scolding gently as she did so. Bouncer instantly assumed the cowed mien of a dog suffering under torture, but upon being released tore round the room three times, at top-speed, sending all the rugs flying, and ended up with a leap on to the sofa, where he sat grinning and panting until turned off it by his master.

The night was eventful. Upon the following morning, Carlyon came over at an early hour to Highnoons, and allowed himself to be lured up to the attic by Nicky, where he made a clearance which would have been very more drastic had not Miss Beccles trotted up a plate of rout drop-cakes (for she believed that gentlemen stood in constant need of sustenance) and rescued from the pile on the floor several old-fashioned dresses, whose stiff brocade, she assured Carlyon in scandalized accents, would cut up to admiration; a large pin-cushion; just such an earthenware bowl as Mrs. Barrow stood in crying need of; a paper full of pins, a little rusted, to be sure, but by no means useless; and a book of Household Hints, which contained such valuable information as how to remove stains from linen by laying on salt of wormwood, and the infallibility of Scotch snuff as a means of destroying crickets.

While she was upstairs, Elinor went out into the garden, accompanied by Bouncer, to give some directions to the gardener, and was trying to convince him of the propriety of his devoting his time to weeding the overgrown carriage-drive, when a job-chaise drove in at the gate. When it pulled up before the house, a burly individual descended from it, with all the look about him of a tradesman. Elinor stepped forward to enquire his business, and was only just in time to prevent Bouncer's seizing him by the calf of his leg. Ruffled by this reception, the visitor abandoned any attempt at civility, and thrust upon her a formidable, and detailed account, which, he loudly asserted, he would have paid immediately or by distraint. Upon learning that his defaulting client lay dead, he looked greatly taken aback, but after a few seconds' astonishment said that he was not surprised to hear it, and would be paid in any event. The affronted widow recommended him to present his demand to Mr. Cheviot's executors, and, when he seemed inclined to think she might well pay him a trifle on account, since he was a poor man, and sadly out of pocket over the business, announced her inability any longer to control the dog. The visitor then mounted into his chaise again with more speed than dignity, and Mrs. Cheviot went up to the attic to inform Carlyon, with no little relish, that just as she had always expected she was now being dunned at the door.

'Yes, I dare say this is but the first of many such encounters,' replied Carlyon. 'A notice is to be inserted in the newspapers, but no doubt it will be missed by many.'

'Charming! So I must accustom myself to being abused at my own door!'

'I cannot understand why you should be answering your front-door bell,' said Carlyon. 'Barrow is well able to deal with such persons.'

'But I was in the garden, and naturally stepped up to the man to know what he might want!' said Elinor indignantly.

'Unwise. You will know better another time,' was all the satisfaction she obtained.

She was happily diverted by Miss Beccles's displaying to her the glories of the brocade dresses she had rescued. 'Oh, I can remember Mama in just such a dress!' she cried. 'It should have a hoop, should it not, Becky? And the hair dressed high, with powder, and a wreath, or feathers, or some such thing! I wonder how anyone can ever have borne to have worn such a garment! Only feel the weight of it! But the brocade is the very thing we need for the cushions in the parlour.' She looked round the attic, marvelling at the collection of worn-out finery, furniture, and rubbish. 'Good God, has everything that needed a stitch, or a nail, been cast into this garret?'

'Yes, indeed,' said Miss Beccles, shaking her head mournfully. 'There has been a sad want of management and economy, I fear. And here is my lord refusing to let me keep back that chair from the bonfire, and all it needs is to have the seat recaned! And only look at that spit, too! I am sure it could be mended, if only he would let me take it down to the kitchen.'

'You *may* take it down, dear Becky,' said Elinor grandly. 'You may save anything you like from the bonfire!'

'Oh, no, my love! If his lordship feels it were better to throw the things away, I would not think –'

'This,' said Elinor, in a very lofty tone, 'is *my* house, and you may tell his lordship that he has nothing to say in the matter!'

'Elinor, my love! Indeed, you let the liveliness of your mind betray you into saying what is not at all becoming!'

'Tell his lordship with your compliments,' corrected Carlyon. 'You should always add your compliments to any message you wish to render excessively cutting.'

She cast him a withering glance, and prepared to retreat in good order. To her surprise, he followed her out of the attic, and downstairs, saying: 'Your unwelcome visitor has put me in mind of something I should have spoken of before, Mrs. Cheviot. Shall we go into the parlour?'

'Now, what horrid surprise do you mean to spring on me?' she asked suspiciously.

'On my honour, none at all! But it occurs to me that it will be proper for me, as my cousin's executor, to advance you sufficient moneys to pay for all those items, I dare say a great many, which it may not be convenient to charge up.'

'No, pray do not! There can be not the least necessity!'

'On the contrary, you are not to be spending out of your own purse.'

'I shall not. Why, what should I spend money on?'

'Depend upon it, there will be a score of things.' He added with a slight smile: 'At any moment a pedlar may come to the door, and you will buy a broom from him, or a chintz patch, or some such thing!'

'Well, if I do that is quite my own affair. I had rather you did not give me any money.'

'You are over-scrupulous, ma'am, but since you have this extreme nicety I will place a sum in Miss Beccles's charge.'

She almost stamped her foot at him. 'I wish you will not treat me as though I were a schoolgirl, my lord!' she said. She read an answer in his eye, and added hurriedly: 'And do not tell me that I behave as one, because it is quite untrue!'

'Certainly not. I know you to be a sensible woman, a little too much in the habit of having your own way.'

She fairly gasped. 'This reproach from *you*, my lord!'

'Very true: we agreed, did we not, that my disposition is overbearing? But you will own that my way is in general more reasonable than yours.'

'Not while I still retain the possession of my faculties!' she declared. 'Indeed, I do not know how you dare make such a claim! It quite takes my breath away! When I consider in what a position you have placed me, and then am obliged to listen to you talking as though you had done nothing out of the ordinary, but on the contrary had acted in the best possible manner –'

'Well, you know, ma'am, given a situation which you will allow to have been excessively awkward, I think I did,' he said.

Mrs. Cheviot sank into a chair, and covered her eyes with one hand.

Carlyon regarded her in some amusement. 'Still regretting Mrs. Macclesfield, ma'am?'

'Oh, no! How could I, sir?' she retorted. 'How dull I must have been in her house! I dare say she had never a French agent within it, let alone a distraint upon the furniture!'

'I am sure hers is a most respectable household. I should be surprised if her husband has ever done anything as mildly reprehensible as to look for a keg of brandy by his back door.' He broke off. 'Yes, that puts me in mind of something else,' he said. 'It is the season when we may reasonable expect to find a few such kegs. I am sure Eustace had his brandy from the free-traders. If you should come upon any kegs, in some unexpected place, such as an outhouse, for instance, just tell me, ma'am! Do not raise an outcry!'

'This only was needed!' said Elinor. 'I am now to enter into dealings with a pack of smugglers! Perhaps, after all, you had better leave some money with me, for I dare say they will wish to be paid for their trouble! And though, to be sure, life at Highnoons has been a trifle flat these past two days, I should not care to be at loggerheads with a set of desperate persons who would not, I dare say, boggle for an instant at murder!'

'Oh, I do not think they will murder you!' he replied cheerfully. 'I will set the word going, however, in the proper quarters, that any consignment ordered by my cousin may be delivered up at the Hall.'

'And I have no doubt whatsoever,' stated Mrs. Cheviot, 'that you are a Justice of the Peace!'

'Yes, certainly.'

'I wonder you should not be ashamed to own it!' she said virtuously.

'My dear ma'am, there is nothing in the least derogatory in being a Justice of the Peace!' he replied, at his blandest.

Mrs. Cheviot sought in vain for words adequate to the occasion, and could only regard him in speechless dudgeon.

Thirteen

*T*he next day, the eve of the funeral, passed in much the same busy but uneventful style. The piles of rubbish grew higher yet: Miss Beccles was made happy by being permitted to make the still-room and the linen-cupboard her particular concerns; Elinor began to think that in time the house might be made very tolerable; and Nicky beguiled the morning by taking Bouncer to a neighbouring farm, and engaging in a rat-hunt which might have been more successful had not Bouncer jumped to an over-hasty conclusion that his first duty was to rid the world of the flea-ridden terrier who should have assisted him in his work of destroying all the rats in the big barn.

Returning from the day's sport midway through the afternoon Nicky strolled up to the house by the short cut that led through the surrounding woodland in time to see an elegant post-chaise-and-four drawn up before the front door. As he paused, in surprise, a very obvious gentleman's gentleman jumped down from it, a dressing-case in his hand, which he tenderly set down in the porch before turning back to assist his master to alight.

A slim and exquisite figure descended languidly on to the drive, and stood with the utmost patience while the valet straightened the numerous capes of his great-coat, and anxiously passed a handkerchief over the gleaming surface of a pair of well-cut Hessian boots. A high-crowned gray beaver, with a curling brim, was set at a slightly rakish angle on the gentleman's head of glossy chestnut curls. He wore one gray glove, and carried the other in the same hand, together with an ebony walking-cane. From under the brim of his hat, a pair of weary, blue eyes gazed in insufferable boredom at nothing in particular. Their expression of wordly cynicism made them sit oddly in a face decidedly round, with a nose inclined to the retroussé, and an almost womanishly delicate mouth and chin.

'Hell and the devil confound it!' uttered Nicky, under his breath, recognizing the visitor.

Bouncer, who had been standing with his tail up, and his ears on the prick, needed no more encouragement than these muttered words to send him forward like a bolt from the blue to execute his clear duty. Barking like a fiend, he launched himself upon the intruder.

The exquisite gentleman whirled about at the first bark, and as Bouncer came at full-tilt across the ill-kept lawn, his ungloved right hand grasped the ivory top of his cane, deftly twisted it, and drew a thin, wicked blade hissing from the ebony stick that formed its sheath.

'*Heel*, Bouncer!' Nicky roared, terror for his pet lending such ferocity to his voice that Bouncer checked in mid-career, dropping tail and ears, and cowering to the earth in startled dismay.

Nicky came striding up, his eyes sparkling with wrath, his countenance flushed, and sternly admonished Bouncer.

The visitor kept his sword-stick poised, but raised his eyes, suddenly very wide open, to Nicky's face. He was breathing a little fast, but his lips smiled, and he said smoothly: 'I do not – like – dogs!'

'By God, Cheviot, if you so much as touch my dog with that blade of yours I'll ram it down your gullet!' swore Nicky, glaring at him.

The smile grew, the arched brows rose; Francis Cheviot restored his blade to its sheath. 'What, Nicholas! Determined to purge the world of Cheviots?'

Nicky's colour darkened, and his fists clenched themselves

involuntarily. Francis Cheviot laughed softly, and patted his shoulder with one white hand. 'There, there!' he said soothingly. 'I was only funning, dear boy! I am sure you would not really ram my blade down my throat.'

'You harm my dog, and you need not be so sure of that!' said Nicky pugnaciously.

'Oh, but I am, Nicholas! I cannot help but be sure of it,' Francis said, in dulcet accents. 'But tell me, dear boy, is it quite – quite in the best of good *ton* for you to be here? Under the circumstances – and pray do not imagine that I blame you for them, for nothing could be farther from my thoughts! – but under these circumstances, do you not feel – No, I see you do not, and indeed, who am I to presume to set myself up as arbiter? The situation is something quite out of my line.'

'I am staying here,' said Nicky curtly.

'Ah, indeed? How very piquant, to be sure! Crawley, I do trust that you have rung that bell, for if I stand in this disagreeable wind you know I shall take cold, and my colds always descend upon my chest. How thoughtless it was in you to have handed me down from the chaise until the door had been opened! Ah, here is that deplorable henchman! Yes, Barrow, it is I indeed. Take my hat – no, Crawley had best take my hat, perhaps. And yet, if he does so, who is to assist me out of my greatcoat? How difficult all these arrangements are! Ah, a happy thought! You have laid my hat down, Crawley! I do not know where I should be without you. Now my coat, and pray be careful! Where is a mirror? Crawley, you cannot have been so foolish as to have packed all my hand-mirrors! No, I thought not: hold it a little higher, I beg of you, and give me my comb! Yes, that will serve. Barrow, you may announce me to your mistress!'

'Ay, just about I may!' said the retainer, glowering at him. 'It queers me what brings you here, sir, but I'll tell you to your head you ain't wanted!'

'Ah, and now that you have told me, announce me, Barrow!' replied Francis affably. 'And pray do not bring that dog in, dear

Nicholas! I have the greatest dread of dogs, and I know you would not wish to upset me. Really an antipathy, you know! Is it not strange? They say that a liking for dogs is such an English characteristic, and I am sure I am quite English. Cats, now! There is something so admirable in a cat, don't you agree? No, of course you do not! Barrow, am I to be kept standing in this draughty hall for very much longer, because if so I must have my coat on again?'

Barrow gave vent to his feelings in a snort, but walked over to the parlour, and flung open the door, saying with bitter ceremony: 'The Honourable Francis Cheviot, ma'am!'

Elinor, who was seated at the escritoire by the window, turned a startled face, and rose quickly. 'The –?'

'Yes, it's Francis Cheviot,' said Nicky sulkily. 'But what he wants here I don't know!'

Francis trod delicately across the room towards his hostess, a hand held out, and his countenance wreathed in smiles. 'My dear Mrs. Cheviot, how do you do? Ah, what a foolish question! How *can* you do in this sad hour? Allow me to offer you my sincerest condolences upon this unhappy event!'

Rather bewildered, she gave him her hand, curtsying slightly. He bowed over it with punctilious grace. She said, stammering a little: 'How do you do? I beg your pardon – I was not expecting –'

'Not expecting me?' he said, in a shocked voice. 'My dear Mrs. Cheviot – or may I call you cousin? – my dear cousin, who can have been giving you such a false, unkind portrait of me? I am sure it was not Nicholas! That little rusticity of manner, which I am persuaded will be polished away in time, hides a heart of gold, you know! No, no, I must hold the dear boy absolved! But my poor Cousin Eustace – you cannot have supposed I should absent myself from his obsequies! I never neglect those gestures which cost one so little, after all! But I am quite put out of countenance by finding Nicholas here! It is not that I am not delighted to meet him: in fact, I am transported: but I do not know just how I should conduct myself towards him.

You see, I am a mourner, and he – dear me, what delicate ground I seem to be on!'

'I wish you will stop humbugging on for ever!' snapped Nicky. 'You never cared a button for Eustace!'

'Now, this is not just, Nicholas! This is not like you! Poor dear Eustace! Such a deplorable character! The very worst of bad *ton!* Always a source of pain to me, but do not let us speak ill of the dead! Death makes the worst of men instantly respectable, you know. Ah, dear Mrs. Cheviot, I should have explained that I am here in a dual role! Yes, indeed: cousin and uncle combined. How odd it seems! I do trust I can carry it off with grace.'

'Lord Bedlington – does not come to the funeral?' Elinor faltered, quite dazed by all this gentle eloquence.

'Alas! His kind compliments, dear cousin – his deepest regrets – I am the bearer of his most heartfelt apologies! Prostrate!'

'Eh?' gasped Nicky.

Francis sighed. 'I left him laid upon his bed, in the greatest anguish. His old enemy, you know: gout, dear boy! The agitation he has suffered – or perhaps it may have been that horridly cold drive: who can say? – brought on one of his most severe attacks. Impossible for him to venture out of his house! So here I am, in my dual role. I do trust – not unwelcome?'

'Oh, no!' Elinor said quickly. 'How could you think – Pray, will you not be seated, sir? You are staying – that is, I expect you are putting up at –'

'You are all goodness, cousin! My father did indeed encourage me to hope that I should find a welcome at Highnoons. But do not put yourself out, I beg of you! I dare say I shall be very comfortable in whatever bedchamber you choose to bestow me, as long as the chimney does not smoke – yes, I retain the most hideous memories of my last visit to this house – and the aspect is not north. My physician warns me particularly against cold rooms, you know, for my constitution is not at all robust.'

She knew not what to say, for the dictates of civility forbade her to utter the only reply that rose to her mind. Nicky, whose notions were not so nice, said bluntly: 'You will scarcely stay here, Cheviot! The inn at Wisborough Green has several decent rooms.'

Francis answered him with unshaken urbanity: 'I should not dare to take so great a risk, for you must know that I have not brought my own sheets with me, and I make it a rule never to stay at an inn without them. One can never be certain that the beds have been properly aired. Dear me, I am quite overcome to think I should be putting Mrs. Cheviot to inconvenience!'

Elinor felt herself obliged to disclaim, and to say that she would give instructions to have a room prepared for him. He thanked her, and said that he should be happy in the Yellow Room.

'Well, you will not!' said Nicky incorrigibly. 'That is Mrs. Cheviot's room!'

'Ah, then, on no account would I wish her to remove from it!' Francis said. 'It really makes not the smallest difference to me, so do not, I beg of you, cousin, dream of giving it up! That would put me quite out of countenance. Put me in poor Eustace's chamber! It is a trifle sombre, perhaps, but I shall not regard that.'

Elinor found Nicky's eyes fixed on her face with so much meaning in them that she felt the colour rise to her cheeks, and got up out of her chair, murmuring that she would tell Mrs. Barrow. Nicky at once followed her, saying hastily that he must take care Bouncer was safely inside the house. He carefully shut the parlour door behind him, and said to Elinor in an urgent under-voice: 'We must not leave him alone on any account, Cousin Elinor! By Jupiter, Ned was right! He has come here to find that paper: there can be no doubt! But we shall be a match for him! Did you ever see such a frippery fellow?'

'Oh, Nicky, I own I cannot like him! He quite frightens me indeed! I wish you will persuade him to remove to the Hall!'

'Frightens you? What, a fellow that would screech if a mouse crossed his path? You cannot be serious! I am sure Ned would say we must allow him to remain here. Only fancy, cousin, if he should know where Eustace hid that paper, and lead us to it! I should not at all wonder if it is in Eustace's bedchamber, for you must have remarked his suggestion that he should have that room. Doing it rather too brown, I thought! I'll tell you what! Do you lock up that room, and have the chamber next to mine prepared! Then if he tries any of his tricks during the night I must hear him. It would be beyond anything great if I should catch him red-handed, and before ever Ned hears of his being here!'

'Nicky, I shall go distracted! I wish you will send a message to your brother, informing him of this arrival! Not,' she added bitterly, 'that he is likely to be of the least comfort to me, for he is as bad as you are, and will very likely say it is a happy circumstance, or something just as heartless!'

'Well, I should not wonder at it if he did. The only thing is that I shall be hard put to it to be civil to the fellow! Do you know he would have killed Bouncer with that sword-stick of his if I had not been there? A fellow that likes cats above dogs! *Cats!*' Nicky uttered, with awful scorn.

'He is like a cat himself. Oh, I wish he had not come here! Or I either!'

'Fudge! It is famous sport!' Nicky said, and went back into the parlour.

The guest, so far from searching the room, was still seated gracefully beside the fire, one slim, gray-swathed leg crossed over the other. He smiled sweetly at Nicky, and made a gesture with his long-handled quizzing-glass towards the silver tassels on his Hessians. 'Observe!' he said. 'I should not say so, for it is an inspiration of my own, but really I am quite lost in admiration. Silver tassels, dear boy, not gold, thus delicately preserving the mourning-note. I shall wear black pantaloons for the ceremony, of course. I hesitated for long before I permitted Crawley to help me into these gray ones, for one would not wish to betray the least disrespect, but I think the relationship just remote enough to allow of my wearing them, do not you? I do flatter myself that my black neckcloth strikes precisely the correct note, however. Or do you think it makes me look like a military man?'

'No,' said Nicky frankly. 'Nothing could!'

'Ah, how delightful of you, dear boy! Really, you have so much relieved my mind!' Francis said, beaming upon him. 'Now, tell me! Must I look my last on Eustace's face, or do I not indulge my optimism too much in trusting that his coffin is already nailed down?'

'Of course it is!'

'I am so thankful. Death is extremely painful to me, and although I am determined not to omit the least – Ah, *not*, I do trust, in this house?'

'No. It lies in a chapel.'

'Again you relieve my mind. I brought my vinaigrette with me, of course, and Crawley knows how to revive me, but I confess I should have been excessively loth to have slept under the same roof with a coffin. My sensibilities have always been extremely acute, and I dare say I should have suffered a spasm. But now, unless I should have taken a chill on the drive, I do trust we have nothing to dread. It is not to be, I collect, a lengthy cortège?'

'Carlyon has arranged for it to be as private as may be,' replied Nicky.

'One cannot but sympathize with him,' murmured Francis. He watched Nicky colour up, and added apologetically: 'I have never known myself to be so maladroit! Really, I intended not the smallest offence, dear Nicholas! Poor Eustace, alas, was not beloved in this neighbourhood! But I do hope sufficient carriages have bespoken, for he had some friends, you know. I feel persuaded that they must honour his obsequies with their presence. Indeed, I have myself advised Louis De Castres of this sad event, and I do not doubt of seeing him here to-morrow.'

Nicky fairly gasped at this effrontery, and could only gaze at him open-mouthed.

'You must be acquainted with Louis?' said Francis, mildly surprised. 'A charming creature! One of my oldest friends!'

177

'Yes,' said Nicky. 'Yes, I fancy I have met him!'

Elinor came back into the room just then, with Miss Beccles, and under cover of the necessary introduction Nicky escaped, to cool his heated head in the gardens. Since town hours were not kept at Highnoons, it was soon time to be dressing for dinner, and the uneasy party separated, Francis to deliver himself into the hands of his valet, Miss Beccles to superintend the laying of the table so that they might not all be shamed before such a fine gentleman, and Elinor to seek out Nicky, once more to implore him to send the groom up to the Hall with a message for Carlyon.

This he would by no means do, insisting the Carlyon's assistance was not needed to deal with such a paltry fellow as Francis, and she went off to her own room quite out of charity with him.

The party which presently sat down to dinner was, with the exception of Miss Beccles, who dignified the occasion by wearing her best lavender silk, as funereal as the most exacting critic could have desired. Francis had arrayed himself in a black coat and satin knee-breeches which looked more fit for Almack's Assembly Rooms than a country house; Elinor wore her black silk; and Nicky, not to be outdone by Francis, had put himself into a similar attire to his, though not, he enviously realized, of such extremely fashionable cut.

Nothing could have exceeded the affability of the guest, but Miss Beccles would not be lured into contributing her mite to the conversation; Elinor laboured under a sense of indefinable alarm; and Nicky's attempts to conceal his dislike of Francis only served to emphasise it. Elinor wondered how they were to get through a whole evening. When she and Miss Beccles withdrew to the parlour, Miss Beccles confided to her that she owned she could not quite like the tone of Mr. Cheviot's conversation, and very much feared he was not a good man.

'I think him a dreadful man!' Elinor said.

'Well, my love, since you say so, I shall not scruple to tell you that I thought that tale he told, about Mr. Romeo Coates – such an odd name, too! – rather too warm, and not at all the sort of thing your dear Mama would have wished you to be listening to.'

'I wish he had not come here! I am afraid of him!'

'My dear Mrs. Cheviot! Oh, dear, dear! My love, *lock your door!* Or, no! I will sleep on the couch in your room!'

Elinor could not help laughing. 'Oh, no, indeed, Becky! I am very sure he has no designs upon my virtue! But now that I have spent a couple of hours in his company I cannot doubt the justice of Carlyon's suspicions. He is the very man to be doing some wicked, treacherous thing! We must not leave him alone in the house an instant! If only that odious boy would have sent to advise Carlyon! And beyond all else, how in the world are we to pass the evening? I was never so uncomfortable in my life!'

'Well, my love,' said Miss Beccles doubtfully, 'if you think he might like it, I could offer to play at backgammon with him.'

Happily, she was not obliged to do so. Hardly had the gentlemen entered the parlour than all the bustle of an arrival was heard in the hall; and within a very few minutes the door was opened to admit Carlyon, his brother John, and a lady and gentleman who bore all the air of being in the first rank of fashion.

The lady, who came in on Carlyon's arm, was decidedly younger than Elinor. She was extremely pretty, with such golden ringlets and such sparkling blue eyes that it did not need Nicky's shout of 'Georgy!' or Carlyon's quiet introduction to 'My sister, Lady Flint,' to inform Elinor of her identity. She rose at once, blushing, and curtsying, and found her hand seized between two warm little ones, and heard herself addressed in a sweet, mischievous voice.

'Mrs. Cheviot! My new cousin! Oh, you are such a heroine! I made Carlyon bring me to see you! This is Flint, my husband, you know! Oh, Nicky!'

Elinor's hand was dropped; the engaging creature was off in a mist of gauze to throw her arms round Nicky's neck; then to bestow hand and smile on Francis; and, upon Elinor's murmuring her companion's name, a handshake on Miss Beccles. She chattered all the while, explaining that she was on her way into Hampshire, to spend a few weeks with the Dowager, but could not rest until she had discovered all the truth of what John had been telling her. Nothing would do but Flint must bring her not so *very* much out of their way, after all, to spend a night with Carlyon. While she rattled on in this style, her husband, a sensible-looking man, some years her senior, stood watching her in fond admiration, and Nicky pelted her with questions which she never paused to answer.

Carlyon took advantage of her vivacity to draw near to Elinor, and to explain that his sister, having heard John's account of her marriage, had had such a desire to meet her that he had set dinner forward an hour so as to be able to drive the whole party over to drink tea at Highnoons. 'I would not bring them to dinner,' he said. 'It must have incommoded you. I trust we are not now unwelcome?'

'No, indeed!' she returned, in a low voice. 'I have been wishing all the evening that Nicky would but have sent over to advice you of *that* gentleman's arrival!'

'It is certainly interesting,' he said, glancing towards Francis, who was conversing with Flint.

'I knew you would say so, provoking creature!'

'Where is Bedlington?'

'Prostrate! With the gout!'

He looked thoughtful, but made no answer.

'For heaven's sake, my lord, what would you have me do?'

'I will discuss it with you at a more convenient opportunity.'

'Meanwhile he may prowl about the house all night, in search of you well know what!'

'I hardly think so. Is not Nicky's dog with you? Let him roam at large!'

There was no time for more. Lady Flint came fluttering up to them, determined to make the further acquaintance of her new cousin. It was soon made plain that John had told her nothing of the strange events which had taken place in the house. It was the marriage which had captivated the lively lady's fancy. She soon drew Elinor to the sofa, and sat down beside her there, engaging her in conversation, interrupted every now and then by her throwing a word to one of her brothers, or to Francis, with whom she seemed to be on excellent terms. But presently, upon some pretext, she flitted up with Elinor to her bedchamber, and said to her with her pretty air of candour: 'Carlyon said we should put you out of countenance, so many of us, and arriving without the least warning! But you do not regard it, do you? Oh, when I saw that notice in the *Morning Post*, you may suppose how ready I was to drop! I sent at once to Mount Street, to John! I declare, I would have made my poor Flint storm the Home Office I was in such a fever to know more! Tell me – do not think me impertinent, though to be sure I am! – how came you to do it?'

Elinor replied with a little reserve: 'Indeed, I scarcely know! Lord Carlyon persuaded me, but I must suppose myself to have been out of my senses.'

Her ladyship gave a little gurgle. 'Dearest Carlyon! how I shall tease him! But what is this story of housebreakers? I declare it is like a romance! How happy it must have made Nicky to be shot at! I have a very good mind to make Flint stay here for an age, for I was never so diverted in my life! But I dare say it will not do. I am in the family way, you know, and my poor dear Flint has taken such crotchets into his head! I was never so well, I vow! But nothing will do but I must go into the country, and ten to one Carlyon will aid and abet him. Do you like him?'

'Indeed,' Elinor said, quite taken aback, 'Lord Flint appeared to me a most amiable –'

'Stupid! Not Flint! Carlyon!'

Elinor was vexed to feel herself colouring. She replied stiffly: 'Certainly. I am sure his manners and address are such as must universally please.'

There was a pout, an arch look. 'Oh –! Sad stuff! Do you quarrel with him? Does he make you very cross?'

'If you must have the truth,' said Elinor, 'he is the most odious, overbearing, inconsiderate, abominable man I ever met!'

She was instantly embraced. 'Famous! How often I have said the same! You will deal admirably together. I am glad I have seen you. Oh, but it is enough to make oneself wish to be a widow to see you look so very becoming in that black dress! How shocking of me to say so, for you must know that I dote on Flint! Does Francis Cheviot stay long with you? I was so much surprised!'

'Only a night, I fancy. It is a little awkward, but he comes as proxy for his father, for – for the funeral.'

The delicate brows rose. 'Ah, you do not like him! But there is no harm in him, you know, and you may meet him for ever! I always invite him to all my parties: everyone does so, for he is the most amusing creature, and such good *ton!* Mr. Brummell says that his tailor makes him: was there ever anything so unkind? He is very good company, and always knows just which colours will set one off best, and how one should furnish one's new drawing-room.'

Elinor returned some non-committal answer, and after some more of this inconsequent chatter Lady Flint allowed herself to be escorted downstairs again. It was soon time for the party from the Hall to be off, if they were to reach home before morning, so as soon as tea had been drunk, and adieux spoken, the carriage was called for. There was no opportunity for Elinor to hold private converse with Carlyon; she could only throw him a very speaking glance as they stood in the hall, and this was received only with a slight smile. She was obliged to go through her part as hostess with a smiling face, and could only whisper, as he shook her hand in farewell: 'How dare you leave me with that creature?'

'My dependence is on Bouncer,' he returned.

He followed his brother-in-law out of the house, allowing her no time to retort, and was soon in the carriage, and driving away from Highnoons.

'My dear Carlyon, she is charming!' Georgiana said, out of the darkness beside him.

'A very well-bred young woman,' pronounced Flint.

'She is a Rochdale of Feldenhall.'

'It is very strange. I do not pretend to understand it.'

'Dearest Flint, where would be the sport if one could?' demanded his wife. 'But, Ned, you did not tell me how very handsome she is! She has a great deal of countenance, and dignity, too – far more than I have, I am sure.'

'Which is to say more than none at all!'

'Very true! It is not in my line: never was! But there is some mystery you have not told me about! It is too provoking!'

'It exists in your own head.'

'No! John is so silent!'

'John is always silent.'

'Pooh! I am not such a fool as to be put off so! *Something* I have discovered, but not the whole: I wish I had not to go into Hampshire!'

He turned the subject with some reference to her projected stay with her mother-in-law; she was diverted, and the conversation turned no more upon Highnoons until the party was set down at the Hall. It was then that John, detaining Carlyon when he would have entered one of the saloons in the wake of his sister, said: 'By God, you were right, Ned! What's to do now?'

'I believe we should have expected to see him here.'

'Ay! But what has he done with poor old Bedlington? How has he persuaded him to remain in London? And what does he intend?'

'To find your memorandum, I collect.'

'You are damned cool, upon my word!'

'No: interested, and as yet unsure of my ground. The case is plainly desperate, and I must indulge the hope that he will betray himself. Hush! do not speak of this before Georgy!'

She had come out of the saloon, and was advancing towards them. 'I shall go to bed. How odious it is in you to be talking secrets!'

'No such thing!' said John. 'Where's Flint? I want a word with him!'

She watched him stride off towards the saloon, and turned her eyes back to her eldest brother, a roguish look in them. 'Oh, Ned!'

'Well, and now what?'

A dimple peeped. 'Gussie and Eliza would be agog if I told them, but I don't know that I shall. But I thought you past praying for!'

'Nonsense! What can you mean?'

She put her arms round his neck, and stood on tiptoe to kiss his cheek. 'You are the best of kind, provoking brothers, and I won't tease you – not a bit! But I think you are very sly!'

Fourteen

The visitors having all departed, Elinor was thankful to find that Francis Cheviot was ready to retire for the night, provided he might be assured that every door and window was secured against intruders. To Nicky's mingled scepticism and scorn, the story of a thief's having broken into the house seemed to have taken strong possession of his mind. He believed himself to be incapable of closing his eyes all night if the least possibility existed of anyone's being able to enter the house, and debated the advisability of commanding his valet to sit up with a loaded gun. 'If only I might trust him not to discharge his piece upon a mere false alarm!' he said. 'But he is the stupidest fellow! If he did not know to such a nicety how to polish my boots I must have turned him off years ago! How difficult it is to decide what to do for the best! Would it be a comfort to us to know him to be standing guard over our slumbers? But, then, if he were to take fright at a shadow, and wake us all with firing at it, how shocking that would be! *My* nerves, I know, could scarcely support it, and I must suppose, my dear cousin, that yours would not readily recover from it.'

'There is no need for the poor man to be kept up all night,' she responded calmly. 'Bouncer is an excellent watch-dog, and we have formed the habit of allowing him to roam over the house at will. At the least sound of stirring in the house he would give the alarm.'

'I should think he would!' corroborated Nicky, with an impish smile. 'Why, when Miss Beccles only opened her door last night he set up such a barking as roused even old Barrow!'

'Did he, indeed?' said Francis politely. 'I do trust I shall not be thought unreasonable if I solicit Miss Beccles not to open her door to-night. If I am awakened out of my first sleep I find it very hard to drop off again, and to be lying awake all night, you know, cannot but harm the most robust constitution.'

Miss Beccles assured him that she would not do so; and the party went out into the hall, where the bedroom candles were set out on the table. Bouncer was lying on the mat by the door, and Francis put up his quizzing-glass to scrutinize him. He sighed. 'A singularly ill-favoured hound!' he said.

'Much you know about it!' snapped Nicky, who could not brook criticism of his favourite.

Either his tone, or the dog's natural antipathy to Francis, provoked Bouncer into uttering a subdued growl. He was in doubt how this would be received, but when no rebuke greeted it, he got up, and barked aggressively at Francis.

Francis shuddered. 'Pray hold him, dear Nicholas!' he begged. 'What a shocking character mine must be! They say dogs can always tell, do they not? I do trust that is yet another of the fallacies one is for ever discovering!'

'Oh, he will not bite you while I am here!' said Nicky cheerfully.

'Then do, I beg of you, accompany me up the stairs!' said Francis.

This was done, and Francis delivered into the tender care of his valet. Nicky confided to Elinor that he should sleep with one ear open, and only hoped that Francis would come out of his room, for he was willing to bet a monkey Bouncer would indeed savage him. Upon this pious aspiration, he took himself off to his own room, there to drop into the deep and sound sleep of youth, from which, Elinor shrewdly judged, nothing less than a cataclysm would rouse him.

But Miss Beccles, for whom Bouncer had no terrors, could not be satisfied, and horrified Elinor by stealing into her room hardly half an hour after the valet's footsteps had been heard retreating to the wing which housed the servants, with the information that she had made it impossible for Francis to leave his bedchamber that night.

'What can you possibly mean, Becky?' Elinor demanded, sitting up, and pushing back the bed-curtains.

'My love, I bethought me of the clothes-line!' whispered the little governess impressively. 'I have securely attached it to the handle of his door, and to the handle of dear Mr. Nicky's door too!'

'Becky!' Elinor exclaimed. 'No, no, you must not! I am sure Bouncer is guard enough! Only think if Mr. Cheviot should discover it! I should never be able to look him in the face again!'

'Dear old fellow!' said Miss Beccles, fondly regarding the faithful hound, who had followed her into the room, and now sat on his haunches, with his ears laid flat, and an expression on his face of vacuous amiability. 'I am sure he is not a nasty fierce dog, are you, Bouncer?'

Bouncer at once assumed the mien of a foolishly sentimental spaniel, and began to pant.

'Becky, when the servants discover it in the morning, only conceive how it must look!'

'Yes, my love, but I am always awake before the servants are stirring, and I shall undo the line, of course. Do not be in a pucker, my dear Mrs. Cheviot! I only thought you would wish to know that I have made all safe. Come, Bouncer, good doggie!'

She glided away again, leaving Elinor to toss and turn on her pillows, rehearsing the lame explanations she might be called upon to make in the morning to a justly offended guest. But the only disturbance consequent upon Miss Beccle's brilliant stroke was caused by Nicky, who, waking betimes, and ascribing this unusual circumstance to some noise which must have penetrated to his consciousness, jumped out of bed, and tried stealthily to open his door. The clothes-line held fast, and Nicky, concluding very naturally that his imprisonment was due to Francis Cheviot's wicked wiles, instantly set up a shout for help. The first to answer the call was Bouncer, who tore up the stairs, and after flinging himself unavailingly at his master's door, set to work to release him by a process of furious excavation.

Miss Beccles, only pausing to cast a shawl over her night-dress, ran out, and seizing Bouncer by his collar, agitatedly begged Nicky to hush! Neither he nor Bouncer paid any heed to this admonition, and it was not until she had with trembling fingers untied her knots, and the commotion had brought not only Elinor, but Barrow, also, to the spot, that the imprecations of the prisoner and the excited barking of the dog abated. The matter being hurriedly explained to Nicky he instantly went off into a shout of laugher, quite sufficient to have roused anyone who had contrived to remain asleep thorough the previous hubbub.

Elinor was in an agony of apprehension, but no sound of stirring came from the guest's chamber.

'Well, it queers me why anyone should take and do such a tedious silly thing!' said Barrow, staring in surprise at the clothes-line. 'A hem set-out it'll be if Mr. Francis comes to hear tell of it!'

Barrow looked from one to the other with such an expression of astonishment on his face that Nicky marched him back to his own wing, favouring him on the way with an explanation which caused him to say with withering scorn: 'Mistress hasn't got no call to suspicion the likes of Mr. Francis! As like as ninepence to nothing, he is!'

'What did you say to Barrow?' demanded Elinor, upon Nicky's return.

He grinned at her. 'I'll not tell you. You would be ready to eat me!'

'Hateful boy! What was it?'

'No, it would make you blush.'

'Oh!' she gasped indignantly. 'Odious!'

'Well, I don't know what else I could have told him!'

'Well, never mind!' She sank her voice to an even lower note, and pointed towards Francis Cheviot's door. 'He cannot have slept through such a noise! Why has he not come out, or called to us to know what is the matter?'

'Hiding under his bed be like,' responded Nicky caustically. 'He is bound to remark upon it!'

'I'll fob him off,' Nicky promised.

In spite of this assurance, it was in the expectation of suffering a considerable degree of embarrassment that the widow descended presently to the breakfast-parlour. But her uninvited guest put in no appearance, and Barrow explained, with a sniff of disapproval, that Crawley had carried up a tray to his bedchamber. Mr. Cheviot, had said Crawley loftily, never left his room until noon.

'Oh, doesn't he, by Jove?' exclaimed Nicky. 'Well, he will, then, for the funeral is at noon!'

He lost no time, after he had consumed his usual hearty breakfast, in going upstairs to break these tidings to Francis. But Francis, who was seated before the dressing-table, wrapped in an exotic robe, and having his nails carefully pared by his valet, remained annoyingly unruffled.

'Yes, dear boy, so I was informed, and you see how early I am up! I grudge no exertion, but how I shall contrive to be dressed in time I know not. After ten already, and I dare say we must set out quite by eleven! Crawley, we must bear in mind that should the Fates be against me, which I do trust, however, will not be found to be the case. I might be obliged to spend an hour over the arrangement of my neckcloth, and that would make me late, you know. Perhaps I should make the first attempts at once.'

Nicky stared at the pile of black cravats, each at least a foot wide, which lay on the table. 'Good God, you cannot need the half of such a stock!' he exclaimed. 'Do you mean to stay here a month?'

Francis eyed the pile anxiously. 'Do you think I shall not?' he said. 'I do hope you may be right, dear Nicholas, but it is by no means unknown for me to ruin a score before I have achieved just the correct folds. It would be so disrespectful to poor Eustace if I were to attend his obsequies in a clumsily tied cravat! You will have to leave me, dear boy; I find it so agitating to be watched while I am engaged on the most crucial part of my toilet. But do tell me, before you go, why was I so rudely awakened this morning?'

'Oh, so you did not sleep through the commotion?' said Nicky.

'My dear Nicholas, I am neither deaf nor a heavy sleeper. One would have supposed a regiment of solders to have stormed the house!'

'I wonder you should not have come out of your room to discover the cause!'

Francis turned a shocked gaze upon him. '*Come out of my room before I had been shaved?*' he said. 'Dear boy, are you mad?'

'Oh, well!' Nicky said impatiently. 'It was nothing, after all! I could not open my door: it was stuck, you know: all the doors in this house are so warped there was never anything like it! Barrow was obliged to thrust his shoulder against it, for I thought if I tugged at it the handle would very likely come off.'

'Dear me!' said Francis mildly. 'What a very violent young man you are, dear Nicholas!'

Nicky went off to find Elinor, and to tell her that there was no making anything of Francis.

'Do you think he can have tried to open his own door?' she asked anxiously.

'Lord, I don't know, but I should not be surprised! He is the smokiest fellow, and lies as fast as a dog would trot, I dare say! But only wait till I tell John of the cravats he has brought with him! John cannot bear a dandy!'

Apparently the cravats were not that day recalcitrant, for punctually at eleven o'clock Francis descended the stairs, dressed, with the exception of a gray waistcoat, in funeral black, and followed by Crawley, carrying his fur-lined cloak, gloves, hat, and ebony cane. His chaise stood at the door, and it had been arranged that he should take Nicky up with him as far as Wisborough Green, where funeral carriages were to await them.

Francis greeted his hostess with all his usual urbanity, assuring her that but for such trifling disagreebles as a mouse gnawing in the wainscoting, Bouncer's predilection for scratching himself on the landing just outside his door, the matutinal habits of apparently a hundred cockerels, and Nicky's unfortunate contretemps with his bedroom door, he had passed an excellent night. The only thing that threatened, in fact, to ruffle his placidity was an ineradicable fear that the wind was backing round to the north-east, in which case, he apologetically warned Elinor, it would be impossible for him to leave Highnoons that day, starting his journey, as he must, at an advanced hour of the afternoon and without the hope of reaching London before night. Her civility obliged her to say what was proper, but her heart sank, and when Francis had been tenderly packed into the chaise, and the door shut upon him and his impatient companion, she went off to ask the gardener what he thought of the weather. He said there was a nasty cold wind a-blowing up. She went dejectedly back to the house, to give Mrs. Barrow due warning, but that competent woman was so delighted to have two girls from the village at her beck and call, not to mention the gardener's wife, whom she had been briskly bullying all the morning, that she merely asked whether her mistress preferred her to make a pheasant-pie, or to serve up a couple of broiled fowls and mushrooms for dinner.

The funeral, meanwhile, passed off as smoothly as could be desired, Francis occupying the first carriage in solitary state, the three Carlyon brothers following in the second; while a scattering of persons of consequence who lived in the neighbourhood, and who had put in an appearance more from a desire to gratify Carlyon than from any regard for the deceased, made the cortège respectable. The tail was brought up by a few humbler personages, chief amongst whom was the doctor.

A cold collation having been prepared at the Hall for the chief mourners, all the more genteel personages repaired there after the interment, when Carlyon had the opportunity to observe that although Louis De Castres was absent, there were present two gentlemen who had come down from London at Francis's behest, and were almost as beautifully arrayed as he was himself. They excused themselves clearly, on the score of having the drive back to London to accomplish; and the local gentry, finding an awkwardness in the occasion, and perhaps oppressed by the demeanour of Mr. Cheviot, who seemed crushed by woe, soon followed their example, the last to leave being Sir Matthew Kendal, who shook Carlyon by the hand, saying gruffly that all was well that had ended well. Feeling that the sentiments underlying this remark might have been more felicitously expressed, he coloured up to roots of his grizzled hair, and sought to cover his confusion by turning to issue a ferocious warning to Nicky to keep that damned dog of his off his preserves if he did not want to see him shot, and hung up as a warning to other such marauders. After this threat, which he palliated by a playful punch in his young friend's ribs, he took himself off, and John was at last at liberty to give vent to the annoyance which had been consuming him ever since the return of the funeral party to the Hall. Speaking with a restraint which only served to emphasize the profound nature of his vexation, he looked Francis up and down, and said: 'I was not aware that you cherished such peculiarly strong sentiments towards our cousin. Your grief, I dare say, does credit to your heart, but, for my part, I should be glad, now that only ourselves remain to be edified by it, if you would abate its violence!'

Nicky, who had just raised a glass of Madeira to his lips, was taken with a fit of choking which, while it for once brought down upon his head no rebuke from his stern brother, earned him a pained glance from Francis. A heavy sigh was the only answer Francis vouchsafed to John. He raised his handkerchief to his eyes, and kept it there.

John's lips tightened for a moment before he said: 'Come, Cheviot, this is the outside of enough!'

Francis shook his head, saying into the folds of his handkerchief: 'Alas, you are mistaken! I have received the most distressing tidings. These unmanly tears are not, I blush to confess, for our unfortunate young relative, but for one nearer to me by the ties of affection. Pardon me! It has cost me a severe effort to bear my part at this feast with any degree of fortitude.

No, feast is not the right word: I should have said wake, but it is odd how often the funeral baked-meats are partaken of in a spirit almost of jollification. My dear John I have sustained a terrible shock, which has quite overborne me!'

Both John and Nicky stood staring at him, the wildest improbabilities darting through their brains. 'Why – what –?' stammered Nicky, setting down his wine-glass.

Francis raised his face from his handkerchief to reply in broken accents: 'You can scarcely fail to have remarked Louis' absence to-day!'

'Young De Castres?' John said impatiently. 'Well, and what of that?'

Francis made a despairing gesture with one white hand. 'Dead!' he uttered, and sank into his handkerchief again.

'*What?*' Nicky gasped. 'But –'

John's grip on his elbow silenced him. John said: 'Indeed! I am sorry for it. I fancy I saw him only the other day in town. I conclude his taking-off was of a sudden nature?'

Francis shuddered eloquently. 'Stabbed to death!' he moaned. 'His body left under a bush in Lincoln's Inn Fields! One of my oldest friends! I am wholly unmanned.'

'Good God!' John said blankly.

Carlyon's quiet voice spoke from the doorway. He had come back into the room from seeing Sir Matthew off just in time to hear this revelation, and paused on the threshold, intently watching Francis. 'Where had you this news?'

'It is in the *Morning Post*, which Godfrey Balcombe was so thoughtful as to bring down to me,' said Francis. 'Poor fellow, he meant it to be a kindness but he little new what a blow he was handing me! He was not acquainted with Louis, you know – scarcely glanced at the fatal paragraph! You must forgive me: my poor Louis! So intimate a friend!'

Carlyon shut the door, and advanced into the room. 'You must feel it indeed,' he said. 'I am aware that you have for long been upon terms of the closest friendship with De Castres. There can be no doubt, I collect?'

'Ah, you would seek to encourage me to hope! But it will not do: 'M. L –. De C –,' you know – *the scion of a distinguished family of French emigrants!* Alas, I cannot doubt it is my poor Louis! That unfortunate turn he had for walking, instead of calling for a chair or a hackney! And never so much as a link-boy to go with him! How often have I warned him of the dangers of this practice, but he would never attend, and now we see the unhappy end of it. And I sending round a billet to his lodging the very day I left London, begging him to lend me his support at Eustace's funeral! Poor fellow, I fear he was even then no more!'

'It is very shocking, indeed. You said he was killed in Lincoln's Inn Fields, I think? Pray, at what hour was he set upon?'

Francis shook his head. 'It is not stated in my newspaper. It was at night, of course, but I dare say it will never be discovered precisely when, or by whose hand. What could have taken poor dear Louis to such a locality at such a time? Stripped of his purse and all his jewellery! Left to welter in his blood! Horrible!'

He shuddered again, and with so much revulsion that it was plain he was a good deal affected. Carlyon signed to Nicky to pour him a glass of brandy, and said: 'Is it thought to have been the work of footpads?'

Francis nodded, and took the brandy from Nicky, thanking him in a broken voice. 'Such a sordid motive! Murdered for a few paltry trinkets, and, I dare swear, no more than five or ten guineas, for he was not a rich man, you know. It must be a warning to us all! And to reflect that – But I must try to compose myself, or I fear I shall be quite unwell! There is something so particularly disgusting to one of my delicate sensibilities in the very thought of bloodshed, and, indeed, all forms of violence! Even at school I could not bring myself to engage even in sparring exercise, for the sight of a bloody nose invariably made me swoon. Yes, I feel sure I must seem a poor creature to you, but so it is, and one cannot help one's nature, after all! I will take a little more of your excellent brandy, Carlyon, and then, if you will pardon me, I think I should take my leave of you. Repose, and – yes, perhaps a glass of hartshorn and water: Crawley shall mix one for me. Mrs. Cheviot, I am persuaded, will respect my desire for solitude until I have learnt to master my emotion. Dear Nicholas, if you mean to accompany me, I wonder if you will be so very obliging as not to talk to me?'

'Thank you, I mean to ride over a little later.'

'Your thoughtfulness does you credit, my dear boy. I am so grateful!'

He drank off his second glass, and rose to his feet. He said earnestly: 'Thank God I brought a black waistcoat with me! This gray one does very well for Eustace, but it is now quite out of tune with my mood. My poor Louis!'

Neither John nor Nicky could find anything to say in answer to all this, but Carlyon replied with his usual calm good sense, and, as soon as word was brought that Mr. Cheviot's chaise was waiting at the door, conducted him out to it. When he returned it was to find that John had picked up from Francis's chair his copy of the *Morning Post*, folded open at the requisite sheet, and was just starting to read aloud, in a slow, stupefied voice: '*A melancholy event happened two evenings since in Lincoln's Inn Fields, where the body of a Young Man, done to death under circumstances of horrid Barbarity, was discovered yesterday morning by Mr. B –, a Clerk employed in the Chambers of a certain well-known Attorney. We understand the unfortunate Young Man to have been M. L –. De C –., the Scion of one of the Distinguished families of French Emigrants with which the Metropolis still abounds. There would appear to be little room for doubt that the motive for this Brutal Murder was robbery, since we learn that M. L –. De C –'s pockets had been ransacked, and watch, fobs, seals, pins, rings – in fact, every adjunct to a Gentleman's apparel, stript from his person. We think it not ineligible to advert yet once again in these columns to the shocking prevalence of pickpockets in the Metropolis, and to demand for our fellow Citizens some better protection from the violence of these free-booters than the* Vigilance *of the Decrepid Dotards who at present patrol our streets, and –* Oh, et cetera, et cetera!' John concluded impatiently. 'My God, Ned, what devilish stratagems have we stumbled on? Pickpockets! I wish it might be so indeed!'

'Is that all it says in the *Post*?' asked Carlyon.

'That's all, save for the usual plaint about the ineptitude of the Watch, and of the constables. It's enough, my God!'

'Nicky, go and enquire of Chorley whether the London papers are yet arrived, will you? There may be something more in the *Times*, or the *Advertizer*.'

Nicky went out of the room at once. John flung down the *Morning Post*, and said gravely: 'Ned, this is a shocking business! I do not wonder that Cheviot should be so overcome. There can be no question but that he is in this affair hand-in-glove with De Castres, and those who must stand behind De Castres. If he fails to discover what is so desperately needed he must shake in shoes to think what may be his own fate!'

'You think De Castres was murdered by French agents?'

'I do not know, but that presents itself to me as the likeliest answer to a riddle which I'll take my oath will never be solved! If De Castres had promised his masters that memorandum, or his copy of it –! He may even have received moneys already, or the suspicion may have entered their minds that he was fobbing them off with a plausible tale, and meant himself to reap all the advantage. I have never believed him to have been a principal in this business: I still do not. Something must have been known against him had that been so, and I cannot discover that he is any more suspect than any other young Frenchman at large in this country.'

'Yes,' said Nicky, who had come back into the room. 'Or he might have been killed by one of our people, might he not? One of our spies, I mean?'

'I suppose it is possible,' John replied reluctantly. 'It would be grossly improper, however, and I prefer to think – not but what the fellows one is forced to employ in that work have necessarily few scruples. Well, what has the *Times* to say, Ned?'

'Nothing more than you have read in the *Post*,' Carlyon answered, handing the paper over to him.

'I can't find any mention in the *Advertizer*,' said Nicky, rapidly scanning the columns. 'What stuff they do print, to be sure! Here's something about Grafted Gooseberry Plants! I should like to know who cares a button for that! *On Friday a butcher exposed his wife for sale in Smithfield Market* . . . Lord! *Curious Incident at Rotherhithe: A young whale came up the river* . . . I wish I might live in Rotherhithe, by Jupiter I do! *A very elegant dinner given by the Lord Mayor at the Mansion House.* . . . Oh, here we have it at last, but the meanest little snippet only! *The body of the unfortunate young man which was discovered in Lincoln's Inn Fields yesterday morning is now established to be that of a distinguished French Emigrant, well-known in Fashionable Circles.* Well! The shabbiest thing! Oh, Ned, I would not have missed this for anything you could offer me! I shall go back to Highnoons at once, for depend upon it Cheviot will only be awaiting his chance to steal that document from us!'

'Yes,' Carlyon said slowly. 'Yes.'

John looked at him narrowly. 'What's in your head?'

Carlyon returned no answer, but after a moment said abruptly: 'I am going up to London. Nicky, will you tell them to bring round the light post-chaise as soon as they may?'

'Going to London?' repeated John. 'What the devil for?'

'To try what I can discover there. I shall come back as speedily as I am able. Do you remain here, John, and keep Nicky from doing anything foolhardy! Nicky, understand me, you may stay at Highnoons, and you may watch Francis Cheviot as much as you please as long as you can do so without his finding you a hindrance he might be tempted to remove out of his path. But on no account are you to run your head into danger!'

'Lord, Ned, I'm not afraid of a fellow like Francis Cheviot!'

'Francis Cheviot is a very dangerous man,' Carlyon said curtly, and left the room.

Nicky blinked at John. 'What the deuce makes him think so?' he asked. 'For of all the lily-livered –'

'I don't know, but he was saying something of the sort to me the other night. Of course, if Francis has engaged himself to hand over a certain document to the French, and knows his partner in this pretty piece of treason to be dead, I dare say he will be as dangerous as a cornered rat. Now, mind you do as Ned tells you, Nick! I shall come over to Highnoons myself presently, but it's not to be expected Francis will make any attempt to search the house during the day, for he would scarcely dare to run the risk of being discovered at that work. I have a good mind to spend the night at Highnoons, quite secretly, of course.'

'Why, he is afraid for his life Bouncer will bite him!' Nicky laughed. 'And he knows Bouncer is loose in the house all night!'

'Take care you do not find that dog of yours has been poisoned!' John said grimly.

Fifteen

*E*linor and Miss Beccles had spent a quiet, housewifely morning, during the course of which Miss Beccles had announced with simple satisfaction that she believed Highnoons would soon be as pretty a resident as one might find anywhere. She so plainly envisaged a prolonged sojourn in it that Elinor was constrained to remind her that as soon as she was at liberty to do so she was to sell the house. Miss Beccles said that she was by no means persuaded of this being her best course. 'We might be so comfortable here!' she said, with a tiny sigh.

Elinor could only assure her that wherever she went there would be a place for her dearest Becky, but that there could be no question of her remaining on at Highnoons. To which Miss Beccles replied that no doubt his lordship would know best what she should do. This goaded Elinor into delivering herself of a pithy condemnation of his lordship's tyrannical disposition, and utter lack of regard for the scruples of a decent female. Miss Beccles said wistfully that she did so much like a masterful man, an observation that sent the widow out of the room with something perilously akin to a flounce.

It was useless to expect Miss Beccles to enter into her sentiments. Indeed, no one with whom she was now in daily contact seemed to have the least appreciation of the awkwardness of her situation. She could not but realize that she was allowing herself to be swept along towards a future that was impenetrably wrapped in a haze of speculation. She could not imagine what was to become of her. It seemed improbable that anything beyond the merest competence would be saved from the wreck of Eustace Cheviot's fortune: indeed, she could not have borne to have found herself living in affluence as a consequence of her marriage, and must, she told herself, have made over any considerable property by a deed of gift. But, since she was an honest woman, she was bound to own to herself that after this interlude in her drab existence she would find it very hard to return to her previous occupation. A little house, which she could share with Becky, in a modest quarter of the town, seemed to be the best she could hope for, and although this, a week earlier, had represented the sum total of her ambitions, for some reason or other it no longer held any attraction for her.

The first fruits of the brief notice of her nuptials, which Carlyon had inserted in the London newspapers, had come to her hand already. Letters from two of her cousins, and her least beloved uncle, had reached Highnoons, brought up to the house from the mail-office at Billingshurst by the groom, who had gone there on an errand. Her uncle's missive, couched in dignified terms, showed him to have taken offence at the secrecy of her marriage, and reminded her, over two crossed pages, that it had not been at his wish or instigation that she had abandoned the shelter of his roof. He had apparently missed the other notice, of Eustace Cheviot's demise, and wrote that he hoped she might not regret an alliance with one of whom all reports spoke ill.

The cousins sprinkled their letters with points of admiration, and were obviously agog with curiosity to learn all that must lie behind the formal advertisement in the *Times*. Both begged her to recall their affection for her, and not to hesitate to invite them to Highnoons if they could be of service to her in her hour of trial. Elinor lost no time in replying to these kind offers, in civil but repelling terms.

The return of Francis Cheviot from the funeral, in a beaten-down condition that made it necessary for Crawley to be summoned to lend him the support of his arm, was a surprise, but as nothing to the surprise occasioned by his faltering explanation of his overmastering grief. Elinor could only gaze at him in horror. As little as Carlyon did she believed that the young Frenchman's murder had been at the hands of pickpockets. Some dreadful and sinister force was at work, and she could not suppose that it would cease with the death of De Castres. She had not the least guess who the assassin might be, whether an English agent, or a French one, but that it was connected with some document which De Castres, and Francis Cheviot, and perhaps others as well, believed to be concealed at Highnoons she did not doubt. In her first dismay, she was almost ready to have torn the house down brick by brick, only to be rid of whatever was so cunningly hidden in it, but soberer reflection gave her thoughts a more proper direction, and she could not but acknowledge that it was the part of a loyal Englishwoman to do her possible to frustrate the enemies of her country, however ruthless these might be. But she wished she had not been the appointed Englishwoman.

Looking upon Francis's pallid countenance, she could not wonder at his discomfiture. Although she might have little dependence on the sensibility which cast him into such apparent woe, she could not doubt that he was labouring under considerable nervous tension. It found expression in a shriller note in his voice, and the testiness with which he rounded on his valet for some fault. His smile seemed forced, and his movements less measured and graceful than they had been before the receipt of the tidings from London. Elinor could almost have pitied him had she not stood in such dread that his fear of the implacable master whom both he and De Castres served might lead him to undertake some desperate action in which she might become involved. She was in a fever to put out the whole to Carlyon, and once Francis had gone upstairs to lie down upon his bed, with smelling-salts and hartshorn and the blinds drawn, she could scarcely drag herself away from the parlour windows, which commanded a view of the front drive. Provokingly matter-of-fact Carlyon might be, but she owned it would be an inexpressible comfort to see his tall figure entering the house, and to hear his quiet voice coolly making light of her alarms.

But it was not Carlyon who at last came riding up from the gate, but only Nicky, who had shed his funeral wear, in defiance of his brother John, for a blue coat with large silver buttons, and very yellow buckskins; and was bestriding a raw-boned hunter which took instant exception to Bouncer's ecstatic greeting of his master. Nicky was fully occupied for a minute or two in a tussle with his horse, but he caught sight of Elinor presently, and waved, shouting: 'I'll just stable Rufus! Isn't he a proper highbred 'un? Just playing off his tricks, you know! He don't care a button for Bouncer, of course. He's been eating his head off in the stable, poor old fellow!'

She nodded, and smiled, able to sympathize, even in her agitated state of mind, with his pride in his horse. He rode on towards the stables, and she resigned herself to a prolonged wait while he saw the noble animal properly rubbed down, and bestowed.

Twenty minutes later he came striding into the house, and, laying down his hat and whip on the table in the hall, said in an undervoice vibrant with excitement: 'Where is Cheviot?'

'In his bedchamber, with the blinds drawn, and Crawley chafing his feet. Oh, Nicky —'

'Hush! Come into the back-room, cousin: we must not be talking here, where we might be overheard.'

'Oh, no!' she agreed, going towards the book-room obediently. 'But indeed I think he is in truth laid down upon his bed. He is suffering the greatest irritation of nerves: I cannot allow that to be called in question.'

'Lord, yes, don't I know it!' he said, shutting the door securely, and treading over to the fire to cast another log on to it. 'Sick as a horse! He told you that Louis De Castres has been murdered?'

'Yes, and the reflections this shocking event conjures up are so horrid that my own nerves are in a sad way. Where is your brother? I had hoped he might have come back here with you!'

'No, no, you will not be seeing Ned to-day!' Nicky replied. 'He has gone up to London – driving post, you know, and taking his own bays over the first two stages! Prime goers, those bays of his! Beautiful steppers!'

'Gone up to London!' she exclaimed in a stupefied tone.

'Yes. He said he would come back as fast as he could, but –'

'Does he know of that Frenchman's death?' she demanded, interrupting him without compunction.

'Oh, yes! Well, of course he does! It is to do with that he has gone to town, though he would not tell us what he meant to do there. John is at the Hall still, and if you should like it he says he will spend the night here, without Francis's being any the wiser, of course. And, by Jupiter, Cousin Elinor, I must take care Bouncer does not eat anything I do not give him myelf, for John thinks Francis, or that tooth-drawer of a valet of his, may seek to poison him! But I have been training Bouncer not to take food from the hand of any stranger, so I dare say there is not the least fear on that score.'

She refrained from telling him that his favourite apparently considered the offer of a bone or a scrap of meat sufficient introduction to put him on terms of acquaintance with the seediest stranger, and said: 'Your brother knew this, and has gone off to town without a word vouchsafed to me?'

'Oh, he knew I was to return here, and should inform you of his journey! It is the most famous affair, cousin! We cannot tell what may happen next!'

'Very true! And for that reason I should have wished to have had speech with his lordship!'

'Well, I fancy he don't know either, but I don't mind telling you this, cousin: he thinks Francis is a very dangerous man! He said so, and bade me take care what I was about here.'

'Oh, he did?' exclaimed Elinor, rigid with wrath. 'I am sure I am very much obliged to him! And am I to take care what I am about, or is that of no consequence?'

Nicky smiled engagingly down at her. 'Bouncer and I will take good care of you, Cousin Elinor.'

'I have a very good mind to pack up my trunk, and to leave this house within the hour!'

'You will not!'

'No, I will not,' she said crossly. 'But it is the most infamous thing! When I see your brother – if ever I do see him again, which very likely I shall not, as I dare say I shall soon be found with my throat cut from ear to ear! – I shall have something to say to him! Oh, when I think of the hideous case in which I am, and all through his crazy schemes, which he has the effrontery to say are very sensible, I could – I could go into strong hysterics!'

He laughed. 'Ay! You will have a spasm, I dare say, like one of my sisters' governesses! But this is no time to be funning, cousin!'

'Funning!'

'Now, be serious! Oh, Cousin Elinor, did you ever suppose – when you were quite young, I mean: in the schoolroom – that you would one day find yourself pitted against French agents?'

'No, Nicky, I did not. Nothing that has happened to me during the past week did I expect, even when I was in the schoolroom – where I very much wish I was now!'

'I am persuaded you do not! Why, how could you? But the thing is, what will Francis do now?'

'That thought has been occupying my mind this past hour.'

'He is such a poor-spirited fellow, you know, that I do not at all believe that he will attempt anything of a violent nature. I wish he would!'

'Yes, I am sure you do.'

'No,' said Nicky, unheeding. 'If Ned is right, and he is indeed a dangerous fellow – but I own I cannot believe that a fellow that prefers cats to dogs, and will not stir without he has his smelling-salts with him can be worth a button! – but if it is so indeed, then I'll sear he will go to work in some devilish cunning way you and I would never think of!'

'You are very likely right, and every word you say adds to my conviction that I had best pack up and be off to Mrs. Macclesfield this very day.'

'Mrs. Macclesfield? Oh, that female you was to have gone to!

It is a good thing Ned would not let you, isn't it? You would not have liked to have missed all this sport!'

Elinor had not consorted with adolescents for six years without learning when it was useless to persevere in the attempt to convey to them ideas that were wholly alien to their minds, and she now made no further effort to bring Nicky to an appreciation of her own sentiments. She agreed that it would have been a shocking thing to have missed spending a week in almost continuous alarm; and was rewarded by his telling her with impulsive warmth that he had known all along that she was a right one. He then did what lay in his power to undermine whatever fortitude was left to her by recounting, with embellishments, John's theories on the murder of De Castres.

'John does not think that it can have been one of our fellows,' he said, striding about the room with all the energetic restlessness of a young gentleman itching to be up and doing. 'He says, of course, there is no knowing what such men will be at, but he inclines to the belief Louis must have been killed by those who employ him.'

'Only for failing to procure what was wanted?' she faltered.

'Oh, no! John has a notion they may have suspected him of not dealing quite honestly with them. You see, he is persuaded that Louis was never a principal, because nothing seems to be known about him, and of course our people are generally pretty watchful, and know more than you would suppose. The thing is that there is very likely someone, and I dare say more than just one man, who is behind it all. I should not be at all surprised if it were someone no one suspects in the least. What capital fun it will be if he comes to have a touch at us himself!'

'Yes, indeed! And to make it even better, I dare say, since he appears to be such a desperate character, he will stop at nothing to obtain his ends.'

'Exactly so! Particularly if he should suppose that we have that paper safely in our possession!'

She could not repress a gasp of dismay, but common sense

came to her rescue, and she suggested diffidently that if they had had the paper they must surely have restored it to its rightful owners.

Nicky, after considering this with some dissatisfaction, was obliged to own that there was something in what she said. He cheered up after a moment or two, and said: 'But only conceive what a famous tangle it is, with the only man who knew where the paper was hid dead, and you living in this house, so that whatever is done to find the thing must be done by stealth! The more I think of it the more I believe they are bungling the affair sadly! The thing to have done would have been to have got into Highnoons by a ruse. By Jupiter, yes! Someone should have been sent to you as a servant, and only think how easily a seeming servant could ransack the place!'

Her mind darted to the two young wenches hired by Mrs. Barrow, to the carpenter who had been sent for to mend defective hinges, and broken chair-legs, and even to the boy who had been engaged to assist the gardener in his labours. She started half out of her chair, exclaiming: 'Good God! You do not think that that man who was working here all the morning – or the maids – or –'

'No, I'm afraid not,' Nicky said wistfully. 'You mean Redditch, do you? I must say it is a first-rate notion, but I have known Redditch all my life. And as for the maids, ain't one of them Mrs. Barrow's niece, and the other a girl from the village?'

'Of course!' she said, sinking back again. 'I do not know how I came to be so stupid! It is your fault, you horrid boy, for putting such dreadful ideas into my head! And now I come to think of it, I have not the least apprehension that any sinister stranger will arrive at Highnoons, for it is not at all reasonable to suppose that the man who employed De Castres can be aware that your cousin was employed as a go-between.'

'Why not?' demanded Nicky, staring.

'Because if this dreadful person knew who was the man from whom De Castres obtained information he must surely have approached him himself! Why should the French Government be paying two persons where one would suffice? I am sure they would never do so!'

Nicky thought this over. 'Well, yes,' he admitted, in some discontent. 'I dare say that may be so. And that is why Francis is forced to act in the matter himself, which I'll wager he never wanted to do! I must say, it will be a dead bore if Francis is the only man we have to reckon with!'

He continued walking about the room, advancing and discarding theories, until relief came to Mrs. Cheviot in the solid shape of Mr. John Carlyon, who, after shaking hands with his hostess, prosaically recommended Nicky to take himself off for a brisk walk.

'Walk! I do not want to go for a walk!' said Nicky, quite affronted.

'Then sit down, and do not be fidgeting Mrs. Cheviot in this way. What has become of your guest, ma'am?'

'He is laid down upon his bed.'

He smiled. 'Well, my brother may say what he likes, but I shall not readily believe that we have anything to fear from Francis Cheviot! I trust you have not allowed yourself to be alarmed by what I make no doubt Nicky has told you?'

She regarded him with patent hostility. 'Dear me, how excessively like your brother Carlyon you are, to be sure!' she remarked.

'Like Ned? No, that I am sure I am not!' he replied, laughing.

'You are mistaken. The resemblance is most pronounced. I might have fancied him to have been addressing me. What a nonsensical thing it would be in me to allow myself to become alarmed by a trifle such as murder!'

'My dear Mrs. Cheviot, nothing of the sort is likely to threaten you, believe me! But I cannot but feel that it is not comfortable for you to be left with Cheviot in your house at night, when he is most likely to make the attempt to possess himself of that memorandum.'

'Hey!' said Nicky, ruffling up. 'I shall be here!'

'Yes,' said John unkindly. 'Falling over suits of armour, I dare

207

say. Tell me, ma'am, shall I come over to you? I may be perfectly comfortable on the sofa in this room, you know. I would set old Barrow to mount guard if it were not an object with us to keep the servants in ignorance of our suspicions.'

She thanked him, but upon reflection declined his offer, saying that she was content to trust in Nicky and in Bouncer, who had taken such a dislike to Francis that he barked whenever he encountered him, and would certainly rouse the household if Francis ventured out of his chamber during the night. Bouncer opened a pair of sleepy eyes, and gently thumped his tail on the carpet.

'Yes,' said Nicky gratefully, 'and if I tie him to the foot of the stairs, after Francis has gone to bed, there can be no fear of his giving him poisoned meat, because he will never be able to come near enough to him to do so. He will have roused the whole house before Francis has had time to reach the head of the stairs.'

'Well, ma'am, I own I think you are wise not to refine too much upon suspicions which may yet prove to be without foundation,' John said. 'Indeed, when I reflect soberly I find myself loth to believe that we are not all of us hunting for mares' nests.'

Such a spiritless remark as this could not have been expected to appeal to Nicky, who was provoked into joining issue with his brother in a very heated manner. But when, a few minutes before dinner was announced, Francis came down from his room, his demeanour gave a good deal of colour to John's prosaic reflections. He wore, besides a complete suit of black, embellished with a crape-edged handkerchief, so woebegone a countenance that it was hard to suspect him of duplicity. His mind seemed to be wholly absorbed by the two evils of his friend's death, and his own incipient cold, and it was difficult to decide which loomed the larger in his brain. Whenever the thought of Louis De Castres came into his head it cast him into a silence broken only by deep sighs; but his conversation turned for the most part on a sore throat which he trusted would not be found to be putrid. He partook sparingly of the pheasant pie, trifled with the ratafia-cream, and declined mournfully to taste the roasted cheese. Nicky, whose ambition was to goad him into betraying himself, divulged to him the discovery of the secret stair, but as the revelation was met with a strong shudder and an urgent prayer to Mrs. Cheviot securely to nail up such an undesirable feature of the house, he could not be said to have got much good by this gambit. Nor did a reference to Eustace Cheviot's papers succeed better. Francis said that he had no doubt of their being in the utmost disorder, but begged no one would ask him to assist in unravelling them. 'For I have no head for business, dear boy: positively none at all! Your estimable brother will do very much better without me. I am so thankful it is he and not I who is an executor of poor Eustace's Will!'

When the party gathered in the parlour after dinner, he very soon detected a draught, and directed Nicky where to place a handsome needlework-screen so that he might be protected from it. But even this did not serve, and with many apologies to Elinor, he desired Nicky to summon Crawley to his assistance. 'For if I were to take one of my colds, you know, I might be tied to Highnoons for a month,' he said earnestly. 'The thought of putting Mrs. Cheviot to such inconvenience is very disturbing.'

Elinor could only hope that her countenance did not betray how completely she agreed with him. Miss Beccles came forward with offers of remedies, and Crawley presently draped his cloak round his sounders, and promised to have ready a foot-bath of hot mustard-and-water when he should come up to bed. This he soon did, leaving Nicky to exclaim: 'He is the paltriest fellow! Why, I think him worse than Eustace, and as for standing in awe of him, pooh!'

Even Miss Beccles allowed herself to be dissuaded from again roping the handle of his door to Nicky's. Bouncer was tethered to the banister at the foot of the stairs, and provided with a rug to lie upon. This, however, was found to be a failure, that free-spirited animal being unable to brook such unaccustomed restraint, and yelping so persistently that Nicky was obliged to untie him.

After this, peace descended upon the house, and remained unbroken until the clatter of dust-pans and brushes showed that the servants were once more at work.

Scarcely had Elinor risen from the breakfast-table than Crawley presented himself to her, wearing a most lugubrious expression, and informing her in suitably grave accents that his master found himself far from well, and begged that a doctor might be summoned. She promised that a message should be dispatched to Dr. Greenlaw, and hoped that Mr. Cheviot had been able to swallow some breakfast.

'Thank you, madam, just a little thin gruel,' said Crawley. 'I have taken the liberty of requesting the cook to make some arrowroot jelly for my master, which he might be able to partake of a little later.'

'Mutton and herbs make a very supporting broth,' suggested Miss Beccles helpfully.

The valet bowed, but shook his head. 'My master, thank you, miss, can never stomach mutton. I took the precaution of packing a pot of Dr. Ratcliffe's Restorative Pork Jelly in the larger valise, and shall endeavour to persuade my master to swallow a spoonful every now and then.'

An enquiry in the kitchen brought corroboration of this tale, and with it a tirade from Mrs. Barrow on the valetudinarian habits of a young gentleman who should, she held, be above coddling himself in such a fashion.

'I disremember when I've seen Mr. Francis here without he took ill,' remarked Barrow dispassionately. 'I mind one time he gave his ankle a twist, and carried on like he was burnt to the socket. I dare say we'll have him here a se'nnight, setting us all by the ears.'

'By Jupiter, we will not!' declared Nicky, when this was reported to him. 'I see his game, cousin: he thinks to remain on till he may take us off our guard, but it will not answer! I'll ride for Greenlaw myself – Rufus needs a good gallop, you know! – and see if I don't get him to have Francis up out of his bed this very day! Yes, and on the road to London, what's more!'

'I wish you may!' she said. 'but I do not know how it is to be contrived.'

His eyes danced. 'Don't you, though? Smallpox in the village!'

She was obliged to laugh, but doubted whether he would be able to persuade the respectable physician into perjuring himself so shockingly.

'Oh, lord, yes, nothing easier!' Nicky assured her. 'I can always make old Greenlaw do what I want. The only rub is that I may have to hunt all over for him. But I dare say I shall discover in which direction he has gone a-visiting. Everyone knows his gig!'

He went off to the stables, accompanied by Bouncer, whom, however, he brought back to the house, firmly shutting him in. Bouncer, having scratched vigorously at the front door for some time, and addressed it in a crescendo of most distressful sounds, was lured away by Miss Beccles, who held out a bone to him as a bait to follow her to the back premises. He there consumed the offering, afterwards departing on a foraging expedition of his own through a low window which he found to be conveniently open. Elinor, who caught sight of him from an upper window, sternly bade him return, a command to which he turned a deaf ear. The chance to enjoy a morning's sport had not come in this way lately. And he was never one to let opportunity slip.

Elinor, accepting defeat, closed the window, and went down to the kitchen for a prolonged conference with its chatelaine. Retreating at last from Mrs. Barrow's volubility, she went into the book-room, to write a careful letter of unconvincing explanation to her Aunt Sophia, who, one of her cousins had warned her, had formed the intention of sending her meek husband into Sussex to discover the truth of her unhappy niece's reprehensibly secret nuptials. She was engaged on this task when Miss Beccles came in with an imposing inventory of all the linen in the house, written out in her delicate copperplate, and copiously annotated with descriptions of rents, darns, and thin patches. Elinor thanked her, and promised to read it carefully, a formality the little governess was insistent should be observed.

Miss Beccles then trotted away again, zestfully determined to compile a further inventory, this time of all the pickles, preserves, dried fruit, and household remedies to be found in the still-room. Elinor finished her letter, folded and sealed it, and laid it by for Carlyon to frank for her. To oblige Miss Beccles, she glanced perfunctorily through the inventory, initialled it, as she had been directed, and folded the stiff sheets neatly. It occurred to her that Nicky should have returned by this time, and she glanced towards the clock on the mantelpiece, only to be exasperated for the fiftieth time since she had come to Highnoons by the realization that it was not going. She got up, the folded inventory still in her hand, and walked over to the fireplace, intending to discover if the clock was broken, as all had assumed, or was merely suffering from lack of winding. The works could only be reached from the back, so she laid the inventory down on the mantelpiece, and carefully shifted the heavy clock round at right-angles to the wall. The door to it was found to be locked, and resisted her efforts to pull it open, so she was obliged to abandon the attempt, and to replace it in position. She picked up the inventory again, and was just adjusting the clock, which she had not set quite straight, when a faint sound came to her ears, as of a creaking board. Her hands dropped; she was in the act of turning round when something struck her a stunning blow on the head, and knocked her senseless.

Sixteen

*N*icky, entering the house by one of the side-doors that opened into an ante-room, hung up his hat and whip, and went striding off to the front hall, calling out to Miss Beccles, whom he saw at the head of the stairs: 'Where is Cousin Elinor? I had such a piece of work to find our doctor! But he is coming, never fear! Why, what's amiss?'

This exclamation was provoked by Francis's voice, agitatedly raised in the back-room. 'Miss Beccles! Crawley! Barrow! Nicholas! Will no one hear me? Come this instant? Oh, dear, what can have happened?'

Three bounds took Nicholas to the door of the book-room. He was brought up short by the sight of his hostess lying inanimate on the hearth-rug, with Francis Cheviot on his knees beside her, distractedly splashing water from a vase of snowdrops over her ashen face. The snowdrops lay scattered beside her; the cushion from one of the window-seats had been cast on to the floor; and the casement was swinging wide on its hinges.

'You villain, what have you done?' thundered Nicky, hurrying forward.

'Do not waste time asking me what *I* have done!' Francis besought him. 'Summon Miss Beccles, my dear boy! Burnt feathers! Where is Crawley? Crawley will know what to do to bring her round! Oh, dear, what in the world can have come over her? My poor nerves!'

By this time Miss Beccles had reached the scene, and with a cry had run towards the group by the fire. 'Elinor, my love!

Mrs. Cheviot! Oh, what is the matter? What caused her to swoon? Pray let me come there, Mr. Nicky! Run quickly to the kitchen and beg a handful of the pheasant's feathers from Mrs. Barrow!'

'Yes, yes, and call to that fool of mine!' Francis begged. 'He is never where he is wanted! I must have my smelling-salts, and the hartshorn brought directly. She looks horridly pale! I do not know when I have sustained such a shock! How long has she been lying here? It is a mercy her clothes have not been set alight by a spark from that fire! Do hurry, my dear boy!'

'What did you do to her?' Nicky demanded hotly.

'Dear Nicholas, what could I do? I had no time to do more than snatch up that bowl of flowers and cast it over her, and it has not answered in the least! Do pray fetch Crawley! He is very knowledgeable, always knows just what to do in case of illness!'

Nicky stood irresolute for a moment, but upon Miss Beccles's adjuring him to make haste, swung round on his heel, and hurried off to the kitchen. By the time he had brought both the Barrows bustling to the book-room, he had had opportunity to reflect on the improbability of Francis's having had any hand in Elinor's plight. He could not imagine any conceivable reason for an assault on her, and began to think that she must have been overtaken by a fainting-fit. She was still unconscious, but Miss Beccles, in answer to an agitated enquiry from Francis, assured them that her pulse was beating. Francis, abandoning his attempts to assist Miss Beccles, had sunk into a chair, and seemed to be almost as much in need of resuscitation as his hostess. So, at any rate, his valet thought, for when he arrived, in response to Nicky's shout, he instantly produced a vinaigrette from his pocket, and held it beneath his master's nose. It was waved away.

'Take it to Mrs. Cheviot!' Francis said faintly. 'I must not be selfish, and I dare say I shall not have one of my spasms if I keep very quiet for a minute or two.'

The draught from the open casement was causing the fire to belch puffs of smoke into the room; Nicky said: 'It's all very well of you to have opened the window, but she's more likely to be smothered by this smoke than to derive the least benefit from such a devilish draught!'

'Open the window! You cannot suppose me to have been so imprudent!' exclaimed Francis. 'Good God, I had not noticed it! Pray shut it this instant, dear boy! Do you wish me to die of an inflammation on the lung?'

Nicky pulled it to, but turned to stare in surprise. 'Did you not throw it open? Who can have done so, then? She would not be sitting here with that wind blowing into the room! And how came that cushion to be on the floor?'

The smell of burnt feathers began to mingle with the smoke; Miss Beccles looked up to say: 'No, no, she would not have sat with the window open on such a day as this! I know it was not so when I came into this room only half an hour ago! Oh, what can have happened? Is it possible someone has been here, and escaped by that way?'

'Not with Bouncer in the house!' Nicky averred.

'Oh, but the naughty doggie has gone off hunting! I should never have left her, but, to be sure, I never supposed – and in broad daylight, too!'

'Are you telling me,' said Francis, in a failing voice, 'that some desperate person has been able to enter this house without let or hindrance?'

'They could have done so, for the side-door is unlocked,' Nicky said shortly. 'I came in through it myself. But that any should have dared –' he broke off, for a bell was clanging in the distance.

'That's the front door, that is,' Barrow said, thrusting the decanter of brandy he was holding into his wife's hand, and going off to answer it.

'Crawley,' said Francis faintly, 'if Miss Beccles is not using my vinaigrette, pray bring it back to me! Thank you – and perhaps a little of that brandy. Yes, that is enough. Now go and secure any door which you find open! I cannot understand how anyone could be so careless, for how can one tell what evil characters may be in the neighbourhood, only awaiting their chance to rob the house? I dare say there may be gypsies! I cannot answer for the consequences if there is any possibility of the house's being broken into again, for already I have the gravest fear that I may be going to have one of my spasms. Perhaps it would be as well if you, dear Nicholas, were to take the precaution of searching the grounds. I cannot be easy until I know that no one is lurking in those dreadfully overgrown bushes, as I feel might so well be the case.'

'Ah, she is coming round!' Miss Beccles cried, fondly chafing Elinor's limp hands. 'There, my love! There, there!'

A quick, firm tread was heard approaching across the hall; another instant, and Carlyon had entered the room, still wearing his caped driving-cloak, and his gloves. One glance took in the scene; he stripped off his gloves, saying: 'What's this? What caused her to swoon?'

'We do not know!' Miss Beccles answered. 'Mr. Cheviot found her lying here, and called to us to come to her. But she is better! See, she is beginning to stir, and to recover her complexion a little! Elinor, my love!'

'Ned, I found this window swinging wide, and that cushion on the floor, as though it had been kicked off the seat! And, look at this! I've this instant seen that the curtain is torn off two of its hooks!'

Carlyon cast a cursory glance towards the window, but strode across the room to the fireplace, to drop on one knee beside Elinor, and to lift her up from the floor. He rose with her in his arms, and walked with her to the sofa. She gave a moan, and opened her eyes, murmuring something he could not catch. He said calmly: 'Do not try to talk, Mrs. Cheviot! You will be better directly. Have the goodness to pile up those cushions a little, Miss Beccles! Nicky, fetch me some brandy for her!'

'It's here, if Francis has not drunk it all!' Nicky said.

'Then pour some into a glass,' Carlyon said, lowering his burden on to the sofa, but keeping one arm under Elinor's shoulders.

Nicky hastened to place a glass into his imperatively outstretched hand. He put it to Elinor's lips, carefully supporting her head, and said: 'Try to swallow this, ma'am! You will feel very much better if you do.'

Her eyes, blurred at first, began to grow clearer; she looked up in a dazed way into his face, and whispered: 'My head! Oh, my head!'

He obliged her to drink some of the brandy. She choked over it, but it revived her. She was trembling convulsively, and one of her hands clutched his wrist. 'Something struck me!' she said hoarsely. 'Oh, I am glad you have come! Do not leave me!'

'No, certainly I shall not leave you,' he responded. 'But you will do better to be quite for a little while. There is nothing to alarm you now.' He laid her down on the cushions as he spoke, and she cried out as her head came to rest on them.

'By God, someone did hit her on the head!' Nicky exclaimed. 'Cousin Elinor, who was it?'

She was lying with closed eyes, and a hand pressed to her brow. 'I don't know. I heard a noise. Then something struck me. I don't know any more.'

'For heaven's sake!' said Francis, in a shrill voice, 'will no one go out to make sure that somebody is not lurking in the garden? How can you be so inconsiderate, Nicholas? Have you no regard for the nerves of others less insensible than yourself? If you will not go, then Crawley must do so, but tell him to arm himself with my sword-stick, for it would be a shocking thing if he were to be injured by some ruffian! I cannot bear to have strangers about me, and if he were to be incapacitated I should be obliged to do so.'

'Well, I will go out to look, but you may depend upon it there is no one there,' Nicky said. 'If there was ever someone he will have made off long since!'

'Go and see,' said Carlyon. He nodded to Mrs. Barrow, who had brought in a bowl of water, and some strips of old linen. 'Thank you, Mrs. Barrow: that is all.' He waited until she had left the room, and then bent over Elinor again. 'Where does it pain you?'

She had turned her head sideways on the pillow, and now moved her hand cautiously to the back of it, just above the neck. Her own touch made her wince; she opened her eyes, saying: 'Oh, I have such a bruise! I can feel the bump already!'

'Will you let me raise you, so that it may be attended to?' he said, slipping his arm under her shoulders again.

She bore it mutely, but her senses seemed to swim, and she was obliged to lean her brow against his arm. Miss Beccles was already soaking a cold compress, and would have laid it to the back of her head had not Carlyon taken it out of her hand, and gently applied it to the bruise. Elinor sighed with relief, and murmured: 'Thank you. You are very good.'

'If someone would call Crawley to me again, I will desire him to mix a glass of hartshorn and water,' said Francis. 'Two glasses, for I think I should take a little myself. My hand is shaking dreadfully still, and I feel quite unwell. The thought of this horrid violence, following, as it does, the shock I have already sustained, had been too much for me. If it were not that I do trust I was able to be of some slight assistance to Mrs. Cheviot, I should be almost inclined to wish that I had not left my room. But I thought it right to make the effort, and so I did. The windows in my room fit very ill: there is a shocking draught, and no good could come of my remaining there.'

'Take a little more brandy, Mrs. Cheviot,' Carlyon said, picking up the glass again, and wholly disregarding Francis's remarks.

'Oh, I had rather not!' she begged.

'Yes, I dare say, but it will do you good. Come!'

She lifted a wavering hand to take the glass, and sipped a little, murmuring between sips: 'I am sure my skull is cracked!'

'I am even more sure that it is not,' he replied. 'You are feeling very dizzy, and I dare say your head aches sadly, but it is only a bruise.'

'I might have guessed you would be odiously unfeeling.'

'Certainly you might, for you know I have not the least

sensibility. Come, you are better already! You begin to talk more like yourself.'

'If my head did not swim so there is a deal I have stored up to say to you! You have used me abominably!'

'You shall tell me in what way I have done so presently,' he replied, in a soothing tone.

'I warned you that I should very likely be found murdered in my bed!'

'Very true, but you have not been so found, and I cannot suppose it probable that you will be.'

'I am sure,' said Francis, rising, and tottering to the table, 'I am happy to hear you speak so confidently, Carlyon, but I cannot share your sanguine persuasions! When I reflect that this, according to what I have been told, is the second time some ruffian has broken into this house, and committed a brutal act of violence, I wonder that you should remain so cool! I envy you your happy disposition, upon my word, I do!' he refilled his glass, and had just raised it to his lips when Nicky came back into the room.

'What, still recruiting your strength?' Nicky said scornfully. 'You may be easy! There is no one in the garden, and Bouncer is not come back. How do you do now, Cousin Elinor? Do you feel more the thing?'

'Oh, yes, thank you! I am better. There is not the least need for you to hold that pad to my head, my lord, for I can very well do it myself.'

'My love, let me wet it again, and then I will fashion a bandage to hold it in place,' said Miss Beccles, who had been hovering anxiously behind the sofa.

'Cousin Elinor, was that window open when you were struck down?' demanded Nicky.

'Oh, no! That is, I have no recollection that it was. The wind was blowing in at this side of the house, and I am sure I must have noticed. Why, did you find it open?'

'Yes, wide open, and the curtain partly torn down!'

She gave a nervous start, and looked fearfully towards the

window. 'Do not say so! Did someone escape through it? But how did he come in? I heard nothing, until a board, as I thought, creaked just behind me. Becky, you shut the door when you left me, did you not? Surely I must have heard it if anyone had opened it!'

'Oh, no, my love!' said Miss Beccles, tenderly binding the pad in position again. 'I wonder you should not have noticed that I had been rubbing soap on the hinges! It squeaked so horridly, you remember, but there is nothing like soap to cure a creaking door!'

'Has anyone thought to see if anything of value is missing from the house?' enquired Francis. 'I do not wish to appear to be putting myself too much forward, but it does seem to me – However, if it does not strike you as being of consequence, pray do not allow any suggestion of mine to weight with you!'

As nobody was paying the least heed to him, this recommendation seemed unnecessary. Nicky was frowning portentously over thoughts of his own; Miss Beccles was busy tying a knot to her bandage; the sufferer lay with closed eyes; and Carlyon stood beside the sofa, looking down at her.

It was Nicky who broke the silence. 'I do not see how it can have happened!' he announced suddenly.

'I dare say I imagined the whole,' murmured Elinor.

'Well, I mean I do not see *why* anyone should hit you on the head, cousin. What were you doing?'

'Nothing,' she replied wearily. 'I had been writing a letter, which I laid by in the hope that Lord Carlyon might frank it for me.'

'I will certainly do so, but do not tease yourself now, Mrs. Cheviot.'

'Yes, but there's no sense in it!' persisted Nicky. His eye alighted on the folded inventory, still lying on the hearthrug. He instantly pounced on it. 'What's this? *Six pairs linen sheets, monogrammed, in good order. Four ditto slightly darned –*'

'It is only the inventory of all the linen, which Becky had just given to me. I must have had it in my hand, but I do not precisely remember. I had gone over to the mantelpiece, to try whether I could not wind up the clock, but it is locked, and I think – yes, I am sure – that I picked up the inventory again, meaning to put it safely by, when all at once something struck me such a blow!'

Nicky was about to say something, his eyes sparkling with excitement, when he caught Carlyon's level gaze, and subsided, flushing up to the roots of his hair in a very conscience-stricken way. His embarrassment was short-lived, however, for Barrow just then looked into the room to announce, with his customary lack of ceremony, that the doctor's gig was coming up the drive.

Carlyon's brows rose in slight surprise, but he said: 'He is very welcome. Desire him to come in here, Barrow!'

'Why, yes, certainly!' said Francis. 'I shall be only too glad to subordinate my claims to Mrs. Cheviot's, but you must know that he is coming to see me, my dear Carlyon. I caught one of my putrid sore throat's at poor Eustace's funeral: I was sadly afraid I should do so, for there was a dreadfully sharp wind blowing, and I should not at all wonder at it if the damp came through my boots while we stood round that depressing grave. I have scarcely closed my eyes all night, I assure you, for the least thing is so apt to bring on my tic, and you know that I have had a great deal to bear. And now this brutal shock, coming hard upon the distressing news of my poor dear Louis! But I should not like to be thought selfish, and certainly the worthy doctor – I dare say an old-fashioned person, but he may at all events be able to make me up a paregoric draught that will not quite poison me – certainly he shall first come to Mrs. Cheviot.'

By the time he had reached the end of this self-sacrificing speech, the doctor was already in the room, and bowing to Carlyon. Francis waved a languid hand towards the sofa, and said: 'You will be so good as to attend to Mrs. Cheviot, sir, before you come up to my room. I shall leave you, now, ma'am, in the fervent hope that you will soon find yourself greatly amended. Ah, Barrow, send Crawley to me, if you please! I shall need his arm to help me up the stairs. Indeed, I cannot imagine why he is not at hand. How callous! It is beyond everything!'

The doctor stared after him in blank bewilderment, and then turned his eyes towards Nicky, in a look of enquiry.

'Ay, that's the fellow you have to hustle out of this house,' said Nicky frankly.

Carlyon interposed, saying quietly: 'You are come just when you are wanted, Greenlaw. Mrs. Cheviot has suffered a fall, and has bruised her head painfully. Pray do what you can to render her more comfortable! I'll leave you, ma'am, for the present.'

She opened her eyes at that. 'Lord Carlyon, if you leave this house before I have had the opportunity of speaking to you, it will be the most monstrous thing ever I heard of, or had thought possible – even in you!' she declared roundly.

'I have no intention of doing so, Mrs. Cheviot. I will return when Greenlaw has done what he may for you. Come, Nicky!'

Nicky allowed himself to be led from the room. He was plainly bursting with something he wanted to say, and could hardly wait until he had dragged his brother into the parlour, and firmly shut the door, before he exclaimed: 'Ned! I see it all! You were right!'

'Was I? In what way?'

'Why, in saying Francis was dangerous, to be sure! For nothing could be plainer! At first, I did not see why he should have done such a thing, but as soon as I found that inventory I had bubbled him! Lord, and you was only just in time to stop me blurting out what I was suspecting! I was so much surprised, you know, I did not consider what I was about. But I fancy there was no harm done!'

'No, none at all. In fact – But go on, Nicky!'

'I am as certain as that I stand here that it was Francis who struck Cousin Elinor down! I don't know how such a puny fellow can have contrived to do it, but –'

'I fancy he may have used the paperweight from the desk.'

'What, you knew, then?'

'No, but I could see no other implement that might have been snatched up when he entered the room.'

'Good God, did you think to look? It did not enter my head, as it chances, but I dare say it might have presently. But only listen, Ned! you do not know the whole!'

'I am listening. I collect already, of course, that you were got rid of by sending you in search of the doctor.'

'Yes, I was – except that that was my own thought, but I dare say he would have found another way if I had let the groom go. I expect he hoped I might be the one to go, when he said he must have Greenlaw sent for. But the thing is, Ned, he gave it out he was a great deal too sick to leave his room, and had Mrs. Barrow make him arrowroot jelly, and would only take gruel for his breakfast – such stuff! And then, no sooner am I out of the way, and Bouncer gone off hunting – though that was the sheerest good fortune, now I come to think of it, but perhaps he hoped I should take Bouncer with me – in any event, there we were, both of us disposed of, and the women likely to be busy about the house, in the way they are at that hour, though I'm sure I don't know what they can find to be doing for ever, and so down comes Master Francis, on the chance of finding no one about. He goes softly into the book-room, and what does he see?'

'Mrs. Cheviot, with just such a document as he is looking for in her hand.'

'Exactly so! He must have supposed her to have come upon it suddenly, perhaps in the desk, in a secret drawer I thought might have been there. And at all costs he was bound to seize it from her, you know, and so he struck her down. Jupiter! I'd give a monkey only to have been able to see his face when he found it was only a list of some rubbishy sheets and towels! And I have made it out in my mind, Ned, that it must have been then that I came into the hall, and set up a shout for Cousin Elinor. He must have guessed I should go straight to the book-room, and so he had no time to make his escape, but flung open the window instead, and created all that havoc, only to make us think someone had jumped out into the garden, and scattered a lot of snowdrops all over Cousin Elinor, and –'

'Did he do so? It seems a trifle premature,' Carlyon said dryly.

'Eh? Oh, I see!' Nicky said, with a laugh. 'No, but he splashed the water from the bowl on her face so that I should suppose him to be doing what he could to restore her. Not that I did think it, for I hope I am not such a gudgeon as that! But what if it *had* been that document, Ned, and I had *not* chanced to have come in just then?'

'I imagine he would have retired to his bed again,' said Carlyon.

'I suppose he might,' conceded Nicky. 'And I suppose we *might* not have set it down at his door. Not but what – However, it don't signify for he is no better off than he was! But what will he do next?'

'What indeed?'

'Ned, have you some notion in your head?' Nicky asked suspiciously.

'I have a great many notions in my head.'

'No, I won't have you baiting me! It is a great deal too serious!'

'So it is, and there, I fancy, is Greenlaw, coming from the book-room. You had better take him up to Francis's room,' Carlyon said, going towards the door.

'Ned! if you don't tell me, it will be quite shameful of you! You always know everything!'

'Yes, Nicky, but you think I know everything because I never tell you anything I am not quite certain of,' Carlyon replied, looking back at him with his faint smile. 'What a sad blow it would be to my vanity if you found I could be just as easily mistaken as anyone else! You must let me keep my own counsel until I *am* certain. And now I must go back to Mrs. Cheviot.'

Seventeen

Mrs. Cheviot was found to be sufficiently recovered to be able to sit up. A rather more professional bandage encircled her head, and she was distastefully sipping an evil-looking mixture. She managed to achieve a wan smile at sight of Carlyon, but she was still pale, and evidently a good deal shaken. But some of her liveliness of mind seemed to have been restored, for Carlyon had not advanced two paces into the room when she observed in a dispassionate tone: 'I have been recalling how you told me I might rest assured no disagreeable consequences would result from my marriage to your cousin. I wish you will tell me, my lord, what you deem a disagreeable consequence?'

He smiled. 'Did I say that?'

'With some other untrue things. Indeed, you as good as told me you were rescuing me from all the horrors of Mrs. Macclesfield's establishment, to set me up in peace and prosperity for the rest of my days. I was never so taken in!'

'I wonder why your mind runs so continually on Mrs. Macclesfield?' he said.

'Oh! One is apt, you know, to think wistfully upon what might have been!'

'My love!' interrupted Miss Beccles anxiously, 'will you not come upstairs, and lie down upon your bed, as good Doctor Greenlaw advised you to do? I know you have the headache, and he has given you that draught to make you sleep, remember!'

'Yes, dear Becky, I will come, but not all the draughts in the world could bring sleep to me until I have had the opportunity to speak with his lordship. Do you go, and desire Mary to put a hot brick in my bed, and I will join you presently!'

Miss Beccles looked undecided, but Carlyon interposed to assure her that he should send Mrs. Cheviot upstairs within a few minutes; so after placing the smelling-salts within reach, and begging Elinor not to forget to finish her draught, she flitted away.

'Well, Mrs. Cheviot?' Carlyon said, walking over to the fire, and stooping to warm his hands at it. 'You have had rather a disagreeable experience, I am afraid, and I am persuaded you blame me for it.'

'What should put such a notion as that into your head?' marvelled the widow. 'When I understand you have been in London since yesterday!'

'Oho! That is it, is it? But it seemed to me expedient that I should go to London, and you will give me credit for having made the best possible speed back to you.'

'I shall give you credit for nothing. I dare say you went to be measured for a pair of boots!'

'No, but if I told you my object you would think it trifling, I dare say.' He straightened himself, and said, smiling: 'Are you very vexed with me for leaving you, ma'am?'

Mrs. Cheviot felt her colour rising, and made haste to reply: 'Vexed! No, indeed! When you were so thoughtful as to inform Nicky that you believed Mr. Francis Cheviot to be a dangerous man! I am sure I ought to be very much obliged to you for the warning, and it must be quite my own fault that I now have a bump as big as a hen's egg on my head!'

'It is a pity Nicky cannot learn to hold his tongue,' he remarked. 'I do not anticipate that Cheviot will be a danger to you, ma'am.'

Mrs. Cheviot recruited herself with another sip of her draught. 'Of course I have dreamed the whole!' she said. 'I was not hit on the head at all!'

He laughed. 'You are refining too much upon the event, Mrs.

Cheviot. I am sure it gave you a fright, but there is not much harm done, and it is unlikely that you will suffer any further annoyance.'

'Oh!' she gasped. 'Oh, how abominable you are! Not much harm done, indeed! Further *annoyance!* Pray, in what terms would you have described my murder?'

He did not answer for a moment, and then he said curtly: 'We are not discussing murder, ma'am.'

'You will be, if you mean to keep me tied to this dreadful house!'

'Nonsense! If it was Francis Cheviot who struck you, as I believe it was, I dare say it was the last thing he wished to be obliged to do.'

'I may take what comfort I can from that! But why should he have been obliged to do anything of the sort?'

He hesitated, and then said: 'You were holding in your hand some folded papers that might have been the very papers he wishes to obtain.'

She gazed up at him, one hand pressed to her temple. 'What, must I now take care never to have a paper in my hand for fear I may be struck down from behind? My lord, it is monstrous! I dare say he must have seen me with papers in my hand half a dozen times already!'

'Yes, possibly, but –'

'But what?' she demanded, as he broke off, and turned away from her to mend the fire.

'Perhaps it startled him, ma'am, and he sprang to a false conclusion. Whatever be the answer, upon my honour I do not believe you to be in any danger!' There was a pause, while she eyed him uncertainly. His countenance relaxed; he said: 'Indeed, my poor child, you have had an uncomfortable time of it at Highnoons, and I am a villain to keep you here. Shall I take you and Miss Beccles up to the Hall?'

The colour rushed into her cheeks at this; she had the oddest desire to burst into tears, and sought refuge in one of her rallying speeches. 'What, and leave that creature to ransack the house at will? No, indeed! I hope I am a little better-spirited than that, sir! If I am to be martyred in this cause, no doubt it was so ordained, and I can depend on you for a handsome tombstone!'

'Indeed, you can!' he replied, smiling, and putting out his hand. 'It is a bargain, then, and you will stay here.'

She laid her hand in his. 'It is a bargain. But for how long am I to endure that creature above-stairs?'

'I should not wonder at it if you were to be rid of him sooner than you expect. I beg you will not tease yourself with thinking of him.'

Her eyes searched his face. 'But will he go without what he came for, sir?'

'I hope he may be prevailed upon to do so.'

'Shall you so prevail upon him?' she asked.

'Perhaps. I shall do my possible. You have been troubled with him for too long.'

She agreed to it, but added, after a moment's reflection; 'And yet, if he does so, who can tell what horrors may next be in store for me?'

'None, upon my honour.'

'Very pretty, my lord, but I have frequently been forced to observe the remarkable disparity that exists between *my* notions of what is horrid, and *yours*. Are you ever put out of countenance?'

'Very often.'

She smiled a little archly. 'Will you think me very saucy, my lord, if I say that that confession gives me an excessively odd idea of the life you must lead at the Hall? For you have treated as the merest commonplaces every shocking event that has occurred in the last week, from your cousin's death at Nicky's hands, to the discovery that you have stumbled upon a dangerous treason. These things appear not to have the power to disturb the tone of your mind! I envy you!'

'Well,' he said reflectively, 'two of my sisters, and my brother Harry, were for ever doing such outrageous things that I think I must have grown out of the way of being very much surprised at anything.'

She laughed, and rose rather shakily to her feet. He put his hand under her elbow to assist her, and escorted her to the door. She parted from him in the hall, declining his offer to take her upstairs. 'Indeed, I am quite well now! You do not mean to go to London again, I hope?'

'No, I am fixed in Sussex for some time, I believe. You have only to send a message over to the Hall if you should wish to speak with me. May I again impress upon you that you have no need to feel any further alarm?'

She looked quizzical, but as the doctor just then appeared at the head of the stairs, returned no answer, but went up, leaning on the banister-rail, and saying: 'You mean to scold me, Dr. Greenlaw, but indeed I am going to my room, and I have drunk all that horrid mixture!'

'I am glad of it, ma'am; I can assure you you will be the better for it. I shall call to-morrow, to see how you are going on, if you please.'

She thanked him; he waited for her to pass him, and then went on down the stairs to where Carlyon stood in the hall. 'If you will pardon an old man who has known you from your cradle, my lord,' he said bluntly, 'I do not understand how that lady came by that bruise on her head, but I will go bail there is some devilment afoot here!'

'I will readily pardon you, but if this is intended as a reproach to me it falls wide of the mark. I assure you I did not give Mrs. Cheviot her bruise.'

The doctor smiled grimly. 'Very well, my lord, I know how to hold my tongue, I hope.'

'How do you find Mrs. Cheviot?'

'Oh, she will do well enough! Someone struck her a stunning blow, however – for all you may say she fell, and so hit her head, my lord.'

'And your other patient?'

The doctor grunted. 'I can find nothing amiss with him, beyond a pronounced irritation of the nerves. I have prescribed a few drops of laudanum, but as for sore throats, I see no sign of such a thing!' He looked up under his brows, and added: 'Master Nick would have me scare him away with a tale of small-pox in the village, but you may tell him, my lord, that whatever it may be that has occurred at Highnoons, it has given him a pronounced dislike of the place, so that I fancy he will not be plaguing Mrs. Cheviot for much longer. As for Master Nick himself, your lordship will like to know that I constrained him to let me take a look at his shoulder when he caught up with me to-day, and I find it healing just as it should.'

'Why, thank you! He was always one to mend quickly.'

'Fortunately for himself!' Greenlaw said, in his sardonic way. 'He tells me you had my Lord and Lady Flint with you for a night. I trust her ladyship enjoys her customary health?'

He lingered for a few minutes, enquiring after the various members of Carlyon's family, and then put on his coat, and departed. Carlyon went back into the book-room.

Here Nicky found him, some fifteen minutes later. Nicky came in with a worried frown on his face, saying that he had been whistling and calling to Bouncer all through the home-wood, and feared he must have strayed on to Sir Matthew's land.

'Then you had best recover him without any loss of time,' Carlyon said.

'Yes, I know I had, and I have the greatest dread that he may be caught in a trap, or perhaps shot by one of those brutes of keepers. For Sir Matthew swore he would tell them to shoot him if he disturbed his birds, and –'

'Well, I fancy Sir Matthew will not proceed to those lengths, but you should certainly go to look for him, or you will find yourself quite in Sir Matthew's ill-graces.'

'I don't care for that if only poor old Bouncer is not in trouble. You know, he did once get stuck in a fox's earth, Ned, and had to be dug out. I own, I would wish to set out to search for him at once, only do you think I ought?'

'Most decidedly I do.'

'Yes, but there is Francis Cheviot to be thought of, after all!' Nicky reminded him.

'I am sure Bouncer is more important than Francis Cheviot.'

'I should just think he was! Why, he is worth a dozen of him! Only fancy, Ned, he barks at Francis whenever he sees him! And I did not teach him to do so! He is most intelligent! I have not let him bite Francis, though, because with such a mean fellow there's no saying what might come of it. I do wish he would come in!'

'From my knowledge of him, he is not at all likely to do so before nightfall.'

'Ned, I *cannot* be dawdling here when he may be caught in some trap!'

'My dear boy, there is no reason why you should.'

'Very well, then, I shall go out after him. But I warn you, Ned, it may be hours before I find the old fellow, and while I am gone Francis may be up to some more of his tricks!'

'Unlikely, I think.'

'Of course,' said Nicky huffily. 'if you do not choose to tell me what you have in your head you need not, but I think it pretty shabby of you!'

Not receiving any other answer to this than an amused look, he left the room with a dignified gait, and was soon striding off in the direction of Sir Matthew Kendal's lands. Carlyon left the book-room, and desired Barrow to send for his chaise from the stables. Miss Beccles found him drawing on his glove in the hall, and said diffidently, and a little anxiously: 'You are leaving us, my lord?'

He smiled, and nodded.

'I dare say there is no need for you to remain, sir?' she ventured.

'None, I believe. I have already begged Mrs. Cheviot to think no more of what has happened here to-day.'

'I am sure if *you* feel it to be safe for her to remain here, my lord, it must be so indeed,' she said simply.

His eyes lit with amusement, but he let it pass, merely bowing, and saying in a perfectly grave tone: 'You are very good, Miss Beccles.'

'Oh, no! When it is you, my lord, who – Indeed, I am all

obligation! Such distinguishing observance! Never backward in the least attention! I am sure we may place every dependence upon your lordship's judgement. And as for – Well, I am sure! when dear Mrs. Cheviot has been in a pucker, I have said to her a dozen times: "Depend upon it, my love, when his lordship comes, everything will being a way to be settled!"'

He looked a trifle rueful. 'And what does Mrs. Cheviot commonly reply, ma'am?'

The poor lady coloured up, and became entangled in a riot of half-sentences, from which it emerged that although dear Mrs. Cheviot had a mind capable of every exertion, indeed something more of quickness than most females, the awkwardness of her situation had inclined her to indulge lately in odd humours.

'I fear Mrs. Cheviot has no very high idea of my management,' he remarked.

'Oh, my lord, I am sure –! She has a king of sportive playfulness which – But your lordship has such a superior understanding! I need not make the least excuse for the occasional liveliness of Mrs. Cheviot's manners!'

'Not the least,' he agreed. 'Does she abuse me soundly?'

'You know it is her way to indulge in a good deal of raillery, my lord!' Miss Beccles explained earnestly. 'Then she has been so much on the fidgets, you know! I am sure it is no wonder! But with every disposition in the world to fancy herself able to contrive all without assistance, and perhaps with a little distaste of submitting to authority, it cannot be called in question that she can only be comfortable when your lordship is so obliging as to advise her how she should go on.'

He held out his hand. 'Thank you. I depend upon your good offices, Miss Beccles. Good-bye! I shall be at Highnoons again to-morrow.'

He was gone, leaving her to blink after him in bewilderment.

Less than an hour later, having assured herself that Elinor lay deeply and peacefully asleep, Miss Beccles, herself conscious of being very much exhausted by the events of the morning, went downstairs with the intention of desiring Mrs. Barrow to send some tea and bread-and-butter to the parlour on a tray. She was brought up short by the sight of Francis Cheviot, standing in the hall, enveloped in his fur-lined cloak, a muffler swathed about his throat, and his hat already in his hand. He was giving Barrow some languid directions, but he turned when he heard the governess's footsteps on the stairs, and said: 'Ah, I am happy to have this opportunity of addressing you, ma'am! I would not have you sent for, in case you should be ministering to poor dear Mrs. Cheviot, but I am glad you are come: very glad! And how does the sufferer find herself?'

'Mrs. Cheviot is asleep, sir, I thank you,' she replied, dropping him a prim little curtsy.

'One hoped she might be. "Great nature's second course," you know. Upon no account in the world will I have her disturbed!'

'Oh, I should not think of doing such a thing, sir!' she said naïvely.

'Ah, I knew I should find you persuadable in this! And yet propriety of taste dictates that I should take my leave of her! How difficult it is to decide what one should do!'

'Are you – are you leaving us, sir?' she uttered, hardly able to believe her ears.

'Alas! With every wish to show dear Mrs. Cheviot attention, I find I cannot remain at Highnoons with any degree of comfort. My nerves are already sadly disordered, ma'am: it would not do for me to stay. I should not be the least use to my cousin.' He raised one white hand. 'Yes, yes, I know what you would say! Am I wise to run the risk of exposing myself to all the hazards of a journey undertaken in this inclement weather? It is very just, but I am persuaded I ought to make the attempt; and if Crawley wraps me up well, and I draw my muffler over my mouth, we must trust that no ill will result – no *irremediable* ill!'

She was thankful to learn that he was indeed leaving Highnoons that she agreed to this with so much eagerness that he frowned, and reminded her gently that the evil properties of the east wind could scarcely be over-estimated. She said hopefully that perhaps the wind would not be found to be so *very* much in the east as he feared. 'But you will not go without a little nuncheon, sir! Oh, dear, if it is not one o'clock already! I am sure so much has happened to-day I have not noticed how the time has flown! I will send to the kitchen directly!'

'You are most obliging, dear ma'am, but if I am to reach London by dinner-time I must remove at once. And I could not support the notion of dining at an inn in my present sad state of health. I could not answer for the consequences! My chaise is called for already; indeed, I cannot imagine why it is not at the door, but these fellows take a delight in dawdling, you know! I wonder if Crawley has procured a hot brick to put at my feet? Where is Barrow? Ah, he has gone to fetch the clock, as I desired him to do! Miss Beccles, I have been searching my mind to discover in what way I may serve my kind hostess, for one must wish to show every observance! That clock, which has vexed her so much by its lamentable trick of declaring the hour to want but a quarter of an hour to five o'clock! A handsome timepiece, and so like my poor Cousin Eustace to let it remain out of order! But *I* will have it set to rights, ma'am, and it shall be attended to by my own clockmaker. I would not trust it to another, for some of those fellows, you know, meddle more than they mend. Pray inform Mrs. Cheviot that her clock shall be returned to her in working order as soon as I can contrive it! Ah, here is Barrow! Place it carefully inside my chaise, Barrow, if you please! You will present my most respectful compliments to Mrs. Cheviot, Miss Beccles, and of course my deep apologies for not making my adieux to her in person. She will, I trust, forgive me! That she will appreciate my anxiety to be safely in my own lodging before nightfall I cannot doubt. She has such exquisite sensibility! I am happy to think such an estimable female should have become one of my family. Ah, and dear Nicholas! Now, where is dear Nicholas? A charming boy, I am sure, if he would but outgrow his taste for savage mongrels. Barrow, you may send for Mr. Nicholas: I know he will wish to say good-bye to me, and not for the world would I wound him by the smallest show of inattention!'

'Mr. Nick has gone off after the dog, and won't be back till anywhen, sir,' growled Barrow.

'How very unfortunate! My kind compliments to him, Miss Beccles. Assure him of the happiness he will confer upon me if he chooses to honour my abode with his presence any time he should find himself in town! But not his dog! I have the greatest dislike of dogs. Is that you, Crawley? Is my chaise ready at last? One would have said it had to be fetched from the Antipodes! Miss Beccles, your very obedient servant! Do not forget to deliver my compliments and thanks to Mrs. Cheviot! Pray do not dream of coming to the door with me! If you were to catch a cold through any fault of mine I could never forgive myself!'

Quite dazed by this flow of gentle eloquence, she could only curtsy again, and assure him that his messages should not be forgotten. He bowed himself out, and was handed up into his chaise by Crawley, who then swathed several rugs round him, and placed a hot brick from the kitchen at his feet.

'A hem good riddance!' said Barrow, when the chaise had moved off down the drive. 'Him and his quirks! What would he be wanted with that old clock, miss?'

'To have it set going for Mrs. Cheviot. I am sure it is very kind, and she will be glad of it!'

'Have it set going!' exclaimed Barrow, in a tone of strong disapproval. 'That old clock's been stopped these dunnamany years! I disremember when I knew that clock to tick!'

It was plain that he objected to having the exciting state of affairs interfered with. Miss Beccles felt herself to be unequal to argument, and merely repeated that it was very kind of Mr. Cheviot. She added that if Mrs. Barrow would make her some tea she would be glad of it, so Barrow took himself off kitchenwards, muttering against the officious ways of some visitors.

The relief of knowing Francis to have left Highnoons was so great that after she had drunk her tea, and eaten some slices of bread-and-butter, Miss Beccles indulged herself with a nap in front of the parlour fire. She was roused by Nicky, who came in just before three o'clock, with the distressing intelligence that he had not yet succeeded in finding Bouncer, in spite of hunting all over Sir Matthew Kendal's preserves, and twice falling foul of his keepers. 'But I thought I should come back, to make sure all was well here,' he said, 'and that fellow Cheviot not playing off any more of his tricks!'

'Oh, but he has gone, dear Mr. Nicky!' said Miss Beecles, hurriedly setting her cap straight. 'Such a mercy, is it not?'

'Gone!' he exclaimed, looking thunderstruck.

'Yes, and do you know, I cannot think it was he who hit poor Mrs. Cheviot, for it was her having been struck down that made him take the resolve to leave us! But I was so thankful, for you know I could not like him, and Mrs. Barrow was growing so cross at being obliged to make so many jellies that I scarcely dared show my face in the kitchen!'

'Oh, very well!' said Nicky, shrugging up his shoulders, and then blinking at the twinge this gesture cost him, 'I suppose it is Carlyon's doing, and no concern of mine! I am sure I am very glad to hear that he has gone, for that puts me quite at liberty to go on searching for Bouncer, which I had a deal rather do than thrust myself in where I am not needed!'

Miss Beccles looked up at him in dismay. 'I fear you are not quite pleased, dear Mr. Nicky!' she faltered.

'Pleased?! No such thing! I am excessively pleased, ma'am! I rate Bouncer a trifle higher than Francis Cheviot, I can tell you! And if Carlyon should enquire after me, you may tell him that I am gone off on my own affairs, and have no notion when I shall be back, but he need not trouble his head over me, for I shall contrive very well by myself!'

Having delivered himself of this embittered speech, he stalked out of the room, leaving Miss Beccles in quite a flutter of apprehension, and unable to hazard any guess as to the cause of his annoyance.

It was four o'clock before Mrs. Cheviot put in an appearance. She came down then, however, looking a little pale still, but declaring herself to be quite restored. 'I must have been asleep for hours!' she said. 'No, indeed, I have not got the headache now, Becky – or only the least little degree of headache: nothing to regard!'

'My love, I wish you had stayed on your bed! And you have removed your bandage! Now, my dear Mrs. Cheviot, is this wise? Is it prudent?'

'You would not have had me continuing to go about looking such a figure of fun!' Elinor protested.

'I am sure it was no such thing! Besides, there is no one to see you but me, my love, for Mr. Nicky is out looking for poor Bouncer, and he said he did not know when he might return. I do not know what should have occurred to provoke him, but the fact is he was sadly out of spirits when he came in an hour ago.'

'Oh, is Nicky cross? Perhaps Mr. Cheviot has vexed him! Has that odious creature taken to his bed again? I have a very good mind to tell Mrs. Barrow not to be making him any more gruel, in the hope that he may thus be induced to leave Highnoons!'

'Oh, my love, there is no need! He has gone!'

Elinor stared. 'Becky! You are trying to take me in!'

'No, indeed, I would not do such a thing! He said he could not bear to stay after what happened to you this morning. I must say, I thought it poor-spirited of him, and not quite manly, but I was so thankful to say good-bye to him I would not put the smallest rub in his way!'

'No, not for the world! But this is marvellous indeed! It is Carlyon's doing! He told me Mr. Cheviot might be gone before I expected it! Now, how may he have contrived this blessed deliverance? It puts me quite in charity with him, I declare!'

'My love, I wish you will not talk in that wild, heedless fashion! It is not becoming in you, when his lordship, I am sure, has shown himself all compliance, and most truly the gentleman! Such a contrast to Mr. Cheviot, too! One cannot but be struck by it!'

Elinor showed a heightened colour, but said lightly: 'Oh, let a man but be well-looking, and domineer over you, and I know you must fall into admiration, Becky! But how came Mr. Cheviot to leave Highnoons in such haste?'

'Indeed, my love, I fear we have wronged him, and it was not his doing that you were hurt. And I think it cannot have been his lordship who sent him off, for he had left the house an hour before, you know. Mr. Cheviot desired his kind compliments to you, and his apologies for not taking leave of you in person, but he would not stay to see you for fear of not being in town in time for his dinner. Though, to be sure, I think he could have had a neat, plain dinner at an inn, but he has such odd fancies!'

'He wants only gruel! I am obliged to him for his civility, and hope I may never be called upon to entertain him again.'

'No, my love, but I do think he meant to be conciliating. He was so obliging as to say that he desired above all things to show you observance, and he had the happy notion of taking away that provoking clock to be mended for you.'

Elinor had been leaning back in her chair, but she sat up with a start at this, and exclaimed: 'Took the clock away? Which clock?'

'Why, the one from the book-room, my love, that has vexed you so! He will have it mended by his own clock-maker, and –'

'Becky, you cannot have let him do so!' Elinor cried, her countenance gown suddenly white.

'But, my dear Mrs. Cheviot, what objection can there be?'

'Objection! When you knew what we have been so much afraid of! What he came here to find!'

'Elinor, this is the merest irritation of nerves! Pray, what has a clock that will not go to do with secret papers?'

Elinor seemed not to be attending. She had both hands pressed to her temples, as though in an effort to concentrate her thoughts. 'The clock was locked,' she said. 'I had been trying to open it. Then I put it back as it was, and – yes, yes, it was then that I picked up the inventory again from the mantelpiece, where I had laid it down! And then I saw the clock was not standing quite straight, and I adjusted it, those papers in my hand! And it was then that I was struck down! Becky, Becky, what a fool I have been not to have perceived it before! *That* was why he stunned me! He thought I had contrived to open the back of the clock, and had discovered the papers in it! I see it all now, and it is too late! He knew they were there, and must have been only waiting his moment to take them out! Oh, Becky, what a piece of work is this! Oh, how could you have let him take the clock away? But the blame is mine! What shall I do? We must get it back! Nicky –' She broke off. 'No, not Nicky! He would dash off in pursuit, and very likely get hurt, and I should never forgive myself, and nor would Carlyon, I dare say! Becky, what must I do?'

Miss Beccles looked very much agitated, and said: 'Indeed, I am very sorry! I do not see what is to be done, and certainly *you*, my love, are in no state to exert yourself! Do, pray, be still! You will bring on your headache if you allow yourself to get into a pucker!'

Elinor said impatiently. 'Headache! What can that signify in face of this disaster – for it is no less! It may be too late to recover that document, but at least it is my duty to advise Carlyon instantly of what has occurred! Oh, why did he leave Highnoons? He might have guessed everything would go awry if he went away! It is just like him! Odious, provoking man! Becky, run to find Barrow, and tell him I must have a carriage brought round to the door as soon as may be! If there is nothing fit for me to go in but the gig, I will go in that, and the groom must be ready to accompany me. Do not sit staring at me, Becky, but hurry, I beg of you! I am going upstairs to fetch my hat and cloak!'

'Mrs. Cheviot!' gasped Miss Beccles. 'You will not be so mad as to venture out! And in a gig! *Elinor!*'

Mrs. Cheviot fairly stamped her foot. 'Do as I bid you, Becky, for I was never more in earnest in my life! And if Nicky should come in, not one word to him, mind, of Mrs. Cheviot's having taken that clock away!'

Eighteen

Once having taken her resolution, not all Miss Beccles's prayers – and she uttered many – had the power to prevent Elinor from setting forth in search of Carlyon. The barouche which the late Mrs. Cheviot had used was still in the coach-house, but so covered with dust that it was obviously useless to expect it to be got ready for Elinor in the little time at her disposal. She adopted instead Barrow's suggestion that she should take Eustace Cheviot's phaeton, a vehicle very much more to her taste than the gig. The groom, rather pleased to have something more in his line to do than the gardening to which he had been set, hurried to put on his livery, and to harness one of Eustace Cheviot's horses to the carriage. When he discovered that his mistress had formed the intention of driving herself, and required him merely to sit beside her, and to direct her, he looked dubious, and ventured to inform her that the mare, not having been exercised for some days, was lamentable fresh. Mrs. Cheviot deigned no reply to this, but took the reins in a business-like way, and drove off at a spanking pace. By the time the groom had watched her loop a rein, as they swung out of the gate on the lane, and catch the thong of her whip without so much as glancing at it, he was very much impressed, and treated her with all the deference she could have desired.

Highnoons was only some seven miles distant from the Hall, but the roads to it were narrow, and full of bends, so that it was nearly three-quarters of an hour before Mrs. Cheviot was drawing up outside the Hall. The drive had done much to steady the agitation of her nerves, and she was able to ask for his lordship in a voice of tolerable composure. The butler and the footman who admitted her were both too well-trained to show any surprise at her unconventional arrival, and she was at once bowed into a handsome saloon, and begged to take a seat while his lordship was informed of her visit. She had not long to wait; the firm tread she was beginning to know soon came to her ears, and she started up out of her chair even as the butler flung open the door for Carlyon to pass into the saloon.

'My dear Mrs. Cheviot!' he said, coming towards her with his hand held out. 'You should be laid down upon your bed! How is this?'

Her gloved hand clung to his urgently. 'My lord, I had to come! I am quite well: the fresh air has even done me good. I was obliged to come had I been twice as unwell!'

'You cannot doubt of my happiness in welcoming you to my house, ma'am. Only the conviction that it cannot be good for you to exert yourself so unwisely has the power to mar it. But will you not come into the library? It is chilly in here, and I think you are cold already.'

'Thank you. It is nothing to signify! I have something of the greatest importance to disclose to you!'

'We shall be perfectly private in the library,' he said, opening the door for her, and leading her across the hall. The footman sprang to open the library door, and was desired to bring wine and cakes to the room.

'Indeed, I require nothing!' Elinor said.

'You will let me be the best judge of that, ma'am.' Carlyon said, closing the door. 'May I take your pelisse? I wonder what you were thinking of to come out in this weather with only that to protect you from the wind?'

She brushed it aside impatiently. 'What can it signify? My lord, Mr. Cheviot left Highnoons this afternoon, while I was sleeping, and he took with him the clock from the book-room!'

'Ah, did he so?' he said, apparently rather amused.

'You do not understand! I did not think of it myself until Becky told me that he had taken the clock upon the pretext of having it mended for me! My lord, I believe that paper to have been concealed in it! He knew it, and now he has it!'

'No, no, Mrs. Cheviot, he has not got it, I assure you!' he said soothingly. 'Do let me take your pelisse!'

She struck her hands together in exasperation. 'You must attend to me, my lord! You have not realized – how should you indeed? – that I had my hands on the clock when I was struck down! And –'

'I did realize it, Mrs. Cheviot. If you remember, you told us so when you recovered consciousness. I am afraid it is you who have not attended to me: did I not tell you that you had no need to feel any further alarm? I think you deserve that I should be a little angry with you for running the risk of injuring your health in this way.'

She gazed up at him in astonishment. 'You realized it! But you did not think what it might mean?'

'On the contrary, it occurred to me that that might be the answer, and when you had gone up to your room I looked to see whether one of my cousin's keys might not fit that lock. It was so, and I found that my suspicions were correct. I removed the papers, and they are now safely in my possession.'

She was bereft of speech, and could only stare at him in gathering indignation. Twice her lips parted, and twice she closed them again before she could regain sufficient command over herself to say: 'You removed the papers! But this is beyond everything! I dare say you thought I should not be interested in such a trifling piece of news!'

'No, but –'

'I have ransacked every chest and cupboard in that horrid house, only to oblige you! I have not enjoyed a moment's peace this whole week! I have been brutally assaulted, and all on account of the papers which are now safely in your possession! Well! I am happy to learn of this circumstance, sir, but I think it

242

monstrous that I should be obliged to drive seven miles to do so!'

'It was certainly imprudent,' he responded calmly. 'You would have been told of it to-morrow, at Highnoons. Now let me relieve you of that pelisse!'

'I shall do no such thing! I desire you will call for my phaeton immediately!' raged the widow.

'Don't be silly, Mrs. Cheviot!' he said. 'I am not so very much to blame, you know, if you will but consider for a moment! Until I had opened the lock, all was conjecture, and I would not, in the very natural condition of nerves you were then in, trouble you any more upon the matter. My first concern was to see you laid down upon your bed to recover for the shock you had undergone. When I found that my suspicion was justified, another consideration strengthened my resolve to keep the discovery to myself. It can hardly need any words of mine to apprise you of the peculiar delicacy of this whole business. I believe I know which course of action I should pursue, but before I take any step in the matter I think it right to discuss the question with my brother John. It was for that reason that I concealed from you, and indeed from Nicky too, the knowledge that the paper was found. Had I found John here when I returned this afternoon, and had settled with him what I should do, I believe I must have gone back to Highnoons to-night, to set all your minds at rest. Unfortunately, however, I found that John had taken a gun out to shoot rabbits, and he is still not come in. I expect him at any moment now. May I take your pelisse, ma'am?'

She let him do so, and was glad to remove the hat from her head as well, but although she was a little mollified by the quiet good sense of what he said, she still felt herself to have been hardly used, and remarked with a good deal of bitterness that she might have known he would have a smooth answer ready.

'I have only told you the truth, ma'am,' he replied. 'I am sorry to have vexed you, however, and I beg you will not hesitate to tell me how odious has been my conduct! You will find that chair tolerably comfortable, I believe, and out of the draught. Is your

243

head easier? I see that you have cast off your bandages. You should not have done so.'

'If I had not been obliged to drive out I might be wearing my bandages still!' said Elinor mendaciously. 'I suppose even you would not expect me to show myself abroad presenting such a very odd appearance!'

'By no means, but I did not expect you to show yourself abroad at all to-day, ma'am, and cannot approve to it.'

She was prevented from uttering a retort by the entrance of the butler with a tray, which he set down upon a table. He withdrew again, and Carlyon poured out a glass of madeira, and brought it to his guest, with a dish of macaroons. She was obliged to take the glass from him, but frigidly declined the macaroons. He put the dish down beside her, and went to pour out a second glass of wine for himself. The widow eyed his back view malevolently. 'I am sorry I did not send Nicky after Mr. Cheviot, if only to spite you!' she said.

'I am persuaded I might rely on your good sense not to do so,' he returned.

'If he had been in the house I dare say I *should* have done so, but he was gone out!'

'Yes, I took care of that,' he remarked, turning, and coming back to the fire.

Her bosom swelled. 'I am obliged to you, my lord! I now perceive the worth of your compliments!'

He smiled. 'Oh, not for fear of anything you might do, ma'am! But whatever Francis Cheviot chose to do I did not wish Nicky to hinder.'

She sniffed, and relapsed into defiant silence. After sipping her wine for a few minutes, her eye alighted on the macaroons, and she absently took one, and began to eat it, realizing that she was hungry, and had not, in fact, eaten anything since breakfast. A couple of these cakes did much to restore the serenity of her temper; she looked up, found Carlyon regarding her with a lurking twinkle, and suddenly laughed. 'Well, you have used me abominably, but to be sure I might have known that you would, for you have done so from the outset! But what will Mr. Cheviot do when he discovers that there is nothing in that clock?'

'That remains to be seen, ma'am. Will you excuse me while I send a message out to your groom? I think he should go back at once to Highnoons, to inform Miss Beccles that you are safely in my charge, and that I shall convey you home in my carriage after dinner.' She made a half-hearted protest, which was not attended to. He left the room, and was giving the butler his instructions in the hall when John Carlyon walked into the house, carrying his gun, and a couple of rabbits, which he handed to the footman.

'Hallo, Ned, so you are back!' he remarked. 'I stayed in all the morning on the chance that I might be obliged to go over to Highnoons, but no message came, and so I thought I might as well see if I could come by any sport while I am at home.'

Carlyon nodded. 'I was informed you had done so. Come into the library!'

'I will do so when I have washed my hands,' John promised.

Carlyon returned to the library himself, saying as he entered the room: 'My brother is this instant come in, and will be with us in a minute or two, Mrs. Cheviot.'

She made as if she would have risen from her chair. 'You wish to be private with him, I know. I will leave you, sir.'

'Indeed, I beg you will not! I may depend upon your discretion. You already know so much that you must know the whole.'

'You are very good, sir, but Mr. John Carlyon may not like to discuss these matters in my presence, and I would not –'

'Mr. John Carlyon will do as he is bid,' he replied.

She smiled. 'Ah, I knew you for a despot upon my first encounter with you, my lord!'

'Very rarely, I assure you! It seems a long time since that day.'

'Yes, I have often feared that I was but tedious company,' remarked the widow affably. 'You must blame my circumstances, sir, which have made me lose the art of making myself agreeable in society.'

'I observe that they have not made you lose your quickness of tongue, ma'am! You have wished to see me put out of countenance, and now cannot doubt that you have had your wish gratified!'

She laughed, but shook her heard. John came into the room at that moment, rubbing his chilled hands together. He stopped short when he perceived Elinor, and said in a voice of surprise: 'Mrs. Cheviot! I had no notion – Ned, you should have warned me you had a guest with you! I would not have come in in all my dirt! Pray excuse me, ma'am! I have been out shooting, and have had no time to change my jacket!'

'Mrs. Cheviot will excuse you readily,' Carlyon said. 'I have been waiting to see you all the afternoon. The memorandum has been found.'

'What! Not at Highnoons!' John exclaimed.

'Yes, at Highnoons, locked in the bracket-clock on the mantelpiece in the book-room.'

'Good God! You do not mean it! It is the actual copy that is missing?'

'I have not perused it, but read enough to convince me it could be none other. You may look at it.' He drew a folded sheaf from his pocket, and handed it to his brother.

John almost snatched it from him, and spread open the sheets, scanning them rapidly, and with starting eyes. 'My God, there can be no doubt! Who found this?'

'I did – through the instrumentality of Mrs. Cheviot,' Carlyon replied.

John's gaze was turned respectfully towards her. She said: 'Yes, indeed, he could scarcely have succeeded without me. You may imagine how happy I am to have suffered a broken head in this cause! To be sure, I was little put out at first, for you must know that from some cause or anther I have not been very much in the habit of being hit on the head, and so was inclined to refine too much on the event. But your brother's powerful reasoning soon showed me how absurd it was in me to be vexed by such a trifling thing! I make no complaint. I see that it was all for the best.'

'My dear Mrs. Cheviot! You are surely jesting!' said John, quite bewildered.

'I do not wonder at your surprise. You would not have supposed I could play so large a part in the recovery of that document! I did not suppose it myself, and I will own that I could have wished my part in the affair to have been of a less *passive* nature.'

John turned his head to direct an imploring look at Carlyon, who said, with a slight smile: 'It is very true, my dear John, but Mrs. Cheviot has her own way of describing what has occurred. She wished to see if she could not wind up that clock, and while she was endeavouring to open it – but in vain, since it was locked, and I held the key – Francis Cheviot must have entered the room behind her. He saw her with a household inventory in her hand, in the act of adjusting the clock, and sprang to a false conclusion. I think he must have used the paper-weight which I observed on the desk to strike her down. I am persuaded that he took care not to hit her with sufficient force to do her a serious injury, but –'

'Are you indeed?' interrupted Elinor. 'How considerate that was of him! I wonder if I should write to express the sense of my obligation to him?'

'Obligation!' John ejaculated, his mind too much taken up with the enormity of the occurrence to be susceptible to irony. 'It passes everything! I hope you have had the fellow laid by the heels, Ned!'

'No. He has gone back to London, carrying the clock with him,' Carlyon replied, taking a pinch of snuff.

John stared at him. 'I think you must have taken leave of your senses!'

Elinor picked up another macaroon. 'I must own I have often wondered when that melancholy suspicion would enter your brain, sir,' she said. 'I saw at the outset that his intellect was sadly disordered, but I dare say it has come upon him gradually, and you might not notice quite immediately.'

'Nonsense!' said John testily. 'Ned has as sound a head as any

247

of my acquaintance! But how is this, Ned? You cannot want more proof!'

'I believe I do not, but I also believe that we shall do well to take care how we proceed in this business. I would do nothing until I had consulted with you. I fancy we can neither of us be anxious to advertise this matter. The connection between ourselves and the Cheviots is too close to be comfortable. If matters can be settled without scandal, I own I should prefer it.'

'You cannot suppose I have not considered that!' John said, taking a quick turn about the room. 'But it will not do! Even if I knew how to restore that memorandum secretly, I would not do it! It is not the part of an honest man to let a traitor remain at large out of considerations of family!'

'Or, indeed, out of any other consideration. But if we could be sure that the traitor was rendered powerless for the future?'

'How?' John demanded, stopping to stare at him.

'I fancy it is in a way to be done.'

'Ned, what the devil have you been about?'

'It is not my doing. I may even be mistaken. That must be ascertained, of course.'

'I do not know what you would be at! Here you have in your possession a document that must be instantly taken to Lord Bathurst, with the full story of its discovery! You cannot be thinking of doing otherwise! It will be hushed up, I make no doubt: no one will be anxious to have it known how easily such a document went astray!'

Carlyon was silent, frowning down at the memorandum, which he had picked up, and folded again. After a moment he raised his eyes, and directed one of his level glances at his brother. 'I think we should do better to give these papers to Francis Cheviot,' he said.

His words struck both his auditors dumb. They regarded him in stupefaction. He had spoken in a reflective tone, as tough debating within himself, and did not appear to notice the effect his words produced.

'You – think – we – should – Ned, are you indeed mad?' John gasped.

'No. I have not had the opportunity to tell you what I discovered – or, rather, verified – in London. Louis De Castres *was* stabbed.'

Real perturbation was in John's face. 'Ned, old fellow, you cannot be yourself! What has that to say to anything? We knew it!'

'We knew it because Francis told us so. It was not in the *Morning Post*, from which he said he had learnt the tidings, nor in any other paper that I can discover. 'Stabbed to death' was the phrase he used. I marked it particularly.'

'Good God, it was what anyone might have said, *assuming* it had been so!'

'But it happens to have been exactly true. You may recall that he spoke of De Castres's body having been left under a bush. That was also true, but it was nowhere stated in the newspapers.'

John sank into a chair, repeating in a dazed voice: 'Good God!'

Elinor said: 'Do you mean to imply – can you possibly mean – that it was *Mr. Cheviot* who murdered that unfortunate young Frenchman?'

'I think so. I have suspected it all along, but some proof was needed.'

'Ned, it's not possible!' John exclaimed. 'De Castres was a friend of his! That is too well-known to admit of question!'

'I don't question it. I told you that Francis Cheviot was a very dangerous man. I have been aware of that these many years. I do not know what he would stop at: very little, I dare say.'

'Damme, I like the fellow no better than you do, but you make him out to villainous beyond belief!'

'Villainous, perhaps, but not, I think, the villain of this plot. That, if I am not much mistaken, is Bedlington.'

'Bedlington!' John ejaculated.

'It was always a possibility, you know, though I admit it seemed unlikely. It was not until I had had leisure to consider the matter more particularly that I realized how very much more unlikely was my first, really rather foolish, suggestion. It could never have been Francis, of course.'

'I do not know what you mean! To suspect a man in old Bedlington's position rather than his son seems to me fantastic!'

'No, I don't think so,' Carlyon replied. 'If Francis, who was De Castres's close friend, had been the traitor, what possible need could there have been to have employed Eustace as the go-between? No go-between would have been necessary. That such a tool as Eustace was employed should have shown me clearly from the start that the man we were trying to discover must be someone who was anxious not to be known by the French agent with whom he was dealing. Then, too, in using Eustace – hardly an ideal choice, surely! – he betrayed a clumsiness that could have nothing to do with Francis.'

John was silent for a moment, turning it over in his mind. 'It is true!' he said at last. 'I do not know how I can have been so dull as not to have thought of it. I own I did not. How long have you been convinced of this, Ned?'

'Convinced! I do not know that I am convinced now. It has come upon me gradually, I suppose. My enquiries into the circumstances of De Castres's death, and the discovery that Bedlington was gone into the country, and was said by his butler to be in such indifferent health as to make rest and quiet indispensable, made me as certain as a man might well be without positive proof – which I will admit I have not. For that reason I would do nothing without consulting with you.'

John nodded, frowning. He walked to the table, and poured himself a glass of madeira, and stood gazing down at it meditatively. 'It is not easy to see what one should do,' he said.

'No,'

'You have said yourself it is conjecture. If you are right how came Cheviot to know what his father was about?'

Carlyon shrugged. 'There might be several answers, but I do not know them.'

John drank some of his wine. 'If Cheviot did indeed kill De

Castres –' He stopped. 'Black waistcoats!' he said scathingly. 'Faugh! The man makes me sick!'

Elinor asked diffidently: 'Pardon me, but if Mr. Cheviot was not himself engaged in the plot, how came he to know the hiding-place in the clock?'

'Again, we cannot know the answer,' Carlyon replied.

John looked up. 'Ay, and if Louis De Castres did not know who stood behind Eustace, how did Bedlington hear of Eustace's death before the notice of it had appeared in the journals?'

'He told us that he had it from Eustace's valet.'

'And I asked you if you believed that, and you said you did not! Did you not think De Castres, upon learning the news from Mrs. Cheviot, had run to Bedlington with it?'

'Yes, I did. I still believe it to have been possible.'

'How so?'

'My dear John, if you had a secret to conceal, would you have entrusted it to Eustace?'

'No, by God!' John gave a short laugh. 'You think he may have told De Castres, when in his cups, that it was Bedlington who was selling information?'

'Very likely. Or it may be that De Castres might have guessed the truth.'

John turned to Elinor. 'When he visited you, Mrs. Cheviot, did Bedlington make any attempt to come near that clock, or to contrive that he should be left alone in the book-room?'

'None whatsoever,' she replied. 'I received him in the parlour, and he showed no disposition to linger. But he did say that he would return, to attend the funeral, and that he should stay at Highnoons.'

'He was frightened,' John said slowly. 'At that time, I did not credit Ned's suspicions, but it is true that he was devilishly ill-at-ease. But Ned thought then that Francis Cheviot might be the man we were after, and I set it all down to Bedlington's having got wind of it. Ned, do you think he can have lost his head, and told the whole to Francis? Or even that Francis has been privy to it from the start?'

'Certainly not that. Had Francis been joined with his father in the treason I cannot doubt that De Castres would be alive to-day. It is possible that Bedlington, finding his schemes to have gone hopelessly awry, turned to Francis for aid, to save him from disgrace. That Bedlington, with affairs in this uncertain state, has retired into the country on a plea of ill-health, seems to me to suggest that Francis has taken the reins into his hands, and is driving his father hard.'

Again John stared down into his wineglass, his brow furrowed. 'And you would give that memorandum to him?' he said.

'Well?' Carlyon said. 'If my conjectures are found to be correct, you will agree that Francis Cheviot leaves nothing to chance. De Castres was his friend, but De Castres is dead. I do not know how he means to deal with Bedlington, but I think, if I were Bedlington, I should deem it well to obey Francis – quite implicitly.'

'Surely he would not harm his own father!' cried Elinor.

'I wonder if his father thinks so?' said Carlyon dryly.

'Ned, this is not a thing to be decided in a trice.'

'No. Turn it over in your mind. If you are set on exposing the whole, very well: it shall be so.' He glanced at the clock. 'You will wish to change your dress before we dine. We'll say no more of the matter at this present. Mrs. Cheviot, if you should like it, I will take you to Mrs. Rugby. We dine in half an hour.'

She thanked him, and rose, but before he had taken two steps towards the door, it opened, and Nicky bounced into the room, looking tired, and dishevelled, but triumphant. 'I've found him!' he announced.

'Good God!' John exclaimed. 'Where, Nicky?'

'Why, you would never believe it! In our own West Wood!'

'*What?*'

'Ay! And I had been searching for ever, but never thought, until I was in flat despair, that he might have come this way! He knew I was after him, too, and in the devil of a temper, for he hid from me under a bush! It was the merest chance that I caught sight of him, and he would not come out, not he!'

'Hid from you under a bush?' John repeated blankly.

'Yes, and I had to drag him out by main force. He is so plastered with mud I have shut him in the stables, and he may roll himself clean in the straw. Lord, how thankful I am to have got him back safe!'

John gave a gasp. 'Are you talking about that damnable mongrel of yours!' he demanded.

'He is not a mongrel! He is a cross-bred! Why, what else should I be talking about, I should like to know?'

'I thought you had been searching for Cheviot!'

'Cheviot! What, with Bouncer lost? No, I thank you! Besides,' said Nicky, recalling his grievance, and suddenly speaking with alarming hauteur, 'I have quite washed my hands of that business, since Carlyon had as lief manage without my help. I'm sure it's no matter to me, and much I care!'

'If I have sunk to being Carlyon I see that I have offended beyond pardon,' remarked his mentor. 'But I think you might bid Mrs. Cheviot good evening.'

Nicky became aware of Elinor's presence, and blinked at her. 'Why, hallo, Cousin Elinor!' he said. 'How came you here? I thought you was laid down upon your bed!' He looked round suspiciously. 'Oh! I suppose something excessively exciting has happened which you do not mean to tell me!'

'Nicky, stop being so out of reason cross! Of course I mean to tell you!'

'You will not do so!' John said hastily.

'Nonsense! This has been more Nicky's adventure than mine, and I think he has a right to know the end of it.'

'The fewer people to know the better. It is a damned serious affair, Ned, but it is just like you to be treating it as if it were the merest commonplace!'

Nicky, who had flushed up to the roots of his hair, said stiffly: 'If you think it unsafe to tell me, you need not do so! Though why you should I don't know, for it was Gussie who always gave away all the secrets, not I!'

Perceiving that he had grievously hurt his young brother's feelings, John said, in a testy voice: 'Now, Nick, don't, for God's sake, be such a young fool! Only you are such a rattle-pate, you may blurt something out without meaning to! However, it is for Ned to decide! I have nothing to say in the matter. The fact is, those papers are found, and Ned will have it that it was Bedlington who was selling them to Boney, and Francis trying only to recover them, and to scotch the scandal if the theft should leak out!'

'Bedlington!' Nicky gasped. '*Bedlington?* Oh, by Jove, if that is not too bad! I kept Bouncer beside me all the time he was at Highnoons for fear he should bite him!'

Nineteen

*I*t was some time before Nicky could be induced to suspend his eager questions, and go upstairs to change his muddied coat and buckskin breeches for attire more suitable for the dinner-table. He was at first incredulous of Carlyon's conjecture, but his incredulity was seen to spring more from a rooted dislike of Francis Cheviot than from any reasonable objection to it. He would have been glad to have known Francis for a traitor, and was inclined to think it a great shame if he were to be exonerated. As for Carlyon's discovery of the memorandum in the bracket-clock, this for a time revived his sense of ill-usage, and he eyed his eldest brother with reproachful severity, and addressed him in terms of such cold civility that it was plain to everyone that much tact would be needed to win him back to his usual good humour. However, it was impossible for anyone with so sunny a temper to bear malice for long, and when Carlyon mounted the broad stairs beside him, and tucked a hand in his arm, saying: 'Don't freeze me quite to death, Nicky!' he melted a little, and replied: 'Well, I do not think it was a handsome thing to do, Ned, I must say!'

'Most unhandsome,' Carlyon agreed.

'As thought I could not be trusted!'

'Absurd!'

'In fact, I think it was excessively high-handed of you, and selfish as well, besides interfering, because it was more my adventure than yours, after all! And then you would not even let me share the most exciting part!'

'I am altogether a shabby and mean-spirited person,' said Carlyon meekly. 'I do not know how you have borne with me for so long. But if I try to mend my ways, perhaps I shall win forgiveness.'

'Ned!' exploded Nicky wrathfully. 'I never knew such a complete hand as you are! A regular right cool fish! And if you think I am such a green one that I don't know when you are trying to roast me you are much mistaken!'

'Abuse me as much as you wish, Nicky: I deserve it all! But there is a roast goose for dinner, and if you are late –'

'No!' exclaimed Nicky, instantly diverted. 'Is there, indeed? Then I declare I'm sorry I thrashed poor old Bouncer, for if I had not been obliged to chase after him all this way I must have missed it!'

He hurried off to change his clothes, and made such haste over his toilet that he joined the party just as they were sitting down to table. While the servants were in the room, conversation had to be kept to such harmless subjects as presented themselves to the minds of four persons preoccupied with one burning topic of interest, and was necessarily a trifle desultory. But when the goose had been removed, and a Chantilly cake placed on the table, flanked by a dish of puits d'amour, and one of sack cream, Carlyon signed to the butler that he might withdraw, with his two minions. No sooner had the door closed behind them than John, who had been sitting in abstracted silence, said heavily that try as he would he could not decide what to do for the best.

'Why should you?' said Nicky cheerfully. 'Ned will settle it!'

Mrs. Cheviot could not repress a smile, but John said: 'I own, I wish I had never heard a word of the business. I should not say so, and of course I don't mean that I would have had the thing undiscovered, but – Well, it is the devil of a coil, and there is something to be said for Ned's wanting us to be well out of it! If only we had not been related to Eustace!'

Nicky said that he did not see what that should signify, and this observation at once led to an argument which lasted until Carlyon, who had taken no part in it, intervened to point out that

256

neither Nicky's rustication nor John's prosiness, both of which fruitful topics had crept into the discussion and threatened to monopolise it, had any bearing on the real point at issue.

'I do not see why I must needs be called prosy merely because –'

'Well, but, Ned, you must admit –'

The door opened. 'My lord,' announced the butler disinterestedly, 'Mr. Cheviot has called to see your lordship. I have ushered him into the Crimson Saloon.'

He stood waiting, holding the door, but as Carlyon rose to his feet, John also got up, saying in an urgent undervoice: 'Wait, Ned!'

Carlyon looked at him for a moment, and then spoke over his shoulder. 'Tell Mr. Cheviot I shall be with him in a few minutes.'

The butler bowed, and went out again. Nicky, his eyes blazing with excitement, exclaimed: 'By God, this is beyond anything! To think he should dare come smash up to us! Lord, he must have opened the clock before he reached town! *Now* the game's your own, Ned! may I come with you, and see what trick he tries to play off?'

Carlyon shook his head. John said: 'Ned, be careful! You will not meet him unarmed!'

Carlyon's brows rose in a quizzical look. 'My dear John! I really cannot be expected to receive my visitors with a pistol in my hand!'

'You said yourself he was a very dangerous man!'

'I may have done so, but I never said he was a fool. Murder me in my own house, having been admitted by my butler? I think your wits are gone wool-gathering, John!'

John reddened, and gave a reluctant laugh. 'Well, perhaps so, but you will at least allow me to accompany you!'

Nicky instantly raised his voice in indignant protest. He was silenced by an authoritative finger. 'No,' said Carlyon. 'I think he might find your presence embarrassing. Moreover, I wish you to entertain Mrs. Cheviot while I am away. I'll see him alone.'

'But, Ned, what do you mean to do?' John said uneasily.

'That must depend on circumstance.'

'Well! I own his having the effrontery to come here does make it seem as though – But I'll have no hand in giving that memorandum to him!'

'Then stay here,' said Carlyon, and left the room.

He found Francis Cheviot standing over the fire in the Crimson Saloon, one foot, in its gleaming Hessian boot, resting on the fender, one white hand gripping the edge of the mantelpiece. He still wore his fur-lined cloak, but he had cast his muffler. There was something rather fixed in the smile with which he met his host, but he said, with all his habitual languor: 'My dear Carlyon, you must forgive me for intruding upon you at this hour! I feel sure you will: your sense of justice must oblige you to acknowledge its being quite your own fault. Do forgive me, but must we remain in this welter of crimson velvet? It is a colour that irritates my nerves sadly. It is also extremely chilly in here, and you know how susceptible I am to colds.'

'I know how susceptible you say you are to colds,' replied Carlyon, at his dryest.

'Oh, it is perfectly true!' Francis assured him. 'You must not think that I always prevaricate, for I only do so when I am obliged to.'

'Come into the library!' Carlyon said, leading the way there.

'Ah, this is better!' Francis approved, looking round with a critical eye. 'Crimson and gold – I dare say very eligible for certain occasions, but this is not one of them.' He unfastened his cloak-strings at the throat, and flung the heavy garment off. The smile faded from his face; he came to the fire, and said: 'You know, my dear Carlyon, I am quite tired – really quite exhausted! – with this game of hide-and-seek in the dark which I have been playing with you. I could wish that you had not so much reserve: it is a fault in you: you must own it to be a fault! If you had but taken me into your confidence I should have been spared a great deal of trouble.'

'And Mrs. Cheviot a broken head?'

Francis shuddered. 'Pray do not remind me of anything so

distasteful to one of my exquisite sensibility! What a horrible necessity! I do trust she is now recovered? I myself am still sadly shaken by the affair. You know, Carlyon, I should find myself with an easier task if you would but cultivate that excellent virtue, frankness. Of course, I perceived at the outset that you cherished suspicions, but although I believe I am not generally accounted an obtuse person, I never could discover the extent of your knowledge, nor how you came by it.'

'I knew from John that a certain memorandum was missing,' Carlyon replied.

'Ah, so that was it! The ubiquitous John, who has no business, I am sure, to know anything about the matter. How shocking it is to reflect on the indiscretion that appears to prevail in certain quarters! By the way, I do trust you have that memorandum safe?'

'I have.'

'Well, I must say thank God for that, at all events. You will allow me to compliment you on your quickness, my dear Edward. I had hoped that Mrs. Cheviot's reference to that clock might have passed unnoticed. I should have remembered that you had always a disagreeable trick of fixing upon the very points one would have wished to escape you.'

'I have the memorandum safe,' Carlyon interrupted, 'and I collect that you are here to try whether you can induce me to hand it over to you.'

'Quite so,' smiled Francis. 'I am persuaded that would be the wisest course to pursue.'

'I shall need to be convinced of that, however.'

'Yes, I was afraid you would, and so I shall have to convince you, in spite of all my efforts – my really painstaking and often distasteful efforts – to obviate the necessity of doing so. Ah, perhaps I should make it plain at once that even though I am susceptible to colds, and infinitely prefer cats to dogs, I have not been selling information to Bonaparte's agents. How degrading it is to be obliged to say so! My interest in this affair is neither personal nor patriotic – you remark, I hope, the example I set you in that admirable virtue we were discussing a moment ago! And yet, am I being perfectly frank when I say my interest is not personal? Let us rather say that I am anxious to avoid a scandal. Somehow I feel reasonably certain that a man of your excellent common sense must be similarly anxious.'

'You are right, but I can be satisfied with nothing less than the whole truth.'

Francis sighed. 'Very well, between these four walls, then, let us lay bare the whole truth. As I fancy you have already guessed, my lamentable parent is the somewhat inexpert schemer you have been trying to unmask.' He paused, but Carlyon only continued to regard him steadily. He sighed again. 'One sees why, of course.'

'Does one?'

'Oh, I think so! His fortune was never large, you know, and he has not the least notion of management. That peerage, which affords him such satisfaction, was unfortunately unaccompanied by a grant that might have enabled him to have supported his new dignity in the style he thought proper to it. My dear Edward, have you ever seen the enlargements he saw fit to undertake at Bedlington Manor? Quite dreadful, I assure you! I have only to tell you that he had the Regent for his architectural adviser to make it unnecessary for me to say more.' He covered his eyes with one hand, and shuddered eloquently. 'There is even a Chinese drawing-room. You might almost fancy yourself in poor Prinny's little summer residence at Brighton. The only consolation is that when it is put up for sale, as it assuredly must be, I have not the least doubt of its fetching a fantastic sum. It is just the thing to appeal to some city merchant with social ambitions.'

'And does your father mean to sell it?' enquired Carlyon politely.

'Yes,' said Francis. 'Yes, dear Edward, he does. I have prevailed upon him to see the wisdom of this course. Happily I have a certain influence over him: not always as much as I could wish, but, if I exert myself, enough, I trust. He is not as young as he was, you know, and it must be acknowledged that prolonged intercourse with the Regent is rarely conductive to health or prosperity. When you add to that a turn for playing whist at Oatlands with the Duke of York, which my poor father has lately developed, I cannot think that you need seek farther for a reason why he should be endeavouring to recruit his fortunes in this very foolish fashion. He has not the head for such a dangerous game. In fact, he has not the head for meddling in public affairs either, and I am happy to be able to tell you that he has been brought to own as much. Yes, he is retiring. His gout, you know, has been very troublesome. He will retire full of years and honours, and from my knowledge of his buoyant temperament I do not doubt that the events of the past few months will rapidly fade from his memory.'

'How came you to learn of his activities?' Carlyon asked.

'He told me of the himself,' replied Francis.

'What?'

'Oh, yes! Upon enquiry, you know. To be sure, I had already begun to feel just a trifle uneasy about him. You see, I am on such gratifying terms of intimacy with so many of his colleagues! I am sure you may meet me everywhere in polite circles: I am very good *ton*, you know. Indeed, I have often wondered if I should not challenge Brummell, for there is a set which holds that my way of tying a cravat is superior to his. The younger dandies are already much inclined to follow my lead.'

'Shall we return to the point of this discussion?' Carlyon suggested.

'Ah, forgive me! How very right of you to recall me to it! Yes, the point! The point is, my dear Edward, that being blessed with a large circle of acquaintances I hear quite a number of things which I expect I should not hear at all. I knew that a little pucker was being caused at the Horse Guards, for instance. Leakage of information is not, alas, quite unprecedented: one is for ever hearing of lapses, but I was induced to give this particular pucker more than passing attention. One or two circumstances, into which I need not drag you, had caused me to feel that all was not quite well with my parent. I told you that he is wholly unsuited to a life of intrigue. It had begun to prey upon his mind. A devoted son, you know, cannot be insensible of uneasiness in his father. My devotion led me to keep a filial eye upon his activities – so far as I was able. I even began to visit him with a frequency as trying to my nerves as I have no doubt it was to his. Alas, we have never agreed quite as one would wish! Our tastes, you see, are so dissimilar. But I don't grudge my visits, however much they may have lowered my spirits. For if I had not formed the habit of calling to see how he did I might never have known of his sudden journey into Sussex. I presented myself in Brook Street to be met by the intelligence that his lordship had been called away suddenly, and the merest lift of an eyebrow elicited the further information that poor Mr. Eustace had met with an accident, and was dead. That in itself did not surprise me: one had always felt that poor Mr. Eustace would, sooner or later, meet with an accident. It was with only polite interest that I enquired how this news had come to his lordship. It was then that I learned of Louis De Castres's visit to Brook Street. The butler thought that he had brought the sad tidings.' Francis paused, and frowningly regarded the nails of his right hand. 'Well, you know, I did find that surprising. So far as I was aware, Louis was not acquainted with my father. Of course, you may say that it was very natural in him to carry the tidings to one who had a value for Eustace. But what – I confess – I was at a loss to understand was how Louis, who had positively informed me only the previous day that he was going into Hertfordshire for a night, to visit his estimable parents, came to be in Sussex.'

'What *I* am at a loss to understand,' interrupted Carlyon, 'is why Eustace was ever employed in the business if De Castres was aware of the identity of the man who stood behind him?'

'My dear Edward, Louis was no fool! I dare say he guessed from the start, for who in the world but my father would have dreamt of using such a doubtful tool! Possibly he had the truth out of Eustace any time Eustace was in his cups. But Louis had such tact! Such exquisite perception! He would be the first to appreciate that my father's little whims must be indulged. But when Eustace died so inopportunely, and he discovered Eustace's widow in possession at Highnoons, and failed so signally to effect an unobtrusive search of the house, then it was no longer the moment to be considering poor father's foibles. By the way, I cannot but be thankful that Nicky missed his shot. Really, the scandal that must have ensued had he not missed would have been more than either you or I could have averted.'

'I had rather, certainly, that the met his end at your hands than at Nicky's,' Carlyon replied.

Francis's eyes lifted swiftly to his face, very wide open. 'So you know that, do you?' he said softly. 'Now, how do you know that, Carlyon?'

'You told me so.'

'Did I indeed? And how did I do so?'

'A slip of your too-ready tongue,' Carlyon said. 'You informed us that De Castres had been stabbed, and his body left under a bush. But it was not so stated in the journal from which you said you had culled the tidings. I discovered it to be the precise truth.'

'Yes, you know, this habit of yours – I have referred to it before – of fastening on trivial points is scarcely endearing,' said Francis, with a slight edge to his voice. 'How glad I am that at least you had the good taste not to introduce a third person into this interview! It is quite true, of course: I did dispose of poor Louis. I regretted the necessity; indeed, the whole episode was most painful, but what else was to be done? One could not permit an enemy agent to continue his vocation; one had no means of ascertaining how much that was in that memorandum he already knew; and one shrank from laying information against a dear friend. Indeed, it would be unthinkable to do so! Every feeling must be offended by such a notion!'

'Indeed!' Carlyon raised his brows. 'I collect that the notion of persuading De Castres, by what false message I know not, to present himself in Lincoln's Inn Fields, so that he might there be murdered, awoke no revulsion in your breast?'

Francis looked a little pained. 'My dear Edward, you misjudge

263

me! Nothing could have exceeded my revulsion! Of all things in this world I shrink most from bloodshed, or, indeed, from any form of violence. Poor dear Louis! Quite one of my oldest friends, you know! So very distressing that he should have taken such an ill-judged step! A man of his birth becoming a spy, and for Bonaparte, of all vulgar persons! One can only wonder at it. I had believed his *ton* to have been almost as unimpeachable as my own. I confess, it has been a dreadful shock to me. Are you acquainted with his father, the Marquis? A truly estimable creature: it must be an object with his friends to keep the sad truth from him. But as for sending false messages to poor Louis – really, I am overcome whenever I think of him! – I had no need to do anything so repugnant to one's feelings as a gentleman. He lodged near the Strand; I had an engagement in Holborn; nothing could have been more natural than for him to give me his company. We walked together in perfect amity. It is the greatest comfort to me to reflect that he can never have known what happened to him. Oh, yes! He died almost instantly: it would have been a shocking thing in me to have bungled. I could not have supported the thought that he had suffered. Friendship carries with it the gravest obligations: I have always been sensible of that. I do feel that I performed the last possible office for him. Only fancy if he had been shot as a common spy! I must not allow my mind to dwell on such a horrid thing: it affects me profoundly.'

Carlyon drew a breath. 'You should be felicitated on your resolution!' he said.

'Thank you, Carlyon, thank you a thousand times! It is always such a mistake to allow sentiment to outweigh judgement, is it not? I knew you must feel it so.'

'Don't credit me with a similar resolution, I beg! I must for ever fall short!'

'You disappoint me,' Francis said mournfully. 'I had thought you must have entered into my feelings upon this event. You have such amazing good sense! Where must sentiment have led me, and, I must point out to you, both our families, and poor

Louis too? I cannot think that you would have had me shut my eyes to treasonable activities! No, no, sentiment must have led Louis to an ignominious death, plunged my family into eclipse, embarrassed yours, and quite shattered the poor Marquis and his charming wife! We shall now brush through the affair quite silently.'

'I do not know that. But pray continue!'

'We have had such a digression that I forget which point I had reached. Ah, yes! Poor Louis' failure to ransack Highnoons, was it not? His subsequent loss of decision encourages me to hope that he had not been for long engaged on that work. No better course suggested itself to him that to post to London, to divulge the whole to my father. Yes, the discovery that his complicity was perfectly well-known to Louis quite overcame his lordship. As you are aware, he at once came into Sussex, but with what purpose in mind I know not. He had not the least idea where he should search for that memorandum. It is a source of constant wonder to me how I came to have such a cork-brained parent. However, I have not the slightest reason to believe that my poor mother played him false. It must remain an enigma. The turmoil his brain was got into by the time he again reached Brook Street was such that I flatter myself he greeted my arrival on his door-step with relief. It needed only a trifle of persuasion – I am very persuasive, you know – to induce him to admit me at last into his confidence. I have seldom found him more ready to listen to my advice. It was most gratifying. I was obliged to point out to him that the state of his health demands that he should retire from public life. I really could not answer for his life if he were to continue in office. Thank God, I was able to bring him to acknowledge the justice of my arguments! He had not been aware of the danger in which he stood: how often a man will go on in his harness long after his friends have perceived that the time has come for his retirement!'

This was said in the gentlest tone, but had the effect of sending a cold shiver down Carlyon's spine. His face remained impassive; he merely said: 'I understand you, I believe.'

'Yes, I thought you would,' smiled Francis, carefully removing a speck of dust from his sleeve.

Carlyon stood silent for a moment, frowning down into the fire. His guest had sunk into a chair, and now crossed one slim leg over the other, and fell into admiration of the silver tassels on his Hessians. Carlyon looked up, saying abruptly: 'How came you to know where the memorandum was hid?'

'My dear Edward, nothing could have been more obvious to me! Eustace assured my father that he had a hiding-place which no one would ever think to suspect. You must know that the poor fellow cherished a touching regard for me. Yes, indeed: he had been trying for years to achieve my way with a cravat, with such distressing results, too! I must confess that his frequent invitations to me to visit him at Highnoons have done much to embitter my life. I have often wished I were not such a good-natured creature. I have felt myself several times obliged to gratify his desire to entertain me in Sussex. And if have no real taste for cognac, you know! But I well remember his placing a valuable snuff-box – I never discovered to whom it belonged – in that clock, and informing me with all the mystery engendered by a somewhat maudlin state of mind that whenever he had anything which he wanted no one to see he put it in his cunning place. He recounted with glee his having once coveted and obtained from your brother Harry some trinket or other which he allowed Harry to search for all over the house, secure in the knowledge that even so suspicious a person as Harry would not think to look in the clock. Fortunately, as it has chanced, he retained no recollection on the following morning of having taken me into his confidence. When I learned that all his papers were in your hands, and that the memorandum was plainly not amongst them, it seemed to me more than probable that the clock had once more been put to a strangely improper use.'

'Good God, Cheviot, why could you not have come to me like an honest man, and told me the whole?' Carlyon demanded.

'Really, my dear Edward, this is not worthy of you!' Francis protested. 'Can you possibly suppose that anything other than the direst necessity has led me to confide in you to-day? Do, pray consider! To be obliged to sit here, recounting to you the peculiar exploits of my father is an experience I shall not easily recover from. *Your* reserve made it impossible for me to discover the precise extent of your knowledge; *my* pre-eminent desire was to recover the memorandum while your suspicions remained unsubstantiated. Had Nicholas not entered the house at a most unnecessary moment, I must have succeeded. Poor boy! I dare say he would be quite sorry to think he had embarrassed me!'

'You are, I'm aware, a reckless gamester, but I would not advise your hazarding any considerable sum on that chance!' replied Carlyon caustically.

Francis smiled, but said nothing. Carlyon bent, and set another log on the fire, and watched the flames curl round it. 'Well, and now?'

Francis sighed. 'I am quite in your hands, my dear Carlyon.'

Carlyon directed a frowning look at him. 'Do you expect me to give that memorandum up to you?'

'You would be very wise to do so.' He saw the ironic gleam in Carlyon's cool gray eyes, and flung up a hand. 'Oh, pray do not misunderstand me! Nothing could be farther from my mind than offering you the least violence! No, no, I meant only to suggest that I can more readily restore that paper than can you. But as long as it is restored, and without scandal, I shall be excessively glad to be rid of it.'

'To be frank with you, so shall I!' said Carlyon.

'My dear Edward, I never doubted that for an instant. How pleasant it is to discard our reserve! Tell me, do you think we might safely entrust it to your brother John, or is he no longer with you?'

'He is here. I do not know what he will say to this, but I will not act in the matter without his sanction. You will not object to my sending for him.'

'By all means send for him!' said Francis cordially.

Carlyon stepped up to the bell-pull, and tugged it. 'Have you dined?' he asked.

'Thank you, yes, if one could call it that. If you mean to invite me to spend the night here, which I trust may be the case, for I make it a rule never to travel at night, be the moon never so full, a little broth, and perhaps a glass of burgundy (for I must strive to keep up my strength) sent up on a tray to my bedchamber would make a fitting end to a singularly displeasing day. I need not, I am persuaded, beg you to direct your housekeeper to satisfy herself that my bed is properly warmed. I dare say she is perfectly to be relied on. And I have Crawley with me, of course!'

Carlyon bowed gravely, and, when the butler came into the room, repeated this request. 'And be so good as to desire Mr. John to join me here,' he added.

John was not long in obeying the summons. He came in with his heavy tread, nodded curtly to Francis, and looked under his brows at Carlyon. 'Well, Carlyon? You wish to speak with me?'

'Yes, I wish for your advice,' Carlyon replied. 'I am satisfied that Cheviot and I are at one in desiring to restore that memorandum without involving either of our families in any scandal. His suggestion to me is that if I prefer not to entrust the matter to him you might be able to take it out of both our hands.'

'Restore the thing secretly, do you mean?' John said. 'No, no, I can have nothing to do with such a course! It would be most improper in me, even if I knew how it might be achieved, which I am happy to say I do not!'

'What an excellent official you are, John!' murmured Francis.

Carlyon smiled slightly, and drew the memorandum from his pocket, and gave it to Francis. 'Take it, then.'

'Ned!'

'Well, John, what would you have me do? I cannot carry it to Bathurst without divulging Bedlington's part in the theft, and if you wish to run into that kind of scandal I can only say that I do not.'

John was silent, his face much troubled. Francis slid the folded sheets into his pocket. 'I shall not thank you,' he said. 'One does not thank a man for handling one a live coal. I think I should make arrangements to journey to Cheltenham Spa when I am at last rid of this business. I have always found the air there to agree tolerably with me.'

'If this were ever to come out!' John exclaimed.

Francis gave one of his eloquent shudders. 'John, my nerves have already been called upon to stand more than they are in any condition to do. Pray do not raise horrid spectres! I dare say I shall not close my eyes this night as it is!'

'Well,' said John bluntly, 'I've no wish to insult you, Cheviot, but I hope to God Ned does right to trust you with this!'

'Indeed, and so do I!' agreed Francis amiably. 'If I were to be held up on my way to London to-morrow by highwaymen, for instance, how shocking it would be!'

'It's very well to turn it off with a jest, but I am sure I do not know who you will contrive to restore that memorandum without being discovered!'

'I expect you will be happier if I do not tell you, dear John. It will not be so very difficult. Really, I have only to make up my mind whom I most dislike at the Horse Guards. It will be a choice, I own, but I do not despair of hitting upon the very man who would be all the better for a set-down.'

John looked horrified. 'I had rather know nothing of what you mean to do!' he said hastily.

'The perfect official!' smiled Francis, rising. 'And now, my dear Carlyon, if I may be permitted to retire? I have had such a fatiguing day, and all this junketing about the countryside is just what my doctor most earnestly deprecates. I wonder if I am in right in preferring Cheltenham to Bath? Dear me, there is no end to the problems that beset one, is there?'

Twenty

*W*hen Carlyon, having escorted his guest upstairs to a suitably warmed bedchamber, and delivered him into the care of his valet, joined the drawing-room party, he found that Nicky was loudly giving vent to his disgust at the outcome of the adventure. Nothing, he insisted, could have been tamer, while as for Francis Cheviot's continued presence in the house, the only circumstance that could in any way reconcile him to such an abominable thing would be if Bouncer were to bite him. Bouncer, who had been released from prison and was stretched out before the fire, wagged a willing but slightly weary tail, and heaved the sigh of a dog who has spent a successful but exhausting day.

It was not to be expected that John could readily accustom himself to the thought of his brother's unorthodox conduct. Nightmarish possibilities kept on rearing up their heads, not the least of these being a doubt of Francis's sincerity. His arguments were met by Carlyon with calm patience, and although he did not quite talk himself out of them he was able at last to admit that he did not know what else could have been done, and was merely thankful the matter had not been left to his judgement.

Elinor, when she heard a brief account of Francis's activities, could only say that she was glad to think she had not known what a desperate character she was harbouring at Highnoons.

'Yes, only fancy if he had had that sword-stick of his in his hand when he found you tampering with the clock!' exclaimed Nicky. 'I dare say he would not have hesitated to stab you with it, for if a man will stab his best friend there is no telling where he will stop!'

'Just what I was thinking,' Elinor agreed. '*I* may be thankful, though I quite see that it would have been a very exciting thing to have happened. How flat it will be at Highnoons now!'

'By Jupiter, yes! There will be no bearing it. You know, Ned, I don't think I have every enjoyed myself more in all my life! Except for the wretched work you have made of the end of it, you and John between you!'

'For heaven's sake, Nick, do not be saying that I had anything to do with it!' John besought him. 'Ned knows how far I am from approving of his conduct.'

The widow looked much struck. 'Is it so, indeed? Can I have heard you aright, Mr. Carlyon?'

Carlyon smiled, but John looked puzzled, and said earnestly: 'I have never made the least secret of my sentiment upon this event, ma'am. But so it is always with my brother! He will always go his own way, be it never so crazy!'

'Now, John, don't be prosing again!' Nicky begged. 'Ned's a great gun – at home to a peg!'

'Yes, that is all very well, and I don't doubt his notions suit you very tolerably, but it will not do! This was not right. *You* are a sensible woman, ma'am: I appeal to you! You must be aware of the whimsical nature of his behaviour throughout this affair!'

'No one,' Elinor assured him, 'is more so, sir! And what I find so particularly disagreeable in him is his habit of making the outrageous things he does seem to be the merest commonplace! I dare say I may not have mentioned it before, but I shall not scruple to tell *you*, Mr. Carlyon, that I consider him to have been ruined by the indulgence shown him by his family, till he had become overbearing, self-willed, ruthless, lawless, set up his own conceit, insensible of the claims of others –'

'Why, Cousin Elinor, I thought you liked him!' Nicky cried, quite shocked.

'I cannot think where you came by such a notion,' said Elinor firmly. 'Pray, what cause have I to like one who has subjected me to all the ills I have suffered at his hands? My credit has been destroyed, my chance of finding a home in a very eligible household foiled, and I have been exposed to all the dangers of a treasonable plot.'

'It is very true, upon my word!' John said. 'Ned, I do not think you have used Mrs. Cheviot well, you know.'

'I cannot agree to it,' replied Carlyon. 'I make it a rule always to get over heavy ground as light as I can, and you will scarcely deny that we have met with very heavy ground from start to finish of this business. We are now safely over it, at the trifling cost of a hole in Nicky's shoulder, and a bruise on Mrs. Cheviot's head.'

'Oh!' exclaimed Elinor indignantly. 'This passes everything!'

'Well, I don't grudge my share in it, I can tell you!' Nicky declared. 'But I know you are funning, Cousin Elinor! You would not have missed such sport, now, would you?'

Carlyon laughed, and rose to his feet. 'You will never prevail upon her to own as much, Nicky. Come, ma'am, it is time I was taking you back to Miss Beccles before you have quite undermined my credit with my brothers.'

'Indeed, my lord, it is quite unnecessary for you to put yourself to the trouble of escorting me,' Elinor replied, getting up also. 'After all I have gone through, a mere drive of seven miles, even supposing I were to be held up by footpads, can hold no terrors for me.'

'Of course you need not come, Ned!' said Nicky. 'She does not go alone! I shall be with her, and Bouncer too. You will not object to having Bouncer in the carriage, will you, cousin? He is too tired to run behind.'

'My dear Nicky, there is no longer the smallest danger threatening Mrs. Cheviot, and it is time that you came back to me.'

'Well, and so I will, Ned, but had I not better return to Highnoons to-night? You see, I left my gear there, and —'

'You have plenty of gear here,' said Carlyon.

'Yes, and what is more you are looking fagged to death!' said

John, in the rough tone he used to conceal any anxiety about his young brother. 'I do not know what Ned was about to be encouraging you to tramp miles in search of that dog of yours!'

'Oh, fudge! I was never better in my life!'

'No! And I dare say your shoulder does not pain you either, and you keep shifting in your chair because you have the fidgets!'

'I wish you will take a look at it, John,' said Carlyon. 'You are very right: I should not have let him go out after Bouncer. It seemed preferable to his falling foul of Francis, however.'

This unguarded remark made Nicky stiffen with shocked surprise. 'Ned! you advised me to go after him only to get me out of the way! Oh, it is too shabby of you! I would not have thought you would have used me so!'

'No, indeed!' said Elinor. 'I am sure we had none of us any reason to expect such solicitude. It is wretched for you, Nicky, and if you like to return with me to Highnoons I shall be very happy to accept your escort.'

'Well, I will!' said Nicky.

John encountered his elder brother's eye, and grasped Nicky's arm. 'Oh, no, you will not!' he said. 'You will come up to bed, and no more of this nonsense. I'll attend to him, Ned.'

Nicky, who was indeed extremely weary, said: 'Oh, very well, but I am not a baby! I do not need to be put to bed! Good night, Cousin Elinor: I shall be riding over to collect my gear in the morning, I dare say. Come, Bouncer!'

John shook hands with the widow. 'I must say good-bye, ma'am, for I set out for London to-morrow, and do not know when I may be in Sussex again. I hope when I see you next you will be comfortably settled at Highnoons, with no more secret entrances discovered! But Ned will look after you!'

She returned some answer, and he then marched Nicky off. Carlyon had fetched her hat and pelisse to Elinor, and she put them on, and let him usher her out to where the carriage was already waiting. 'I wish you will not put yourself to this trouble, my lord!' she said, as he handed her in. 'Indeed, I am not at all afraid to go alone!'

'But I wish to go with you,' he replied, spreading a fur rug over her knees, and taking his place beside her.

The carriage moved forward. Mrs. Cheviot said: 'I do trust Nicky may not be found to have done his shoulder an injury!'

'I do not think it.'

There was a pause.

'Well, it will seem strange not to be going in terror of my life any more!' remarked Elinor. 'So much has happened this week that there has been no opportunity for me to discuss with you what next I must do. But this must now be thought of, my lord, as I am persuaded you must realise.'

'There is little that you can do until probate has been granted,' Carlyon replied.

'You mean to keep me at Highnoons until then?'

'Surely that was agreed between us?'

'Was it?' she said doubtfully.

'Certainly. You are to sell Highnoons, and we must hope that my cousin's debts will not swallow all the purchase price.'

She turned, but could only dimly discern his face in the darkness. 'My lord, that is no matter to me! I could not reconcile it with my conscience to benefit by that dreadful marriage! Please to understand that I mean that!'

'As you wish,' he said indifferently.

She was surprised, for she had expected him to argue the matter, and had braced herself to resist his persuasions. After another slight pause, she said: 'I do beg you will agree to let me leave Highnoons at once, sir. You are ware of my situation; I must look about me for an eligible engagement, and it will not do for me to be lingering on in this way.'

'Mrs. Macclesfield,' he murmured. 'I thought we should return to her.'

She laughed. 'No, alas! I fear my credit with Mrs. Macclesfield cannot be high! But do be serious, sir! I dare say it may be many months before a purchaser is found for Highnoons, and then what shall I do, with so much time wasted?'

'I have considered that, ma'am, and if you should not like to return for a space to your own relatives I think it would be an excellent scheme for you to go on a visit to my sister, Lady Hartlepool. You will like her, I fancy. She has a sweetness of disposition which must always please. I do not suggest that you should go to Lady Flint, for she is expecting to be confined. And my sister Augusta is for ever racketing about town in a way that would hardly be proper for you during the period of your mourning. My sister Elizabeth will be visiting me shortly, and if I may do so I will bring her to make your acquaintance.'

'But – but does Lady Hartlepool require a governess?' asked Elinor.

'Oh, no! Her children are all still in the nursery.'

'Then – My lord, I do not know what scheme you may have in your head, but –'

'I hope you will think better of this determination to seek another post as governess.'

'Well, I shall not, I assure you, sir! I told you once before that I would not become your pensioner, and I beg of you to believe that I meant it!'

'I hope that you will become my wife,' he replied, with all his usual calm.

She was stricken to silence, and was aware of nothing but the hammering of her heart in her chest.

He continued after a moment. 'I should not be making such a declaration to you yet, but I think my sentiments cannot be unknown to you.'

'Quite – quite unknown, my lord!' she said, in a voice which did not seem to be her own.

'I have tried to conceal them. It is too soon, and I would not upon any account embarrass you. But when the period of your strict mourning is over it is my very ardent desire to be permitted to pay my addresses to you.'

She could only say: 'It is absurd! I am persuaded this is one of your *whimsical* turns, my lord!'

'My whimsical turns! No, indeed! I was never more serious in my life. You are the only woman I could think of asking to be my wife. You must be aware, at least, that I have found no common delight in your company.'

'No! No, no, I had not the least notion – Oh, pray do not, my lord! This is some chivalrous conceit! You cannot mean it!'

He sounded amused. 'My dear child, when have you ever known me indulge in such romantic folly as a chivalrous conceit? Indeed, my fear is that my overbearing, self-willed ways may have given you a distaste of me which not all my future efforts may serve to eradicate. Is it so?'

'No,' said Elinor. 'Oh, no! But –'

He found her hand, and raised it to his lips. 'Well, I have used you quite abominably, but I will not do so any more. I mean to take the greatest care of you, if you will let me.'

She was obliged to hunt hurriedly in her reticule for her handkerchief. Trying to speak in a collected way, she said: 'It will not do! You are so very obliging, my lord, but do, pray, consider!'

'I have already considered, and it is absurd to say that I am obliging.'

'Oh, stop, stop! It is madness! Only think of your sisters. What would they say? You to marry one who is nothing but a penniless governess!'

'What in the world is this new flummery? Do you forget that until a week ago you were Miss Rochdale of Feldenhall?'

'No, I do not forget it, but I think you must forget the circumstances of – of my father's death!'

'I remember them perfectly, but what they have to do with you, will, I fear, always remain a mystery to me.'

She was silenced, but after a moment managed to say: 'I am persuaded your sisters would not say as much. Only think what a shock it would be to them to learn of such tidings as your betrothal to me!'

'If I know anything of my sister Georgy,' he responded, 'she has already written to tell both Eliza and Gussie, and very likely Harry too, that Ned has fallen head over ears in love at last.'

She blushed rosily in the darkness. 'Oh, no! do not say so! She cannot have thought such a thing!'

'Well, she said I was very sly, but that she would not tease me.'

'I must not listen to you!' Elinor said, much shaken. 'Oh, it is the most ridiculous thing! You only met me a week ago, and then you constrained me to marry your horrid cousin!'

'It is a fortunate thing that I did not know you better, for if I had I should certainly never have done so.'

She uttered a laugh that broke in the middle. 'Odious, odious man!'

'I depend on you to teach me to be less odious. I shall be very happy to learn of you.'

Elinor gathered her forces together. 'Lord Carlyon!' she began.

He interrupted. 'Do you know, it has of late become an ambition of mine to hear my name on your lips instead of my title?'

'Certainly not!' said Elinor, with resolution.

He was silent.

'And when I think of the hateful way you have of calling me Mrs. Cheviot, when you know I dislike it,' added the widow, quite ruining her effect, 'I wonder that you should ask it of me!'

'Very well. When we meet in public, I will call you cousin, as Nicky does. But here, in the privacy of my carriage, I need not scruple to say, Elinor, I have fallen very deep in love with you, and I beg that you will honour me with your hand in marriage.'

'You are talking a great deal of nonsense, and you will thank me one day for not attending to you!' said Elinor, in a scolding tone.

'Now you are being uncivil,' he said imperturbably. 'I shall have to teach you how to reply to a declaration with more propriety, my little love.'

She trembled. 'Oh, no! pray – Oh, will you only think for one moment! If you were to marry me, everyone would say you had done it to obtain possession of Highnoons!'

'Certainly not. You are going to sell Highnoons, and we shall not trouble ourselves to put it into any but reasonable order. It will go for a song, I dare say. If any money is left when Eustace

Cheviot's debts have been paid, you will buy your bride-clothes with it, and so we shall be rid of the whole concern. Have you any other objections to put forward?'

'Oh, if only I knew what I ought to do!' Elinor cried.

'You had better let yourself be guided by me, for I have no doubts at all on that subject.'

'Oh, my lord, how can I help believing that you have made me this offer because of some nonsense I have talked – the merest raillery! – of your having ruined all my prospects?'

Carlyon moved, and firmly pulled the agitated widow into his arms. 'You know, I never thought you could be such a simpleton!' he said, and kissed her.

Elinor tried rather half-heartedly to thrust him away, but finding this an impossibility, appeared to resign herself, merely saying, when she could say anything at all: 'Oh, Edward, no!'

'Elinor, I have spent a great deal of my life in listening patiently to much folly. In my sisters I can support it with tolerable equanimity; in you I neither can nor will! Will you accept of my hand in marriage, or will you not?'

Recognizing that his lordship's disordered intellect was beyond mending, the widow abandoned the attempt to reclaim his wits, leaned her cheek thankfully against his shoulder, and said with the utmost meekness: 'Yes, Edward, if you please! I would like it of all things!'

Sprig Muslin

Finding so young and pretty a girl as Amanda wandering unattended, Sir Gareth Ludlow knows it is his duty as a man of honour to restore her to her family. But it is to prove no easy task for the Corinthian. His captive in sprig muslin has more than her rapturous good looks and bandboxes to aid her – she is also possessed of a runaway imagination . . .

April Lady

When the new Lady Cardross begins to fill her days with fashion and frivolity, the Earl has to wonder whether she did really only marry him for his money, as his family so helpfully suggests. And now Nell doesn't dare tell him the truth . . . What with the concern over his wife's heart and pocket, sorting out her brother's scrapes and trying to prevent his own half sister from eloping, it is no wonder that the much-tried Earl almost misses the opportunity to smooth the path of true love in his marriage . . .

The Spanish Bride

Shot-proof, fever-proof and a veteran campaigner at the age of twenty-five, Brigade-major Harry Smith is reputed to be the luckiest man in Lord Wellington's army. Yet at the siege of Badajos, his friends foretell the ruin of his career. When Harry meets the defenceless Juana, a fiery passion consumes him. Under the banner of honour and with the selfsame ardour he so frequently displays in battle, he dives headlong into marriage. In his beautiful child-bride, he finds a kindred spirit, and a temper to match. But for Juana, a long year of war must follow.

arrow books

ALSO AVAILABLE IN ARROW BY GEORGETTE HEYER

Lady of Quality

Independent and spirited, Miss Annis Wychwood gives little thought to finding herself a suitable husband, thus dashing the dreams of many hopeful suitors. When she becomes embroiled in the affairs of the runaway heiress Lucilla, though, she encounters the beautiful fugitive's guardian – as rakish and uncivil a rogue she has ever met. Although, chafing a bit at the restrictions of Regency society in Bath, Annis does have to admit that Oliver Carelton, at least, is never boring.

False Colours

The Honourable Christopher Fancot, on leave from the diplomatic service in the summer of 1817, is startled to find his entrancing but incorrigibly extravagant mother on the brink of financial and social ruin – and more than alarmed to find that his twin brother has disappeared without trace. The unfortunate Kit is forced into an outrageous masquerade by the tangled affairs of his wayward family – his rigid uncle, Lord Brumby, the surprisingly wily Sir Bonamy Ripple, the formidable old Lady Stavely and Evelyn's betrothed, Cressy – but in the face of Evelyn's continued absence, Kit's ingenuinty is stretched to the limit.

arrow books

ALSO AVAILABLE IN ARROW BY GEORGETTE HEYER

The Unknown Ajax

Miles from anywhere, Darracott Place is presided over by irascible and short-tempered Lord Darracott. The recent drowning of his eldest son has done nothing to improve his temper. For now he must send for the unknown offspring of the uncle whom the family are never permitted to mention. Yet none of the beleaguered family are prepared for the arrival of the weaver's brat and heir apparent.

Cotillion

The three great-nephews of cantankerous Mr Penicuik know better than to ignore his summons, especially when it concerns the bestowal of his fortune. The wily old gentleman has hatched an outrageous plan for his stepdaughter's future and his own amusement: his fortune will be Kitty's dowry. But while the beaux are scrambling for her hand, Kitty counters with her own inventive, if daring, scheme: a sham engagement that should help keep wedlock at bay . . .

The Talisman Ring

The legend of the Headless Horseman and a proposed *marriage de convenance* both have their impact on the mystery of a golden talisman ring and Lord Lavenham's young heir, Ludovic. Neither Sir Tristram Shield nor Eustacie, his young French cousin, share the slightest inclination to marry one another, and yet it is Lord Lavenham's most fervent dying wish. For there is no one else to provide for the old man's granddaughter while Ludovic remains a fugitive from justice.

arrow books

The Convenient Marriage

When the eligible Earl of Rule offers for the hand of the Beauty of the Winwood Family, he has no notion of the distress he causes his intended. For Miss Lizzie Winwood is promised to the excellent, but impoverished, Mr Edward Heron. Disaster can only be averted by the delightful impetuosity of her youngest sister, Horatia, who conceives her own distinctly original plans . . .

Powder & Patch

In an 18th-century England of wit, womanising and powdered wigs, provincial Philip Jettan runs the risk of irreproachability unlike Cleone Charteris, who certainly stands in no such danger. Golden-haired, headstrong and the despair of all men within reach, she seeks a husband who can duel and dice with the best of them. So Philip leaves for Paris, where his father's hopes and his lover's ideals are realised, but with unforeseen consequences for them both.

Bath Tangle

The Earl of Spenborough has always been noted for his eccentricity. Leaving a widow younger than his own daughter was one thing. Leaving his fortune to the trusteeship of the Marquis of Rotherham – the one man the same daughter had jilted – was quite another.

arrow books